THE HOUSE OF THE HANGED WOMAN

Derbyshire, 1921. When an MP goes missing in a Derbyshire village, Scotland Yard detective Albert Lincoln is sent to investigate. A grim discovery has been made in a cave next to an ancient stone circle: the naked body of a middle-aged man mutilated beyond recognition. The local police assume it is the missing politician but when Albert arrives in Wenfield he begins to have doubts. Two years earlier he conducted another traumatic murder investigation in the same village and he finds reminders of a particularly personal tragedy as he tries to help a vicar's widow who claims her husband was murdered. Then there is another murder in Wenfield. Could there be a link between all of Albert's cases?

KATE ELLIS

THE HOUSE OF THE HANGED WOMAN

Complete and Unabridged

CHARNWOOD
Leicester

First published in Great Britain in 2020 by
Piatkus
an imprint of
Little, Brown Book Group
London

First Charnwood Edition
published 2021
by arrangement with
Little, Brown Book Group
an Hachette UK Company
London

A catalogue record for this book is available
from the British Library.

ISBN 978–1–4448–4688–1

Published by
Ulverscroft Limited
Anstey, Leicestershire
Set by Words & Graphics Ltd

To everyone who works in public libraries and book shops, those wonderful people who can transport us to other worlds.

1

Wenfield, High Peak, Derbyshire

March 1921

The man stumbled on, barely aware of his surroundings or his unfamiliar, ill-fitting clothes.

His limbs felt uncontrollable like the spindly legs of a newborn foal. They said the war was over, but they were wrong. Some could put the horrors behind them — they could drink, laugh and dance as if the world was about to come to an end — but others would never forget. They were doomed like him to relive the terrors over and over again each night in the silence of darkness.

Gas. Gas. The shouts; the mortar fire that made the eardrums bleed. The bodies ripped apart, limbs hanging on barbed wire, red and dripping like meat in a butcher's shop. Too much for a human soul to bear.

For so long he'd been a dead man; a man with no identity, no history and no future. Then, once the hazy memories began to crawl from the fog of his brain, he'd gathered what little courage he had left and embarked on the quest for his old life. He'd searched for the man he used to be, following the half-remembered shreds of his past that returned in brief, vivid flashes like shell blasts. And when he'd reached

1

Wenfield all hope had died.

As he rose to his feet and dragged his body towards the stones that protruded from the ground like the crooked teeth of some monstrous, long-buried creature, pictures ran through his mind, some clear, others hazy. Recollections of that perfect summer when he'd married his young bride. Heat and kisses and sweet wedding flowers. Then the horror of a shell landing in the trench, killing his comrades and emptying his head of memories, leaving him an empty shell, cared for by nurses with kind faces. An unknown soldier without a tomb.

His head was spinning and he hardly felt the jolt of bone against hard earth as he fell to his knees again and the nausea rose in his chest. He no longer knew where he was and his soul seemed to float above him. Or perhaps he no longer had a soul because it had been made quite clear to him that he didn't exist.

He began to crawl towards the largest stone, the one in the centre of the circle. A faint memory told him that the stone was called the Devil. And that it was he who commanded the eternal dance before he dragged the unwary straight down to hell.

The Devil loomed over him, bent as though he was playing the fiddle for the helpless dancers, controlling their every move as they writhed in their frozen agony. The nausea eased a little and he crawled towards a crevice in the wall of rock that towered over the circle. Not far now. He was hardly aware of vomiting. He felt numb, all pain gone as he edged inside the cave, escaping the

2

Devil before he was drawn into the terrible dance. He was cold now, so cold, but his head was clearer, as though all the confusion of the past couple of years had suddenly vanished. He felt strangely at peace as he lay down and fell asleep, his heartbeat slowing almost to a stop.

He didn't hear the stealthy footsteps at the cave's entrance. He didn't feel the rock crashing down into his face. Once. Twice. Three times. Destroying his features. Ensuring that he no longer existed.

2

Rose

I lie awake and my hands finger the smooth fabric of the paisley quilt my mother gave me as a wedding gift as I listen to him breathe. Snuffling like a night creature making its way through undergrowth, sniffing its way blindly in search of sustenance — or prey.

Each night I dream of his death and I think of it every waking hour. I know I must be evil because I have murder in my heart. Murder. The taking of a life. The sin of Cain. I imagine that terrible, wicked act over and over again, and sometimes I think it can't be so wrong because it is the one thing that will release me from the misery of this existence.

I turn over, finding myself trapped in my twisted nightgown, and I open my eyes to watch him in the moonlight that trickles in through the thin curtains. Asleep, he looks so harmless. Almost innocent. Almost like the little boy he must once have been. There's no trace now of the raised voice, the clenched fist, the accusations, the words intended to wound and humiliate. If only he could stay asleep for ever.

He is handsome, there is no denying that. I was eighteen when we met and, because of my youthful naivety, I fell in love with his fair curls and boyish face. I saw him then as a character from one of the novels I love so much; the stories that whisk me far away from Derbyshire and land me in a different, warmer world where the plucky girl wins the brooding hero, tames him into a husband and lives happily ever after. That's what I believed in when I walked up the aisle of Cheadle church that day just before Christmas in 1919, so grateful that he had come home safe from the war, so relieved that both of us had escaped the dreadful influenza that finished off so many of the young and strong.

It rained on our wedding day and the bare trees around the churchyard waved in the wind like the fleshless arms of the long-dead. They looked as though they were signalling me to stop, telling me not to take another step towards the old stone porch. It was an omen. I should have obeyed.

Bert stirs and my eyes open again. Sleep refuses to come and I know it never will until he is no longer lying there beside me. I slither out of bed and place my naked foot on the bare floorboards. Their chill makes me rise on tiptoe as I creep towards the door. I try the icy brass doorknob, doing my best to make no sound because I know he'll be angry if I wake him up. The knob twists noiselessly in my hand and I pull it towards me but the door won't budge. He has locked it again and put the key beneath his pillow. I am a prisoner.

But one day soon I'll know happiness. One day soon my husband will be dead.

5

3

Detective Inspector Albert Lincoln had once heard someone say that November was the month of the dead — but he wasn't so sure. It was early spring now and the earth was returning to life and yet death still haunted his waking thoughts.

There were so many dead for him to mourn; hundreds of them, all khaki-clad, all smiling, all swearing it would be over by Christmas. All trying to stay cheerful, keeping their chins up as the great adventure turned into a nightmare of blood, mud and rotting flesh. Sometimes he felt guilty that he had survived, even though a shell had left him maimed — his left hand reduced to a reddened stump, half his face burned away and his leg mangled. He had been lucky. Or so everyone told him. Now, three years later, it didn't always feel like that.

From the office in Scotland Yard with his name and rank etched on the glass door he could see his sergeant, Sam Poltimore, sitting at his desk, frowning with concentration as he spoke on the telephone. Sam was a wiry man, nearing retirement, with a face that always betrayed his emotions. Albert could tell that the person on the other end of the line was imparting bad news.

Things had been unusually quiet recently with only a few unimaginative robberies and a couple of easily solved domestic murders over the Christmas period to break the monotony. Albert knew he should be glad of the lull in criminal activity now that his wife, Mary, was so ill, but things weren't that simple. Over the past couple of years he had taken refuge in his work and at that moment he was hoping a case would come his way; some vicious and complex crime that would release him from the trap his home had become. A cage as strong as a prison with invisible bars and a phantom warder.

He closed his eyes and took a deep breath, experiencing a pang of guilt that he felt this way. It wasn't Mary's fault. She had lost a child — as had he. Part of her had died when their son, Frederick, had breathed his last; a small sad victim of the influenza that had ravaged the country, as though the bitter losses of war hadn't been enough to sate Death's appetite for human flesh. Albert had grieved with her and tried his best to support her, but she'd pushed him away, seeking other means of comfort. Since her loss she was no longer the woman he'd fallen in love with. It was as though, for Mary, Albert had ceased to exist.

Perhaps that was why the loyalty he'd always assumed was part of his nature had failed him. In 1919 the consequences of that failure had been disastrous. Then when he'd been investigating the strange death of a woman in the Cheshire village of Mabley Ridge last September he'd met Gwen Davies, the village schoolmistress. Gwen had seemed to understand what he'd been through. But after the traumatic events they'd experienced together she'd made the decision to return to her home city of Liverpool. At their final meeting she'd given him her parents' address. He'd kept it with him, although he was sure he would never attempt to contact her, however much he was tempted. It had been a tantalising possibility which would come to nothing because of the vows he'd made to Mary when the world had been different. He'd been unfaithful to her once and that had been enough.

When Albert opened his eyes he saw through the glass that Sam was heading for his office. He shuffled the papers on his desk, trying to look busy, trying to look as though he wasn't thinking of what happened last year in Mabley Ridge. His investigation there had been a qualified success: he had solved the case and brought one of the dead woman's murderers to justice. He had even discovered who had been responsible for the death of a child in the same village before the outbreak of the war. However, another killer had evaded justice and that failure still nagged at him. The man could well be dead and one day his body might be found reduced to dust and bone. Or maybe he had survived, although Albert couldn't bear to think of this particular culprit escaping justice after the evil he'd brought to that small Cheshire community.

Sam gave a token knock on the etched glass and Albert looked up from his false industry, hoping for something, anything, to take his mind off the mistakes he'd made in the past; mistakes he feared could never be put right.

'A letter's come for you in the second post,

8

sir,' Sam said with a sheepish look on his face.

'The second post must have arrived a couple of hours ago.'

'It did but . . . ' Sam Poltimore looked like a guilty schoolboy summoned before the headmaster.

'What's wrong, Sam?'

Sam held out a pale blue envelope, unopened. The handwritten address was neat, possibly a woman's hand. 'I recognised the postmark, sir.' He paused. 'It's from Wenfield.'

Albert froze. Just the name of that village in Derbyshire's High Peak set his heart racing. There were times when he'd almost convinced himself that what had happened there in 1919 had been his punishment for being unfaithful to Mary when she'd been in need of comfort.

As a result of his stay in Wenfield, Albert had gained another son, although he had never set eyes on the boy, only learning of his existence through third parties. He had no idea whether the child was living safely with a loving family or whether he had been placed in some grim orphanage — the unwanted offspring of a mother who'd committed the ultimate sin and paid the price demanded by the law. It was something he tried not to think about, although more often than not he failed. The boy kept bobbing back into his mind. His lost son. His own flesh and blood.

The previous September he'd taken the train from Mabley Ridge to Wenfield in the hope of discovering the truth. But when he'd arrived he'd found that the Reverend Bell, the one

9

person who might have known something about the boy's fate, was dead. Albert had returned to Cheshire despondent. Even so, a tiny glimmer of hope still remained in his heart. A little flame, so small that it could be easily extinguished. In optimistic moments he vowed he would find his son one day. But he knew all too well that reality often disappoints the hopeful.

'Shall I open it, sir?'

Sam's question broke through his thoughts like an explosion. 'No, Sam. It's addressed to me. I'd better . . .'

He took the envelope from Sam, noting that it wasn't cheap, nor was it the most expensive stationery one could buy in the better London shops. He didn't recognise the handwriting, although it looked to him like an educated hand, and he stared at it for a while, putting off the moment of revelation. Then he slit open the top with the paperknife lying near his inkwell — a dagger confiscated from a member of an East End gang.

Dear Inspector Lincoln, it began:

I'm not sure whether you will remember me from the time you spent in Wenfield in 1919. I am the widow of the Reverend Horace Bell, the vicar of that parish, who died unexpectedly last September. I gather you learned of the tragic news when you called at the vicarage while I was away staying with my sister. I am sorry I was not there to receive you but I'm sure you will understand that I needed some time

10

away from Wenfield following my grievous loss. When my husband's former curate, the Reverend Fellowes, was appointed as the new vicar he moved into my old home and I purchased a smaller house nearby which suits me very well.

I hope you do not mind me writing to you, but I did not know who else might be in a position to advise me. I recall that my late husband spoke highly of you, choosing to overlook your friendship with Flora Winsmore. I still find it hard to believe she was a murderess. She seemed such a sweet young woman. How appearances can deceive.

I hope you will not think me foolish but I fear that murder has visited our village again. It is my belief that my husbands death was not natural and that he was poisoned by some wicked hand. There, I've written the words that have dominated my every waking thought since I laid him to rest. As to the perpetrator of this dreadful crime, I have my suspicions but no proof. A vicar is privy to so many secrets and it may be that somebody wished to ensure that theirs was never revealed to the world.

The coroner concluded that Horace died of natural causes yet with each passing day I grow more and more certain that somebody ended my dear gentle husbands life.

Since those terrible murders of 1919 it is as though a cloud of distrust and suspicion hangs over Wenfield like the mist that so

11

often shrouds our Derbyshire hills. It
would put my troubled mind at rest if you
were to advise me as to my best course of
action. While I have no doubt that Ser-
geant Teague and Constable Wren are
good men, I do not trust them to under-
stand my fears or to act upon them.
I await your reply.
Yours sincerely,
Caroline Bell (Mrs)

Albert found it hard to absorb the letter's
contents on the first reading so he read it
through again. When he looked up he saw that
Sam was still there, watching him as though he
feared the letter might send him into a state of
shock. Sam was the only person in London who
knew the truth of what had happened in
Wenfield. He was the one person Albert had
been able to trust to keep the information to
himself. And he'd had to share his burden with
someone.

'It's from Mrs Bell, the widow of the vicar of
Wenfield. Remember I told you he'd passed
away last September?'

Sam nodded. 'What does she want?'

Albert hesitated before answering. 'She thinks
her husband might have been murdered. I met
her, Sam. She's a sensible woman — not the sort
to let her imagination get the better of her. She
was very well thought of in the village . . . and
. . . the woman always spoke highly of her.' He
found he couldn't bear to utter Flora's name.
'Mrs Bell was one of the few people to stand up

12

to that Society for the Abolition of Cowardice — those dreadful women who sent white feathers to soldiers suffering from . . . '

'I know, sir. Some people had no idea. What does Mrs Bell expect you to do about it?'

Albert sighed. 'She's asking for my advice but I'm not sure how to reply to her. The coroner's verdict was natural causes and she has no proof that it was wrong. Not that I'd ever want to set foot in that village again anyway.' His last words were half-hearted and the possibility that Mrs Bell might be privy to information about his lost son kept flitting through his mind, even though he tried his best to ignore it.

Albert pushed the letter to one side and picked up one of the files on his desk, a signal the subject was closed. Mrs Bell's communication had taken him by surprise and he needed time to consider his response. Sam sidled out of the office and shut the door behind him.

Albert stared at the file in his hand without really seeing it. Mrs Bell suspected, rightly or wrongly, that the coroner's verdict was wrong and that her husband had been murdered. However, she was over two hundred miles away and if she had any doubts about her husband's death it was only proper that she should share them initially with her local police. Besides, he had his duties to attend to . . . not to mention the heaviest duty of all: his duty to Mary, his wife.

He put the letter out of sight in his in-tray, resolving to consider the problem tomorrow. Perhaps his mother's old adage, that things

13

always seemed clearer after a good night's sleep, would prove correct in this instance.

The following morning, however, he was to receive a message that would take the decision out of his hands. The late Reverend Bell would most likely have said it was Divine Providence. But Albert blamed coincidence.

14

4

Rose

Bert went to the mill first thing as usual, complaining that his shirt cuffs were still grubby. He said he was senior clerk and the slovenly way I keep house makes him look bad in front of his juniors. I was afraid he'd hit me again but he didn't. I promised to have a word with Betty about the laundry but, to be honest, she frightens me. I am the mistress and she is the maid, but she is older than me and more confident. She knows I haven't been married long and I'm sure my inexperience exasperates her. I've seen her watching me as I sit in the parlour reading my book and I wonder if she thinks of me as a spoiled child. A child who has nothing to do all day but read tales of romance while she blacks grates, sweeps crumbs and cleans clothes.

I imagine it's hard to get Bert's cuffs clean when there's so much soot in the air from the village fires and the mill chimneys belching out smoke. But I've never tried to wash a shirt so that's all I can do — imagine.

Mind you, it's probably a good thing Betty's always kept busy. While she's busy she can't poke her nose in where it's not wanted. She can't know what I do or who I meet when I leave the house. I know she can't be trusted to keep my

15

secret and I think she'd most likely take my husband's side and betray me. I think she's a sly one; an enemy to be feared just like the wicked housekeeper in the book I finished yesterday.

I close my eyes and think of my lover. My Darling Man. He's so attentive; so exciting. He makes me feel alive again, as if I were a corpse risen from the grave into the marvellous light the vicar talks about in his sermons.

When I think about the loving words in my darling's letters a smile comes unbidden to my lips. The very thought of him warms my heart and he's told me he's willing to do anything for me. Anything.

Bert doesn't like me going out and if he wasn't at work he'd probably try to stop me. But I promise him I only visit the shops and the library and what would I do all day if I didn't have books to read? When he sees my books he gets annoyed and talks as though the library is a den of sin and iniquity filled with dangerous ideas, but he hasn't forbidden me to go there, provided I'm always home when he comes in for his dinner at twelve thirty.

I confess that his restrictions have made me cunning and the library provides the perfect excuse for me to communicate with my Darling Man. He too has his obligations, but we have learned to overcome all obstacles. And we write to each other such loving words and such secret plans. Plans of freedom. Plans of murder.

Before I set off for the library I have to speak to Betty. I can hear her clattering pans in the kitchen and I hold Bert's shirt, summoning the

16

courage to tell her about the cuffs. But it has to be done or I might suffer for it. Bert doesn't like to be thwarted, especially by women. Especially by me.

When I walk into the kitchen Betty looks up from her work. She is peeling potatoes for tea and her hands are filthy with the soil that clings to the skins. I mutter Bert's instructions, expecting to see contempt in her eyes. But instead I'm surprised to see pity and she says she'll see to it after dinner. Perhaps Betty has begun to realise what my husband is. Perhaps she will be my ally. Although I won't trust her until I know for sure. If Bert were to suspect the truth, I might be called upon to pay with my life, for he has a terrible temper.

Before I leave the house I adjust my hat in the mirror. My hatpin is long and sharp, lethal in murderous hands, and as I push it into the fabric of my hat to secure it onto my head, I fantasise about pushing it into Bert's heart. Perhaps I'm a wicked woman for having such thoughts but my life with him is hard to bear.

I leave the house, carrying my basket over my arm like any other housewife making for the village shops. I pass the library, which is a grand building built of red brick rather than the local stone. The words Public Library and the date 1897 are picked out in ornamental brick above the entrance and at once I feel as though I am being drawn inside that place of stories and escape. But today I have other plans. I hurry past, glancing round, relieved when I see that everyone in Wenfield seems to be absorbed in

17

their own business so I might as well be invisible. I walk on, making for the edge of the village, passing the mill where my husband spends his working day, and taking the footpath out to the open countryside.

If I had been raised in Wenfield my actions would no doubt be fraught with danger because everyone would know me and report back to their family and neighbours. But as it is, I was born in the village of Cheadle in the north of Cheshire so my face is unfamiliar. How I long for Cheadle and those days before my marriage, but I can never go back there because my parents are dead and my brothers were both killed at the Somme. I thought marriage to Bert would give me a new and happy beginning, but it wasn't long before my hopes of bliss were shattered.

But now I have fresh hope. If everything works out as I want, Bert will soon be gone and I will have a new husband; a kind, clever, wonderful man who will carry me away from Wenfield and love me for the rest of my life. One big sin will set me free for ever. Though the smell of smoke clings to my clothes and hair long after my husband's mill with its belching chimneys has faded from view, I find myself skipping over the grass like a child.

I've heard people talk about the place we've agreed to meet, but I have never been there myself. It is some way from the village and when it was described to me I felt a chill, as though I had encountered something evil. The place is known as the Devil's Dancers; a circle of stones

18

so ancient that nobody knows their age or how they came to be there. The Devil stands in the centre with his fiddle while the dancers swirl in a circle around him. I don't know why anybody would go dancing with the Devil. Perhaps they were witches. Or maybe it's just a fanciful tale because people love stories. I've heard there's a curse on the place and that anybody who goes near the stones at midnight will be dragged down to hell. I wonder if it's ever happened.

There is a sharp chill in the March air and I pull my coat around me. The grey clouds glower over the tops of the hills and as I climb the hill I look back at Wenfield. The houses look tiny now, like dolls' houses, and I can see people, small and diminished. From here everything seems so harmless.

There are sheep in the fields I walk through but they show more interest in grass than in a faithless woman meeting her lover. They ignore me and carry on grazing. I had thought to see some sweet little lambs but there are none. Perhaps they and their woolly mothers are in another field. These sheep I pass look thin and their fleeces are dirty grey and hung with mud — or something worse, as if the Devil has put a curse on them too.

The ground dips and I find myself running down a hill into a valley. On the other side of the dip a grey cliff face rises up like an impenetrable barrier and in front of it I can see the circle of stones: the Devil's Dancers cavorting to their eternal tune.

As I approach, I pause to glance back.

19

Wenfield is on the other side of the hill now, I can see nobody and nobody can see me. My heart beats faster as I lift my watch to check the time. I am five minutes early but I don't care. The stench of smoke is gone and the open countryside smells of freedom.

I walk slowly around the circle and I understand how the place acquired its name. There is a movement in the stones, as though they are dancers frozen suddenly in the course of their dance. The stone in the centre looks like a thin, bowing figure towering over the others and the protrusion from its centre has the look of a fiddle. I close my eyes and the sound of the crows becomes the raucous tune of a violin. But that is my imagination. My mother used to say it was my curse.

My Darling Man has arrived and my heart beats faster as I watch him hurrying down the hill into the hollow to meet me. I hold my breath and wait, holding out my arms. There is a smile on his lips, although he looks wary, as though he fears discovery.

'Did anyone see you come here?' he says breathlessly, taking both my hands in his.

'No. I was careful.'

'Good. You know what villages are like.'

I put my hand up to his head and remove his trilby. 'You worry too much.'

He takes the hat from me and smiles. 'You could be right. But we can't take the risk. We have to be discreet. You're a married woman.'

I long to remind him that if all goes to plan I'll soon be a widow. A respectable widow with a house and a good income. In his letters he says he longs for that day as much as I do, but now we are face to face his boldness seems to have vanished. But feelings can often be expressed better in the written word.

'We haven't much time. It's almost eleven and Bert will be back for his dinner at half past twelve.'

'Last time I was walking here I noticed a cave in the rock face. We'll be safe there.' His voice is thick with longing and I feel a thrill of excitement. My heroines never describe the moment in words, just feelings. A warm oblivion. A sweet surrender.

He leads me towards the towering rock face and points to a small circle of darkness. 'In there,' he whispers. 'We can lie on my coat.'

He takes my hand gently and I follow in a dream, the basket still in the crook of my arm. He has to stoop to access the cave, but the entrance is high enough for me. There is an unpleasant odour that I can't quite place but I try to ignore it. He takes out his cigarette lighter and sweeps the light around our new refuge. Then I hear him gasp.

'What is it?' I ask. I haven't been paying attention to my surroundings, only to him and what we are about to do.

When he doesn't answer I hold my breath, hoping all my plans aren't about to be thrown into disarray. He walks towards the back of the cave, his body blocking my view. Then he kneels and holds the lighter aloft.

I follow him slowly and then I see it. A body,

grotesquely swollen and the colour of a bruise. It is a man and he is naked. How did he come to be here, I wonder, and where are his clothes? Why did his life end in such a lonely place? Did he take off his own clothes or did somebody strip them off him? There are so many questions and I want to know the answers.

As my eyes adjust to the gloom I see that the face is a mess of dried blood and broken flesh and something has gnawed at his fingers so that here and there white bone pokes through. Then the smell hits me hard. The stench of rotting meat. I feel sick. As I turn away, I notice a dried-up pool of vomit near the cave entrance. It horrifies me that I must have stepped in it and I recoil, shuddering.

'What are we going to do?' I ask. My voice is feeble from shock and I feel ashamed. The heroine I want to be would know what to do.

He turns to me, his eyes gentle and patient. Bert would have mocked my confusion; told me I was useless.

'We must tell the police,' I say. 'We have no choice.'

'But how do we explain . . . '

'I can say I was walking in the hills; that I needed fresh air and solitude. I will say I looked into the cave out of curiosity because I've never been to this spot before.'

'I won't let you do that. What if your husband gets to hear? If anybody reports it, it should be me.' He pauses and smiles. 'Then your name will never be mentioned. Your reputation won't be sullied.'

'People will guess.'

He thinks for a moment. 'Perhaps you're right. Perhaps there's some other way. Or maybe someone else will find him so we won't have to become involved.'

I touch his back; a fond touch. Grateful. He understands everything. My position; my fears; my terror of discovery and punishment. He is the man I will kill for.

He studies me earnestly in the flickering lighter flame as though he wishes to remember every feature when we are apart. He stoops to kiss the top of my head. He is so much taller than me and I feel protected. But I know that he cannot protect me from Bert.

'Go now. Go home,' he whispers.

He kisses me, a kiss that hints at the potential bliss our grim discovery has prevented.

I obey at once without question and run out of the cave across the damp grass. The clouds have thickened and the stone dancers stand out stark against the grey sky. The Devil is still in the centre, still giving out his eternal, infernal tune. I swear I see him move but I run on, up the slope and out of the little valley, back towards the village. I almost trip on a small outcrop of granite and drop my basket. But I manage to stay upright and when I reach home I take a deep, calming breath before I open the front door.

I must play the innocent. I have been to the village. I have not met my lover. I have not seen a dead man.

5

Since his return from the war in 1918 Albert hadn't slept well. The pain in his leg and injured hand more often than not robbed him of sleep until he fell into a fitful slumber in the early hours of the morning. Then he'd wake with a start, the sound of gunfire ringing in his ears, and it would take him a while to understand that he was safely in his small house in Bermondsey and not in a trench sliced into the French mud.

These days each morning began the same way. He woke up alone, just as he'd done since Frederick's death. In her grief, Mary had banished herself from the bed they'd shared in happier days to sleep in Frederick's bed, saying it made her feel closer to him. And now Mary wasn't there at all. She was in a sanatorium in Margate where she could benefit from good sea air well away from the London smoke.

When the doctor had prescribed fresh air, Mary had argued against it. She hadn't wanted to leave London because in London she was near to the man who called himself the Reverend Gillit, whose League of Departed Spirits claimed to be able to contact Frederick in the hereafter. In spite of Albert's insistence that the man was a charlatan, Mary was in his thrall, egged on by her mother, Vera, who was also a member of Gillit's so-called 'church'.

Albert had struggled to persuade his wife that

the move to Margate was for the best. Although there were times when he wondered whether he'd encouraged her to heed the doctor's advice because their home had become a sterile wasteland since Frederick's death, devoid of all affection and hope. In some ways it was a happier house without Mary's burden of misery, but this very thought caused Albert another pang of guilt.

It was a Wednesday, four days to go until he paid his weekly Sunday visit to Mary, whose sole topic of conversation these days was the Reverend Gillit and what Frederick was doing in the Afterlife. Even the move to Margate hadn't been enough to extract her from Gillit's oily clutches. Vera insisted that Gillit was Mary's only comfort now that Albert was incapable of supporting her. Vera was a poisonous woman, but he knew there was some truth in her words.

He rose from his bed and straightened the sheets and rough grey blankets — the habits of army life never leave you. After dressing, shaving and making himself a breakfast of bacon and fried bread he left the house and caught the tram to Scotland Yard. The air was cold and the streets still moist from overnight rain, so he buttoned his overcoat to the neck and pulled his hat down over his face. He could smell the horse manure mingled with fumes from the motor cars that trundled past, more now than there had been before the war. Some said they were a fad that would never catch on. He himself wasn't so sure.

Sam Poltimore had arrived in the office before him and he greeted him at the door. Albert could tell he was bursting with urgent news.

'The superintendent wants to see you.' He lowered his voice. 'Something to do with a missing Member of Parliament.'

Albert raised his eyebrows. If Sam had got this right, and there was no reason to believe he hadn't, this was bound to be a high-profile case. Unless it was to be treated as hush-hush to avoid some kind of scandal.

'The Super says you're to go up right away. He said he'll have the commissioner with him.'

Albert removed his hat and coat and deposited them on the stand in his office. He was aware that he'd been wearing the same shirt collar for two days on the run; if he'd known he'd have to appear before the top brass he'd have made more effort. As it was, he hoped it wouldn't be noticed.

He made his way upstairs to the superintendent's office where he found his superior sitting stiffly almost at attention. Another man in a pristine uniform sat on the visitor's side of the large oak desk. He turned his head when Albert entered but made no effort to acknowledge him.

The superintendent stood nervously and told him to come in. Albert had never actually spoken to the commissioner before, although his face was familiar. Once the introductions had been made the man studied him as though he was assessing him for some important task.

'You wanted to see me, sir,' said Albert.

'Sit down, man,' the commissioner said impatiently. He was a large, bald man whose forehead was furrowed with a worried frown, as though all the problems of the world were resting on his shoulders.

Albert obeyed, perching himself uncomfortably on the edge of the only other chair. He looked expectantly at his superior officers, but neither spoke.

Finally the commissioner broke the silence. 'It's a delicate matter, Lincoln.'

'Yes, sir,' said Albert, hoping for enlightenment.

'Henry Billinge, Member of Parliament for Liverpool East, travelled to Derbyshire last Thursday to stay with a colleague. He went out on the Saturday afternoon, saying he was going for a walk, and never returned. He completely disappeared.'

'Surely the local police can deal with the matter.'

'It seems they've made no progress and the Prime Minister . . . '

'Wants him found.'

'Precisely, Inspector. He thinks it's high time Scotland Yard stepped in. The friend Billinge was visiting is Sir William Cartwright. His house, Tarnhey Court, is in a village called Wenfield. I understand you investigated a series of murders there in 1919. Since you know the place — and Sir William . . . '

'Yes, sir, but — '

'As you're familiar with the lie of the land, so to speak, you're the perfect man for the job. You'll need to liaise with the local police, of course, but I expect they're no strangers to you. Chance to renew old acquaintance and all that,'

27

the superintendent said with forced bonhomie as the commissioner nodded in approval. 'I told the prime minister I'd be sending my best man. How soon can you get up there?'

Albert attempted to smile but suspected it looked more like a grimace of pain. Although he'd once vowed that he'd never again set foot in Wenfield, he thought of Mrs Bell's letter and knew the task he'd just been given might provide him with an opportunity to resume his quest for his lost, living son.

Revisiting Wenfield would be painful but it seemed he had no choice. It was as though it was meant to be.

6

Rose

As soon as I got home yesterday morning I scrubbed my new boots clean of mud while Betty was busy elsewhere. I didn't want her to start asking questions.

I feel restless and I long to get out of the house. A pile of library books awaits my attention but I can't concentrate on stories of love and triumph. Instead I need to find out whether the police have discovered the body in the cave. And if they have, do they know who he is? His lack of clothes and battered features suggests that someone doesn't want him to be identified, although surely if he is from around here someone's bound to miss him.

Bert's due back at half past twelve for his dinner, which means I have two hours of liberty. I leave the house without telling Betty where I am going; she pries too much into my business as it is. I carry my basket as though I am visiting the shops but instead I make for the library. As soon as I enter I pretend to look for a new book, glad that Miss Hubbard is busy behind the counter stamping the books of an elderly lady. I wouldn't want her to know that I'm really there to see whether he's left a letter in our secret place — his and mine. I look around before shifting the loose piece of wood at the end of the far shelves and my heart beats fast as I pull out the envelope he's put there for me. How I love him.

I place the letter in my basket and hurry out, as though I haven't found any books I wish to borrow. Then I walk quickly through the village towards the lane leading to the Devil's Dancers because I want to find out what's happening. Once in the lane I look round to make sure I'm alone before tearing the envelope open and reading the precious words he has written.

My darling Rose
  How I regret that we were so rudely dis-
turbed by our friend yesterday. My every
waking hour since then has been filled with
thoughts of our next meeting, anticipating
our kisses and our sweet union.
  How I wish you were with me living as
my wife, sleeping in my bed — and not
only sleeping, my love. How I long for us
to be together, sweet Rose.

I read on, his loving words warming me, giving me the strength to face Bert over the silent dinner table. I hate mealtimes, the fear that saying anything wrong might bring on a tirade of bitter words — or worse. But as I read on my spirits soar with new hope.

My darling, ground glass might not work.
It would take very sharp pieces of glass to
do enough damage to kill. But I beg you
to do nothing hasty, even though we both

fear it might be the only way to win your freedom from the torment you endure so bravely, my sweet one.

I kiss his letter and hold it to my heart, tucking it into my bodice before I carry on walking towards the Devil's Dancers. When I reach the top of the hill that overlooks the stones and the rock face I stop. Below me I can see policemen, five in all, two bearing a stretcher. On the stretcher is a blanket and I know that the shape beneath that blanket is my dead man, about to be borne off to the mortuary at the cottage hospital.

The other three policemen are milling around the cave entrance. I wonder if they found the dried vomit. And I wonder what it means. Was the man ill? But if he was, why did he die in that lonely cave and not seek help in the village? Why was his face destroyed like that and why wasn't he wearing any clothes? Suddenly I long to find out what happened to him. And who he was.

Perhaps the police will discover the truth and the news will eventually reach the ears of the village gossips. As long as nobody learns that my Darling Man and I were the first to find the body.

When I arrive home I hurry upstairs and hide my letter with the others in my secret place. I know I should destroy it at once, but it would feel like destroying part of him.

7

Albert had no idea how long he'd be up North. The missing MP might be found before his train journey was over, alive or dead, or the search could take weeks. He recalled that the area around Wenfield held hidden perils; ancient mine workings and potholes that could devour the unwary. Farmers lost sheep that way so the landscape could easily lose a Member of Parliament.

There was a call he knew he ought to make before he set off. Mary was his wife and he owed it to her, whatever difficulties they'd had to endure. He was tidying his desk, preparing to leave the office early to prepare for his journey to Derbyshire first thing the following morning, when the telephone on Sam Poltimore's desk began to ring. Albert stood in his hat and coat watching Sam's face as he spoke into the instrument, wondering if it was news he needed to know.

After a few moments Sam beckoned him over. 'It's a Sergeant Teague from Wenfield,' he whispered, covering the mouthpiece with his hand. 'Isn't that the . . . ?'

Albert nodded and took the telephone from Sam's hand.

'Sergeant Teague. What can I do for you?' He could visualise the officer on the other end of the line: a man with a long thin face and an officious manner.

When Teague replied, Albert remembered something else about him — his voice was unusually loud. He held the telephone receiver away from his ear.

'You've been told there's a man gone missing up our way?' Teague began. 'A Member of Parliament? Well, a body's been found. It matches our man's description but ... his clothes have been removed and his face has been bashed in.'

Albert was momentarily lost for words. He quickly gathered his thoughts and replied, 'You mean someone's gone to a lot of trouble to try to conceal his identity?'

'That does seem the most likely explanation, sir. The doctor says he'll do the post-mortem in due course, but our Super thought — '

'My superiors have already spoken to me about it, Sergeant. I'll be coming up first thing tomorrow.'

Teague made a noise that sounded like a grunt before clearing his throat. 'Well, at least you know the lie of the land, sir,' he said as though he was glad someone was about to relieve him of the responsibility.

After speaking to Teague, Albert suspected he'd be up North for some time — unless the doctor found the unfortunate Henry Billinge had died of natural causes or as a result of some tragic accident which, in view of the strange circumstances, seemed highly unlikely. And while he was in Wenfield he would be able to speak to Mrs Bell. The idea of anybody wanting to kill the harmless Reverend Bell seemed ludicrous, but he knew from bitter experience that human wickedness knows no limits.

He told Sam he was going home to pack for his journey, but as he left Scotland Yard it occurred to him that, since he would be unable to pay his usual visit to Mary on Sunday, perhaps he ought to head for the railway station and catch a train to Margate tonight. But the journey would take over an hour and a half, so by the time he arrived there it would be dark and the nurses would be settling their charges for the night. It looked as though he would have to leave it to Vera to explain the situation and ask her to pass on his regrets to Mary. Knowing his mother-in-law, there was every likelihood she would twist his words and tell her daughter he hadn't come because he couldn't be bothered making the effort.

Vera's house stood in the next street to his own and when he arrived he found that she already had a visitor. He'd met the Reverend Thomas Gillit before; a plump man with a small moustache and an oily manner, dressed in a suit that looked more expensive than anything a policeman could afford. Albert had to fight the urge to drag him to Scotland Yard and demand to know what became of the donations his congregation, mostly ladies, bestowed on him for his words of comfort. Before she'd been admitted to the sanatorium, Mary had been one of those generous benefactors — using his hard-earned money. She'd insisted it was worth paying any price to speak to their little Frederick once more.

'Good to see you again, Mr Lincoln.' The words slithered from Gillit's mouth as he gave Albert a smile that didn't spread to his eyes.

Albert didn't reply. Instead, he turned to Vera. In honour of Gillit's visit she had shed the crossover apron she usually wore and kept smoothing her shapeless brown dress with nervous hands.

'If I could have a word in private . . . '

Gillit seemed to take the hint. He took his hat and overcoat from the hook on the wall and said he had to be going. He had other needy souls to visit. Albert watched him take both Vera's hands in his while she gazed at him in adoration.

'Be strong, dear lady. And I promise to visit dear Mary this week. Please tell her she's always in my thoughts and prayers. I'll see you at the meeting on Sunday.'

'Of course, Reverend.'

If the king himself had summoned her to Buckingham Palace, Vera's manner couldn't have been more obsequious . . . and grateful. Once Gillit had gone, Vera donned her apron again and stood with her arms folded.

'What do you want? You haven't been to see Mary for over a week.'

'I've been busy at the Yard and Margate's a long way — '

'You'll be there on Sunday.'

'I'm afraid I have to go up North. Suspicious death and a missing Member of Parliament. Tell her I'm really sorry.'

'I don't know what the attraction is. They say the North is a horrible place.'

'It's work, Vera. Not my choice.' He knew his words sounded defensive, but unwittingly she'd spoken the truth. There had been two occasions when he'd been tempted to stray from his marriage vows, and both times he'd been up North — far from home. In 1919 in Wenfield he'd been unfaithful to Mary with Flora Winsmore. The second time, the previous September in the Cheshire village of Mabley Ridge, the adultery had been only in his thoughts. Although some would say that was almost as bad.

'Mary needs to see you. She wants to tell you what Frederick's been doing.'

'Frederick's dead.' As soon as he'd uttered the brutal words he felt as though he'd been hit by some unstoppable force. The grief for his son he'd tried to suppress bubbled up without warning and he felt his eyes stinging with tears.

'Mary knows otherwise and so do I. I've heard his voice at the reverend's meetings. I've spoken to him.'

'You've spoken to Gillit or one of his tricksters.'

Vera stepped forward, challenging. 'Do you think Mary doesn't recognise her own child's voice? You're a cruel man, Albert Lincoln. I warned Mary against you, but she wouldn't listen. Go up North. Go to hell for all I care.'

She turned her back on him.

'Tell Mary I'll see her as soon as I get back,' Albert said before letting himself out of the front door and shutting it behind him. As he stepped out into the street he thought he saw a

36

movement out of the corner of his eye, there for a second then gone. He looked towards the alleyway that ran beside Vera's house. Had someone been there, waiting, watching? He peered into the unlit alley. Nothing there. His imagination had been playing tricks again. Or was it the sign of an uneasy conscience?

As he walked home the smoke hanging in the damp yellow air hit his lungs and made him cough. When he let himself into his house he found the place in darkness and, with no fire in the grate, it was as cold as a tomb.

He thought of Wenfield and the comforts of the Black Horse where he'd stayed on his previous visit. Suddenly he couldn't wait for morning to come.

8

Rose

The book I'm reading at the moment is so wonderful that I'm trying to get through it as slowly as I can because I don't want it to come to an end. It's sometimes like that with books, I find.

It's about a poor servant girl who's working for a heartless master. The girl's father is in grievous debt to the master, so he has the power to ruin her family, thus keeping her enslaved. She meets a handsome young blacksmith who truly loves her but the wicked master wishes to make her his mistress, although she keeps resisting him. The story reminds me a little of my own situation. But soon that will be resolved and I will have my happy ending. I know I will. The library is full of happy endings. How I wish I could live there.

News of the body in the cave has spread through the village. Nobody speaks in the library, of course, because it's a place of blessed silence, but I heard a woman in the butcher's say the police think it's murder. Someone else said they're calling in Scotland Yard but I don't know whether that's true.

I do worry in case someone saw me there that morning. What if the police find out and me and my Darling Man come under suspicion? What if

Bert finds out about our meeting? I don't know who I fear most — my husband or the police. But I've got to stay calm and behave as normal. There's no other way.

My Darling Man thinks ground glass might not work so tonight I might put some larger pieces in Bert's stew. Is that very wicked of me?

9

Vivid memories flashed through Albert's mind as the train chugged into Wenfield station. He had made the same journey in the spring of 1919, wondering what he would find in that Derbyshire village. All he had been told was that it stood in the High Peak, which had conjured visions of Swiss mountains, snow-capped and treacherous. There were hills there all right, some almost mountains, green-grey with granite outcrops. At this time of year the snows of winter had mostly vanished, leaving a few stubborn patches near the peaks. The lower slopes were laced with drystone walls and dotted with sheep but there were no Alpine passes or flower-decked chalets; only grey stone villages like Wenfield that looked as though they'd been carved from the rugged landscape itself.

In 1919 he had been called up there to investigate a series of bizarre murders; the female victims had been stabbed through the heart and dead white doves had been stuffed into their mouths. Bringing the killer to justice had come at great personal cost and as he alighted from the carriage with his small brown suitcase, he felt a wave of nausea, wishing he could have passed the job to one of his colleagues. But it was too late to turn back now.

The smoke from the engine dispersed and Sergeant Teague loomed out of the mist, a tall figure in helmet and serge cape. Two years ago the scene had been identical, the local sergeant greeting the man from Scotland Yard on the station platform. Back then, however, Albert had had the advantage of being an unknown quantity.

Teague hurried up to him, hand outstretched. 'Sir. Good to see you again,' he said, although his manner belied his words. Albert guessed that he resented the man from London descending again on his little kingdom. 'You'll be staying at the Black Horse?'

'If Mrs Jackson has room.'

'I'm sure that won't be a problem, sir. Do you want to go straight there, or do you want to call in at the station first?'

Normally Albert would be keen to learn the details of the case as soon as he arrived, but on this occasion he wanted to gather his thoughts. All he knew were the barest facts — a missing Member of Parliament and an unidentified body. He wanted more information before he faced the assembled officers at the village police station.

'Tell me what happened. Who found the body and where?'

'The doctor was going for a walk, something he likes to do after his afternoon surgery, he says.'

Albert caught his breath. 'Dr Winsmore's replacement?'

Teague nodded. 'That's right, sir. Dr Winsmore left the area after his daughter's trial. Couldn't stay . . . not under the circumstances.'

Albert had never enquired what had become

41

of Flora's father. He hadn't wanted to pick at that particular wound. Now the mention of the man made the next question stick in his throat.

Eventually he summoned the strength to carry on. 'What's the new doctor's name?'

'When Dr Winsmore left, Dr Bone from New Mills took over for a while. Then a year ago Dr Kelly arrived. He's young. Well liked.'

'You believe his story about how he found the body?'

'No reason not to, sir. He's going to do the post-mortem once you've settled in. Is tomorrow morning convenient?'

'Yes. I understand the body matches Henry Billinge's description?'

'He's around the same age and build. But the face . . . It wouldn't be right to ask his wife to identify him, would it?'

'I can see that. I believe he was found without any clothes?'

Teague cleared his throat. 'That's right, sir. He was . . . naked.'

'No sign of his clothing nearby? The area has been searched?'

'Of course, sir.' Teague pressed his lips together as though he suspected Albert of questioning his professional abilities. 'No sign of it. Bit of a mystery.'

'Wasn't Mr Billinge staying at Tarnhey Court? Perhaps Sir William would be able to identify him.'

'I'm reluctant to ask him. The body's not a pretty sight.'

'I'm sure Sir William would be prepared to do

42

his civic duty.' Albert had met Sir William Cartwright and thought Teague's consideration of his finer feelings was misplaced. Cartwright had a well-developed ruthless streak and he guessed Teague's motive was a desire not to offend his social superiors. There were some things the war hadn't changed.

'If you say so, sir.' Teague didn't sound happy.

'I'll ask him, if you wish.'

'Would you, sir? Thank you, sir.'

'I need to speak to him anyway about Mr Billinge's last-known movements.'

'I've already asked him, sir.'

'Even so, I want to ask him myself. Is . . . er, Lady Cartwright well?'

'As well as she ever was, sir. She's never been a healthy lady as you'll remember.'

'Do you see much of Roderick?'

'Master Roderick's moved to Manchester, sir. Since Flora Winsmore . . . went we haven't seen much of him. They were friends, I understand, and I heard he was upset about what happened so he upped and left. Working in some theatre.' The word 'theatre' was said with distaste.

'That's right. His name cropped up in an investigation I was called to in Cheshire last September. Just a loose connection. I didn't actually get to see him again.'

Teague nodded. They had reached the Black Horse. It was a solid old inn midway down the High Street with an archway to one side that had once allowed coaches access to the cobbled courtyard at the rear. The paintwork was fresh and, under the management of Norman Jackson and his capable wife, it was the best place to stay in Wenfield.

When he told Teague to return to the police station the man took his leave reluctantly, as though he didn't want to let Albert out of his sight. Albert watched him walk off down the street and took a deep breath before opening the front door of the Black Horse and ringing the bell in the entrance hall. Mrs Jackson came hurrying through from the back and when she saw her new guest a look of surprise passed across her face, swiftly replaced with a welcoming smile.

'Mr Lincoln. Well I never. I didn't expect to see you around these parts again.'

'Neither did I, Mrs Jackson.' He smiled. 'I know I should have telephoned from London, but I came up in rather a hurry. I hope you have a room for me.'

'You're lucky, sir. Two gentlemen left this morning. They had business at one of the mills. Would you like a room at the front? I know you get the noise from the street but . . . '

'That would be most satisfactory, thank you.' A room at the front of the building would give him a good view of the comings and goings on the High Street, which might be to his advantage.

The room was clean and neat, just what he needed. The last time he'd stayed there he'd been along the corridor and he was glad of the change of location. The original room would have brought back too many memories of that spring two years ago. He walked over to the window and looked out. The High Street was busy. There were women hurrying in and out of the shops, tiny children in prams and pushchairs and old men in flat caps watching the world go by while they waited for the pubs to open. A public library stood almost opposite the inn, its red-brick frontage jarring with its stone-built neighbours. It was a grand building for Wenfield, a symbol of civic pride. Learning brought to the masses; Wenfield as a bastion of culture and education.

Down the street he could see the tearoom where a spinster called Miss Forrest had once presided like a queen; the empress of gossip and vinegar words. It was still a tearoom but under its new management it had acquired a new coat of blue and white paint and had been renamed 'The Willow Pattern Tearooms'.

Albert wondered whether Mrs Bell still frequented the establishment. He recalled that she had never liked Miss Forrest and her poisonous talk, although she'd been as shocked as the rest of Wenfield at the woman's violent death. For a brief moment he was tempted to go down and see if she was there. But Teague would be expecting him to put in an appearance at the police station.

On his way to the station he slowed down as he passed the teashop but he couldn't see Mrs Bell at any of the neat tables with their crisp white cloths. He needed to speak to her but in the meantime his priority was to discover who might have killed a Member of Parliament and left him battered and naked in a Derbyshire cave.

He was greeted at the station's front desk by Sergeant Teague and Constable Wren, who shook his good hand earnestly while trying hard not to look at the left hand hanging by his side, a reddened stump with only the thumb and forefinger remaining.

'Good to see you back, sir,' said Wren. It had always seemed incongruous to Albert that such a large man should bear the name of Britain's tiniest bird.

Albert nodded in reply. If he'd given the conventional response that it was good to be back he'd have been lying.

'I've given you the office you had last time, sir,' said Teague. 'I hope that's satisfactory.'

'Thank you, Sergeant.'

As he settled into the familiar office that held so many memories, he hoped his stay in Wenfield would be short. The sooner he was out of there, the better.

10

Rose

I put a small piece of glass in the stew we had for tea but he found it at once and called me a stupid slut. He said anyone with half a brain would have noticed and I told him I'd broken a glass earlier and some must have fallen into the stew. He was angry and slapped me across the face. At least he didn't realise I'd done it on purpose.

I don't think I'll make a good murderer. I'm too easily frightened, but my Darling Man says that's a nice thing about me. He says he wouldn't like to love a Messalina. Only I don't know who Messalina is. Perhaps she was very wicked. I'd ask him to tell me about her, but I don't want to appear ignorant. My Darling Man is so clever. Whenever I visit the library I try to read some books on history and science but I don't find them as gripping as my novels. Learned volumes don't take me away from Wenfield and Bert like my love stories do.

I've heard that a writer's moved into a cottage just outside the village. A lady, someone said. I wonder if I've read any of her books. If she comes into the village, I might meet her, although I don't know what she looks like. I expect she's glamorous like a film star, but I haven't seen anyone like that in Wenfield. It's possible she looks quite ordinary, which would be a little disappointing.

Ground glass might not be as effective, but I think I'll try it anyway. I have a pestle and mortar in the kitchen and at least Bert won't realise because it will be as fine as salt. And he likes salt with everything.

The villain in the book I'm reading at the moment reminds me of Bert. He's good-looking and charming to the world but underneath all that he's cruel to the beautiful wife he keeps locked up in the attic so that he can get his hands on her fortune. How I hate Bert. How I wish he was dead.

11

Albert left the police station at eight o'clock and returned to the Black Horse for his evening meal. Mrs Jackson had made something specially — meat pie and mashed potatoes — because the hour was late. In Wenfield most people ate their tea at six o'clock.

He had Mrs Bell's new address and it was just a matter of finding the time to speak to her. But after he'd finished eating he decided that it was far too late to call on the vicar's widow. He'd have to curb his impatience and save his visit for another day.

He didn't sleep well. Being back in Wenfield with its echoes of past sins unnerved him. He'd endured the horrors of war; he'd seen his comrades blown to pieces in the trench beside him, as well as suffering pain and injury himself, and there were times in the silence of the small hours when mortar fire still echoed through his head. And yet these things seemed almost bearable compared to the agony of betrayal he'd experienced two years before in that very village.

The following morning he climbed out of bed, his head aching, knowing he had to attend the post-mortem of the man from the cave. Long ago he'd learned to detach himself from the procedure; to view the body on the mortuary table as a specimen to be studied rather than a human being. But it was still something he dreaded. Strangely it had been the doctor himself who had come across the body while taking a walk near a place called the Devil's Dancers; an ancient circle of stones whose purpose and origins had been lost in the mists of time and legend.

When he went down for breakfast he found Mrs Jackson scurrying around, clearing dirty crockery from the tables. Albert nodded to his fellow breakfasters — two men in cheap suits sitting at separate tables, probably there to visit one of Wenfield's three mills, whose tall, smoke-belching chimneys dominated the far end of the village. They nodded back warily and turned their attention to their bacon and eggs, the deep concentration on their faces suggesting that they wanted to avoid conversation at all costs.

He remembered Mrs Jackson's breakfasts from his last stay and all of a sudden he felt hungry. After so long having to cater for himself in Mary's absence, he savoured each mouthful of the perfectly cooked meal as he tried not to think too hard about the day ahead.

As he was leaving the inn, Norman Jackson, the landlord, emerged from the back carrying a crate of beer bottles. When he saw Albert he came to an abrupt halt, a look of alarm on his face. Two years ago he'd been treated as a murder suspect. Albert had questioned him at length and the memory had clearly left a lasting and unpleasant impression.

'Good morning, Mr Jackson,' Albert said, attempting a reassuring smile.

Jackson grunted in reply and vanished back through the door. Perhaps Albert hadn't been forgiven. But he'd only been doing his duty.

He walked through the cobbled streets towards the police station, aware of curious looks from the people he passed. He'd become a well-known figure in the village back in 1919; the man from Scotland Yard who'd come to sort out their difficulties. Now all he wished for was anonymity.

When he arrived at the police station Wren was waiting for him, standing to attention behind the front desk. Sergeant Teague joined him and, after the good mornings had been said, Albert asked what time the post-mortem had been arranged for.

'Dr Kelly says half past eleven, sir. He has patients to see first.'

'I wouldn't want to keep Dr Kelly from his patients. I'll bring myself up to date with the details of the case while we're waiting.'

Wren lumbered off, leaving Albert with Teague, who followed him into the office that had once been so familiar. Albert hesitated before taking the seat behind the desk like a king assuming his throne. He was in charge now and he noted a fleeting look of resentment on Teague's face.

There was a file in the middle of the desk and Albert opened it before inviting Teague to sit. The file would probably contain everything he needed to know, but he preferred to hear it from Teague's lips. In his experience, you could learn a lot from the observations of the local force.

51

'You've already told me the bare bones of what happened. Now I want to hear the whole story.'

Teague cleared his throat. 'As I said, Mr Billinge was staying with Sir William at Tarnhey Court. He'd been there a couple of days when he told Sir William he was going for a walk. Sir William warned him not to stray too far. There are grouse moors up beyond the village and the gamekeepers up there have had trouble with ruffians from Manchester trespassing and having to be chased off. If Mr Billinge had been mistaken for one of them . . . '

'It might have caused some embarrassment, but I'm sure Mr Billinge would have told them that he was a guest at Tarnhey Court.'

Teague grunted. 'Some of those fellows shoot first and ask questions later, if you know what I mean. Like I said, they've had a lot of trouble with folk who think they have the right to wander anywhere they please, and with the young birds — '

'You were telling me about the day Mr Billinge was last seen.'

'Right you are, sir. Mr Billinge left Tarnhey Court around three o'clock and was expected back for dinner. Only he never returned and nothing more was heard of him.'

'Did he have a motor car?'

'He came up by train. Sir William met him at the station in the Rolls.'

'And you think it was him who ended up in that cave?'

'Well, no one else has been reported missing around here so I don't see who else it could be.

Sir William sent out a search party, but I don't know if they got as far as the Devil's Dancers. Some people are superstitious about that place.'

'Why?'

'All sorts of rum things have been reported there over the years. There's talk of a curse.'

'Do you believe that?'

Albert saw Teague's cheeks redden a little. He was local. He'd been brought up to be wary of that particular place and old habits die hard.

'There are potholes and old mine workings round about. Sir William thinks Mr Billinge might have . . . He was a city gentleman, not used to walking in the hills.'

'I need to speak to Sir William. Telephone Tarnhey Court to make an appointment, will you.' Then Albert suddenly realised that it might work to his advantage if Sir William was unprepared for the interview. 'On second thoughts, forget that last order.'

'But surely, sir . . . '

'That will be all, Sergeant. Let me know when it's time to set off for the cottage hospital.' As Teague turned to go, Albert spoke again. 'Have you seen anything of Mrs Bell, the Reverend Bell's widow?'

'Not much, sir. Since the reverend died she's kept herself to herself, although I hear she still arranges the flowers in church. Nice lady. Her mother passed away a couple of months after the reverend and her children are grown up and making their way in the world so she's all on her own.'

'I might pay her a call if I have time.' Albert

53

hesitated. 'Has she said anything to you about the reverend's death not being . . . ' He searched for the right words. 'Not altogether straightforward?'

Teague raised his eyebrows. 'No, sir. Nothing like that.'

'Was there a post-mortem?'

'I don't think Dr Kelly thought it necessary, sir.'.

Teague left the room reluctantly and Albert started to study the file. He took out the photograph of the missing MP. He was a handsome man, probably in his late thirties or early forties, straight-backed and distinguished, with hair that showed signs of turning grey at the temples. In the photograph, carefully posed in an exclusive photographer's studio, he wore a well-cut dark suit and his hand was resting on a pile of books, a signal that he was a serious-minded, learned man. The name of the studio was on the reverse of the photograph, the address Bold Street, Liverpool. It was a portrait taken to impress, but then a Member of Parliament has to look important and learned in front of his supporters and constituents. Appearances have to be kept up.

Albert studied the file for a further ten minutes before rising from his seat and plucking his hat and coat from the stand in the corner. Before he witnessed the examination of the unfortunate victim's body, he wanted to know more about him.

He left the police station without telling Teague where he was going.

12

At first it seemed that Tarnhey Court had been frozen in time since Albert's last visit. Then he began to spot some subtle changes. The house looked a little more neglected, so perhaps times were hard . . . even for the Cartwrights. Or maybe they'd simply lost the will to keep up the standards expected of people of their social class. In addition, one member of the family would be missing; Sir William's son, Roderick, no longer lived there, having chosen the world of the theatre in Manchester over the life of a rural son and heir and the career in government or the law that would have been his father's choice for him.

Albert recalled that Roderick had had secrets of his own; secrets that would have seen him arrested if the truth about his sexual preference had ever come to light. Albert had kept the secret to himself because, as far as he was concerned, it was Roderick's business and his alone. Although if Teague and Wren had got wind of it they wouldn't have been so understanding. Roderick had been devastated when the truth about the murders there in 1919 came to light. The young heir to Tarnhey Court and Flora Winsmore had grown up together, they'd been friends. Albert suspected that Roderick had felt almost as betrayed by what happened as he had.

He passed through the gateposts topped by

their moss-covered stone eagles, and as he walked up the drive he noticed that the crocuses were in bloom beneath the overgrown laurels, providing some welcome spring colour. Here and there rotting autumn leaves lay in drifts and weeds protruded through the gravel of the path. Before the war the Cartwrights had employed an army of gardeners but since 1918 their staff had dwindled in number. These days, men — those who had survived — preferred jobs in factories where they could call their free time their own.

He knocked on the front door and waited. After a while it opened to reveal Mrs Banks, the Cartwrights' housekeeper, a stout, grey-haired woman dressed in black with an intelligent face and kind eyes. Last time he was there the door had been answered by the maid, Sarah, who had later met her death in a terrible way. Albert suspected that the Cartwrights hadn't bothered to employ a replacement.

Mrs Banks recognised him at once. 'Mr Lincoln. My word, I didn't expect to see you up these parts again!'

'How are you, Mrs Banks?'

'Well enough. Although with Sarah not being replaced . . . Girls don't want to go into service these days, but the work's still there to be done.'

Albert gave her a sympathetic smile. 'Is Sir William at home?'

'He's at a meeting in Manchester this morning. I expect you've come about Mr Billinge?'

'Would I be keeping you from your work if I asked for a cup of tea?'

Mrs Banks caught his meaning at once and led the way past a row of silent servants' bells to her sitting room next to the kitchens. It was a cosy room, cosier than the family's grander accommodation. Albert felt comfortable there. It reminded him of his own home, before the war and Frederick's death had destroyed his and Mary's brief domestic idyll. His eyes were drawn to the motto hanging above the glowing fireplace: *God sees all our sins*. Albert hoped this wasn't true.

'I can send Martha to see to Her Ladyship if she rings,' Mrs Banks said after placing the kettle on the gas ring in the corner of the room. 'In a place this size it's not easy making do with one maid and a couple of women from the village who come in to do the heavy cleaning and sort the laundry. But you don't want to listen to me moaning on about my problems. You'll want to talk about Mr Billinge.'

'I could do with you at Scotland Yard, Mrs Banks.'

Her face was suddenly solemn. 'I was shocked about . . . I heard you and Flora Winsmore were friends.'

'We were all shocked.'

'They say it's a good thing she was hanged before she could kill any more. Mind you, Master Roderick took it bad.' She turned her head away. 'I heard talk that she had a baby before she . . . Wonder who the father was.'

Her words almost made Albert gasp. 'Perhaps it's best not to speculate,' he said quickly. If Mrs Banks had been looking closely at his face, he

57

feared she might have guessed the truth.

'There were some who thought it might have been Master Roderick but . . . I can't see it myself.'

'No,' Albert leapt in. Sensing that, if he didn't change the subject he'd give himself away, he added a prompt: 'You were going to tell me about Mr Billinge.'

'Fine gentleman he is. He and Sir William stayed up till all hours smoking cigars and drinking brandy in the billiard room. Discussing matters of state, I shouldn't wonder.'

Albert could tell Henry Billinge had made an impression on the housekeeper. She smoothed her dress and leaned towards him as though she was preparing to share a confidence.

'Although I did hear them having words on the night before Mr Billinge left.'

'Words?'

'Raised voices. Almost midnight it was. Her Ladyship had gone to bed and I was afraid they'd wake her. She needs her sleep, does Her Ladyship. She hasn't been too good since Master Roderick left. I think she misses him. They say his theatre in Manchester is doing well. He's showing moving pictures now, so I've heard,' she said proudly.

'Did you hear what Sir William and Mr Billinge were arguing about?' Albert asked, not wanting to be distracted by talk of Roderick's career.

She hesitated, torn between sharing her knowledge and being revealed as a listener at keyholes. 'I think it was something to do with votes for women. Whether the voting age for women should be lowered to the same as for men.'

'What's Sir William's opinion?'

'He's all for keeping it at thirty, but I don't think Mr Billinge agreed with him.'

'Are you sure their argument was just about lowering the voting age for women? There was nothing more . . . personal?'

Mrs Banks inclined her head to one side, considering the question. 'When they were arguing, I'm sure I heard the name Clara. 'Don't bring Clara into this,' I think he said — Sir William, that is.'

'Who's Clara?'

'I've no idea. Perhaps it's somebody they both know in London. Sir William spends a lot of time down there, him being a Member of Parliament.'

'Can you tell me exactly what happened on the day Mr Billinge went off?'

Mrs Banks took a deep breath. 'There wasn't much talk over breakfast, I can tell you that. Her Ladyship tried her best to make conversation and Mr Billinge answered politely enough. But I sensed bad feeling between Sir William and Mr B. Not that they said anything, but there was definitely an atmosphere.'

'And later in the day?'

'The two men went into Sir William's study and stayed there until luncheon was served.'

'And the conversation over luncheon was . . . strained?'

She nodded. 'Although Mr B did his best to be charming to Her Ladyship. Like I said, he's a real gentleman. Then at three o'clock he said he was going for a walk. He was dressed for the countryside in tweeds and sturdy brogues and he was wearing a good overcoat, so we thought nothing of it. Some gentlemen like to walk in the countryside, don't they, especially if they live in the town.'

'Of course. And you expected him back?'

'That's right.'

'Did you ever hear him mention that he knew anybody round these parts?'

'Not in my hearing. Maybe you should ask Sir William.'

'Did he have anything with him? A suitcase or . . . ?'

'I didn't see him go out, but he left some things in his room. I'm not sure what he brought with him because he saw to his own luggage and unpacking. Not like the old days.'

'Where was Sir William while Mr Billinge was out?'

'He went out shortly afterwards, took the motor car to Stockport. He said he had someone to visit.'

'Did the chauffeur drive him there? Is Pepper still with you?'

'Oh no, sir, Mr Pepper left us a year ago to set up his own garage in Stockport. Sir William drives himself now.'

'Could it have been Pepper he was visiting?'

'I'm sure I've no idea, sir. He doesn't confide in me.'

'Perhaps I should have a word with Her Ladyship. Is she at home?'

'She's lying down at the moment. If you want to talk to her you'll have to come back another time.' Mrs Banks seemed protective of her mistress. Albert remembered Lady Cartwright as a frail, almost fey woman, so it was possible the housekeeper's concern was justified.

'What time did Sir William return home that day?'

'Around six o'clock. His shoes were dirty. Took me ages to clean them, it did. And he seemed rather . . . distracted.'

'Was he worried when Mr Billinge didn't come back?'

'Not at first. But he was later. And the next morning Her Ladyship insisted on calling the police when we found Mr B's bed hadn't been slept in.'

'Why weren't the police notified at once?'

'I told Sir William they should be, in case the gentleman had got into difficulties. What if he was stranded somewhere? Or even injured? Sir William said he was a grown man and he didn't want to cause him embarrassment by sending the police on a wild goose chase.'

'I'd like to speak to Sir William. What time is he expected home?'

'Not till this evening, sir. He said he wouldn't be home for luncheon. Her Ladyship will have something on a tray in her room.'

He thanked Mrs Banks. She had been helpful; had perhaps told him more than she'd intended about her employer and his dealings with the missing man. He took his leave with a feeling of dread. Shortly he'd have to witness the

61

post-mortem on the as yet unidentified man. And he needed Sir William to confirm whether or not the body was indeed that of Henry Billinge MP.

As he walked down the drive he could hear his feet crunching on the sparse gravel but when he stopped he thought he heard another set of footsteps, following some way behind.

He turned but there was nothing to see, only a pair of doves flapping towards the dovecot in the walled garden. His wife would have said it was a ghost. And, for him, Wenfield was a place of ghosts; the sort he could never lay to rest.

13

Rose

I cannot see him today and I'm worried. What if the police discover that we were there together in the cave that morning? But my Darling Man assured me that they'll only be interested in finding the truth about the dead man. They'll just want to know who he was, how he died and why. And so do I. Whenever I shut my eyes I see that face reduced to nothing but blood and bone, and that body, dark purple like a massive bruise, naked and glistening in the flame of my darling's lighter.

It's horrible to think that someone hated that man enough to do that to him. I imagine that whoever killed him didn't want anybody to find out who he was. The police have been searching to see if the murderer hid the clothes nearby. I wish my Darling Man had a way of finding out, then he could share his knowledge with me. We have no secrets from each other. It is as though we are one person.

I tried the ground glass in Bert's dinner last night but it seems to have had no effect. Perhaps I have to wait longer for it to work. Bert wanted me to do my duty as a wife last night and I had no choice. I lay there as he grunted like a pig on top of me, closing my eyes tight and trying to imagine it was my Darling Man. I failed because he is so different — so gentle and thoughtful. Just like the heroes in my books.

I'm going to meet him tomorrow. I cannot wait. I am counting the moments.

14

Albert had vivid memories of the cottage hospital and as he entered he glanced upwards at the sign above the door: *Endowed by Sir William Cartwright MP*.

He remembered the way to the mortuary where he had witnessed the postmortems on the victims back in 1919 all too well. It was there that he'd watched Dr Winsmore extract the bedraggled, bloodstained doves from the women's mouths and slice into their prone bodies. Dr Winsmore had had no inkling of the truth and Albert wondered whether he could have proceeded so calmly if he had.

This time Dr Kelly was in charge, dressed in his surgical gown with his scalpel at the ready to make the initial incision. First, however, he stood back to make a visual examination of the corpse.

'Late thirties or early forties at a guess,' he began. 'Fairly well nourished. Hair appears to be neatly cut and washed. Dirt beneath his fingernails and on his hands, but that's to be expected if he crawled to the cave where he was found. He's not a man who's been living rough. I'd say that in the period before his death he'd been well cared for — which means that someone's bound to miss him.'

'Anything else?'

'There's a shrapnel wound to his left arm. Some of it's still in there, by the look of it. And there's scarring on his scalp — probably the result of a head injury.'

'War wounds?'

'I'd say this man served his king and country, yes.'

Kelly fell silent and as he began to cut the body open Albert's eyes were drawn to the mutilated face.

'What about the face? What kind of weapon was used?'

'Our old friend the blunt instrument. There are fragments of stone in the wounds, so in my opinion his killer used a rock — there are a lot of them about up there. But although it made a hell of a mess I don't think he was bludgeoned to death. I think the damage was done post-mortem.'

'Someone wanted to make sure he wouldn't be recognised. Which suggests he's known in these parts.'

'Or someone hated him enough to want to obliterate his face,' Kelly said, before resuming his exploration of the man's internal organs. After a couple of minutes he looked up from his work. 'It's been suggested that he could be that missing Member of Parliament?'

'That's one possibility, Doctor.'

'I met him, you know.'

'Really?'

'I was invited to dinner at Tarnhey Court along with what passes for the great and the good in Wenfield.'

'Who else was there?'

'The vicar and Mrs Bell, the last vicar's

widow. Then there was a couple who have a big place outside the village . . . and the manager of Gem Mill and his wife. And another lady was invited to even up the numbers — a novelist.'

'Do you think this is Henry Billinge?'

Kelly stood back from the corpse, staring at it intently. 'I'm sorry, Inspector,' he said after a few seconds. 'I can't be sure. I hardly said a word to him all evening and I was called away to see a patient before the gentlemen had their brandy and cigars.' He thought for a moment. 'But, you know, it could be him. Similar hair, similar build. As for the shrapnel wound, we weren't on such intimate terms. Sir William knew him best, of course.'

'If he wasn't bludgeoned, what was the cause of death?'

'There was a pool of dried vomit in the cave, which makes me think of poison. Perhaps he went to the stone circle with his killer, who tricked him into taking the noxious substance — from a hip flask — or it might have been something slow-acting he'd ingested earlier and he and his killer made their way up there for some reason.'

'But why go to the trouble of disfiguring him like that?' said Albert, thinking aloud.

'Fortunately, Inspector, that's your problem not mine.' He paused. 'There's one thing that might interest you. From the dried-out contents of his stomach, I'd hazard a guess that his last meal contained steak, potatoes and peas eaten an hour or two before death and washed down with a generous helping of whisky. One thing I do recall about Billinge is that he enjoyed his drink. I'll send the vomit off for analysis and we'll have to keep our fingers crossed that the laboratory comes up with an answer. There are reliable tests for some poisons, but others . . . ' The doctor shrugged his shoulders helplessly, which made Albert fear that they might never learn the precise cause of death.

When the post-mortem was over he left the mortuary alone, looking back at the building that held so many bad memories. Then he set off at a brisk pace for the police station. There were things he needed to do.

15

Albert's route back to the police station took him past the doctor's house, a building which had become so familiar on his previous visit to Wenfield. The brass plate next to the front door that had once borne the name of Dr Winsmore now said Dr Ronald Kelly MD but the house looked the same. The same front door; the same ivy growing up the rough stone wall; the same wrought-iron gate that Albert had pushed open so many times, his heart pounding with anticipation. He slowed down, peering at the house, half hoping to see the housekeeper, Sybil, who had run Dr Winsmore's household, cooking and cleaning for the doctor and his daughter, Flora.

After what had happened there in 1919 he wondered whether Sybil had stayed on to work for Dr Kelly — or if she'd left to seek employment elsewhere, away from the scandal and the memories. He remembered that she and Flora had been fond of one another, but that fondness had probably vanished as soon as the truth emerged.

If it hadn't been the doctor's house, where the village went to be cured of their ills, he knew it would have become known as the murderer's house, tainted forever by its history. But the association obviously hadn't bothered Dr Kelly too much. He had taken over the practice from

Dr Winsmore and, presumably, enjoyed the same trust and success. Although he wondered whether the new doctor lay awake in the early hours and thought about the traumatic events that had occurred under that very roof.

He carried on walking, trying to put the doctor's house out of his mind. With any luck he'd never have to enter that front door again. As he walked his leg began to ache. In an effort to take his mind off the pain, he lifted his eyes to the surrounding hills, newly green as they recovered from their winter coating of snow, just as they'd been two years before. The eternal circle of nature carried on oblivious to man's problems.

When he reached the police station he hesitated at the entrance, standing beneath the blue lamp suspended above the door. Sergeant Teague wouldn't know what time the post-mortem had ended so if he turned round now he could visit Mrs Bell. Her letter intrigued him, but he needed to know more before he took any action.

He had kept the letter with him in the inside pocket of his overcoat and, once he was out of sight of the police station he took it out. The address was in a small street near the church, on the way to Pooley Wood where most of the victims had died two years before. The woods were a popular spot with courting couples back then but he wondered whether what had happened there had put a stop to all that.

His route took him past the entrance to Tarnhey Court. Sooner or later he'd have to return and question Sir William, and perhaps ask him to view the body in the mortuary in the hope he could identify it. But, according to Mrs Banks, he wasn't expected home until that evening, so Albert's second visit would have to wait.

When he reached Mrs Bell's address, he was surprised at how small the cottage was. It must have felt cramped after Wenfield's spacious vicarage but nowadays she would have no need of a large house in which to entertain and conduct parish business.

The cottage was stone-built like the rest of the village, with small-paned windows and a budding rambling rose by the green front door. It was attached to another, identical cottage and separated from its neighbour by a low wooden fence. The square front garden was neatly planted. When summer came it would be a riot of cheerful colour. It was every city dweller's vision of an English country dwelling; the sort of place they'd been told they were fighting for back in 1914.

He raised the lion-head knocker and it fell with a crash. As he waited, shuffling his feet, he felt a sudden rush of anxiety. If Mrs Bell hadn't seen fit to share her suspicions about her husband's death with the local constabulary, how much proof did she have? He feared this might prove to be an unwelcome distraction from a politically sensitive case. Then there was his other problem: if it turned out that Mrs Bell knew the whereabouts of his lost son and could be persuaded to share that information with him, what was he going to do about it?

When the front door opened his first thought was that the vicar's widow looked older than when he'd last seen her. Thinner and more strained. Her grey hair was scraped back into an untidy bun and her shapeless dress was black, the colour of mourning. Albert took off his hat.

'Inspector Lincoln. When I wrote to you I wasn't expecting you to come in person. Thank you so much. Please come in. Don't stand there on the doorstep.'

She stood aside to let him pass. The little hallway was decorated with pictures; watercolours of local scenes and a few dark oils. He recognised some of them from his last visit to the vicarage. He was shown into a front parlour crammed with furniture, including a large upright piano. At Mrs Bell's invitation he took a seat near the cast-iron fireplace.

'I received your letter,' he began after she'd rung a small brass bell to order tea from a spotty girl who hurried in from the kitchen.

'That's Joan,' she said quietly when the girl had gone. 'She started at the vicarage shortly before the reverend passed away and I felt obliged to keep her in gainful employment. She's not the brightest candle in the box,' she said with what looked like a wink. 'Grace has stayed on to look after the new vicar. I do miss her, but she's a regular visitor.'

Albert smiled, feeling foolish that he'd been so apprehensive about their meeting. 'I was surprised when I read your letter,' he said after the girl had come in with the tea tray and

72

scurried out again like a frightened mouse.

'I'm very grateful that you've come all this way.'

'Your letter isn't the main reason I'm here. I'm sorry.'

'Don't be. I'm just glad to see you. I did hear about that body being found at the Devil's Dancers but I thought it was some sort of accident or . . . '

She clearly wasn't aware of the Henry Billinge connection and Albert didn't feel it was his place to enlighten her. 'I'm afraid the death is being treated as suspicious and it was thought that as I was familiar with the area . . . '

'Of course.' She hesitated. 'These two years have passed so quickly, don't you think?'

'Indeed.' He wondered how much she knew about his relationship with Flora. In her letter, she had mentioned their friendship, but had she known the whole truth? The keeping of confidences had been part of her late husband's calling so Albert was sure he wouldn't have let even his wife in on the secret. 'I was so sorry to hear about your husband. He was a fine man. And much loved in the village.'

'Yes, he is greatly missed. The Reverend Fellowes has replaced him, but in my opinion he lacks Horace's warmth.' She raised her hand to her mouth, as though she feared she'd been indiscreet. 'Oh, please don't tell him that if you see him. He's a good man, really, and I'm sure he does his best. He served as a padre in the Somme, you know, and I think he's still troubled by what he saw there.'

'That's to be expected,' said Albert, glancing down at his own maimed hand. 'You wrote that you thought your husband's death wasn't altogether . . . straightforward.'

She put down her teacup and gave a long sigh. 'Horace died quite suddenly, you see, and before that he'd been a picture of health, rarely darkened the doctor's door. He used to say the Lord had blessed him with a good constitution. He hadn't been ill at all before his death. Not even a cold. When I wrote to you, it had been preying on my mind for months.'

'People do die suddenly. It's a tragic fact, I'm afraid.'

'Dr Kelly said it was his heart, but Dr Winsmore always said he had the heart of an ox.' At the mention of Winsmore's name she lowered her eyes.

'Even oxen are obliged to meet their Maker one day,' said Albert before draining his teacup. As soon as the words had left his mouth he wondered if they'd sounded flippant, but to his relief Mrs Bell smiled.

'You're quite right, Inspector. But he'd gone out the evening before he passed away without telling me where he was going, which wasn't like him at all. He always let me know where he was and who he would be visiting — just in case I needed to contact him urgently.'

'He didn't mention where he'd been when he returned?'

'No. He went straight into his study and when he came to bed I was already asleep. In the early hours of the morning he woke me up and told me he hadn't felt well since he'd arrived home, but he hadn't wanted to worry me. He said he felt dizzy and he was finding it hard to breathe. Then he was very sick and he died shortly after.'

Albert could see tears glistening in her eyes and he knew it pained her to recall that terrible night when she had lost her dear husband and her life had been changed for ever.

'You didn't believe it was his heart at the time?'

She shook her head and took a clean white handkerchief from her sleeve. After dabbing her eyes she spoke again. 'I couldn't contradict the doctor, could I? He seemed convinced, although he did ask me whether Horace could have eaten something that disagreed with him. I told him that we'd dined together and we'd both eaten exactly the same things — as had our maid and our cook.'

'Unless he ate something while he was out on this mysterious evening visit of his?'

'That's possible, of course, but he never mentioned anything. Dr Kelly said there was no need for a postmortem. I think he wanted to save me from more distress. He's a very thoughtful young man.'

'Your husband was buried?'

'Here in the churchyard, yes. The bishop himself took the service. It was a beautiful day and the whole village turned out. It was a comfort to me to know how much he was loved.'

'But you still think he was poisoned?'

She straightened her back. 'I fear so.'

'And you said in your letter that you have a

suspicion as to who might be responsible.'

She said nothing for a few moments and Albert sat on the edge of his seat and waited. In the silence he went through everyone he'd met in Wenfield, searching his memory for anyone who struck him as a potential murderer. However, he knew that, given the right circumstances, anybody is capable of the ultimate sin. Two years ago he'd discovered that the girl he'd fallen in love with had been responsible for a series of cruel deaths, yet he hadn't harboured the slightest suspicion until the very end.

'Maybe I was too hasty when I wrote that letter. I don't think it's right to accuse anybody without evidence.'

'It's up to the police to find the evidence, Mrs Bell. If you tell me where we should be looking.'

'I can't. It wouldn't be right.'

'Then I'm afraid I can't help you.'

He sat watching as the emotions passed across her face, changing like the Derbyshire weather, cloud and mist one minute, brightness the next. Eventually she looked him in the eye. 'Will you be discreet?'

'You can rely on me.'

'And tactful?'

Albert nodded.

'I think he might have gone to Tarnhey Court that night. I think he might have called on Sir William.'

'You're not suggesting Sir William poisoned him?' Albert said with disbelief.

'When you put it into words, it sounds ridiculous. But Horace had been visiting Tarnhey rather a lot around that time and he never said why. At first I thought Lady Cartwright might have been ill but word has it in the village that she's as well as she usually is.'

Albert caught her meaning. Lady Cartwright was known to be 'delicate', but such women often outlived their healthier contemporaries.

'I've absolutely no proof. As far as I know, Horace and Sir William were on good terms. He even read a lesson at the funeral. I'm probably being foolish.'

'Sometimes our instincts are right, however unlikely they may seem. I'll make enquiries.' He saw a worried frown pass across her face. 'And don't worry, I'll be the soul of discretion. Sir William will never learn of your suspicions from me.'

'Thank you. I knew I could trust you. Horace always spoke well of you.'

'Did he receive any telephone calls that night? Or perhaps a letter that arrived earlier in the day?'

'He did receive a letter. He opened it in front of me and I saw that it contained a photograph but before I could ask him about it he'd put it in his pocket.'

'Did you ever find it after . . . ?'

She shook her head. 'He might have put it away in his study when he got in, but I didn't have the heart to go through his things after his death. And by the time I returned to Wenfield the Reverend Fellowes — Simon — had moved into the vicarage.'

'Did you ask him about it?'

'Yes, but he said there was no letter of the right date — and certainly no letter with a photograph enclosed.'

Albert glanced at the carriage clock ticking away on the mantelpiece. He knew he should leave but he had another question, one he'd been longing to ask since he entered the house.

'Your husband arranged for an orphaned child to be found a home. The mother was Flora Winsmore and I understand the child was a boy. Do you know what became of him?'

He thought he'd succeeded in making the enquiry sound casual, as if he'd only asked out of mild curiosity, but Mrs Bell was staring at him as though she could read his thoughts. He took a deep breath and awaited her reply.

'Horace said he'd found the unfortunate child a good home and that he was sure he'd always be kept in ignorance of his unhappy origins.'

'Somebody adopted him?'

'Why do you want to know?'

It was the most difficult question Albert had ever been asked. Aware that Mrs Bell was watching him closely, he paused to consider his answer.

'I was the officer who arrested her. It might seem foolish to you, but I can't help feeling responsible for the poor mite. I had a son myself. He died of influenza shortly after the war. So you see . . .'

She bowed her head. 'I'm sorry for your loss, Inspector. There are few things worse than losing a little one. As for Flora's baby, I'm afraid I can't help you.'

The flame of hope that had flickered inside Albert ever since he'd discovered the previous September that the Reverend Bell might know what had happened to the child was suddenly snuffed out. Anxious not to betray his disappointment to Mrs Bell, he took a deep breath and changed the subject.

'Have you heard that Sir William's guest, Mr Billinge, is missing?'

'Yes. Poor man. You don't think it's him they found . . . ?'

'We can't be sure yet. I believe you dined with Sir William and Mr Billinge the night before he disappeared.'

'There were a number of people there.' She smiled. 'Prominent members of the community, I suppose you could call them. I found Mr Billinge a pleasant man and I assure you that I recall nothing about that evening that could have led to murder. It was a convivial dinner and I left early, along with Dr Kelly, who was called to see a patient. I'm sorry I can't be more help.'

Albert thanked her and took his leave.

Sir William was due back that evening so he'd pay him a visit. If Mrs Bell's suspicions about her husband's death were founded in fact, he needed to know.

16

Rose

Bert is due home from work any time. I have made a pie with the steak and kidney I got from the butcher's today. Steak and kidney's his favourite. There's no ground glass in it today because I don't think it works. My Darling Man was right — and I suppose he should know, what with all his learning. I haven't been able to see him for a while and I really miss him. But I must be patient. I have to think of the future. Our future.

I hear the front door open and close with a bang. Bert is home and my heart is beating like a drum. My book's lying on the sideboard and I rush to hide it because he hates to see me reading. Filling my head with nonsense, he calls it. My Darling Man would never speak to me like that. Never.

He's standing in the parlour now, sniffing the air. 'What's for tea?' he says. No greeting. No kiss hello.

'Steak and kidney pie,' I say, trying to smile. 'Your favourite.'

'I can't smell nothing.'

I rush into the kitchen and look at the oven. It isn't lit. I put the pie in earlier but I forgot to light it and now I feel like crying.

I turn and see him looming like a monster in

the doorway. I want to scream because I know what's coming but it would only make him more angry. I back away. 'Sorry. We can have fish and chips instead. I'll go and get 'em. We can have the pie tomorrow. It won't spoil.' I try to sound cheerful, as though it doesn't matter. But he's taken a step towards me. Then another. I can see his fists are clenched and I close my eyes.

'Stupid bitch. Stupid useless cow,' he shouts as the fist meets my stomach and I fall to the floor.

'I'm off out to the Carty Arms,' he shouts as he lumbers from the room, leaving me sobbing and winded.

It takes me half an hour to gather the strength to stagger out of the house and over to the telephone box on the corner of the street. The door is heavy and the inside smells of sweat and tobacco. I dial the number before pressing my coins into the slot. It has to stop before he kills me.

17

Albert telephoned Tarnhey Court from the Black Horse. Mrs Jackson was very proud of her telephone and the fact that businessmen visiting the mills only had to make a call from their offices in distant parts of the country to secure a respectable room for the night when the demands of commerce kept them from their own beds.

It was Mrs Banks who answered, formal now as though their meeting earlier that day had never happened. Albert had noticed that speaking on the telephone often had that effect on people. She confirmed that Sir William had now returned home but Albert declined her offer to fetch him. He would call on him in person. His business wasn't something that could be conducted over the telephone wires with the operator listening in.

He knew that he ought to tell Sergeant Teague what he was planning to do but he couldn't face the sergeant's inevitable attempts to interfere. To Teague the Cartwrights were untouchable; his social superiors who had to be treated with the respect they'd enjoyed for centuries. So far as Albert was concerned, those days were gone.

By the time he reached Tarnhey Court it was dusk and the archway of laurels seemed to press in on him as he made his way down the drive. He could see the old stables, once home to the

Cartwrights' chauffeur, standing in darkness, and he made a short detour. Sir William's Rolls-Royce was there and when Albert put his hand on the bonnet he felt a slight warmth. Sir William hadn't been home long.

The Rolls was the only vehicle in there and it looked small and insignificant in that large dim space designed for a selection of horse-drawn carriages. Albert looked around before climbing the stairs in the corner that led to the chauffeur's quarters. The door was unlocked and he pushed it open. Last time he'd been there Sydney Pepper had been in residence, a former soldier who had suffered his own losses. Now the place was empty, although some basic furniture remained — an iron bed, stripped to the stained mattress, and a couple of chairs standing beside a shabby wooden table. The light was fading so Albert took his torch from the pocket of his overcoat as he crossed the room. He opened the door of a built-in cupboard only to find that it contained nothing but junk, the unwanted possessions Pepper had left behind when he quit Sir William's employment for a new, and hopefully better, life. Albert pushed the things to one side; old newspapers, half-empty containers of hair oil, a pair of driving gloves with holes at the fingertips.

Then something on a lower shelf caught his eye. A blue bottle, the glass ribbed as a warning. When Albert took it out he saw that it was half full — and that it bore a skull and crossbones on the front below the word 'poison'.

Albert wrapped the bottle in his handkerchief

and dropped it carefully into his pocket before making his way downstairs again. Sir William would be expecting him.

He knocked on Tarnhey Court's grand front door and waited, surprised when Sir William himself answered. He was a thin man with sparse hair and an amiable face and if it wasn't for his natural air of confident authority he might have been mistaken for a country solicitor. But now, for a split second, he looked wary, almost as though he feared that Albert had come to arrest him. However, he invited Albert in with the cool confidence he had shown during their previous meetings.

'Mrs Banks said you wanted to speak to me. I presume it's about Henry Billinge. Terrible business. We were all very worried about him and now this body's been found. It's a tragedy. Terrible business,' he repeated before leading Albert through to his study. Once Albert was seated he picked up a heavy cut-glass decanter and poured out two glasses of whisky. He handed one to Albert, then he drank his own down in one and poured himself another.

'I did warn him to take care. What with old mineshafts and disused quarries, this landscape can be extremely hazardous to the unwary.' He paused for a few seconds. 'I must say I never expected to see you back in these parts again, Inspector.'

Albert ignored the comment, not wishing to be distracted from the matter in hand.

'You and Mr Billinge had a disagreement, I believe.'

Sir William's eyebrows shot up. 'Where on earth did you hear that?'

Albert didn't answer the question. He had no wish to get Mrs Banks into trouble with her employer. 'Is it true?'

'We had a bit of a debate over policy,' Sir William said smoothly. 'Women's votes and all that. Nothing personal, I assure you. I've already given a full statement to Sergeant Teague.'

'I realise that, sir, but I would like to know more. What kind of man was Mr Billinge?'

'Clever. Ambitious.' He hesitated. 'Before the war I would have said he was a little ruthless; the sort of man who liked to get his own way and usually did, if you get my meaning. But I had noticed a change in him recently.'

'Since the war?'

'He served with distinction, but I think his time at the front affected him as it did so many. That's not to say he wasn't an effective politician.' He leaned forward. 'Am I right to use the past tense? Do you think it's him?'

Albert decided not to answer the question. 'He's married, I believe.'

'Yes. His wife's the daughter of a baronet.'

'Is the marriage happy?'

'How should I know? It's not the sort of thing gentlemen discuss.'

'You must have formed an impression. You must have sensed whether he and his wife were close by the way he spoke about her.' It suddenly hit Albert that the words might apply to himself. How did he talk about Mary? The answer was that he avoided the subject if at all possible.

85

'If you want the truth, Inspector, I'd say the marriage was a socially advantageous one rather than a love match, if that's the phrase.'

'I believe it is, sir. You've been in touch with Mrs Billinge?'

'Of course. Naturally she's very distressed and I told Teague not to tell her about the body until the identity was certain. No point in upsetting the lady more than is necessary. I understand you need someone to identify the body.'

'That's right, sir. But . . .' He searched for the right words. 'I'm sorry to have to tell you that somebody battered the face with a blunt instrument.'

Sir William looked shocked, although Albert wondered whether the emotion was genuine. 'Who would do a thing like that?'

'That's what we want to find out, sir.'

'If you're saying someone hated Henry enough to want to destroy his face? I can assure you that I know of no one who — '

'Did he have a mistress, one with a jealous husband, perhaps?'

There was a brief moment of hesitation. 'Not as far as I know.'

Albert fought the impulse to take the man by his expensively tailored lapels and tell him he knew he was lying. Instead he spoke calmly, inclining his head to one side. 'Are you absolutely sure about that, sir?'

'I dare say there will have been moments of temptation. But then we're all men of the world, aren't we, Inspector?'

Albert took a sip of whisky, trying his best not

86

to show that Sir William's last statement had made him squirm with guilt. 'Was there anyone in particular?'

'I believe there was a certain lady in Kensington, although I heard that all finished over a year ago.'

'Anybody else?'

'Not that I'm aware of,' he said, avoiding Albert's gaze.

'Was he in possession of any important papers when he vanished?'

'Confidential papers, you mean? None as far as I know. And certainly nothing worth killing for.' Sir William shook his head, the ghost of a smile on his lips. 'Not unless his killer was interested in the government's policy on fisheries. The matters Henry dealt with had absolutely no connection to the country's security, I assure you.'

'Did he receive any letters or telephone calls while he was here?'

'You'll have to ask Mrs Banks. If there were any letters, she would have given them directly to him.'

Sir William poured himself another glass of whisky, his third, and waved the decanter in Albert's direction. 'More, Inspector?'

Albert held out his half-full glass for a top-up. He knew he wasn't meant to drink on duty but it was the evening. Besides, he felt he needed the warm, hazy comfort the amber liquid gave him.

'I understand the Reverend Bell made frequent visits here shortly before his death.'

'That's right. He came to see my wife. A

family matter concerning her niece.'

'How is Lady Cartwright?'

'Well enough, thank you.'

'Having a guest in the house must have been a strain for her.'

'She understands that a man in my position is expected to entertain from time to time.'

'You had people to dinner while Mr Billinge was here.'

'We gave a small dinner for neighbours on the Friday night, yes. Dr Kelly was here and the vicar, the Reverend Fellowes, although the man's not really one for conversation. Mrs Bell, the late vicar's widow and Mr Jones, the manager of Gem Mill, together with his good lady. And the Ogdens, who have a place between here and New Mills, were there too; Ogden's a decent sort and his wife makes an effort to speak to Lady Cartwright, which is much appreciated. There was also a lady called Peggy Derwent who writes novels. She took the Eames's place outside the village when they left.'

'The Eames have moved away?' Albert remembered David Eames, the artist, and his sister well from his last visit.

'They left shortly after Flora Winsmore's trial. Eames was friendly with the woman, I believe.'

'Where did they go?'

'Yorkshire, or so I heard.'

'I'd like to speak to everyone who was at your dinner that night,' said Albert.

'It was the first time they'd met Henry, so I'm sure they won't be able to tell you anything. It was an amiable evening, I assure you. Nothing controversial and certainly nothing that might provoke murder.'

Albert took a deep breath. This agreed with what Mrs Bell had told him but he still wanted to speak to the other guests. 'Dr Kelly suspects the person we're assuming is Mr Billinge might have been poisoned.' He watched Sir William's reaction and saw only mild surprise.

'You said he'd been battered to death with a blunt instrument.'

'I said someone disfigured him so he couldn't be identified. They also took his clothes.'

Sir William's mouth fell open. 'Sergeant Teague never mentioned that.'

'Was Mr Billinge wounded in action, sir?'

'I believe he was, yes,' Sir William replied, staring at Albert's own scars.

'How?'

'He never spoke about it.'

'Shrapnel in his arm?'

'It's possible.'

Albert stood up. 'Can you come to the mortuary tomorrow morning? First thing.'

Sir William drained his glass again and nodded. 'As long as you contact Mrs Billinge. I don't think I can face . . . '

'Of course, sir. That's a job the police are accustomed to. Although it might be wise to delay breaking the news until his identity has been firmly established. We wouldn't want to distress the lady without good cause. Would nine o'clock sharp at the cottage hospital suit you?'

Sir William made a show of consulting the diary on his desk. 'Yes, that will be convenient. I will meet you there.'

Albert stood to leave but when he reached the study door he turned. 'I believe the Reverend Bell visited you here on the night he died.'

'You've been wrongly informed, Inspector. I never saw Bell that night.'

'Does the name Clara mean anything to you?'

Sir William hesitated for a moment. 'No.'

Albert was sure he was lying.

As he made his way down the drive once again he had an uncomfortable feeling he was being watched from the shadow of the bushes. As he neared the gates he heard a rustling to his right and he stopped, taking out his torch and shining the beam into the undergrowth.

Though the dim light revealed nothing, he was sure something was lurking, possibly an animal — or maybe a human being, the most dangerous of all nature's predators.

18

The following morning Albert found a letter from Vera lying on the breakfast table between his knife and fork where Mrs Jackson had placed it. Even when Mary was too sick to write, Vera took it upon herself to make sure she wasn't forgotten.

His fellow guests in the dining room made no attempt at conversation, each apparently fascinated by their own breakfast, so Albert calculated that he could safely open the letter without being watched. He picked up the butter knife on his side plate and slit the envelope open, letting the cheap lined paper inside flutter down onto the table.

I hope you are well, began the stiff school-girlish greeting:

The Reverend Gillit visited Mary in the sanatorium yesterday and something wonderful happened. I know you are not a believer but if you had seen it with your own eyes you would have changed your mind. When the reverend and I arrived Mary was asleep and she looked poorly. Then she woke up and the reverend held a special seance, just for the three of us. Frederick was there in the room talking to us. There was no trickery. It was his own sweet voice. He said Mummy was going to get better and she should go home because he liked to be near his bedroom and his toys. Afterwards Mary seemed so much improved. She even had some colour in her cheeks. She hardly coughed at all and I'm sure she's on the mend. I'm going back there today to bring her home. She doesn't like it at the sanatorium and she says she's missing Bermondsey. When you come back she'll be home again. I told her you'd be pleased.

I will write again soon.

Yours truly,

Vera Benton (Mrs)

Vera's strangely formal way of signing a letter used to make Albert laugh, but there was no smile today. The contents of the letter made him uneasy. Against all medical advice and on the dubious say-so of the Reverend Gillit, Mary's mother was taking her out of the sanatorium. Gillit's growing power was no longer merely annoying — at worst, it might eventually prove dangerous. Still, there wasn't much he could do about it because he had lost all influence over Mary a long time ago. Even if he'd been on the spot, he doubted whether his advice would trump that of Gillit.

He returned the letter to its envelope and stuffed it into his jacket pocket before starting on the breakfast Mrs Jackson had just placed in front of him. He ate hungrily and washed the meal down with Mrs Jackson's strong tea, the tannin setting his teeth on edge. He had an appointment with Sir William at the cottage hospital and he didn't want to be late.

Sir William was waiting for him at the hospital entrance, studying his gold pocket watch to make the point that Albert had kept him waiting five whole minutes. Once inside the mortuary, a gnarled man in brown overalls led them to the room where the corpse lay beneath a white sheet. At Albert's signal he folded back the sheet to reveal the top half of the body and Sir William gasped.

'He doesn't smell too good, I'm afraid, sir,' said the man, still holding the edge of the sheet. He turned to Albert. 'Does the gentleman need some smelling salts?' he asked in a low voice, nodding towards Sir William.

'That won't be necessary, thank you, my man,' said Sir William, taking a snowy handkerchief from his pocket to cover his nose. He stared at the body, frowning.

'Is this Henry Billinge?' Albert asked, anxious to get the ordeal over and done with.

Sir William shook his head. 'Hard to say. He's a similar height, but this man's hair looks greyer and not as neatly cut. Billinge was very particular — used a lot of pomade. I always thought him vain, to tell you the truth. And this man appears to be plumper, although his body's swollen so . . . It's difficult to tell.'

'He stayed at your home. You must know.'

'It's impossible to be certain with his face like that.' He paused, deep in thought, then said, 'His ring. Billinge wore a signet ring on the middle finger of his right hand.'

Albert drew closer to the corpse on the slab and studied the right hand. There was no ring there but whoever killed him might have taken it, along with his clothes. More significantly, he could see no mark where a ring had been, although this might be explained by the swelling and discoloration of the body. However, without a positive identification from Sir William, he felt he was still working in the dark.

The likelihood was that the remains in front of him were those of Henry Billinge MP, but he had to know for certain. The one course of action left to him now was to invite Billinge's wife up from London to view the body. It was something he would have preferred to avoid, but only a wife would possess the required intimate knowledge to confirm it one way or another. He would ask his colleagues at Scotland Yard to undertake the unpleasant duty of breaking the news.

It wasn't until later that day, after several hours spent bringing himself up to date with the details of the case and speaking to Teague and Wren about possible lines of enquiry, that he heard back from Scotland Yard. Mrs Billinge was travelling up from London the following day and would arrive around five o'clock in the afternoon. But she was refusing to believe that the dead man was her husband.

19

Rose

It's seven o'clock on Sunday morning and I spent the night wide awake listening to the clock on the bedside table. Tick tock, tick tock. Ticking away the hours until the light started to creep through the curtains and the birds began their dawn chorus. You'd think I'd have slept better without him snoring there beside me. But I didn't.

Bert went to the Cartwright Arms last night but he never came home and I don't know what to do. Maybe he stayed out because he's angry with me. Maybe he's got another woman — I wouldn't mind if he has. Or maybe something's happened to him.

I thought I'd be pleased not to have him here but instead I'm worried. What if the ground glass has worked at last and he's lying dead somewhere? What if I get the blame?

Once I'm up and dressed I'm going to go to the telephone box to call my Darling Man. He'll know what to do.

20

The last thing Albert expected during his breakfast on Sunday morning was an interruption from a lady. He hadn't been aware of her arrival and when he looked up from his plate of egg and bacon she was standing beside his table wearing a smart hat and a black bouclé coat whose length had been fashionable before the war. Albert guessed it was her best outfit, reserved for church on Sunday, but the widows of vicars aren't usually renowned for keeping up to date with the latest modes.

Mrs Bell looked nervous as Albert invited her to take a seat. It was only eight o'clock and he couldn't help wondering what had brought her to the Black Horse at such an early hour. He put down his knife and fork, looking regretfully at the fried egg congealing on his plate.

'Oh, please carry on with your breakfast, Inspector. I'd feel guilty if I stopped you eating. A man needs a hearty meal at the start of the day. I know my dear late husband always did.'

He shot her a grateful look and resumed eating. Many, in his experience, wouldn't have shown so much consideration. She sat patiently, watching him as he ate. A comforting presence, almost like a mother. No wonder she'd been a popular figure in her husband's parish; the person people went to with their problems when confiding in a man of the cloth seemed too daunting.

'How can I help you?' he said, once he'd pushed his plate to one side. At that moment Mrs Jackson appeared to clear the table and he asked for tea and a second cup.

Mrs Bell waited for the tea to be poured before she began, lowering her voice so they wouldn't be overheard by Mrs Jackson or her other guests who were taking their breakfast nearby.

'Something rather odd occurred yesterday evening and I wanted to ask your opinion.'

Albert sipped his tea and waited for her to continue. He was tempted to sneak a surreptitious glance at his watch because he'd promised Sergeant Teague he'd be at the police station by half past, but he resisted, suspecting that what Mrs Bell was about to tell him might be important.

'I visited the vicarage, my old home, and I didn't expect . . . ' She didn't finish the sentence, as though she was trying to make sense of what happened and needed time to think. 'You know I never like to speak ill of anybody and I wouldn't want to throw suspicion on someone without good reason.'

'I know that, Mrs Bell. Why don't you tell me what's troubling you and let me be the judge?'

'Yes, of course.' She gave him a weak smile, then took a deep breath before she spoke again. 'I called at the vicarage last night in the hope of looking through my late husband's correspondence for some clue as to who he might have met shortly before he died. I thought it a straightforward request.

97

'As I said before, dear Horace's death was so sudden and I was far too upset to spend hours trawling through his correspondence at the time. At Grace's suggestion, I went to stay with my sister, and by the time I returned a few weeks later Simon had moved into the vicarage — which he had every right to do. I moved all my things to the cottage, but the study had been Horace's domain so I left it as it was.'

'You didn't see whether there were any personal papers left in there?'

'Simon said that if he found any he'd bring them round to the cottage, which he did. But . . . ' She hesitated. 'My late husband was a very open man, Inspector. He had no secrets from me. But last night when I asked Simon Fellowes if I could take a look through the papers in the study he reacted very oddly. I told him I wanted to look for the letter with the photograph Horace received on the day he died, but Simon insisted there was no such letter and that all the correspondence in the study was private. He said he couldn't allow just anybody in there.'

Albert sighed. 'Mrs Bell, you have no proof that your husband was murdered. The doctor said — '

'I think Dr Kelly made assumptions at the time and if I'm able to find new evidence then perhaps Horace's body can be exhumed and his death can be investigated properly. Why didn't he tell me where he was going that night? He always told me where he'd be, so it wasn't like him at all.'

'The police will need more evidence before we

can order an exhumation. I'm sorry.'

He drained his teacup. The woman sitting on the other side of the table didn't seem the type given to fanciful theories, and part of him was inclined to believe her. But he needed more before he could take action.

'I haven't finished telling you about last night,' she said.

'Well?'

'When I pointed out to Simon that I'd lived at the vicarage for twenty years and was well aware of the need for discretion, he told me some cock and bull story about losing the study key. I knew he was lying and he wasn't very good at it. He didn't want me poking around in there. Why was that, do you think?'

'How long have you known him?'

'He came here as Horace's curate just after the war, and when my husband died he took his place.' There was a hint of bitterness in her words, as though she viewed the new man as a usurper.

'Tell me about him.' Albert glanced at his watch. It was eight fifteen but he would have to be a few minutes late. He was sure Sergeant Teague could cope until he arrived.

'I told you he served as a padre during the war, didn't I?'

Albert nodded.

'He's in his thirties and a bachelor. There's never been any mention of a sweetheart, as far as I know. A man in his position needs the support of a wife. At least, that's what my husband always used to say,' she added with a sad smile.

99

'You think Mr Fellowes is hiding something from you?'

'I'm sure he is.' The certainty in her statement was convincing. 'And I thought that if a Scotland Yard detective asked him for access to the study he could hardly refuse.'

Albert considered her suggestion, unsure how to reply. Then a selfish thought crept into his head. It was possible that some record of his and Flora's son's whereabouts might be among the papers the Reverend Bell had left behind and a search might give him a chance to find his own child. And yet it was a matter that would require delicate handling. 'I'll have to think about it,' he heard himself saying. 'I'm afraid I can't make any promises.'

Mrs Bell stood up stiffly. 'I've wasted enough of your valuable time, Inspector.'

Albert rose to his feet and took her hand in his. 'It's always a pleasure to see you, Mrs Bell. And I will give your problem some thought. By the way, does the name Clara mean anything to you?'

'I had an aunt Clara, but she died many years ago. And there's a Clara Meadows who teaches at the village school. Apart from that . . . '

'Thank you. It's probably not important.'

As she left she stopped for a word with Mrs Jackson on the way out and he checked the time. Even though it was Sunday, the murder investigation carried on and he needed to be at the police station. The sooner the problem of Henry Billinge was cleared up, the sooner he could leave Wenfield for good.

21

Sergeant Teague raised his eyebrows when Albert said he wanted to view the cave where the body believed to be that of Henry Billinge had been found.

'It's a fair walk,' he said, as though he presumed a man from the capital whose leg had been injured in combat wouldn't be up to such exertion.

'That won't be a problem,' said Albert, quickly, wondering whether others who saw his injuries made assumptions about his capabilities, especially those like Teague who'd never faced the realities of war.

Teague grunted in reply and Albert suspected his reluctance was because he didn't fancy the walk himself. The stunning, hilly landscape might be a novelty to visitors from the smoky streets of Manchester but to Teague, who had lived there all his life, it was probably as unremarkable as the grimy streets of Bermondsey were to Albert.

'Mrs Billinge will be arriving on the five o'clock train,' Albert said as they walked. 'I'll meet her at the station. I've had a word with Mrs Jackson and there's a room for her at the Black Horse.'

'I thought she'd be staying at Tarnhey Court.'

If Sir William was to be considered as a suspect it would hardly be appropriate for the victim's widow to stay under the same roof, Albert thought, although this wasn't something he felt he could share with Teague, who deemed the Cartwrights to be above all suspicion. 'I think she'd be more comfortable at the Black Horse. Besides, I don't expect she'll want to stay in Wenfield more than a night or two. Mr Billinge is MP for a Liverpool constituency. Does he have a house there?'

'I believe there's a bachelor flat he uses when he has to stay on constituency business, but it would hardly be a suitable place for his lady wife. And I understand he owns a couple of other properties there as well and rents them out.'

'Has anybody been to his flat?'

'The local lads in Liverpool gave it the once-over but they found it empty. No clue to his whereabouts.'

Once beyond the confines of the village they soon reached the path leading to the Devil's Dancers. The stone circle couldn't be seen from where they were walking; there were a couple of small hills to climb first, with the land forming hollows in between. The path up the first hill was rough but well trodden. Farmers kept their sheep up there and this was their route into the village.

'People don't like coming this way, especially after dark,' said Teague.

'You mentioned a curse. What's the story behind it?'

'They say that hundreds of years ago a group of women from the village wanted to rid themselves of their husbands and take younger lovers so they turned to witchcraft and took to meeting up there to cast spells and dance. One night when they were up there a handsome young man turned up and offered to play the fiddle for their dance. They thanked him and when he started to play the music was so beautiful they found they couldn't stop dancing. On and on they danced, and even when they grew tired their feet wouldn't stop moving and the fiddler wouldn't stop playing. The dance got faster and faster until the music suddenly stopped and the women found they were rooted to the spot. They couldn't move and they saw that their handsome young man had turned into the Devil. They never returned home to their husbands because they'd been turned to stone. Ever since, people have said the place is cursed.'

This was the longest speech Albert had ever known Teague to make. It was obvious he knew the story well, as many others in the village probably would.

'What form does this curse take?'

For the first time Teague looked unsure of himself. 'Well, like I said, nobody goes up here in the dark.'

'But it looks as though Henry Billinge might have done. Why would he do that, do you think?'

Teague fell silent. They had reached the crest of the hill and below Albert could see a dip before the land rose again to form another smaller hill. As they carried on the path became rougher and Albert's injured leg began to ache, although he wasn't going to admit this hint of weakness to Teague.

'It's quite a way from the village.'

'About a mile,' said Teague.

'So who usually comes up here? Walkers? People who don't know about the story — or don't care?'

Teague shrugged.

'Courting couples?'

'Suppose so. But I'd never have brought my missus this way when we was courting. Wouldn't have seemed right.'

'If they knew it was a place people from Wenfield tend to avoid, it might attract couples with something to hide. Illicit liaisons.'

'Married men meeting their fancy women, you mean.'

Teague's suggestion, voiced with such obvious disapproval, made Albert smile.

'If locals are frightened of the place they'd most likely have it all to themselves. The perfect way not to be caught.'

'You can't think Mr Billinge was meeting a fancy woman? He's a respected man; a Member of Parliament.'

Albert was tempted to point out that the outwardly respectable often hide the worst sins, but he thought he'd allow Teague to live with his illusions until the truth became necessary.

'It's a possibility we have to bear in mind, Sergeant. Although it might be best not to mention it to Mrs Billinge when she arrives.'

They'd just reached the top of the second hill and below, in the small valley, he could see a circle of standing stones, harsh grey and weathered by time into strange, swirling shapes. He could see how the legend had started, because they did look as though they were dancing, caught in movement, frozen in their eternal dance while the Devil fiddled his diabolical tune in the centre of the ring. On one side of the dip a tall rock face rose up, grey to match the dancers. It looked as though it might have been a quarry in centuries past but now greenery sprouted from the stones here and there, relieving the brooding darkness of the rock.

'The cave's down here,' Teague said, as he started along the path, his shiny boots setting fragments of loose stone skittering down the slope.

Albert followed. His leg felt more painful now but he was determined to keep up. He soon found himself by the stones, which seemed smaller now he was close to them. The dancers barely reached his shoulder, although the Devil himself, the master of the dance, was a good two feet taller.

Teague was making straight for a small gap in the rock at the base of the cliff. He stopped and looked round, waiting for Albert to catch up with him.

'What would make Billinge come here?' Albert asked once they were both in the cave. When he looked around, his eyes were drawn to a patch of dried vomit still visible on the ground near the entrance.

'Curiosity? To meet somebody?'

'Sir William said Billinge went out for a walk. He didn't mention that he'd arranged to meet someone.'

'If it was a . . . ' Teague cleared his throat. 'A lady, he might not have wanted Sir William to know.'

'Who else, apart from Sir William, did Mr Billinge know in these parts?'

'I understand Sir William hosted a dinner in his honour, but — '

'Perhaps he met someone that evening, a lady . . . ?'

Teague blushed. 'I'm sure the type of people Sir William would invite wouldn't behave like — '

'You'd be surprised at how our so-called betters behave, Teague,' said Albert, irritated at the sergeant's assumptions.

Since the war he'd sensed deference slipping away, being shed like a restricting garment. Working men and gentlemen had shared the same trenches and ordeals, and they'd seen the best and worst of each other. One man, they'd discovered, was as vulnerable as the next. It was impossible to unlearn those lessons and go back to how things used to be.

He turned to Teague. 'Why don't you go back to the station, Sergeant. I'd like to stay here for awhile.'

Teague looked mildly alarmed. 'Are you sure, sir? I wouldn't fancy being here alone, I really wouldn't.'

'I'm sure I can take care of myself. You must have duties to attend to.'

'If you're sure, sir.'

'I am.'

Teague left Albert in the cave, glancing back

once he reached the entrance as though he was reluctant to go. Teague's presence had been getting on Albert's nerves and he wanted some time by himself to consider what he'd learned.

He felt he knew very little about Henry Billinge but, with luck, he'd learn more from his widow. Then there was Mrs Bell's dilemma. If Billinge had been poisoned, as the doctor suspected, then maybe she was right and Horace Bell had been as well. Which would mean there was a poisoner at large in Wenfield. They said poison was a woman's weapon, but he knew this wasn't necessarily true. Anybody might resort to it if they wanted to kill at arm's length.

He emerged from the cave into the weak spring sunlight and walked around the stone circle, stopping in the middle, face to face with the Devil. The first thing that struck him was the silence. There was no birdsong here, not even the raucous cries of the crows who populated the countryside round about. The silence unnerved him. It was the kind of silence he'd experienced before going over the top. There had been no birdsong in the trenches either.

Unusually for that part of the world, it hadn't rained much since the body was discovered. Albert's eyes were drawn to the ground, which had been disturbed near one of the stones: the tallest of the dancers, nearest to the cave. It looked as though there'd been some sort of scuffle. Or perhaps the scuffs in the rough grass had been caused by the dying man's death throes as he was led, struggling, towards the shelter of the cave to vomit out the contents of his stomach before dying his painful death.

Albert suspected the man had been taken there to die. Somebody had guided him away from all possible help and left him naked and disfigured with nothing to betray his identity. He could imagine the killer leading Billinge there, offering him a swig from a hip flask on the way, a drink of poison. Then waiting for it to take effect. Watching the man suffer and die.

Albert had hoped that the killer would have left some trace. But he'd seen nothing and he felt despondent. He retraced his steps towards the village and when he reached the summit of the second hill he could see Wenfield laid out below; the stone cottages and the three mill chimneys to his left. With the church bells ringing in the distance the scene looked so innocent. But this had once been a killing ground. And it seemed it might have assumed that role again.

He stopped and when he turned he saw a movement to his right, something that had suddenly crouched down in the shelter of the wall. He was about to investigate when a large sheep emerged from the hiding place, leaving Albert feeling foolish. His time in the company of the Devil's Dancers was making him see things that weren't there.

22

Rose

'I don't know where Bert is.' That's what George Yelland told me earlier when I caught him passing the house in his Sunday best.

I saw him from the front window and ran outside to ask him if he'd seen my husband but I should have known he wouldn't have been with Bert in the Carty Arms last night. He's not the type to be one of his drinking cronies. George is the youngest of the clerks, a nervy creature who looks as though he's frightened of his own shadow.

George looked really nervous as he stood on the doorstep twisting his hat in his hands like a frightened orphan in a play. As if he was scared that Bert might appear and be angry at being disturbed. I often wonder what Bert is like at work. Is he a bully, the way he is at home? Maybe people are scared of him there too. My Darling Man insists that I'm not to do anything. If I keep calm everything will be all right. He tells me I'm not to worry, but I can't help it.

There's a knock at the door. A heavy knock like a portent of doom. My heart begins to pound so loudly that I can hear the blood rushing in my ears. It can't be Bert because he has a key. Unless he's been drinking all night and lost it. I straighten my apron and when I walk into the hall I see a large shadow behind the stained glass in the front door. Then the knocking starts up again and I have no choice. My hand is shaking as I open the door and when I see Constable Wren standing there as solemn as an undertaker's mute, I know the worst has happened.

Or perhaps it's not the worst. Perhaps it's the best.

23

'Who is he?'

'A clerk at Gem Mill, name of Bertram Pretting, known to everyone as Bert. He's a regular in the Cartwright Arms. Likes his drink, by all accounts.'

Albert leaned back in his chair, studying the young constable standing in front of him. He didn't look more than eighteen and still possessed an aura of innocence. In his job, any residual naivety was unlikely to last long.

'Where was he found?'

'In an alley near the Cartwright Arms. He'd been stabbed. Just once in the heart.'

Albert raised his eyebrows. Somehow he'd been expecting — or perhaps hoping for — a drunken fight that had got out of hand; an ill-judged punch; a fall against a wall.

'Have you spoken to the landlord?'

'Sergeant Teague has, sir. Mr Dawkins, the landlord, said Pretting left last night at closing time but there'd been no altercations. It was a quiet night, he said. No trouble.'

'Was Pretting the type to have enemies?'

'Not that Mr Dawkins knows of, sir. He's never seen him arguing with anyone. Quite hail-fellow-well-met, he says.'

This was all the local police needed when they had the Billinge case to deal with. Still, if this particular murder stemmed from drunken

111

resentments, he hoped it wouldn't be a case that required the expertise of Scotland Yard.

'The sergeant's out taking statements and Constable Wren's gone to break the news to his wife,' said the young man. 'He's going to ask her to make a formal identification.'

'Good,' said Albert. 'I take it this poor chap's fellow drinkers are going to make statements.'

'Most of them'll be at work at the moment, sir, but Sarge said we'll catch them tonight in the Carty Arms.'

Albert, hearing the abbreviation, wondered how Sir William would feel about the mangling of his family name. 'So who's he speaking to now?'

'Retired clerk from the mill who was drinking with the victim last night.'

'Is this man a suspect?' he asked hopefully. If this was a settling of scores, local knowledge would probably win the day.

'Not that I know of, sir. But I'm sure Sarge'll have a few in mind,' said the young man with a knowing smile.

The telephone on Albert's desk began to ring. It was Constable Wren calling from a telephone box.

'Hello, is that Inspector Lincoln?' he began, shouting into the mouthpiece so that Albert had to hold it a few inches from his ear.

Once Albert had answered in the affirmative, the constable carried on. 'You've been told about Bert Pretting?'

'Yes, I heard as soon as I got back to the station. I believe Sergeant Teague's dealing with the matter.'

112

'That's right. I've asked Mrs Pretting to make a formal identification of the body and I thought you'd like to be there.'

'Is that really necessary? Sounds like a local matter to me; can't you and Teague deal with it? I'm here to investigate the Billinge case.'

In the silence that followed, Albert could imagine the crestfallen look on Wren's face. 'It is a murder, sir. A stabbing. I thought you'd . . . I'm sure it'd reassure the widow if someone from Scotland Yard was present.'

Albert examined his pocket watch. Half past two. He had plenty of time before Mrs Billinge arrived and he supposed there was a chance, albeit a very slim one, that this latest murder might be linked to the death of the man at the Devil's Dancers. However, if it turned out to be a simple case of a drunken fight that had got out of hand, he would be able to leave the investigation to the locals.

'Very well. I'll come down to the mortuary.'

'We'll meet you there, sir.'

Albert felt he had no choice if he was to keep the local force on his side. He looked up and saw that the youthful constable was still standing there to attention, his eyes sparkling with anticipation. He'd be too young to have been involved in the events of 1919, so this might be his first murder case.

'What's your name, Constable?'

'Smith, sir. Daniel Smith.'

'Well, Daniel Smith, it seems I'm needed at the hospital. Hold the fort here, will you.'

'Yes, sir. Of course, sir.'

Albert set off, leaving Smith bristling with pride. At least he'd made one person happy that day. He trod the familiar route to the mortuary and found Wren waiting for him inside the entrance. With him was a small woman, not much more than five feet tall, with a slim, shapely figure. She was wearing a fashionable royal blue dress, low waisted with a hemline just on her knee, the outfit finished off by a pair of high-heeled patent leather shoes and a long string of white beads. Beneath her hat, her light brown hair was bobbed and straight, the latest fashion. He had seen women dressed similarly in London but somehow he hadn't expected a clerk's wife in Wenfield to be quite so stylish. She had a pretty face and her delicate features reminded him of a doll's.

He shook her hand, holding it for slightly longer than necessary. 'Mrs Pretting, I'm Inspector Lincoln. Scotland Yard. I'm sorry we have to meet under such circumstances.' He looked at Wren, who gave him a small nod. 'Are you ready to go in?'

'Yes,' she said in a whisper. 'I want to get it over with.'

Albert allowed Wren to lead the way to the tiled room where the body lay covered by a sheet, reminding him of the last time he'd been there when he'd viewed the mortal remains of the man everyone assumed to be Henry Billinge MP. He would be there again in a few hours' time with Mrs Billinge and the prospect made him feel slightly sick.

When the sheet was drawn back he heard Mrs Pretting gasp.

'That's him. That's my husband Bert.'

'You're sure?'

She nodded and drew a delicate lace handkerchief from her sleeve. It looked expensive and it crossed Albert's mind that Bert Pretting must have been well paid because his wife appeared to have a taste for the finer things in life.

'What happens now?' she asked with a hint of a sob.

'The constable will walk you home.'

Albert looked into her eyes, expecting to see glassy tears.

But there were none there.

24

Mrs Billinge's train was on time and Albert watched it chug into the station in a cloud of steam. It pulled up beside the platform with a hiss and there was a banging of doors as the passengers alighted under the station master's watchful gaze.

The last person to emerge was a tall woman with a long but attractive face. She wore a well-cut coat with a fox-fur stole draped around her neck, the unfortunate creature's face and paws still visible and its glass eyes glistening. Like Mrs Pretting before her, her shoes were patent leather, only these were no doubt the dearest London had to offer. Her cloche hat was also the pinnacle of fashion and she was younger than Albert had expected. Probably in her thirties. She had the confident manner often endowed by the security of wealth and he remembered Sir William saying she was the daughter of a baronet. He took a step forward and removed his hat.

'Mrs Billinge?'

'You must be Inspector Lincoln.' She studied him, her eyes drawn to the scarring on his face, then to his left hand. 'You were in the war. Our country owes so much to men like you. Heroes.'

Albert wasn't sure how to respond. He'd known many a lot braver than himself.

'Thank you, ma'am. And thank you for

making the journey up here. I've booked you into the Black Horse. It's very clean and comfortable and the food is plain but well cooked.' He paused. 'I'm staying there myself.'

'That's reassuring,' she said with a hint of humour. Something in her manner told Albert that she wasn't exactly grief-stricken at the loss of her husband.

'I'll take you there now and you can get settled in. Mrs Jackson, the landlady, says she'll do everything in her power to make you comfortable.'

'That's very kind.'

She allowed him to carry her crocodile-skin suitcase and he led her out of the station and up the road. As he passed the doctor's house he averted his eyes, avoiding the memories that had been flooding into his head ever since his arrival in Wenfield. He was almost glad that he had the responsibility of escorting Mrs Billinge to distract him.

'I've taken the liberty of asking Mrs Jackson to provide an evening meal. I hope that's in order.'

As there had been no invitation forthcoming from Tarnhey Court, Albert had seen no alternative, but he thought it best not to mention it.

'I'm sure it will be,' Mrs Billinge replied, much to Albert's relief.

'Do you know the Cartwrights? The people your husband was staying with?'

'I've never actually met them, although Sir William and I spoke once on the telephone after my husband went missing.' There was something guarded about her answer, as though Cartwright was more than merely a parliamentary acquaintance of her husband's who was a stranger to her.

'I did wonder if you'd prefer to stay with them at Tarnhey Court,' he said, curious about the lack of invitation from the man her husband had been staying with.

'No.'

The monosyllabic answer told him the subject was closed.

'When do I see my husband?'

For a moment he had the impression she was talking about the man as though he was still alive. 'Tomorrow morning. I can be there if you wish.'

'Thank you. That will be a comfort.'

When they reached the Black Horse, Albert went on ahead to smooth things with Mrs Jackson, who came out and greeted her new guest with almost simpering sympathy. If there was anything Mrs Billinge needed she had only to ask, Albert heard her say as she led the newcomer upstairs to her room, the best the Black Horse had to offer.

Albert went up to his own room to prepare for dinner, putting on a clean shirt as he'd be in the company of a lady. On his return he'd half expected Mrs Jackson to present him with another letter from Vera. When he was away she usually considered it her duty to keep him abreast of any news from home. But to his relief there'd been nothing waiting for him, which meant he could forget his domestic worries for that evening. If anything was wrong, Vera would be sure to let him know.

People tended to eat early in Wenfield and Mrs Jackson had the meal ready by six fifteen sharp. Albert and Mrs Billinge shared a table. She had shed the coat and fox fur and was wearing an emerald green dress of elegant simplicity, the sort of simplicity that doesn't come cheap. When the dinner arrived, she pushed the braised steak and onions around her plate with her fork as though it was some unfamiliar and exotic dish she wasn't quite sure she'd like. Eventually she tasted a forkful, then another, until the plate was clean.

They ate in silence but as soon as she'd finished Albert spoke. 'You enjoyed that. Mrs Jackson will be pleased.'

'I haven't eaten anything like it since I was in the nursery with my nanny.' She smiled at the memory. 'There's something very comforting about childhood tastes, don't you think?'

Albert's childhood had been tough; bread and dripping — poor man's fare. But he nodded in agreement.

'You're sure this man you found is my husband, aren't you?' The question was forthright, almost blunt.

'He matches your husband's description and we think he died around the time he went missing from Tarnhey Court.' Albert looked into her eyes and saw no shock or grief there. 'Sir William viewed the body but was unable to make a positive identification. I'm sorry.'

'Save your sympathy, Inspector. My husband

119

and I weren't exactly close. I lead my life and he leads — led — his.'

'You have children?' Albert asked, surprised by her candour.

She shook her head. 'We were never blessed. Perhaps that's why we grew apart.'

At that moment Mrs Jackson bustled up to take the plates and inform them she had jam roly-poly and custard for afters. More comforting nursery food. Mrs Billinge gave a brittle smile and said that would be lovely.

When the pudding came she ate heartily. 'I wish my cook in London was as good as Mrs Jackson,' she said once she'd finished. 'She's a dab hand when it comes to dinner parties, but sometimes I long for something . . . simpler.'

Albert said nothing. Fancy cooking had never been in Mary's culinary repertoire and she'd never really mastered the more basic offerings either. The thought of his wife hit him with a jolt.

'Are you married, Inspector?' Mrs Billinge asked, almost as though she'd read his thoughts.

'Yes.'

'Children?'

'No.' He couldn't face explaining about Frederick and his other lost son, so a negative answer was easier.

He considered it was time to bring the conversation round to murder before she probed any further. 'Did your husband have any enemies?'

'He was a Member of Parliament. I would say making political enemies goes with the job. He's very much for lowering the voting age for women

120

to twenty-one, and that doesn't go down well in some quarters.' She took a gold cigarette case from her handbag and offered one to Albert. He accepted gratefully and delved in his jacket pocket for his lighter. But she produced her own first, gold encrusted with diamonds and sapphires, and lit Albert's cigarette before her own.

'I'm not talking about the cut and thrust of debate. I meant enemies who might want to kill him.'

'As I said before, we lead our separate lives,' she said, inhaling the smoke and blowing it out slowly. 'All I can say is that I'm not aware of anybody. Certainly nobody up here.'

'Do you know anybody called Clara?'

For a moment her expression froze. Then she took another drag on her cigarette, perfectly composed. 'We had a maid called Clara. Pretty little thing.'

'You say had. Is she no longer with you?'

Mrs Billinge looked Albert in the eye. 'I suspected she was sleeping with my husband, Inspector. I caught them whispering together.'

'Just whispering?'

'They looked as though they were sharing secrets — things they were keeping from me. As far as I was concerned, that was enough. I told him she had to go.'

'What did he say?'

'He said he'd deal with the matter and assured me I had nothing to worry about.'

'You didn't believe him?'

'Would you?' She took a long drag on her

121

cigarette then stubbed it out.

'Do you know where she went?'

'No. She was gone from under my roof and that was my one concern. What the silly floozy did after that is none of my business.'

Albert couldn't leave the subject there. Sir William and this woman's husband had been overheard arguing about someone called Clara and he needed to know the truth.

'You must have some idea what became of her. Perhaps you wrote a reference for a future employer?'

'I left that to my husband. By that time I couldn't bear the sight of her and the only character I'd have given her would have been a truthful one: 'Don't trust this girl and whatever you do, don't leave her alone with your husband.''

She stubbed her cigarette out in the glass ashtray with a violence Albert found surprising. Despite her claim that there was no love between her and Billinge, it seemed his infidelity had bothered her very much indeed. From her manner, he assumed the subject was closed, but it turned out he was mistaken.

'I suspect one of his friends found a position for the little tart. I heard Henry speaking on the telephone to somebody he addressed as William, and I'm not ashamed to say that I listened in on the conversation. I was standing at the top of the stairs so Henry didn't know I was there.' A satisfied smile appeared on her lips. 'He was talking about Clara and he said I was making waves, as he put it. When the call ended he seemed very pleased with himself, so I presumed the matter had been brought to a satisfactory conclusion.'

'Do you think he might have been speaking to Sir William Cartwright?'

'It's possible. I know they've been friends for a while. But I'm sure there are a lot of Williams about.'

Albert pondered this as he finished his cigarette. Sir William said he'd never heard the name Clara, but now it seemed he might have been lying. He had another question: 'Your husband was wounded in the war?'

'Yes. Ypres. He was brought back to Blighty and treated at a hospital in Lincolnshire. Then he went back.'

'Did he have shrapnel in his arm?'

She frowned. 'Yes. His right arm — and his leg, although they managed to get that out. He always said he was lucky. Not like some.'

'Are you sure it wasn't his left arm?'

She took the gold case out again and lit another cigarette. Again Albert accepted one, but this time he was ready with his lighter.

'Of course I'm sure. I fancy a drink. Will you keep me company?'

Albert needed company himself, so he led the way into the little snug Mrs Jackson reserved for guests, relieved that the men from the mill hadn't commandeered the space. The Black Horse didn't run to cocktails or fine wines and he thought the limited choice of drinks might present difficulties — until Mrs Billinge requested half a pint of the local beer.

They spent the rest of the evening talking about London and her childhood in Cheshire. He asked her if she knew Mabley Ridge and she said she did. She'd been brought up near Wilmslow and had taken walks on the Ridge with her parents as a child. She had stood on Oak Tree Edge and gazed at the mills of Manchester in the grey and smoky distance. Albert listened in silence as her words conjured memories of the previous September. He was a good listener, which had often proved an advantage in his job. When she asked him to call her Anne he knew he'd gained her trust and he hoped she'd have more to tell him. Things she hadn't liked to reveal to a stranger. She retired to bed at half past nine, saying the day had tired her. Albert ordered another pint and sat down alone to consider what he'd learned.

The next morning he met Anne Billinge at breakfast and once more they shared a table.

But when they arrived at the mortuary he was quite unprepared for the shock he was to receive.

25

Anne Billinge looked down at the body and shuddered. 'I don't know who this man is, but he definitely isn't my husband.'

Albert caught Teague's eye and saw that the sergeant looked as confused as he felt. They'd both been sure the man in the cave was the missing MP but now the certainties of their case had been shattered.

If this wasn't Billinge then presumably the MP was still out there somewhere, alive or dead. They'd already checked with the station master, who'd confirmed that he hadn't caught a train out of Wenfield so an accident remained a strong possibility. If he'd gone walking and fallen down an old mine working, he might never be found; Albert was reluctant to mention this possibility to the man's wife until they'd exhausted all other possibilities.

'Are you absolutely sure it's not him?' Albert asked her gently.

'First of all, this man's wound is to his left arm rather than his right, and the injuries are far more extensive than my husband's.' She nodded to Dr Kelly, who had folded the sheet back to reveal the upper body. 'May I see his legs, please, Doctor?'

Albert couldn't help admiring her cool manner. Many women he knew would have found the sight of a corpse distasteful. Perhaps, he thought, she had nursed in the war like Flora and had become used to seeing horrors of this nature.

Kelly hesitated before he drew back the sheet further to reveal the rest of the body. Anne Billinge stepped forward and studied the legs, then the groin. Albert was surprised to see her smile.

'My husband has a birthmark just above his private parts. And he has a scar on his leg where a bullet was removed. This man has neither. Then there's that large birthmark on the back of this man's left hand. My husband has no such mark. It's definitely not him.'

'Then who is he?' Teague asked nobody in particular.

'I'm afraid I can't help you with that, Sergeant,' said Mrs Billinge before sweeping from the room. Albert told Teague to follow her and once he was alone with the doctor he asked another question.

'How soon can you do the post-mortem on Bert Pretting?'

'Will this afternoon suit you? I'll fit it in after my rounds.'

Albert paused before leaving the room. 'Have you found any clues to this poor man's identity?' he said as the corpse was being covered again by the sheet. 'Anything at all, however small?'

'Sorry, but there's nothing I haven't already told you,' said the doctor. 'Has nobody else been reported missing around here?'

Albert shook his head.

So the missing Member of Parliament was still

lost out there somewhere. And now, to further complicate matters, he had a body without a name.

26

Rose

It was definitely Bert. I said there was no doubt about it. Constable Wren had offered to ask one of the men he'd been drinking with to identify him, in case the sight of my husband lying dead on a slab proved too upsetting for me. I knew he was being thoughtful but I told him I could cope and when I said I needed to see him he seemed to understand. What I didn't tell him was that I felt nothing but relief.

Last night I slept better than I've done for a long time. It was good to know he wouldn't expect me to do my wifely duty, the way he usually did when he'd had a skinful in the Carty Arms. 'You're my wife,' he always said. 'I've got rights.' Well, not any more. A dead man has no rights. A dead man can't hurt you.

I changed the sheets because they smelled of him and I lay there in the fresh ones, stretching out in the big bed which is now mine and mine alone. My Darling Man says we have to be careful. Discreet, was how he put it. He always knows the right words.

He says it's best we don't see each other for a while. I dread the thought of it, but I know he's right. The time will pass quickly and then we'll be together for ever. I'll fill my lonely days with reading about the triumph of love, dreaming of the time when my own love will overcome everything. *Amor vincit omnia*, that's what my Darling Man told me, although I don't know what it means.

Bert is dead and I am alive.

I can hear a pounding on the door and the sound makes me jump. I don't want to answer it but I know I must. Everything has to look normal. Everyone has to think I'm grieving.

27

Anne Billinge decided not to stay in Wenfield for another night. There was no point in prolonging her visit, she told Albert when he saw her off at the railway station, especially as Sir William and Lady Cartwright had made no effort to offer her hospitality; something that still struck Albert as odd in the circumstances.

He found it hard to gauge how she felt about her husband's disappearance. She belonged to a class who'd been raised from childhood not to show their true emotions, so he guessed that she might be more worried than she seemed. In Anne's world, appearances had to be maintained at all costs.

He watched her train chug away from the platform in the direction of Manchester where she was to catch the London train. Despite their different positions on the social ladder, he'd liked her and he'd found her easy to talk to. He hadn't revealed anything about his own private life over their drinks the previous night, although he suspected that if she'd stayed another night, that situation might have changed. It was probably a good thing that she'd returned to London.

He found himself wondering why Sir William had failed to do what would surely be considered by many to be his social duty. Perhaps he was embarrassed that he'd let Billinge wander off into the countryside without taking steps to ensure his safety; perhaps he felt responsible, even guilty. Or was there a more sinister explanation? He needed to speak to Sir William again. It looked very much as though he'd lied about Clara and he knew exactly who she was. But why hadn't he told Albert when he'd asked?

Before escorting Mrs Billinge to the train he'd ordered one of the constables to telephone all the police stations within a hundred-mile radius. The man in the mortuary must have been missed by somebody; possibly somebody further afield. The young constable looked daunted by the task, but Albert gave him an encouraging pat on the shoulder and told him that if they could establish the identity of the man in the cave, they would be one step closer to discovering who was responsible for his death.

He left the railway station, wondering whether to take the road to Tarnhey Court or to return to the police station and see whether anything new had come in in his absence. He had to attend Bert Pretting's post-mortem later, but hopefully it would be straightforward, although a knife in an alley was something he associated with his native London or a big city like Manchester rather than a quiet Derbyshire village.

Perhaps Pretting had gambling debts or he'd been involved in some sort of dispute he'd kept from his wife. If he was one of those men who led a secret life unbeknown to his wife and colleagues, it was possible he had acquired enemies no one knew about. Albert resolved to raise the possibility with Teague later, if the culprit wasn't swiftly apprehended.

He almost turned into Tarnhey Lane, but then decided to delay his visit to Sir William until he'd had more time to consider the questions he needed to ask. Besides, the longer he left it, the less prepared Sir William would be. He knew from experience that suspects made mistakes when they didn't know what was coming. And Sir William now had to be treated as a suspect, whatever Teague and his deferential Wenfield colleagues might think.

As Albert arrived at the door of the police station he saw a familiar figure walking down the street towards him. Mrs Bell was carrying a wicker shopping basket, as yet unfilled, and as soon as she spotted him she gave an enthusiastic wave, her footsteps speeding up almost to a trot.

He stopped to wait until she caught up, breathless and holding on to her hat.

'Inspector, just the man I wanted to see. Can we talk in private?'

'Of course. Please come into my office.'

She hesitated for a moment, glancing up at the blue lamp above their heads. He guessed she'd never crossed the threshold of the police station before.

'Would you like a cup of tea?' he offered.

'That would be most welcome.'

As she followed Albert through to his office behind the front desk, Constable Wren shot him a quizzical look but Albert responded by asking for tea. This was between him and Mrs Bell; it wasn't a police matter yet.

'How can I help you?' he asked after inviting

her to take a seat. Though her suspicions continued to intrigue him, he wasn't sure how to proceed. He leaned forward, hoping she was about to give him something solid at last.

'I visited the vicarage again yesterday and repeated my request, but Simon Fellowes stuck to his story about losing the study key. He says he's been preparing his sermons on the table in the parlour.'

'So the situation hasn't changed since our last meeting?' he said, disappointed.

She leaned towards him, lowering her voice. 'I had a word with Grace. You remember she used to work for me and my husband,' she added with a knowing smile which told Albert that the maid's loyalty remained with her former mistress. 'She says Simon's lying. He *is* using the study. Goes in and locks the door behind him, she says. And she's not allowed in there to clean, which I think is rather peculiar. She always cleaned in there in Horace's day. She was very careful not to disturb his things.'

'Does she think there's something in there he doesn't want anyone to see?'

'I don't know.'

There was a long silence before Albert asked his next question. 'You think Mr Fellowes might have had something to do with your husband's death?'

Mrs Bell sighed. 'It sounds ridiculous when you put it like that. And if it was poison that killed Horace it seems so calculating, doesn't it. But I must say, when he was the parish curate, Horace always found him . . . ' She searched for the right word. 'Difficult. And I know they had words shortly before Horace died.'

'What about?' This was something she hadn't mentioned before.

'Horace thought Simon wasn't sufficiently sympathetic to the problems of his parishioners. He told him he wasn't there to sit in judgement on them as sinners and tell them they were damned to burn in hell without the mercy of God. He said he should understand their struggles like Our Lord did. I've spoken to people who knew Simon before the war and they said he wasn't like that then. The war changed him. Hardened him.'

'It changed a lot of people, Mrs Bell. But I can't see it as a motive for murder.'

'Then why doesn't he want me to look for evidence of where my husband went that night?'

'Could Horace have had a meeting with Fellowes?'

'The curate's house is just a short distance from the vicarage. Perhaps that's why Horace didn't bother telling me where he was going. Because he didn't think he'd be long.'

'But he was?'

'A good two hours.'

'I'm sorry, Mrs Bell, but at the moment I have no legal reason to order Fellowes to let me into that study, you do realise that? We don't even know for sure that your husband was poisoned.'

For a moment she looked crestfallen. She'd been so convinced that the man she'd devoted her life to hadn't been taken from her by the God she trusted. 'Of course. You're right,

Inspector. All I have is suspicions. I need proof.'

Albert picked up the fountain pen that was lying in front of him on the desk and turned it over and over in the fingers of his good hand. This situation required further thought — and tact. 'Leave it with me, Mrs Bell. I'll think of something. What time is the Reverend Fellowes likely to be out of the vicarage?'

Mrs Bell gave Albert a knowing smile. 'I'm not sure, but I can find out from Grace.'

Albert had had an idea. It was something he was used to deploying against London's criminal fraternity rather than in a northern vicarage, but it might be the only way of finding the answers he needed.

She stood up to go. 'I'll be in touch, Inspector. And thank you. I feel so much better now I've shared my suspicions with you.'

Albert watched her leave, Constable Wren acknowledging her with a little salute as she passed him. What he was planning was irregular. But if the Reverend Horace Bell's death hadn't been natural, he needed to get to the truth.

The telephone on his desk rang. Bert Pretting's postmortem was about to begin. And he had to be there.

But before he could leave, Constable Smith knocked on his door. He looked as though he had news.

'I didn't like to disturb you while the lady was here, sir.'

'What is it, Smith?'

'A woman came in while you were out, sir. Betty Legge. She's the Prettings' maid. She said

135

Mr and Mrs Pretting weren't on good terms and that she thinks Mrs Pretting has a fancy man.'

Albert sank down into his chair again. He'd nursed a hope that he wouldn't have to become involved in the Pretting investigation. But it seemed it might be hard to avoid it.

'Sergeant Teague's gone round there, sir. Just thought you should know.'

28

Rose

When Sergeant Teague and Constable Wren turned up at the door and asked if they could come in, I had no choice. If I'd said they couldn't, it would have looked suspicious and that was the last thing I wanted. I was feeling so pleased with my performance at the cottage hospital but now I don't know where to turn because my Darling Man and I have agreed not to see each other for a while.

I need a drink, something stronger than tea. My heart's beating so fast I think it'll burst out of my chest, but I have to stay calm. I have to convince them I had nothing to do with Bert's murder.

The policemen took off their helmets and when I showed them into the parlour the sergeant asked if they could take a look in the bureau. I said they could if they could get it open. I told them I don't have a key because Bert said he kept confidential things in there. I keep my private things in one of the bedroom drawers. I've got all my old school reports in there and I get them out to look at sometimes. A for English and A for Arithmetic. I used to be quite clever once, before I married Bert.

To my surprise, the sergeant produced the key — said he'd found it in Bert's jacket pocket — so

I left them to search because they told me it was just routine; something that had to be done when someone's murdered. I pretended to start crying again and he said why didn't I put the kettle on. Betty was in the kitchen. I don't know what she has to be so smug about. And insolent. I told her to fetch the milk jug and she smirked at me and banged the jug down on the table. Perhaps I'll get rid of her now Bert's gone.

When I went back into the parlour, Constable Wren was stuffing things from the bureau into a brown paper bag and he told me he'd have to take it back to the police station. I could hear the kettle whistling so I dashed back into the kitchen and when I came back with the tea I found the constable on his own and Sergeant Teague was nowhere to be seen. I thought he must have left, but then I heard footsteps upstairs.

I didn't panic at first. He was hardly likely to start rooting around in my wardrobe. Even Bert never looked in there. That's why he never discovered my hiding place.

I climbed the stairs, calling out Sergeant Teague's name. When there was no answer I began to feel nervous. I thought of the loose board at the bottom of my wardrobe, but I knew he'd never find it because it's so well hidden and my shoes were lined up on top of it.

When I reached the bedroom I found him looking through Bert's wardrobe. He said it was just routine but I could tell he was lying. It takes one to know one, as my dad used to say.

I told him his tea was ready and if he didn't come down it'd get cold, hoping he wouldn't bother with my wardrobe. He said he'd come when he was finished, and started on the chest of drawers by the window, taking out the contents of each drawer and laying them on top of the eiderdown. I watched as he handled my smalls and stockings, trying not to blush. Then he started on Bert's shirts and underwear. Once each drawer was empty he slid it out and looked behind and underneath. His thoroughness made me nervous.

Once he'd finished with the drawers he opened my wardrobe, pushing back my dresses and taking my hat boxes from the top shelf and opening them one by one.

'Be careful,' I said. 'Those weren't cheap.'

He turned to me and smiled. 'I know. Mrs Teague's always after new hats. Costs me a fortune.'

'How is Mrs Teague?' I hoped the question would distract him. 'I saw her at the library the other day.'

'She's very well, thank you.' His answer was formal and I knew he wasn't going to be put off, although my presence must have made him uneasy because instead of taking my dresses out and laying them on the bed he pushed them to one side and then the other and as the hangers screeched against the rail I could see his face was flushed with embarrassment. Then he looked down at my neatly arranged shoes and shuffled them around before shutting the wardrobe door. His fingers hadn't searched for the little knothole in the wardrobe floor as mine had done so often. In my mind's eye I could see the plank coming loose and the letters lying there, ready for him to pluck out as I watched, frozen to the spot, turned to stone like the Devil's Dancers.

My heart had been thumping so loudly that I was afraid he'd hear it, but as soon as he shut my wardrobe door I knew the danger was over and my secret was safe.

Then I heard Constable Wren's voice from downstairs.

'Sarge! Come and see what I've found.'

29

Albert didn't have time to wait for Teague's return. He was due at the mortuary and, as Kelly was Wenfield's only doctor and therefore a busy man, it would be unfair to keep him waiting. He told Constable Smith he'd speak to Teague when he got back, and set off for his second mortuary visit of the day.

Albert thought Dr Kelly seemed tired as they shook hands on his arrival. His youthful face looked strained, but he imagined that doctors — the good ones — often worried about their patients' problems.

Kelly began the post-mortem with a visual examination of Bert Pretting's corpse. Healthy male in his thirties. Five feet nine. Heavily built. Well nourished and showing excess weight around the middle, possibly a result of heavy drinking. There was no emotion in the doctor's voice as he recited his observations and when the post-mortem began in earnest he said nothing while he conducted the procedure under Albert's watchful gaze.

When it was over he removed his gown and gloves before giving his verdict.

'It's as I expected. Cause of death: a knife wound directly to the heart. He was stabbed once in the chest and the knife slipped between the ribs and hit its mark. The killer used something like a kitchen knife. I estimate that the

141

blade was around eight inches long and an inch wide at the base; pointed with one sharp edge.' He cleared his throat. 'It's the sort of knife found in kitchens everywhere. Have you any suspects?'

'It's early days,' said Albert noncommittally. 'I believe his fellow drinkers have been questioned but nobody's fallen under particular suspicion so far. Wenfield's a small place, though, so I'm sure it won't be hard to root out any people he's offended. Can you tell me anything about his attacker?'

The doctor frowned, took a scalpel and probed the wound, calculating the angle of entry. Eventually he looked up. 'I'd say his killer was at least as tall as the victim. You can tell by the wound. If he'd been smaller, the weapon would have been thrust upwards — instead it was slightly downwards.'

'A man?'

'I'd say so. Some force was used.' He paused. 'How's his wife? Sorry — his widow.' The question was casual but Albert sensed more than a passing interest in his answer. 'She's a patient of mine,' Kelly said. 'I'm wondering whether she'll be needing something to help her sleep or . . . '

'That's very thoughtful of you, Doctor. I'm sure the lady'll be grateful for any support you can give her.' In view of her maid's revelations, Rose Pretting was bound to come under suspicion. Her diminutive stature probably ruled her out as the attacker, but an accomplice might have done it on her behalf. However, this wasn't something he was inclined to mention just at that moment.

Kelly returned his attention to the corpse. 'There's really nothing more I can tell you, Inspector. It's a straightforward case of murder. A lucky strike after a drunken quarrel would be my guess.'

There was a short silence before Albert spoke again. 'Actually, there is something I'd like to ask you, Doctor. You examined the body of the Reverend Bell, who died last year.'

'That's right.' Kelly looked uneasy.

'You said he died of a heart attack.'

'Man in late middle age, overweight, sudden death.'

'You didn't suspect foul play?'

'I had no reason to at the time.' The answer sounded a touch defensive.

'You didn't consider poison?'

The doctor sighed. 'You've been talking to Mrs Bell, haven't you? She asked me the same question and I'll give you the same answer I gave her. No, I didn't suspect poison at the time. Although . . . '

'You did have doubts.' Up until now, Kelly had been giving him the authorised version. Albert hoped he was going to tell him what he'd really been thinking.

'A few, I admit. I thought his pupils showed signs of . . . ' He swallowed hard. 'It's true, I did suspect poison, but I was afraid it might have been a case of suicide and I wanted to spare Mrs Bell any distress.'

'Why would you think of suicide? Did you

143

know of any problem that might have led him to take his own life?'

'No. But I couldn't think of anybody here in Wenfield who would want to kill him. He was well loved. Highly thought of by everyone. He tended to take the burdens of others on his shoulders, which can prove a strain for some. Of course I'm not saying he did take his own life. It might have been a tragic accident. Even so, I wasn't going to risk dragging his good name through the mud.'

'He was too old to serve in the war.'

'I know what you're thinking, Inspector. A lot of men came home with damage that can't be seen. But, no, in this case you can rule out a delayed reaction to the horrors of the trenches. Bell wasn't even there.'

'You served yourself?'

'In a military hospital on the front. Fresh out of medical school and wet behind the ears. I grew up fast.'

'The reverend visited somebody on the night he died. Was it you?'

Kelly shook his head. 'Absolutely not, Inspector. I hadn't seen him since church the previous Sunday.'

'If it was poison, what would you say was used?'

The doctor considered the question. 'Certainly not cyanide. And the symptoms were wrong for arsenic. There are a few possibilities. Morphine, perhaps. There's plenty of laudanum still around in cupboards all over the country, I imagine, and the appearance of the pupils was consistent with that particular substance.' He walked over to the cupboard that stood against the far wall. 'I didn't conduct a full post-mortem because I didn't want to distress Mrs Bell, but I did take the precaution of taking a few samples.'

A slow smile spread across Albert's face. He had been dreading the fuss and explanations involved in obtaining permission to exhume the Reverend Bell's body, but now it seemed Kelly had relieved him of that burden.

'I have a friend at Liverpool University, where I studied. I can ask him to take a look at Mr Bell's samples, if you wish. I've already sent him the stomach contents of the man in the cave.' He grinned. 'He says I send him the nicest gifts.'

'If it does turn out that Bell was poisoned and we're ruling out suicide, that leaves us with two possibilities,' said Albert. 'Accident or murder.'

'I'm well aware of that, Inspector.'

Albert thrust his right hand into his trouser pocket and drew out the little blue bottle he'd found in the empty flat above the stable block at Tarnhey Court. The bottle bearing the skull and crossbones and marked poison. 'Can you get the contents of this bottle analysed?'

The doctor took it from him. 'Where did you find it?'

'I'd rather not say for the time being,' said Albert before taking his leave.

30

On the way back from the hospital, Albert was strongly tempted to pay another visit to Tarnhey Court because he was sure Sir William knew more than he'd admitted about Henry Billinge's disappearance. However, he decided to call at the police station first to see whether there'd been any new developments. As soon as he walked in, Constable Smith hurried from behind the front desk to meet him.

'Inspector, there's someone to see you. A woman. I asked her to wait in your office. I hope that's all right.'

Albert made straight for his office where he found Grace, the elderly maid from the vicarage, perched on the edge of his visitors' chair. When she rose to greet him, she looked overwhelmed by her surroundings, but Albert gave her a reassuring smile before inviting her to sit and shutting the door behind him.

'What can I do for you?'

Grace looked round as though she was afraid of being overheard. 'I didn't like to use the telephone at the vicarage, in case . . . I just wanted to tell you that the reverend's gone to see the archdeacon and he won't be back till this evening. Mrs Bell said you'd want to know.'

Albert hadn't expected Mrs Bell's plans to come to fruition so quickly. Emboldened by the suspicions Dr Kelly had shared with him about the Reverend Bell's untimely death, he convinced himself that he wasn't agreeing to this course of action in order to find his lost son. He was doing it to uncover the truth about a possible murder.

He consulted his pocket watch. It was three o'clock, so they had plenty of time. 'Thank you. Can you let Mrs Bell know I'll meet her there in half an hour?'

Grace nodded and made a swift exit from the police station, as though she feared she might be tainted by being in the place where wrongdoers were interrogated and imprisoned.

Albert wasn't sure whether what he was planning to do was wise. He needed to see inside that study, although he knew Sergeant Teague would be bound to. disapprove if he ever found out. He had lost Frederick but there was a chance the vicarage study might contain a clue to the whereabouts of his other son. His and Flora's. His heart began to beat faster at the prospect, but this wasn't something he could ever share with anybody. Not even Mrs Bell.

31

Rose

I lie on my bed at three in the afternoon, reading, because there is nobody to chastise me for my idleness. I answer to nobody apart from my Darling Man, but he says we should not meet for a while, so all I have is my books. My stories of love and triumph.

The police found money in the bureau; a lot of money — over two hundred pounds in a brown envelope. Sergeant Teague asked me where it came from and I told him the truth: I didn't know.

I slide off the bed and look at my reflection in the mirror. My eyes are brighter and I cannot help smiling at my new self. I cup my breasts in my hands and turn this way and that. I am beautiful and now my body is mine to do with as I please. He cannot touch me any more because he's dead. I am proud of the act I put on in the mortuary. A star of the moving pictures couldn't have done better.

I gather my books up and go downstairs to put them in my basket, smiling as I go. But I must wipe the smile from my face when I step beyond the front door. I am a recent widow, wearing black. I rub my eyes with my knuckles to make it look as though I've been crying. Everyone I meet will feel sorry for me. Even in the library, my safest place, nobody must guess how joyful I am.

As I open the front door Betty comes out of the parlour, a duster in her hand. She says nothing but looks at me with those sly eyes of hers. I am so tempted to give her notice, but they say that servants are hard to come by since the war.

32

'Even if your husband was poisoned, as you suspect, surely you can't think the Reverend Fellowes had anything to do with it?'

Now Albert was standing beside Mrs Bell and Grace outside the study door in the vicarage he was beginning to doubt the wisdom of what they planned to do. He was a detective from Scotland Yard sent there specifically to deal with the case of a missing, possibly murdered, Member of Parliament. He wondered whether he would have been so keen to take Mrs Bell's suspicions seriously if they hadn't offered him the possibility of making his own, more personal, investigation.

Grace passed Albert the key and he opened the front door, hoping they weren't being watched by curious eyes. He allowed the two women to enter the hall before him and waited. Grace nodded towards the study door to his left; polished mahogany and sturdy as the tree from which it was made. Albert fumbled in his jacket pocket and took out the tools he always kept with him for such occasions. He'd used them many times in the course of his police career to break into anything from thieves' dens filled with stolen goods to locked Mayfair rooms where a body had lain rotting until the wealthy neighbours could no longer bear the smell. He'd never before had occasion to use them in a country vicarage.

He put the thin instrument into the lock and manoeuvred it until he heard a satisfying click. The door opened smoothly and he entered the study, the two women following.

'It doesn't seem to have changed much since Horace's day,' said Mrs Bell. She sounded slightly disappointed.

Albert paused, wondering where to begin. He was supposed to be searching for anything that might tell him who Bell visited on the night he died. A note, perhaps. Or a letter. Or an entry in an old diary. He took a deep breath and started on the desk drawers. As soon as he opened the top drawer he found the leather-bound diary for the previous year. He took it out and handed it to Mrs Bell.

'This is the one he wrote all his appointments in,' she said, flicking through the pages. Then she stopped and passed the open diary back to Albert. 'There's nothing for that day. Wherever he went, he didn't write it down.'

'If I can look through his correspondence, I might find something there.'

'He kept everything in that big cupboard,' she said, pointing to a monumental cupboard that occupied one wall of the room. 'He was always very organised. Everything in date order.'

Albert opened the cupboard door and took out a cardboard file dated the previous September, the month of the Reverend Bell's death. But when he searched through the correspondence he found nothing requesting a meeting on that particular evening. And certainly no letter with a photograph enclosed.

'Perhaps he received a telephone call,' Albert suggested.

The two women exchanged looks.

'I don't remember any call,' said Mrs Bell. 'In fact I'm sure the telephone didn't ring that night, and I know nobody called at the door. But I definitely remember the letter — it came in the late post.'

'Did the reverend take his bicycle when he went out?'

'I'm not sure,' said Mrs Bell, looking at Grace enquiringly.

'As I recall, I heard the shed door opening. It needs oiling, so it creaks something awful. You were in the parlour at the back of the house, ma'am, so you wouldn't have heard. But I can't be sure. I wish I'd paid more attention.'

'Neither of us was paying much attention,' said Mrs Bell, putting a comforting hand on Grace's sleeve. 'How were we to know at the time it might be important?'

Albert returned to the desk. Ignoring the top drawer where he'd found the diaries, he opened the other drawers and examined the contents with dawning realisation. No wonder the Reverend Fellowes hadn't wanted anybody to enter his study. Three drawers were crammed with photographs of women in various stages of undress. Albert had seen a lot worse in his time, but in a small place like Wenfield such photographs would cause quite a scandal if they were discovered.

He looked up and saw the two women watching him expectantly. He smiled at them and shut the drawer. The reverend was entitled to his private vices. 'Nothing in there. I'll have another look through the files in the cupboard, if I may. The person whose letter arrived on the day the Reverend Bell passed away might have written to him earlier. I'd feel more comfortable if someone kept watch in case the reverend's meeting finishes early. Perhaps you could guard the back door, Grace, while you station yourself at the drawing-room window, Mrs Bell.'

The women nodded conspiratorially and left the room. As soon as he was alone, Albert went to the cupboard, selected the files for the appropriate dates and took them over to the desk. The information he wanted had to be in there somewhere.

Giving silent thanks for Bell's meticulous filing system, he flicked through the papers. Minutes of parish meetings. Letters from charities. Correspondence from the headmaster of the village school. Personal letters from parishioners. As he searched, he began to despair of ever finding what he was looking for.

Then he found it. A letter dated late February 1920 from a woman called Charlotte Day (Mrs) assuring Mr Bell that the little one had settled in well, in spite of his unfortunate start in life, and was thriving under the care of his nursemaid. Albert's hands shook as he took the letter from the file. It was on expensive notepaper and the writing was well formed, an educated hand. As he reread the letter he caught a slight whiff of perfume. Mrs Day ended by thanking Bell for what he'd done and saying she was enclosing a contribution to the work of the church.

Albert read the letter again before putting it in his pocket. The Reverend Fellowes was hardly likely to miss it and it might be his only opportunity.

He replaced the 1920 file and went through the more recent correspondence for any clue to who Bell had met on the night he died. The fact that he might have taken his bicycle widened the field slightly, but as he examined the contents of the files, the truth about Bell's death seemed as elusive as ever. Try as he might, he couldn't find even the smallest clue and he knew he was going to have to disappoint Mrs Bell.

But his visit to the vicarage hadn't been in vain: he now had a name and an address. As he locked the study door behind him, he wondered whether Charlotte Day would have the answer to the question that had tormented him for the past eighteen months — and whether he would ever be able to summon the courage to approach her.

33

Rose

How hard it is to pass the building and know that my Darling Man is inside but we cannot yet be together. Especially now we are both free to live and love as we choose. I recall that line in the final chapter of the book I've just been reading — *The Scarlet Maiden* by Gloria Phipps. Rowena, the heroine, escapes from her wicked stepfather and, when she meets the young viscount who has waited so patiently for her, she says those very words — free to live and love as we choose. I think they're the most beautiful words I've ever read.

I had an appointment with Mr Jennings, the solicitor in the High Street earlier. He told me that, according to Bert's will, I inherit everything and will not have to worry about money in the future. There was a large life insurance policy and with the house and what he inherited from his father, I am now a wealthy widow. Well, not exactly wealthy, but certainly comfortably off. Then there's the money in the envelope the police found. I suppose that's mine too — although I've no idea where it came from.

Betty says one of Bert's colleagues from the mill called to express his condolences while I was out. He says he'll call again, so I'll have to play the grieving widow. My aunty always said I should have gone on the stage.

How time drags. I have finished *The Scarlet Maiden* and *The Duchess's Valentine*, so I need to visit the library again for more romance to feed my appetite until I can experience the real thing.

As I climb the stairs I can hear Betty singing to herself while she cleans the bathroom I insisted Bert had put in so I could enjoy all the modern conveniences. Sometimes Bert could be generous — if it made him look as if he was going up in the world. She's singing 'Pack up your Troubles' and she sounds more cheerful than usual. Perhaps she's glad Bert's no longer with us too.

When I reach my bedroom — how good it is to call it mine rather than ours — I pick up the books from the bedside table. Then temptation overwhelms me and I go to the wardrobe. Sergeant Teague never found my hiding place and the memory makes me smile. I smile a lot these days.

I remove my shoes from the base of the wardrobe and place them neatly on the rug. I can see the knot in the wood and I hook my finger into it and lift. The board comes up easily and I lean over to see the precious chocolate box, the container of my happiness.

Then my heart skips a beat because the box has gone.

34

Albert's fingers kept touching the letter in his pocket, yearning to read it again but resisting the temptation. The little one was thriving under the care of his nursemaid. The date fitted perfectly and the child was a boy. But was it his boy?

He checked his pocket watch. He'd been intending to pay Sir William Cartwright an unannounced visit, but he'd been sidetracked by Mrs Bell's request.

He had been sent to Wenfield to find the truth about Henry Billinge MP and he knew he shouldn't allow anything to deflect him from his purpose, however strong the temptation. He was intrigued by the nameless man at the Devil's Dancers but Billinge had to be his priority, and that meant another interview with Sir William.

His route back from the vicarage to the police station took him past the gates of Tarnhey Court and as he turned left through the gates, he rehearsed the questions he needed to ask.

It was Mrs Banks who answered the door with a welcoming smile.

'Inspector, come in. You're in luck. Sir William's at home. I'll let him know you're here.' Mrs Banks had obviously taken a liking to him. It was often good to have friends below stairs.

Five minutes later he was shown into Sir William's study. It was hard to read the man's expression, but if he was irritated at another visit from the man from Scotland Yard he was hiding it well.

'What can I do for you, Inspector?'

'I take it you've had no word from Mr Billinge?'

'Sadly not. Although it came as a great relief that he wasn't the unfortunate man in that cave. You've no idea who he was?'

'We're still making enquiries, sir,' he said, unwilling to admit they were no nearer identifying the mysterious naked corpse than they had been on the day he was found. Contacting forces within a hundred-mile radius about missing persons had, as yet, produced no results. Albert had ordered the search to be expanded further afield.

'Strange business,' said Sir William. He seemed tense, Albert thought. As though the identity of the mystery man was bothering him more than the fate of his missing parliamentary colleague.

'Mrs Billinge confirmed once and for all that the man in the cave wasn't her husband, which means he's still a missing person.'

'I've told you everything I know, Inspector. Henry went out for a walk and didn't come back. Simple as that.'

'Last time I was here I asked whether you knew anybody called Clara.'

'And I told you I didn't.' There was a warning note in his voice. *Don't enquire any further.*

But Albert carried on. 'Mrs Billinge told me she once had a maid called Clara. She also said she suspected this maid was having an affair with her husband.'

Sir William shifted nervously in his seat. 'I don't see what that has to do with me.'

'You were arguing over somebody called Clara on the night before Billinge disappeared. And Mrs Billinge overheard her husband speaking on the telephone to somebody called William and Clara's name was mentioned. Were you the William he was talking to?'

'Certainly not. Now if you'll excuse me, Inspector, I have work to do.'

Albert was certain the man was lying to him. Sir William knew who Clara was all right, and if he was lying about that it was possible he knew where Billinge was and was choosing to cover for him for some reason. Albert had met plenty of 'gentlemen of honour' in the course of his work, but there hadn't been many he'd been inclined to trust.

'I understand Mr Billinge left his things here.'

'Mrs Banks put them in the box room. Sergeant Teague had a look through them when we first reported Henry missing, so . . . '

'I'd like to see them for myself.'

Sir William rolled his eyes impatiently. 'Very well. I'll ring for Mrs Banks.'

Sir William had abandoned politeness now and it was clear he was keen to get rid of the interfering policeman.

Mrs Banks led him to the box room, where he opened Henry Billinge's two leather suitcases. He lifted out the clothes and placed them on a nearby trunk. Then he turned to the housekeeper who was standing behind him, watching.

'Are these all the clothes he brought with him?'

'I don't know. As I said, he did his own unpacking. Before the war, a valet would have seen to it, but . . . '

'From the photographs I've seen of him, he doesn't have a beard.'

'No.'

'What happened to his razor?'

'Isn't it there?'

Albert didn't answer. He'd seen enough and he wanted to get away from Tarnhey Court and its memories. Besides, he needed an antidote to the artificial respectability of the Cartwrights; he longed to be among straightforward working people again, and where better to find them than at Gem Mill where Bert Pretting had worked as senior clerk.

35

The mill stood at the other end of the village and although Albert knew that Teague and his underlings had already spoken to Pretting's work colleagues he wanted to meet them for himself. He'd always prided himself on being able to tell when people were lying to him. His instincts had gone badly wrong in that very village back in 1919, but he chose to think of that as an aberration. Back then he'd been blinded by love.

On his way to the mill he passed the doctor's house, just as a middle-aged woman was entering the open front door, probably a patient. He carried on walking, passing the side street where Bert Pretting had lived. It was lined with stone-built terraced houses, larger than the average Wenfield homes and respectable with small front gardens beneath the bay windows. It seemed that Pretting had been doing well for himself.

As he neared the mill, the houses he passed were built of the same stone but they were smaller, more cramped, with front doors that led straight onto the street. Gem Mill itself lay at the end of a cobbled roadway wide enough to accommodate the lorries that took goods to and fro. When Albert turned the corner he saw the mill's vast many-windowed facade with a tall chimney at one end, belching smoke up into the clean Derbyshire air. Even from outside he could hear the rhythmic clatter of looms and when he entered the door marked 'Office' in gold lettering they could still be heard, distant and muffled. He supposed the people who worked there day in, day out became used to it. Perhaps in the end they didn't even notice.

The clerks' office was painted in dull green and brown with a pair of windows that gave a view over a cobbled courtyard. Albert counted eight desks in all, arranged in rows of four and all occupied — apart from one at the front of the room. The men working there were all smartly dressed and ranged in age from their twenties to verging on retirement. He could hear the sound of typing from behind a door in the corner which bore the words 'A.Jones, Manager' in gold on a wooden plaque. The clack-clack of the keys echoed the noise of the looms he'd heard on the way in.

The clerks, busy with their work, didn't raise their heads as he made for the manager's office and opened the door after giving a perfunctory knock.

The secretary who sat at a wide desk in the small outer office looked perfectly serene. She was a smart, slim young woman whose clothes looked as though they'd been freshly pressed that morning. Her brown hair was styled in a neat bob and her fashionably short skirt looked rather out of place in those utilitarian surroundings.

As he entered the office she removed the letter she'd been typing from between the typewriter rollers, along with its carbon copies. When Albert had introduced himself, she stood and asked if he'd like a cup of tea. Albert thanked her. This was better treatment than he'd received at Tarnhey Court.

She tapped on her boss's door and as soon as she'd announced the visitor, Albert was invited to step into the oak-panelled inner sanctum. The manager, Arthur Jones, was a tall red-faced man with receding hair. He looked uneasy and Albert wondered whether Pretting's untimely death was causing him problems — or whether he had something on his conscience. When Albert explained what he wanted, the man's expression was hard to read.

'My staff have already been interviewed,' he said, fingering his collar nervously. 'How long is this going to take? There's work to be done and we're a man short.'

'I promise I won't keep your staff any longer than necessary,' Albert replied. 'I'd like to speak to your secretary first, if I may.' He'd read the statements of Pretting's work colleagues but he hadn't noticed one from a woman.

'Miss Reynolds has only just got back from visiting her sister in Yorkshire. She was away when . . . the tragedy occurred, so I'm sure she won't be able to tell you anything.'

'Even so, I'd like a quick word.' He looked the man in the eye and said, 'You gave a statement yourself.'

'Yes, but I couldn't tell Sergeant Teague very much. I know nothing of what Pretting got up to outside working hours.'

'You were at home on the night of his murder, I understand.'

163

The manager was sweating now, perspiration beading on his forehead. 'Er, yes. With my wife. I'd prefer it if she wasn't bothered. Her health is rather delicate.'

'I'm sure there'll be no need to disturb her.' Albert suddenly changed the subject. 'You were invited to dinner at Tarnhey Court while Henry Billinge, the MP, was staying there.'

'Yes, indeed. I heard Mr Billinge is missing, but I can't help you, I'm afraid. I barely said two words to the man.'

'What was your impression of Mr Billinge?'

'A civilised man. He talked a lot to the ladies.'

'Did you sense any bad feeling between him and any of the other guests?'

'Absolutely not.'

Albert decided to let the matter rest for the time being, even though he suspected Jones wasn't telling the whole truth.

He was allowed to use a small side office, which proved to be little more than a storeroom. But there was a desk in there and two chairs, so it was adequate. He stood up as Miss Reynolds entered with the promised cup of tea, which she placed in front of him with a professional smile. Her confident manner led Albert to suspect she would soon outgrow the mill and go on to better things.

'You must hear a lot of gossip in your job,' Albert began.

'That's true, Inspector,' she said as she sat down, crossing her legs neatly.

'You weren't interviewed with the others?'

'I wasn't in Wenfield at the time, so the

sergeant didn't think it necessary.'

Albert didn't comment on Teague's decision. It didn't matter to him that she had been absent at the time of the murder; there were things he wanted to know and he reckoned there was little that went on in that office that escaped her notice.

'You must know the clerks quite well.'

'Some of them better than others.'

'The young, single ones?'

She blushed. 'There are a couple who keep asking me to the cinema.'

'They must have served in the war?'

She nodded. 'I did my bit too. I nursed in a big house near Altrincham. I might have carried on, but my father passed away, so I had to come back to Wenfield to look after Mother,' she said matter-of-factly, seemingly without resentment at the curtailment of her ambitions. 'I was only eighteen. Saw things that no young girl should see. You were injured yourself, Inspector.'

Albert didn't reply. He had no wish to revisit the subject he found so painful. 'Miss Reynolds — '

'My friends call me Janet,' she said, looking him in the eye.

'Janet. How well did you know Bert Pretting?'

She smoothed her hair, playing for time as though she wanted to consider her words carefully. 'He wasn't someone you could avoid. He was senior clerk, but he liked to be one of the boys, if you know what I mean. I can take care of myself — I don't stand any nonsense. But sometimes Bert Pretting . . .'

'He made advances?'

'He was a married man, Inspector. And even if he wasn't, he was hardly my type. Thought he was God's gift to women — only I'm sure the Almighty has better taste than that. Bert Pretting used to make remarks, rub up against me. I slapped his face once,' she said with a hint of triumph. 'He wasn't so forward after that.'

'His colleagues seemed to like him.'

She shook her head. 'I suppose that's what they said. Don't speak ill of the dead and all that. But the truth is he was a bully. There's a boy in the office who came back from the war suffering badly with his nerves. Bert used to tease him and get the others to laugh along with him.'

'Did you ever meet his wife?'

'No, but I imagine she's a mouse of a woman. Pretting's type always need somebody to pick on, don't you think? I felt sorry for her, to tell you the truth.'

'Can you think of anybody who'd want him dead?'

She considered the question for a few seconds before replying. 'Anybody he pushed too far. Like I said, Bert Pretting had a vicious side. Maybe his wife, if the worm finally turned.'

'It was a knife in an alley rather than a domestic murder. He was drinking with some of his colleagues, but they have people who can vouch for them after they'd left the pub. They say he hadn't been arguing with anybody in the Cartwright Arms that night.'

'That might be true but, in my opinion, he was the kind of man who made enemies. He could be smooth — charming even, when he wanted to be. He certainly had Mr Jones fooled. That's how he got his promotion. I saw through him, though there were others who didn't.'

Albert thanked her and told her she could return to her duties. Her honesty had been more useful than she'd probably imagined. As she left he asked her to send in the rest of the clerks one by one. But they just repeated what they'd said in their statements. All except one.

The last clerk to enter the room was called George Yelland and he was the youngest in the office — a thin, pale lad who looked no older than a schoolboy. And yet Albert could see something else in him — old eyes that had witnessed unimaginable horrors. Even if his body hadn't been damaged, the same couldn't be said of his mind. His hands shook slightly and plucked restlessly at his trousers when he sat down.

'You know why I'm here,' said Albert gently.

'Bert Pretting. You want to know who killed him.' The words came out in a rush.

'You saw action. So did I. I know what you went through.'

The young man had been avoiding Albert's gaze, but now he looked up, sensing he was in the presence of a sympathetic soul. 'Some don't. If they weren't there, they can't imagine.'

'Bert Pretting?'

'He had a cushy time in some training camp down south. Said he was on the Somme, but I knew different. He didn't like that.'

'He used to tease you.'

'Who told you that?'

'It doesn't matter. It must have made you angry — after everything you've been through.'

'He used to copy me, make his hands shake like mine. The others laughed.'

'Probably because they were afraid that if they didn't he'd start picking on them. That's how bullies operate, George. Did you ever go to the Cartwright Arms with your colleagues?'

He shook his head. 'I don't drink much these days and my mother doesn't like me going out at night and leaving her. She's a widow and, since my sister got married, she's on her own.'

'She must have been relieved when you came back from the front alive.'

George gave a small smile and nodded.

'Where were you the night Bert Pretting was stabbed?'

'I was at home. I told Sergeant Teague.'

'So you did. Is it true?'

The young man didn't answer. And Albert noticed that the hands that had been shaking before were now perfectly still.

36

Sergeant Teague looked like a cat who'd caught a particularly large and juicy rat. The smug expression on his face as Albert walked through the door of the police station suggested that either he'd caught Bert Pretting's killer or he'd just inherited a fortune from a distant relative.

Teague lifted the flap in the front desk to admit the inspector, waiting until Albert had removed his hat and coat before he spoke.

'I've had a visit from the Prettings' maid. If we can talk in private, sir . . . in your office.'

Albert bowed to the inevitable and led the way, his mind still on the interviews he'd conducted at the mill.

'Well, Teague, what is it?' Albert said as he took a seat, leaving the sergeant standing.

'You know I told you about all that money we found locked away in Pretting's bureau?'

'There's no evidence he didn't come by it legally, is there?'

Teague's face turned red. 'Not at the moment, sir. But we've had a stroke of luck.' Teague's eyes glowed with untold news. 'I reckoned that if Pretting had secrets, something he wanted to hide from his wife, he'd keep them well hidden 'cause she was at home all day with plenty of time on her hands to nose around. I thought he might have had a fancy woman. He had a bit of a reputation, did Bert Pretting.'

169

'You've found proof he was involved with a woman?'

Teague's grin widened. 'That's where the luck comes in. The Prettings' maid — Betty, her name is — came to see me while you were out. She told me it was the other way round.'

Albert wondered what Teague meant by 'the other way round'. Then his overloaded brain began to make sense of the sergeant's words. 'You mean it wasn't Mr Pretting who had the fancy woman — it was Mrs Pretting who was involved with someone else?'

'I must say, I was surprised. I mean, Mrs Pretting's always struck me as being such a nice lady. Regular at the library, she is. Wife's always bumping into her there. According to the missus, she must spend most of her time reading.'

'But she finds time for other pursuits.' Albert noticed the sergeant's eyes gleaming as though he was imagining what these other pursuits might be. 'Is this just idle gossip or have you got evidence? And what about the money?'

'That's probably irrelevant, sir. He might have been saving up for something, for all we know.'

Teague had been standing to attention with his hands behind his back. Now he brought them forward and Albert saw that he was holding a box. He placed it on the desk in front of Albert with the satisfied look of a dog presenting a ball to its much-loved master. It was a chocolate box with a picture of a cottage on the front, thatched with roses around the door. Puppies were playing in its colourful front garden and a lady in a crinoline was watering flowers with an impractically small watering can. An idealised picture of village life that bore little resemblance to Wenfield.

'Betty's a sharp one. She says Mrs Pretting's been getting billets-doux for a while. She thinks they must have been left somewhere for her to find because she's seen her reading them but there's been nothing through the door. She thinks they might have been left in the library. All sorts of things go on in libraries, so I've heard.'

Albert, who had never considered public libraries to be dens of iniquity, raised his eyebrows.

'Betty found the box hidden under the bottom of Mrs Pretting's wardrobe.'

'Her search must have been more thorough than yours.'

Albert saw that Teague's cheeks had turned an unattractive shade of red as he reached for the box and opened the lid. Inside he found a pile of letters fastened together with a pink shiny ribbon.

'You've read them?'

Teague shook his head. 'No, sir. I thought I'd bring them straight to you.'

'Then how do you know they're not from her husband? Keepsakes of their courtship?'

'That's not Bert Pretting's handwriting, sir. He was senior clerk at the mill and his writing was very neat. This writing isn't his, I'm sure of it.'

Albert raised his eyebrows. Teague was right. The writing on the envelopes was round and

171

almost childlike. 'We'll make a detective of you yet, Sergeant.'

Teague stood there bristling with pride.

Albert pulled the end of the ribbon and it unravelled, flopping onto the desk like a dead pink worm. He took the first envelope from the pile. There was no address, only a name. Rose. As Betty claimed, it had obviously been delivered by hand — or left somewhere for the recipient to find. He slid out the contents and scanned them. First one envelope, then another until he had read them all as Teague watched, craning to see but unwilling to interrupt his superior's concentration.

Once Albert had finished reading he looked up. 'I think we need to speak to Mrs Pretting. Let's bring her in.'

Teague hurried away, triumphant.

★   ★   ★

They didn't find Rose Pretting at home. Perhaps, said Teague, he should have arrested her right away. Albert pointed out that they didn't know about the letters at that stage, so he'd done the right thing. Seeing how crestfallen the sergeant looked, he told him he'd have done exactly the same himself.

'We'll bring her in for questioning as soon as she returns home,' said Albert. 'She won't have gone far.'

'If she's found out the letters are missing she might be meeting her fancy man. Warning him off.'

'In that case you should send someone to the railway station — make sure she doesn't leave the village.'

'The fancy man might have a motor car.'

Albert knew Teague could be right. 'Very well. Tell your constables to be on the lookout. If she's a passenger, they won't be able to miss her.'

However, there was one place Albert thought they should look before be contacted all the other police stations in the area. And Wenfield public library was only a short walk away.

37

Rose

The box has gone; the box containing my most precious secrets; my story of romance in this grey and loveless place. I feel sick and my heart's beating so fast and hard that I'm sure everyone I pass can hear it.

I was so distracted that I barely remember putting on my coat and placing my hat on my head in front of the hall mirror, securing it with the hatpin that looks so lethal. How many times have I dreamed about plunging that hatpin into Bert's sleeping body so I could be free? A hundred times, maybe a thousand. There were nights when I lay awake thinking of little else.

I pick up my basket. It is heavy, filled with books. *The Countess's Lover, The Secret Arbour, Love in the First-Class Carriage.* All written by authors with glamorous names like Lavinia Lovelace and Bettina Devereux. I imagine what those women must be like; tall and willowy smoking expensive cigarettes in ivory holders and sipping champagne at their literary soirees. Their lives must be so different from mine and I wish I could be them for just a day, just to see what it's like.

The front door slams behind me and I wonder where Betty has got to. She said she was going to the butcher's, but she was wearing her best coat.

Was she the one who took my letters? Perhaps she's a blackmailer like the wicked butler in *The Duchess's Valentine*. How long before she starts asking me for money to guarantee her silence like he did?

I try not to think about it as I hurry down the street to the library. As soon as I see the building my spirits lift. It is my place of refuge and I don't know what I'd do if it wasn't there, standing on the High Street like a fortress. I think I might die of sorrow.

I enter the beloved portal with my basket of books over my arm. And something else. My urgent message. The letters have gone. What shall I do?

I arrive at the counter and smile at Miss Hubbard, the librarian, hoping that she's put some new books on the shelves — fresh treats for me to enjoy. Miss Hubbard gives me a faint smile in return. I am one of her most loyal customers, so it is as much as I deserve. She takes the books and after a brief check of the stamps to make sure they're not overdue, she returns my tickets. As I walk away I can hear my heels clicking in the library hush as I approach the shelves. I make for Fiction, licking my lips as I see the volumes lined up like soldiers on parade, waiting for me to make my choice.

But first I locate my hiding place, the narrow gap between the shelves and the wall in the corner. After looking around to make sure nobody's watching, I take the note from my pocket and slip it inside the gap. As I entered the building I placed a small pebble beneath the green railings by the library steps, our agreed signal, and I know he will come soon to collect my message. I need to see him more than ever.

I select three books and carry them to the counter under Miss Hubbard's watchful eye. 'More romance today, Mrs Pretting?' she whispers.

I nod and smile. She has no idea about the hiding place between the shelf and the wall and all of a sudden I feel guilty about the deception.

Once she has stamped the books and taken my tickets, I fill my basket with the new delights and make for the door. But as I'm about to leave my way is blocked by Sergeant Teague.

'I'd like you to come with me,' he says in a loud whisper that echoes through the hushed building. Then he takes hold of my elbow, his grip so tight that it hurts.

I drop my basket and my books spill onto the floor with a clatter, shattering the silence.

38

Rose Pretting had been arrested on suspicion of involvement in her husband's murder and the letters found by the maid, Betty, were sitting in their box on Albert's desk. They had, presumably, been written to Rose by her lover. Some mentioned potential methods of ridding her of her husband. It was beginning to look as though one of the cases at least had a simple solution.

However, the body of the unknown man was still lying, unclaimed, at the mortuary. Then there was the reason he'd been called up to Derbyshire in the first place — the disappearance of Henry Billinge MP.

Since Anne Billinge's brief visit to Wenfield he'd learned that her husband had failed to turn up for an important meeting in his Liverpool constituency. And the sole clue Albert had to his whereabouts was the name Clara, possibly the Billinges' former maid and the missing man's mistress.

The telephone on his desk began to ring and he pushed the box of letters to one side to pick up the heavy black receiver. It was Constable Smith saying there was a call for him from a lady who wouldn't give her name. Curious, Albert told Smith to put her through.

The faint voice he heard a few seconds later was high-pitched and girlish with a slight lisp. It sounded familiar although he couldn't quite place it.

'This is Jane Cartwright,' the voice said. 'We met a couple of years ago — when you came here to investigate that unpleasant series of deaths in 1919.'

That was why he'd recognised the voice. He'd spoken to Lady Cartwright, Sir William's delicate wife, during his last stay in Wenfield. He remembered her as a fey woman with an other-worldly manner.

'What can I do for you, Your Ladyship?'

'I need to speak with you. In private. My husband will be at his constituency office for the next two hours.'

Lady Cartwright's request sounded like an order. A steely command wrapped in soft silk. The Cartwrights ruled the village, so the summons wasn't something he could ignore. Besides, it was possible she knew something about the fate of Henry Billinge. Women like Jane Cartwright often knew more than people realised.

When he arrived at Tarnhey Court the door was opened at once by Mrs Banks, who wore a conspiratorial expression that suggested she was in on the secret, whatever it was. She led him to the drawing room, which hadn't changed one iota since his visit two years before. At that time the Cartwrights had made efforts to eliminate any evidence that Tarnhey Court had been used as a military hospital during the war, but some telltale clues remained: scuff marks on the walls where the iron beds had stood and paintwork chipped as the young heroes were moved in and out of the room on trolleys and in wheelchairs. Some might not have noticed, but Albert, who had been treated in a similar establishment himself, recognised the signs.

Lady Cartwright was reclining on a chaise longue and at first Albert thought she was wearing a nightgown. Then he realised she was wearing a long day dress, the kind that had been fashionable ten years before. She waved a languid hand in the direction of a velvet-covered sofa a few feet away. Albert took his seat as Mrs Banks left the room, shutting the door quietly behind her.

'You wanted to see me, my lady.'

The eyes that focused on him were sharper than first impressions would suggest. 'I believe you've been questioning my husband about our missing guest.'

'That's right. In view of Mr Billinge's position, my superiors at Scotland Yard have sent me up here to investigate his disappearance.'

'I would have thought the events of two years ago would have put you off coming to Wenfield ever again. Those dreadful murders.' She shuddered. 'My son, Roderick, was most upset about what happened. He'd known the . . . young woman responsible since he was a child and it affected him badly' She looked down, studying the handkerchief she was twisting in her fingers. 'I see little of Roderick these days, I'm afraid. He's busy with his own life in Manchester. The theatre and his moving pictures take up all his time.' She paused. 'The village still

179

hasn't recovered from the shock of so many senseless deaths, you know.'

For a moment Albert wasn't sure whether she was referring to the murders that had occurred there in 1919 or the death toll of the war itself. 'I don't suppose it has. But duty is duty and Mr Billinge must be found.'

She let out a long sigh. 'Yes, he's an important man, just like my husband. If he was a farm labourer, I doubt Sergeant Teague would have gone to the trouble of calling in Scotland Yard.'

Albert knew there was truth in her words, but he said nothing and waited for her to continue.

'I suppose you want to know whether I can tell you anything about his disappearance.'

'Can you?' He was beginning to suspect she was playing a game with him, maybe to relieve her boredom.

'Not really. Mr Billinge was very charming, you know. And very entertaining at dinner. And he had impeccable manners — I like that in a man.'

'You invited a number of guests to dinner while Mr Billinge was here, I believe.'

'We don't entertain often these days but, as leading members of local society, my husband said it was expected of us.'

Her words made Albert wonder how long it would be before she realised how much the world had changed since the war ended. The old social order was dying but the Cartwrights seemed determined to carry on as though nothing had happened. 'I trust it was a pleasant evening?'

'Tolerable. The new vicar lacks the social graces of his predecessor, I'm afraid. Then there was the new doctor — so young but so clever. And Mr and Mrs Jones. He runs the mill, but his wife seems somewhat out of her depth — socially, I mean. Her husband claims she's delicate but I suspect she's as fragile as an old army boot.'

Albert raised his eyebrows at this harsh judgement.

'The Ogdens are charming though. She comes from a good family, although I believe he was in trade. Then there was dear Mrs Bell and the lady novelist who's moved into David Eames's old place. Peggy Derwent she's called. She seemed rather restless and I wondered whether our dull provincial conversation was boring her.'

'Did Mr Billinge talk to any of your guests in particular?'

'He divided his attentions fairly equally, I think. He's used to moving in society . . . unlike the new vicar, who was lecturing the poor Jones woman most of the evening. But Mr Fellowes is a prominent man in the village, so Sir William was obliged to invite him.'

'What about the lady novelist?'

'She drank a lot of wine and said very little. I expected her to be more . . . interesting.'

'And the Ogdens?'

'They've taken a large property outside the village — been in the district for two years. They're a very nice couple.'

Albert had heard enough about Wenfield's social hierarchy. It was time to steer the conversation back to her missing house guest. 'I believe Mr Billinge was overheard arguing with your husband.'

She hesitated before answering. 'Oh, William enjoys arguing for arguing's sake. It was most likely something to do with women's suffrage. A policy matter.' She looked Albert in the eye. 'I hope you don't suspect Sir William of any wrongdoing. I assure you . . . '

'Does the name Clara mean anything to you?'

She froze. 'No, it doesn't.'

The woman in front of him wasn't a good liar. Albert couldn't imagine she'd ever had much need to use subterfuge, so she lacked practice.

'The name's come up in the course of my enquiries, that's all. Mrs Billinge thinks she was a former employee of theirs who began a relationship with her husband. Sir William was overheard talking about her to Mr Billinge.'

'My husband is hardly likely to share gossip about his colleague's infidelities with me, Mr Lincoln. He knows I wouldn't approve.'

'Of course.' He paused, watching her as she stared out of the window at the garden, apparently deep in thought. 'Why exactly did you ask me to call?'

She sighed and turned her head to look at him. 'Because I wanted to make it clear that my husband has absolutely nothing to do with Mr Billinge's disappearance. We're both quite sure that Mr Billinge has met with an unfortunate accident. There are so many old mine workings and potholes around here; places where people and animals can vanish and never be found. Sir

William feels very guilty that he neglected to warn him of the hazards. If something has happened, I know he'll feel responsible and find it hard to forgive himself, but I can assure you he has no idea what has befallen Mr Billinge. If he knew anything he would have told the police straight away. That goes without saying.'

Albert stood up. 'Thank you, my lady. I'm sure you're right.' Jane Cartwright wasn't the only one who could lie. Her unconvincing protestations had just moved Sir William a little higher up his list of suspects.

As he left the room he spotted a photograph in an elaborate silver frame sitting on the grand piano that dominated the bay window. It was a picture of an attractive young woman with a handsome child — a fair-haired boy about a year old.

Jane Cartwright saw him looking at it. 'My niece and her son. A blessing from God,' she added wistfully.

Albert left by the front door but he made a quick detour to the back of the house to seek out Mrs Banks. He found her in her sitting room and she offered tea.

They drank in amicable silence for a while before Albert asked the question that had been on his mind since he left the drawing room. 'Her Ladyship has a niece with a baby. Do you know her name?'

'Yes. It's Charlotte. Mrs Charlotte Day.'

39

The silver pocket watch had been a wedding present from Mary, so Albert was reminded of her whenever he checked the time. Their wedding had been a happy occasion. Neither of them could have known how things would turn out. Perhaps that was a blessing.

He checked the watch now and realised time was moving on. The mention of Charlotte Day's name had shaken him. Though he would have liked to glean more information from Mrs Banks or even Lady Cartwright, he didn't see how he could do so without arousing suspicion. When he let his imagination wander he convinced himself that it all fitted: an infant whose mother had died by hanging, another woman who longed for a child, and a kindly clergyman who'd arranged an adoption. But he had no proof and he was reluctant to take the matter any further and seek the woman out. The situation was far too delicate to go barging in.

To take his mind off his son, he focused on the investigation into Bert Pretting's murder. It had happened so soon after Billinge's disappearance and the discovery of the unidentified body in the cave that he felt obliged to take charge — at least until it had been firmly established that there was no connection between the three cases. Hopefully, the stabbing of Bert Pretting in an alleyway would be an easy one to sort out.

People who commit such murders are rarely expert at covering their tracks.

His first priority was to speak to Rose Pretting, who was languishing in a cell at the police station, but he didn't relish the prospect of interviewing the suspect in her cell so he asked for her to be brought to his office. Somewhat reluctantly, Constable Wren obeyed.

Ten minutes later Rose Pretting entered the room with Wren walking closely behind as if he was afraid she'd make a run for it. She looked tiny and vulnerable, almost childlike. When Albert told him to leave them alone, Wren opened his mouth to protest. It took a stern look to make him retreat, leaving the door open behind him. Albert got up to close it and invited Rose to sit.

Albert took the seat on the other side of the desk. He'd seen her at the mortuary but now he had a chance to study her more closely, he was struck by how young she looked. Her eyes were wide and a bright, cornflower blue with long lashes and, like last time, she was dressed in the latest fashion. He'd seen such dresses on women in London, but he guessed that Rose's version was home-made. He imagined her working on it at a sewing machine which was probably her pride and joy.

He gave her a reassuring smile. 'I hope your stay in the cells hasn't been too uncomfortable, Mrs Pretting.'

'They're saying I killed Bert.' The words came out in a whisper.

'Did you?'

'No. I was at home. I went to bed around ten o'clock and fell asleep. I didn't realise he hadn't come home until the next morning.'

'Can anyone confirm that?'

'No. Our maid, Betty, doesn't live in 'cause we haven't got the room. I was on my own.'

He leaned forward and gave her a reassuring smile. 'Tell me about Bert.'

She took a deep breath. 'He was ten years older than me. Worked as senior clerk at the mill. It's a good job.'

'I'm sure it is. Where did you meet?'

'I lived in Cheadle with my mother. It's not far from Stockport — you won't know it.'

'I do, as a matter of fact. I was there last year,' he said, recalling the time when he went to the village to interview a witness while he was investigating the murder of a woman in Mabley Ridge near Wilmslow.

Rose looked surprised. 'Bert was a clerk at Cheadle bleach works. He wasn't there long before he got the job in Wenfield. It meant more money.'

'Has he always lived in the area?'

She shook her head. 'No. He comes from the Wirral — that's across the river from Liverpool. Then after he did his bit in the war he changed his job and moved to Cheadle. The bleach works job was a step up, he always said. Then he got the post here in Wenfield. Senior clerk.' She leaned forward as though she was about to share a confidence. 'He reckoned that when Mr Perkins, the chief clerk, retired he was bound to step into his shoes.'

'He was ambitious.'

She nodded. 'I suppose he was.'

'What about your marriage? Were you happy?'

The answer was a long silence.

Albert hadn't thought of Mary all day, but his last question brought her to the forefront of his mind. Had she been taken out of hospital as Vera intended? Was she lying at home as they spoke, with Vera and the Reverend Gillit watching over her? He felt a sudden stab of conscience, asking himself how he could sit in judgement on the woman in front of him when his own shortcomings as a husband were so great. But he had a job to do so he carried on.

'How did you and Bert get on?'

'All right, I suppose.'

'I've heard he was a bully.'

Rose bowed her head so Albert couldn't see her expression.

'He picked on one of the junior clerks at work and his colleagues were wary of him,' he continued. 'In my experience, men like that often take their frustrations out on their wives when they get home. You must have had a lot to put up with.'

When she looked up, Albert saw gratitude in her eyes, as though she was glad someone understood at last.

'He made you unhappy. And then you met someone else. A man who was everything Bert wasn't. Kind, loving, thoughtful.'

A small smile played on her lips but she didn't answer.

'If this man loves you, he must have been

187

furious about the way Bert treated you.'

She said nothing.

'Who is he, Rose? I'm not judging you for what you've done, but I want to speak to him. I need to eliminate him from our enquiries.'

She straightened her back and jutted out her chin. 'I won't betray him. I'd never do that.'

'I understand. But I do need to ask him some questions.'

'Why? Bert fell out with someone in the Carty Arms and got into a fight.'

'With the man you're seeing?'

'No. Definitely not. He would never stoop so low. Never.'

'Anybody's capable of murder, given the provocation.'

She shook her head vigorously. 'Not him. Never.'

'Or did you wait for him that night and stab him yourself? I'd understand if you did. You must have been desperate.'

'It's not true. I never harmed him.'

'But you wanted to.'

'That's not the same.'

'Did you put glass in his food?'

She looked up at him, tears glistening in her eyes. 'That's not true.'

'Letters were found hidden in the bottom of your wardrobe. Who wrote them?'

Her cheeks turned red, but she didn't answer.

'Who were the letters from?'

Another silence.

'They mention ways to get rid of your husband. Ground glass in his food. Broken glass.'

'Bert was a brute. I dreamed of him dying but I never did nothing. Honest.'

She began to sob, looking around her for escape like a cornered animal. Albert knew he'd get nothing more out of her that day, so he went to the door and called for someone to take her back to the cells. He suspected that she knew more about Bert Pretting's death than she was admitting and he knew any jury was bound to judge her harshly. A woman who conspires with another man to kill her husband can expect no mercy, whatever she has had to endure at his hands.

It was getting late and Mrs Jackson was expecting him back at the Black Horse for his evening meal. Before he left he asked Constable Wren for Rose Pretting's door key and put it in his pocket.

40

The library in Wenfield was a fine building and before returning to the Black Horse Albert took advantage of the late opening hours and called in. He had a question to ask and if the answer was yes, he would know for sure. If not, there was a chance he was wrong. When he thought of Rose and her innocent blue eyes he hoped the answer would be no.

But Miss Hubbard the librarian, a severe-looking woman in a crisp white blouse, gave him an answer that seemed to confirm his worst suspicions. Mrs Pretting had renewed *The Garden of Secrets* by Cecilia Yarmouth five times in all, which was surprising because she was normally a fast reader. The librarian answered the question matter-of-factly without asking why Albert wanted to know.

He was about to turn away from the handsome mahogany counter when the librarian spoke again. 'I hear Mrs Pretting has been arrested.'

The woman's bright eyes were focused on his face. She would detect a lie in a second, he thought. He could have done with her at Scotland Yard. 'We have been questioning her, yes.' He paused. 'Have you ever seen her with a man?'

Miss Hubbard smiled and the impression of severity vanished in an instant. 'You mean a man who wasn't her husband? No, never.'

Albert thanked her, putting on his hat as he left the building. It had begun to drizzle and he asked himself whether he should be putting so much effort into the Pretting case. He was there to find Henry Billinge — but there was something about Rose Pretting that made him want to protect her. He suspected that if Teague had his way she'd meet the same fate as Flora Winsmore, and this was something he wouldn't allow to happen if he could help it.

He couldn't help wondering whether Henry Billinge was really out there trapped somewhere underground in the wild, hilly landscape. Was he suffering a slow and agonising death at that moment — or had death already claimed him? According to Teague, a search of the nearby countryside had been made, but had it been thorough enough? Albert had no choice but to trust the men with local knowledge, and there were still more lines of enquiry he had to follow before he could reach any sort of conclusion, pessimistic or otherwise.

When he reached the Black Horse, Mrs Jackson was waiting for him with a letter. He recognised the handwriting on the envelope as Vera's and he felt his hand shaking as he took it, hoping Mrs Jackson hadn't noticed.

'It's stew and dumplings tonight,' she said.

Stew with dumplings was his favourite so at least this was one piece of good news. He hoped Vera's letter would contain more — although he wasn't optimistic. Before dinner he went to his room to read it.

Mary is home. She didn't like the hospital and the nurses were very rude to the Reverend Gillit when he called. They said he was upsetting her but that was a terrible lie because the reverend has always been a great comfort to her; her only comfort because you think nothing of going away and leaving your wife in her hour of need. I have not called Dr Hughes because Mary doesn't want him. She says she hopes it won't be long now before she passes to the other side to be with Frederick but I tell her not to be so foolish.

He and Mary had long since stopped being a loving couple but Vera's words made his eyes prick with tears as memories of their courtship and early marriage flashed through his mind. He had loved Mary once.

He stared at the paper and saw a drop of water land on it, blurring the ink. Then he realised it was a tear. His own tear, shed for a woman who'd been his world in happier times. He wiped his sleeve across his face, annoyed with himself. Mary had done nothing wrong. He was the one who'd been unfaithful, both in reality and in his heart. He'd failed as a husband.

He ate alone, barely tasting Mrs Jackson's stew and dumplings because possible solutions to his multiple dilemmas kept running through his head. When he thought of work, he didn't have to think of what was happening to Mary.

The mystery of the naked man in the cave intrigued him the most. Someone had robbed him of his clothes and beaten his face to a pulp. But had that been an act of spite or had the motive been to hide his true identity? And if so, why go to such lengths? He was still awaiting Dr Kelly's verdict on whether the victim was poisoned. If the test results confirmed that was the case, it would make the case even more puzzling.

Once he'd cleared his plate he thanked the landlady automatically before retiring to his room where he undressed and fell asleep right away. And when he slept he dreamed of Charlotte Day, the woman he'd seen lovingly framed in silver at Tarnhey Court, with her child. She was in a field, monochrome as in the photograph and frozen to the spot, while the baby boy crawled towards him calling out 'Father' in Frederick's voice.

41

When Albert arrived at the police station the next morning he was still undecided about returning to London to be at Mary's bedside. Despite Mary's dramatic pronouncements about the imminence of death, Vera had said nothing to support this, so he felt it was safe to delay his trip back to the capital until his investigations in Wenfield had made more progress. But just to be on the safe side, he asked Smith to look up train times for the following day. If it turned out Mary was indeed nearing the end, he would never forgive himself if he wasn't there with her. Teague would have to manage on his own.

In the meantime it was good that he had a distraction from the dark thoughts whirling around his head. Albert knew from long experience that as soon as Rose Pretting was charged it would attract the more undesirable kind of newspaperman to Wenfield. There was nothing the press relished more than a young woman with the face of an angel accused of slaughtering her innocent and unsuspecting husband. The fact that Bert Pretting was an unpleasant piece of work wouldn't matter. Once the press had finished with him, he'd be a candidate for sainthood.

And once they'd descended on Wenfield in force, reporters would soon get wind of the Billinge story. Until now the affair had been dealt with discreetly, but within days it would be headline news if he didn't find the missing MP — alive or dead.

He opened the file on Henry Billinge's disappearance and began to read and reread the statements of the people who had attended the dinner party at Tarnhey Court. Teague's initial questioning had been discreet and superficial, as though he hadn't wanted to offend his social superiors by delving too deeply. Albert, however, had no such qualms. He'd already spoken to Mr Jones, the mill manager, but as his wife had also been at the dinner he wanted to question her too. Women are often better observers than men, he'd found — and her husband had observed that Billinge preferred to speak to the ladies.

He pulled on his overcoat and told Smith, who was manning the front desk, that he wouldn't be long.

He knew Jones would be at work so he made for the manager's house, which was a short walk from the mill. The large stone-built house stood on the edge of the village, double fronted and imposing with sparkling paintwork and a flight of wide stone steps leading up to a glossy red front door. Some people of the wealthier sort expected a police officer to use the tradesman's entrance, but Albert had no time for such snobbery. He climbed the steps, ignoring the stiffness in his leg, then raised the door knocker, let it fall three times and waited.

The young maid who answered wore an immaculate starched apron and a wary expression. She looked him up and down suspiciously, but he removed his hat, gave her a reassuring smile and asked whether Mrs Jones was at home.

'Who shall I say is calling, sir?'

'Detective Inspector Lincoln of Scotland Yard. Tell her there's no need to worry. It's a routine matter.'

He was admitted into a wide hallway and asked to wait. Five minutes later the girl returned and led him into a handsome drawing room where a slender woman with a face that reminded Albert of a cat's sat on a sofa by the fireplace, flicking through a glossy periodical. With her short skirt and fashionably styled blonde hair, she looked as though she belonged on the pages of a magazine herself. When she set her reading matter to one side and invited Albert to sit, he observed that her accent was a more pronounced version of Gwen Davies's, which suggested she was from the Liverpool area. She appeared considerably younger than her care-worn husband, and far from the delicate creature portrayed by Mr Jones.

'What can I do for you, Inspector? I hope you haven't come to arrest me,' she said with a coquettish smile.

'I'm hoping you might be able to help me, Mrs Jones.'

'Jacqueline, please. Mrs Jones makes me sound so old. Was it you who questioned my husband about that clerk who got himself killed?'

'Yes. But this is about another matter.'

She took a silver cigarette case from the table to her right and offered it to Albert. He took a cigarette and as she lit it with her silver lighter he

196

caught a whiff of her perfume; something heavy and expensive.

'I don't know whether you've heard that one of the guests at the dinner you attended at Sir William Cartwright's house has gone missing. Mr Billinge went out for a walk the day after you met him and never returned.'

Mrs Jones suddenly looked solemn. 'Yes, I heard. Sergeant Teague asked my husband if he knew anything. He didn't, of course. They say the countryside round here can be dangerous. They say sheep disappear down potholes and are never found again.' She shuddered. 'I sometimes wonder why my husband wanted to come here. It's a dull place. And cold.'

'You're from Liverpool.'

She looked at him curiously. 'How did you . . . ?'

'I knew someone from there once. I recognised the accent. How did you and Mr Jones meet?'

She sniffed. 'If you must know, I was a waitress. Met him when he was there on business.'

'Bert Pretting came from the Wirral.'

'Did he? I never met him.' She hesitated. 'I do hope poor Mr Billinge hasn't met with an accident. If he wandered onto private land I've heard some of the gamekeepers aren't slow to use their shotguns on trespassers. There are people from Manchester who think they have a right to walk anywhere they like.' She sniffed again. 'Good on 'em, if you ask me.'

'All the gamekeepers on the estates round here

have been questioned and nobody has admitted to seeing Mr Billinge up on the grouse moors. Did you speak to Mr Billinge over dinner?'

'I tried to make small talk, as you do, but he seemed a bit distracted, as though he had things on his mind.'

'You told Sergeant Teague this?'

'He never asked me. The vicar was seated to my left, so the evening was hard work,' she added meaningfully. 'Reverend Fellowes is rather an odd sort of man — he kept staring at me in a way that made me very uncomfortable. But of course you're not interested in what I think of the local clergy, are you? You're looking for Mr Billinge.'

'Have you heard about the man who was found in a cave near the Devil's Dancers?'

She lowered her eyes. 'There's been talk of it in the village, I believe,' she said, taking a drag on her cigarette.

'You haven't seen any strangers hanging around the area?'

'I have, as a matter of fact. I was walking back from church and I saw a man going into Pooley Woods.'

'When was this?'

'On Saturday. We ladies do the church flowers on Saturday so they're fresh for the Sunday services. My husband's been nagging me to do something — to make a contribution to the village, as he puts it. He says it's expected of people in our social position,' she added with a dismissive sniff, stubbing out her cigarette then taking another from the silver case before offering it again to Albert. This time he shook his head.

'Turns out I'm quite good with flowers. I enjoy it.'

'Was this before or after the body was found in the cave?'

'Before.'

'Can you describe him?'

'He was a big man. Full beard. Army greatcoat. I thought he was a tramp. And he was behaving like he was up to something. Furtive, that's the word.'

From the description she'd given there was no way that the stranger she saw could have been the mystery man at the Devil's Dancers, but Albert pressed her for more details.

'It was getting dark so I hurried past as quickly as I could, but I could feel him watching me from the trees.' She shuddered. 'There was something . . . desperate about him. To tell you the truth, he scared the life out of me.'

42

Rose

I know Sergeant Teague's highly thought of in the village but I don't like him. He spoke to me very roughly, almost as roughly as Bert used to. He said he'd read my letters and he kept asking me the name of my fancy man. I didn't tell him anything, but I know he'll be back later.

I hate this cell. It smells foul and the blanket they've given me is filthy and damp, but I mustn't cry. I mustn't let them get the better of me. Sergeant Teague says I'm a loose woman but that's not what they call the women in my books who escape from their evil captors. They call them heroines. I wish I could have some books to read. I asked that nice young Constable Smith, but he said I wasn't allowed. If this was a book, a lovely man would come and rescue me. I don't like real life. Nothing's ever fair in real life.

The door's opening and Sergeant Teague's looming in the doorway like an ogre in a fairy tale. He used to smile and touch his helmet when I met him in the street but now he's looking at me as though I'm a piece of dirt he's stepped in; something that's just ruined his shiny big boots.

'Are you ready to tell the truth yet?'

He stands over me so I have to look up at him. I want to hit out at him with my fists, but I know it would only make things worse. He grabs me by the elbow and hauls me to my feet.

'You're coming with me. Either you killed him yourself or someone did it for you. Nobody here likes murdering little sluts who go with other men behind their husbands' backs.'

I can't hold back the tears any more. They've been burning my eyes as I try to keep them in but now they tumble out and stream down my cheeks. And I'm ashamed of myself for giving in.

43

Albert could hear sobbing; the forlorn sound of despair and lost hope.

'What's going on?' he asked Constable Smith, who was standing behind the station's front desk making a great show of studying the register open in front of him.

'The sergeant's interviewing a suspect, sir. Mrs Pretting. Her that did in her old man.' He looked sheepish, as though he was dismayed by the noises coming from the room behind him but was determined not to show it.

Albert removed his hat. 'You know that for a fact, do you, Constable?'

'Her fancy man wrote her those letters. They plotted to do away with her husband, then he was found dead. Stands to reason either he did it or she did, but she won't say who he is.'

'This isn't London, Constable. It's a village in Derbyshire. You're not telling me there's nobody around who hasn't seen her with this so-called fancy man of hers.'

As he waited for Smith's reply, it struck him that he himself had carried on an illicit relationship in that very village two years earlier without anybody being aware of what was going on. But he was a policeman, long skilled in the art of subterfuge. Rose Pretting, if his judgement was correct, was a naive woman to whom stories of adventure and romance had become more real than her daily existence.

It was possible, of course, that Rose's lover, whoever he was, might prove more worldly and cunning. If Albert could discover his identity they might get at the truth. Even so, he suspected that Teague's bullying wasn't the best way to produce results.

He could hear Teague's voice raised in anger as the woman's sobs grew louder and more uncontrolled. He signalled to Smith to lift the counter flap to let him through to the back and marched towards the room where the interrogation was taking place. Without knocking, he burst in and saw Teague towering over the seated suspect, whose face was blotchy and soaked with tears.

'I'll take over now, Sergeant, thank you.' The words were barked as an order and Albert saw a brief flash of defiance in Teague's small brown eyes before the man straightened up and sloped from the room. If he'd been a dog he would have given a parting growl.

Albert took his place opposite Rose at the table as her shoulders heaved with sobs of despair. He handed her a handkerchief and gave her an encouraging smile as she wiped her eyes, giving a final shuddering sob.

'The sergeant was wrong to speak to you like that,' he said gently. 'You've just lost your husband.'

She nodded vigorously, glad of a sympathetic ear at last.

'I expect you want to get home.'

Another nod.

'Is there anything you'd like? Books, perhaps? I know you're a regular at the library.'

'Thank you. I'd like some books. There are some in the house. I only took them out yesterday.'

'I'll get someone to bring them over for you,' he said, remembering he still had Rose's key in his pocket. 'There's one I believe you've borrowed several times. *The Garden of Secrets.*'

She blushed. 'So?'

'Any particular reason?'

'I like it, that's all.'

'Sergeant Teague thinks you're guilty. He wants to know the name of your lover.'

She raised her chin, suddenly defiant, but said nothing.

'Those letters we found — I expect the man who wrote them is everything Bert wasn't. Kind. Clever. Gentle. Someone everyone respects.'

She gave a secretive smile as though she was reliving happy private memories.

Albert quickly ran through some of the likely candidates in his head. The factory manager and Sir William seemed too mature for the role. The schoolmaster too, he recalled, had been too old to fight in the war. That left a number of possibilities, including one that he was reluctant to consider because he'd met young George Yelland from the mill and taken a liking to him.

'Thank you, Mrs Pretting. I'll ask someone to bring your books over.'

Albert rose to his feet. He had other things to attend to; promises to keep. There was a visit he needed to make. It would be an awkward encounter but, because of what he already knew, he was certain he'd get the truth out of the Reverend Fellowes this time.

He instructed Constable Smith to return Mrs Pretting to her cell and told him to go over to her house to fetch her books without letting Teague know what he was doing. As he handed over the key to Rose Pretting's house, the constable looked uncertain but he didn't argue.

A fine veil of drizzle was starting to fall as Albert left the station and hurried down the cobbled street towards the vicarage, hoping he'd find the vicar at home.

He walked in the direction of the tall church tower; God's acre where the dead of the village were laid to rest after their earthly toil in the mill or the farms round about. Sir William's late relatives lay inside the church; a social divide in death as in life.

When he reached the path that led to the vicarage door all he could hear was the wind stirring the fresh green tree branches nearby. He looked around and caught sight of a figure standing some distance away beneath a tall yew in the churchyard that stood beside the low drystone wall separating the vicarage garden from the land of the dead. The man was too far away to see clearly but he could tell he was large and bearded, and he wondered if it was the same man who'd frightened Mrs Jones. There was something familiar about him, although Albert couldn't think what it was, and when the figure hurried away in the direction of Pooley Wood he told himself it was probably someone visiting the churchyard to pay their respects to a dead relative. Perhaps his past experiences in that village were making him see villainy around every corner.

When he knocked on the vicarage door it was answered by Grace, who greeted him with a smile.

'Is the reverend at home?' he asked as he took off his hat.

'He's in the study. Said he found the key in the vestry, but he still says there's no need for me to clean in there. Says he doesn't want his things disturbed,' she added with a knowing wink.

'Does he suspect we were in there?'

'He's mentioned nothing to me, sir.'

'Looks as though we've got away with it, then.' Their eyes met and she gave him a conspiratorial grin. Grace had clearly relished the excitement of her first venture into breaking and entering.

Before he could say anything else, the Reverend Fellowes appeared in the hallway. He was a tall, stooped man in his thirties with a thin, anxious face, fine fair hair and a habit of fidgeting with the lapels of his jacket. Albert introduced himself and shook hands.

'I heard about that poor man at the Devil's Dancers. If his family can't be found, I'm happy to allow him to be buried in the churchyard here.'

'Thank you.'

'It's my Christian duty,' said Fellowes piously. 'I'm not sure when the police will allow the burial but . . . Perhaps you would be good enough to find out for me.'

'Of course.' Albert decided to come straight to

the point. 'Are you aware that Mrs Bell thinks her husband's death might not have been natural?'

'She has mentioned it to me, yes. But I served under the Reverend Bell as curate for a short time before his death and I can assure you he was well loved. He had no enemies who might wish him harm, Inspector.'

Albert considered his next move. If possible, he wanted to keep Grace and Mrs Bell well away from any suspicion of snooping.

'I'm told Mr Bell received a letter on the day he died — possibly a letter with a photograph enclosed. Mrs Bell hadn't the heart to look for it just after his death and by the time she returned to Wenfield you'd moved into the vicarage. Have you come across any such letter and photograph?'

'No.'

'Would you mind if I looked for myself?'

'I thought you were in Wenfield to find Mr Billinge.'

'The two things might be connected.'

Albert saw panic in Fellowes' eyes.

'I promise you I'm only interested in one particular letter. Nothing else.' He looked straight into the vicar's eyes. 'Most of us have things we'd rather others didn't know about and in my job I've learned to be discreet.'

Fellowes swallowed hard and Albert saw his Adam's apple bob up and down. He was a cornered man. Albert knew the signs.

'If you must.' He nodded towards the study door.

Albert made a show of searching through the files of correspondence in the hope there would be something he'd missed last time he was there. But again he found nothing. He ignored the desk, making the excuse that he was sure, if there'd been anything of interest there, the Reverend Fellowes would have found it and reported it. The vicar couldn't conceal his relief.

'You must have known the Reverend Bell well,' he said, looking Fellowes in the eye.

The vicar nodded warily. 'I suppose . . . '

'I wonder whether he discovered things about you — things you'd rather keep private.'

The vicar's face reddened. 'I don't know what you mean.'

'We all have our little secrets, Reverend,' Albert said with a smile. 'Even a Scotland Yard detective has things he'd rather keep to himself. What is it you have to hide, Mr Fellowes? A weakness for drink? A love of gambling? A liking for the ladies — real or imagined?'

A look of sheer horror passed across the vicar's face, as though Albert had seen into his very soul and found it stained and filthy. 'I don't know what you mean,' he said weakly.

'I'm just thinking that if Mr Bell found out about your . . . weakness, you might consider it best if he wasn't around to betray your secrets.'

'That's absolute nonsense, Inspector. Even if Horace Bell had known things about me, he was a kind and discreet man. I would have trusted him with my life.'

The words were said with honesty and somehow Albert believed them. But he had to be sure. 'Where were you on the night Mr Bell died?'

'At home — the curate occupies a small house at the other side of the churchyard. Currently empty, awaiting its new incumbent. I was working on my sermon and reading that night. I saw and heard nothing.'

'You didn't go out at all?'

'No.' Fellowes was a hopeless liar.

'Are you sure?'

He nodded, avoiding Albert's gaze.

Albert decided on a change of subject. 'I believe you attended a dinner at Tarnhey Court while Mr Billinge was staying there?'

'There were a number of people there.'

'The great and the good of Wenfield.'

'If you want to put it that way. Mr and Mrs Jones were present, as were Dr Kelly, Mrs Bell and Mr and Mrs Ogden. And a lady novelist who's recently moved to the area.'

'What happened that evening?'

'Nothing happened. It was a dinner, that's all. And before you ask, Mr Billinge gave no indication that he was planning to disappear or that he'd arranged to meet anybody. Although I admit he did seem rather distracted.'

'You spoke to him during the evening?'

'We began to discuss the spiritual state of the nation since the war, but I don't think the subject appealed to him overmuch. He spent more time talking with Mrs Ogden. A charming woman.'

'I haven't met the Ogdens yet. What can you tell me about them?'

'They live about a mile outside the village. They seem to be a very nice couple, although they're not regulars in my congregation.'

Albert suspected that Mrs Odgen was favoured with the MP's attention because the alternative was being interrogated by the earnest Reverend Fellowes about spiritual matters. 'If Mr Billinge spent some time talking with Mrs Ogden, I'd like to speak to her.' Albert took out his pocket watch and checked the time. 'By the way, do you know a lady called Charlotte Day? She's Lady Cartwright's niece?'

The vicar didn't answer but Albert saw the colour drain from his cheeks. The name Charlotte Day meant something to him. And the memories the name brought back probably weren't pleasant.

44

It was three o'clock and Rose Pretting was still weighing heavily on Albert's mind. Since their earlier meeting he'd been picturing what would happen to her. She would inevitably face a trial — a diminutive figure standing in the dock with the full force of the law ranged against her; men in dusty black peering at her like predatory beasts. Then, if she was found guilty, she would be incarcerated in a prison cell before facing the ultimate penalty. He pictured her being led into the execution chamber, the rough hood thrust over her head and the noose placed around her slender neck while the chaplain intoned his prayers. He felt her terror as she waited for the last drop. He'd loved a woman who'd met the same fate and the memory made him shudder.

As he walked towards Wenfield's main street he wondered whether Constable Smith had fetched Rose's library books as he'd asked. He wasn't far from her house, so on impulse he decided to check. As a police officer it wasn't his place to provide comfort to a woman accused of conspiring to commit a brutal murder but his past experiences in that very village had softened his heart. Although he wondered if what he planned to do was an act of simple kindness — or a sign of weakness.

As soon as he reached Rose's front door he realised that Smith was still in possession of the key so he was relieved to find the maid, Betty, at home. She opened the door and greeted him with a broad smile. She looked happy, almost triumphant.

'Has the constable been to pickup Mrs Pretting's books?'

She shook her head. 'Don't know what she needs books for. She's for the hangman.'

'You think she killed Mr Pretting?'

Suddenly Betty didn't look so sure of herself. 'She couldn't stand him. You could tell.'

'That doesn't mean she killed him.'

She folded her arms, ready for gossip. 'She had a fancy man, so I reckon they did it together. Stands to reason, doesn't it.' She looked round as though she feared she'd be overheard. 'I think they met at that library. Always there, she was. Dolled up to the nines.' She spoke of the library as though it was a house of ill repute.

Albert decided on flattery. In his experience, it normally worked a treat. 'A bright girl like you must know what goes on in this village.'

She blushed. 'I suppose . . . I grew up in Disley and I only started working here a year ago, so I missed all the excitement with those terrible dove murders.'

Albert had been doing his best to concentrate on the present, but Betty's words plunged him back into that terrible time; a time of secrets, betrayal and pain. He took a deep breath.

'Did you ever see Mrs Pretting with a man other than her husband?'

A look of disappointment passed across Betty's face. 'Can't say I did. She must have been careful. But everyone in the village talked about how she always dressed in the latest fashions. She couldn't be bothered mending her husband's shirts or darning his socks — she left all that to me — but when she wasn't reading those books of hers she'd be working away on that sewing machine, making clothes for herself. She got the patterns from Manchester; I know that for a fact.' She sniffed. 'Village shop wasn't good enough for her. Always giving herself airs and graces, she was. Reckoned she was better than everyone else.'

'I believe the letters you found were well hidden. How did you know they were there?'

'She left the bedroom door open once and, as I was passing, I saw her putting the plank back in the bottom of her wardrobe. She had no idea I was watching her,' she added with a smug smile.

'You read the letters before you told the police about them?'

'Might have done.'

'So you could have told someone about them and maybe saved Mr Pretting's life.'

'I didn't know she'd actually do it. I thought it was a joke.'

He was running out of patience with Betty. Her spite towards her mistress was plain to see and he wondered why she'd kept silent about the letters. She could have made no end of trouble for Rose if she'd chosen to tell Bert Pretting about them. Unless she was well aware of Pretting's violent nature and drew the line at condemning Rose to a beating at best — or death at worst. Or perhaps she had her own

213

reasons for keeping Rose's secret — those letters would have given her a perfect opportunity for blackmail.

'Where are Mrs Pretting's library books?'

When Betty showed him into the parlour he saw a pile of books on the sideboard. All novels. Mostly romances, along with a few detective stories. Albert picked them up one by one and studied the titles. 'I'll take them,' he said.

Betty stared at the titles and pointed to one at the top of the pile. 'That one — *The Garden of Secrets* — I reckon that's her favourite. She's read that a few times that I know of. Keeps renewing it from that library.'

'It must be good,' said Albert casually, curious to know what was so special about that particular book.

Without being asked, Betty hurried off to fetch a length of string to keep the books together and then tied them with practised efficiency.

When he returned to the police station he gave Constable Smith the pile of books to take to the prisoner. However, he kept one back. *The Garden of Secrets* by Cecilia Yarmouth.

He flicked through the pages and found it was a romance with a smattering of crime thrown in. A young woman, sold into a loveless marriage to an older man by her heartless parents, falls in love with the young doctor who's treating her husband for a riding injury and they plot together to kill him, first by putting glass in his food then later with poison. They exchange letters and as Albert scanned the page he was struck by the similarity to the letters hidden in

214

Rose Pretting's wardrobe.

It was as though Rose had used *The Garden of Secrets* as a template. A guide to murder.

45

Albert wanted to see Rose's reaction when he produced *The Garden of Secrets* and placed it on the table in front of her. But that would have to wait. First he wanted to head back to the Black Horse to find out whether there had been another letter from Vera; a fresh bulletin on Mary's condition.

As he walked into the hotel he half expected Mrs Jackson to hurry up to him with an envelope in her outstretched hand but, as it turned out, nothing had arrived for him in the later post. Albert felt relieved. If Vera hadn't put pen to paper, perhaps the situation wasn't as grim as she'd made out. He had the train times and he intended to travel down the following evening. Unless he could find Henry Billinge in the meantime, his visit might have to be a short one, but he was determined to see Mary.

He hated eating alone. Anne Billinge's company had provided a much appreciated respite, but that evening he sat at his solitary table as usual, eating his braised liver and mashed potato, casting envious glances at the two businessmen seated at the next table, deep in conversation. He heard them discussing the price of cloth and raw materials and caught the name Jones a couple of times. He wondered if they'd ever encountered Mr Jones's senior clerk Bert Pretting on their previous visits — and whether they were aware of the nature of his death. He supposed it wasn't something Jones would want to become common knowledge among his customers and suppliers.

He retired to his room early, there being little else for a lone stranger to do in Wenfield. And as he lay beneath Mrs Jackson's heavy blankets, longing for sleep, the cases kept running through his mind. Albert was starting to wonder whether the popular theory that Billinge had met with an accident in the treacherous countryside round about would turn out to be right after all.

Hopefully Dr Kelly would soon be able to confirm whether the naked man in the cave had been poisoned, but he still needed to establish why someone had gone to such lengths to conceal the dead man's identity. Albert's instincts told him that the unidentified corpse was somehow linked to Billinge's disappearance, but he couldn't for the life of him think of any possible connection between the two.

The death of the Reverend Bell also nagged away at him, especially as he felt duty-bound to provide Mrs Bell with a definitive answer. Until Dr Kelly received the results from the samples he'd taken, there was no evidence to support Mrs Bell's belief that foul play was involved. He hoped that it would turn out to be a case of a grieving widow, unable to accept that God had claimed her beloved husband before 'his time'. Because, if it was murder, he was at a loss as to what the motive might be. Even if the late reverend had been aware of Simon Fellowes' sexual peccadilloes, Albert thought it unlikely the curate would have killed him over some risqué photographs. The only other avenue of investigation was the visit the vicar made on the night of his death; but had he called on Sir William Cartwright or someone else entirely?

His fourth problem was the murder of Bert Pretting, which seemed on the face of it to be the most straight-forward of the lot. The stabbing of a man whose wife had plotted with her lover to kill him should be a simple matter to clear up. But Albert wasn't satisfied with the obvious solution. Or perhaps he just had a weakness for a pretty face. It was a weakness that had led him into trouble before. When he closed his eyes he saw Flora's face and he tried his best to put her out of his mind by thinking of Mary. But as soon as he'd replaced Flora's face with his wife's, he felt a wave of misery so strong that, combined with a throbbing pain in his injured leg, it robbed him of sleep until the early hours.

Eventually he drifted into a fitful slumber and when he awoke the next morning his head was pounding and his leg ached but he forced himself to go down for breakfast.

The two visitors to the mill he'd seen the previous night were leaving as he walked in, which meant he ate his breakfast alone that morning. Mrs Jackson bustled in and out with his food, chatting cheerfully while he made polite replies, his mind on the day ahead.

He hadn't yet spoken to the Ogdens about Henry Billinge's disappearance, so that would be his first port of call after he'd dropped by the police station to see whether anything had come in overnight. As far as he knew, the couple had met the MP for the first and only time at Sir William's dinner party, but there was always a chance that Billinge mentioned something to them that evening; a throwaway comment perhaps that might provide some clue to his intentions.

As soon as he reached the station he asked Constable Smith for directions to the Ogdens' residence. The young man was eager to help. 'Turn right out of the station, walk past the mill towards the road to New Mills, then turn right. The Ogdens live in a big house at the end of a long drive, but you can see it from the main road. Do you want someone to go with you?' he added hopefully.

Albert declined the offer. He fancied walking there alone, without the need to make small talk. Though it wasn't far, his injured leg hurt more with each step; he carried on, trying to ignore the throbbing pain, telling himself that many had things worse than he did. In London he saw them every day.

Smith had been right about the Ogdens' long driveway. When Albert reached the fine stone gateposts the house seemed some distance away. He stopped to gather his thoughts and get his breath back after the walk. The wrought-iron gates were firmly shut and when Albert pushed them they swung open silently. The drive was straight and if the occupants of the house were to look out of the front windows, they'd be able to watch their visitor's approach. The thought of being observed made Albert feel vulnerable. He preferred the element of surprise.

The house itself was built of local stone; a handsome gentleman's residence with freshly painted sash windows and a glossy black front door, sheltered beneath a stone portico supported by two grand columns. He knocked and the door was opened by a maid in a clean, starched apron.

'I'll tell them you're here, sir,' she said flatly before hurrying off, leaving him in the spacious hallway. There were portraits on the wall — Georgian military officers; regency beauties; haughty Victorian gentlemen and their richly dressed wives. Albert wondered whether they'd been purchased to give visitors the impression that this was the home of a family with a long and distinguished lineage. Art to impress and maybe to intimidate. Or maybe they'd come with the house.

It seemed an age before the maid appeared again, adjusting her linen cap. 'If you'd like to come this way, sir.'

Albert followed her into a generously proportioned drawing room which made Sir William's accommodation seem shabby in comparison. The furniture looked new, as did the carpet, and Mrs Ogden sat on a blue brocade sofa while her husband occupied a chintz armchair next to the marble fireplace. Ogden rose to greet him. He was a tall man in his forties, straight-backed with an athletic figure and dark hair peppered with grey.

'Alastair Ogden,' he said, shaking his hand. 'And this is my wife, Margaret. I presume this is about Henry Billinge.' He formed his features into a puzzled frown. 'We've already told the constable everything we know, so I don't see how I can help you any further.'

Albert smiled. He could see Mrs Ogden watching him. She was a handsome woman, slightly younger than her husband, with flawless skin and fair hair swept back into a neat bun. Her gaze was focused on the red shiny scars that had marred Albert's face ever since the shell had exploded in his trench. He'd noticed how people's eyes were drawn to his acquired imperfections, a subconscious reaction. He saw her look away.

'I appreciate that, Mr Ogden, but I was hoping one of you might have remembered something more about that night. Something Mr Billinge said, perhaps. What about you, Mrs Ogden?'

'It was a pleasant evening, Inspector,' she said. 'If there was any bad feeling it certainly wasn't obvious.'

'But might there have been an undercurrent, a tension in the air, something that came to a head after you'd left?' Albert tilted his head to one side and awaited her reply.

She glanced at her husband. 'I did sense a coolness between Sir William and Mr Billinge. It's possible they'd disagreed about something.'

'Mr Ogden, was anything said after the ladies retired to the drawing room?'

'Not really,' said Ogden. 'If there was an argument brewing between Billinge and Sir William I'd guess it would have been about lowering the voting age for women.' Ogden sounded bored, as though he was longing for the interview to be over. 'That seemed the only bone of contention between them. There were one or two pointed remarks about Sir William's outdated attitude to the fair sex, and I overheard Billinge telling Sir William he was a fool where women were concerned. It was said lightly but, with hindsight, there could have been some animosity there, I suppose.'

'You didn't mention this to the officer who spoke to you.'

'I didn't think it was important. People tend to have different opinions about these things.'

'Was that the first time you'd met Mr Billinge?'

'That's right. Our paths never crossed before Sir William invited myself and Mrs Ogden to dinner.'

'You know Sir William well?'

'Not well. But there are few people of substance in Wenfield.'

'And you seek out each other's society. I understand. You have a profession, Mr Ogden?'

'I was in the import-export trade, but now I've passed on my business concerns to others.'

'A well-deserved retirement, I'm sure,' Albert said, watching the man's face as he nodded, his expression impossible to read.

'Indeed.'

'You must have had a lot to talk to Mr Jones about.'

'Not really. I decided to sell up my business interests after the war.'

'Mr Billinge's constituency is in Liverpool.

222

Have you ever been there?'

'I've been there on business numerous times. But, as I told you, I never encountered Mr Billinge.'

In the awkward silence that followed, Albert's mind started to stray. The mention of Liverpool reminded him of Gwen Davies, who had given him her parents' address the previous September, saying she intended to leave Mabley Ridge and move back to her native city to seek employment. He saw the Ogdens watching him, bracing themselves for further questioning. But he couldn't think of anything else to ask so he thanked them and took his leave.

Albert walked back to Wenfield in a trance. He felt as though the cares of the world were weighing him down, pressing on his heart with no hope of relief. He knew his duty was to Mary, but whenever he thought about her, he experienced an overwhelming feeling of guilt and regret.

He walked on, barely aware of the hilly landscape around him or the stares he received once he reached the village. People knew who he was; in such a small community the man from Scotland Yard was easily recognisable. But nobody greeted him as they passed.

He had one more visit to make, the only person at Sir William's dinner he hadn't yet spoken to. The house that had once belonged to David Eames and his sister, Helen, held a lot of memories but it was now the home of Peggy Derwent, the novelist. Albert wondered fleetingly whether she was one of Rose Pretting's favoured authors. Miss Derwent wrote detective novels, but did this mean she knew more about murder than the average person? He wouldn't find out unless he spoke to her.

46

Albert knew the way to Peggy Derwent's house. He had been there with Flora.

The place looked different now. The outbuilding that had once been David Eames's studio looked empty and abandoned. Last time Albert had seen it, it had been filled with paintings, both finished and works in progress. David had been injured in the war but he'd continued to serve in his own way by using his skills to create portrait masks to conceal the hideous facial injuries suffered by some of the men being treated at Tarnhey Court when it was a military hospital.

There was no sign of life when Albert knocked on the front door. He and Flora had come to this house in David's absence. They'd met in secret and they'd made love in one of the upstairs rooms. The memory bubbled to the surface of Albert's mind but he suppressed it when the door was opened by a thin, nervous-looking woman with unfashionably curly hair and large green eyes. She was in her thirties, or possibly her early forties. Albert wasn't sure why he'd been expecting someone older.

Once he'd introduced himself he was invited into a living room that had changed a great deal since his last visit. David Eames's bright pictures had gone from the walls and the furniture was sparse and the rug threadbare. The desk in the window bore evidence of Miss Derwent's profession. A typewriter and a stack of paper as well as a glass which Albert suspected contained something alcoholic.

'I'm sorry to bother you, Miss Derwent, but I need to ask you some questions. You met Henry Billinge at a dinner given by Sir William Cartwright at Tarnhey Court.'

'Yes. What about it?' Her hands were shaking as she lit a cigarette, neglecting to offer one to her visitor.

'You're aware he's disappeared?'

'I don't know what that has to do with me.' Her words sounded defensive.

'You're a writer.'

'There's no law against that, is there?' she said, avoiding his gaze.

'No, there isn't, I'm glad to say. What kind of books do you write?'

'Detective stories,' she said with a sigh, as though she'd been asked the same question countless times before. 'And romantic mysteries.'

'Your books are in the library here?'

'I presume so.'

'Did you speak to Mr Billinge at Sir William's dinner?'

'We exchanged pleasantries, but the dinner wasn't really my thing, though the food wasn't bad. I left as soon as I could. I was surprised to be invited, to be honest.'

'Why did you move to Wenfield?' He asked the question out of curiosity.

'I lived in a big city. I needed to escape to somewhere quieter.'

'Escape from what?'

There was an awkward silence. 'The past,' she said eventually.

'You lost someone in the war?'

She looked away. 'You're not a detective for nothing.' She took a drag on her cigarette. 'I'd rather not talk about it.'

His eyes were drawn to the books on the shelves. To one book in particular.

'You have a book by Cecilia Yarmouth, I see.'

A secretive smile appeared on her lips.

'Do you know her?'

'Oh yes, I know her well. Intimately, you could say.'

'What's she like?' He couldn't resist asking.

She took a long drag on her cigarette, looking as though she was enjoying a private joke. 'Bitter. Lonely. Scared people will find out things about her she'd rather they didn't know.'

'Are her books any good?'

'I bloody hope so. I wrote them.' She smiled at the look of surprise on Albert's face. 'It's one of the noms de plume I use. Different names for different kinds of book. Cecilia Yarmouth tends towards the Gothic romance, whereas Peggy Derwent sticks to detective stories — although I don't suppose you'd consider them very realistic.'

Albert looked her in the eye. 'Do you know a woman called Rose Pretting?'

She shook her head. 'Never heard of her. Who is she?'

'They're saying she murdered her husband and I think she took one of your books as her inspiration.'

'Every author's nightmare. I don't know the woman, so you can't possibly blame me.'

'I'm not blaming anyone.' He paused. 'You said you had secrets. What secrets are you keeping, Miss Derwent?'

'Mind your own business.'

'As long as you haven't done anything illegal, I can promise that anything you tell me won't go further than these four walls.'

She hesitated as though she was tempted to confide in him. Then the moment passed and she stubbed her cigarette out with a violence that surprised him.

'Look, I'm sorry but I can't help you. I don't know where Mr Billinge is. Why should I?'

The conversation was over. As he made his way out, Albert had an uneasy feeling about the woman — but then again, it might just have been the memories conjured by the house.

47

Rose

They're keeping me in this cell which is more a cage than a room. It has a barred window so high up that I can't see anything apart from the sky. I watch the grey clouds moving. The weather is as miserable as I am.

If it weren't for that nice inspector from London I wouldn't even have my books. I'm making them last, eking out every precious page because I don't know if I'll be allowed any more. But I need my books. I need something to take my mind off what's happening. I wish they'd let me have *The Garden of Secrets* which is my favourite. It tells my story like no other book I've ever read. It is almost as though Cecilia Yarmouth, the author, knows the ordeal I've been through. Although if the police get to read it they might guess the truth. Maybe it's for the best that the inspector didn't bring it here.

Why won't they believe that I didn't kill Bert? I told them I'd thought about it but I said dreaming isn't the same as doing it. The police say I should name my accomplice and they won't believe me when I tell them I haven't got an accomplice. Perhaps I should make up a name. Someone from one of my books.

If they want me to betray my Darling Man,

they're going to be disappointed. I'll never give him away. Never.

I've had no word from him and I cannot send a message to him in my current situation. I wonder whether he's heard of my troubles. If anybody can rescue me, ride to my aid like a perfect knight, it will be my Darling Man.

The cell door opens with a loud clatter and I know it's Sergeant Teague again. I know he's not going to give up bullying me until I confess, but I've got to be like one of the women in my books. Determined. Defiant. I'll tell them nothing. I must keep faith with my Darling Man.

48

Albert returned to the police station to find Constable Smith standing proudly behind the front desk. As soon as he spotted Albert, he reached beneath the counter and took out an envelope which he waved in the newcomer's direction.

'Telegram for you, sir. Marked urgent. It was delivered to the Black Horse and Mrs Jackson brought it over. Thought you should see it right away.'

Albert took the telegram, hardly daring to look at the thing, fearing it would contain bad news.

'Anything come in while I've been out?' he said, trying his best to sound casual.

'A report of a missing bicycle. I said I'd make sure someone went up there to see what was going on.'

Albert gave the young man a weak smile. 'I'm sure I can leave that in your capable hands.' There was nothing wrong with a bit of encouragement every now and then.

Smith was hovering, eager to discover what the telegram contained. But Albert hurried into his office and tore the envelope open. As he expected, the message was from Vera and his hands were shaking as he read.

'*Come home now,*' was all it said. But the meaning was clear. Mary had been right. She was near death and he needed to be with her.

He told Smith to let Sergeant Teague know that he was returning to London. He was sure they could manage without him for a few days. Then he called Sam Poltimore to tell him he was returning to London for a while. Sam said he'd be working late so he might be there if he called in at the office. Albert didn't mention Mary — or that he might not be in a position to make it to Scotland Yard that evening.

He was about to leave the station to pick up some things from the Black Horse for the journey south when he heard raised voices. One of them was Teague's, the other a woman's, and they were coming from the small room used to interview suspects. As soon as he recognised the voice of Rose Pretting, and registered how distressed she sounded, he made for the room and threw open the door.

Teague was towering over the woman, who had shrunk back into her seat, sobbing. Her face was wet with tears and there was a shiny trail of mucus between her nose and her lips. Even though she was obviously distraught, Teague wasn't letting up. He was banging his fist on the table and shouting.

'That's enough, Sergeant!' Albert barked the words.

Teague backed off, like a dog who had been prevented from savaging a rabbit. He trailed out of the room after Albert, his resentment palpable.

'I was about to get the truth out of the murdering bitch,' Teague hissed once the door was closed.

'She's clearly distressed.'

'So she should be.'

Albert checked his pocket watch. His train departed in an hour. 'We'll discuss this when I get back from London. In the meantime, go easy on her. She'll be far more likely to talk if you don't frighten her out of her wits.' He looked Teague in the eye. 'Is that understood, Sergeant?'

Teague grunted and Albert feared his words hadn't got through. But he had no time to reiterate his instructions. He'd made a written list of lines of enquiry to be followed up and he handed it to Teague, adding that he would be back in a couple of days. He tried to make the words sound like a warning.

Two hours later he was on the London train, staring out of the window and thinking about Rose Pretting. The case against her seemed straightforward, and yet Albert had his doubts. Rose lived in a fantasy world, seeing herself as a romantic heroine. It seemed strange that the author of the book that inspired her murderous plot had turned up to live in the same village. But coincidences happen, and he couldn't think of any link between the two women.

His mind turned to the search for Henry Billinge. There was still no sign of him, alive or dead, even though men had been out combing the surrounding countryside. Neither had they managed to discover anything about the elusive Clara. The police in Liverpool had promised to keep an eye on Billinge's flat, just in case he returned to his constituency, and Scotland Yard were checking regularly on his London pied-à-terre, but his whereabouts remained a mystery.

As for the problem of the man found in the cave near the Devil's Dancers, the investigation was no further forward. Albert told himself that as soon as he returned to Wenfield he'd concentrate on giving the victim back his identity and bringing whoever ended his life to justice. But he feared it would not be easy.

When he arrived in London he left the train at Euston and caught the tram and a bus home to Bermondsey. It was dusk by the time he turned the corner onto his street. It had been a long journey and he felt exhausted as he dragged his aching body towards home, dreading what he would find in the house that had once been his refuge from the world. He wasn't aware of the man following him, keeping to the shadows, darting into the shelter of the alleyways they passed.

It wasn't until he was fifty yards from his address that he felt a blow to his back that sent him flying forward. He landed on his knees and the pain shot through his body, knocking the breath from his lungs.

Helpless, he floundered on the pavement, his tired brain trying to work out what was going on. When he twisted his head to look up he saw a dark shadow looming over him, outlined against the moonlit clouds that scurried across the sky. It was a man but he couldn't see the face and for a second both of them froze as though time itself had been suspended.

Then the blow came. A fist in his face. Once.

Twice. Followed by a rough shout: 'Eh. What you doing?' Then his attacker was gone in an instant, vanished into a nearby alleyway. But not before he'd bent to whisper in Albert's ear.

'That's just for starters. You're a dead man.'

49

Albert thanked his rescuer, a builder who'd been on his way to the pub when he'd seen Albert being attacked and had been brave enough to intervene. However, the man had no idea where the attacker had fled to and he'd been unable to provide a description.

'After your wallet most likely, mate,' he said cheerfully. 'Lot of it about these days.'

Albert didn't feel inclined to contradict his good Samaritan, but he suspected robbery hadn't been his assailant's motive. As he watched the man walk off, he looked around in case his attacker was still lurking in the shadows. But there were more people around now so he began to limp home, every muscle aching while his grazed hands smarted as though they'd been stung by a thousand wasps. He was in no state to comfort a dying wife. He was in need of comfort himself.

He tried to place his assailant's voice, certain that he'd heard it before. *That's just for starters. You're a dead man.* The man hadn't sounded local but his accent had been difficult to place. Had someone tailed him from Wenfield? More than once he'd had a feeling that he was being followed while he was up there. However, he thought it far more likely that it was someone he'd arrested in London — a villain with a grudge. It was an occupational hazard.

When he reached his front door he saw a light on in the front parlour — a gaslight. Mary had never wanted electricity, even though he'd offered to have it installed; she'd been afraid it would crawl out of the wall sockets during the night and kill her. He took out his key and put it in the lock, hesitating for a moment before pushing the door open.

The heavy silence in the house was broken from time to time by a hushed male voice, muttering what sounded like a prayer. The door to the front parlour was shut. It was a room kept for best so whoever was in there was a visitor — and Albert was sure he knew who that visitor would be.

When he opened the door the scene that greeted him reminded him of a painting — *The Deathbed*, or *Her Last Words*. The tableau looked as though it had been carefully posed. Mary was lying on the shabby chaise longue she'd inherited from an old aunt and Vera was kneeling beside her, clasping her hand in her own. At the end of the couch stood the Reverend Thomas Gillit, a prayer book in his hands and his eyes raised to heaven. The founder of the League of Departed Spirits was looking every inch the clergyman Albert knew he wasn't.

As soon as he entered the room, Vera and Gillit turned to look at him. Mary, on the other hand, lay perfectly still, her face ash pale and her eyes closed; a picture of peace.

Vera rose to her feet painfully, clinging to the edge of the chaise longue for support. 'You're too bloody late. She passed over to the other side half an hour ago.'

Her words hit Albert like a physical blow, more devastating than anything his attacker had meted out. He knew he hadn't been the best of husbands. He had abandoned Mary in her grief for their son and had fallen in love with another woman — a transgression that had ended in disaster. His failings weighed heavily on him and he stood gaping at his wife's dead body, trying to find the words that wouldn't come. As Vera glared at him like an avenging angel he experienced an overwhelming feeling of shame. He'd betrayed her daughter. What she didn't know was that he'd already been punished for his wrongdoing with the loss of Flora and the son she'd borne him. That was a secret he'd never shared with anybody but Sam Poltimore.

An unctuous voice broke the silence. 'I've already spoken to dear Mary on the other side. She's very happy and she's playing with little Frederick. He was so pleased to see his mother again. Overjoyed.'

Albert turned to face the man and saw a smug smile on his lips.

'I think your work here is done, Mr Gillit.' He couldn't bring himself to address the man as 'Reverend'. 'You can go now.'

But Vera had other ideas. 'No, Reverend. You must stay. There's the funeral to arrange and — '

'Of course, dear lady. Whatever you wish.' He gave Albert a sideways look as if to say that Vera was head of the household now. The husband who'd neglected Mary in life had forfeited the right to dictate what happened now she was dead.

'If you would be good enough to conduct the service, Reverend,' Vera simpered. 'It's what Mary would have wanted.'

No matter how much he disapproved, Albert found it hard to contradict Vera's last statement. It would indeed have been Mary's wish for her final farewell to take place at the League of Departed Spirits, the place where she'd found so much comfort in her final years.

He stood in silence, staring at the woman who had been his wife, events from the past running through his brain like a moving picture. Their first meeting, in a park; he'd been a young constable on patrol when he'd seen a pretty girl trip on the path. He'd helped her up, playing the chivalrous gentleman, and asked her to go for a walk with him the following Sunday.

He'd fallen in love with her and in the early days of their marriage they'd been happy. When Frederick was born, that happiness had seemed complete. Until Albert went away to war and came back maimed, a man with a scarred face, half a hand and an injured leg. They would have overcome all that if Frederick hadn't died of influenza. Mary's appetite for life and love had evaporated the moment Frederick breathed his last. After that she was no longer the girl he'd fallen for, she was a mother in mourning. She'd never recovered from her loss, seeking comfort from any charlatan who promised to bring Frederick back to her. He'd felt Frederick's death too but his life hadn't been ended by it as Mary's had been.

When he looked at her now he felt a wave of anguish; of regret for those lost years. When he'd met Flora Winsmore back in 1919 she'd reminded him so much of the Mary he'd once known. But he banished this inappropriate thought from his mind. He needed to concentrate on mourning Mary. He owed her that at least.

The sound of Vera's voice roused him from his reverie. 'The reverend and I don't think it would be appropriate for you to attend the funeral — seeing as you're not a believer.'

Albert looked round and his temper simmered when he saw Gillit wearing the same smug look on his face as Vera gazed at him adoringly.

'I'm not an unbeliever. I go to church like everyone else,' Albert said. Vera's words had shocked him and he felt he had to defend himself.

'I mean a believer in the League of Departed Spirits. The reverend says the parish church is full of those who reject his work. The mockers and scoffers.' She looked to Gillit for support and he nodded sagely.

Albert felt his fists clench. 'Mary was my wife. I've every right to come to her funeral. I refuse to stay away, and you can't make me.'

'You were no husband to her,' said Gillit smoothly. 'You abandoned her in her hour of need. I was there for her — which was more than you were.'

Albert's anger boiled within him and before he

knew it he'd lost control and was punching Gillit in the face. The fact that the man's words had been uncomfortably accurate only made things worse. It was as though Gillit had seen into his soul.

Gillit sprawled on the floor and while Albert was nursing his sore fist Vera knelt beside the self-proclaimed clergyman, asking if he was all right. Albert could see blood streaming from Gillit's nose and Vera took a handkerchief from her pocket to wipe it away.

She looked up at Albert, furious. 'Get out. Just get out and don't bother coming back. The reverend's right. You're not welcome when we lay Mary to rest. I never want to see you again. Never.'

Her words shocked Albert into silence and he couldn't think of a suitable response. There was only one thing to do and that was to leave; to get away from his mother-in-law and the oily charlatan who called himself 'reverend'. He left the house, slamming the door behind him.

50

Rose

They say the inspector has gone back to London, which is a pity because he was the only one who seemed to believe me. Sergeant Teague thinks I'm a scarlet woman. A murdering bitch, he called me.

He asked me about that money they found in the bureau. He wanted to know where Bert got it and I told him I didn't know, but I think I can guess. When he'd had a few beers in the Carty Arms he sometimes boasted that he knew secrets about people — things they'd rather no one else knew. I never took much notice because he was always coming out with stuff like that. He used to say how he knew things about Mr Jones — secret things — and that meant he was bound to be promoted to chief clerk when Mr Perkins retired. He was going to make himself a fortune, he said. But even if he'd been the richest man in the world I couldn't have loved him — not like I love my Darling Man.

Teague still has no idea of my Darling Man's identity. He said he'll be able to find out from the handwriting on the letters, which made me laugh. He didn't like that at all.

He says I'm going to be charged with Bert's murder. But they can't charge me for something I didn't do, can they?

51

Desperate to get away from the house, Albert caught the tram to Scotland Yard. He needed to talk to Sam — one of the few people he trusted in this world — and he hoped he'd still be there.

But when he reached his office Sam was nowhere to be seen. He'd been called out on a case — a robbery, one of the constables told him.

Albert went into his office, shut the door and slumped down on his chair, head in hands, fighting back tears. Past experience had taught him that work was the best distraction from his grief, so he raised his head and looked about him for some task to occupy his mind. Through the mist of tears he saw a note on the desk in Sam's handwriting. He wiped his eyes with his handkerchief and read: *Please call Mrs Anne Billinge*, followed by a Mayfair telephone number. The message had been received two hours ago and Albert took a deep shuddering breath before asking the operator to get the number for him, hoping Mrs Billinge would still be there.

He was in luck. Anne Billinge answered almost immediately.

'You wanted to speak to me, Mrs Billinge.'

'I did. The policeman who answered told me that you were expected in later, so I left a message. I have some information for you.'

'News of your husband?' Albert suddenly felt hopeful that one of his cases was about to be brought to a satisfactory conclusion.

'I'm afraid not. I've been in touch with everyone we know and nobody's heard from him.' She hesitated. 'I'm beginning to fear the worst.' For the first time he detected some emotion in her voice.

'You said you had some information,' he said gently.

'You asked about Clara, my former maid. An acquaintance of mine says she saw her in Liverpool. She was in a tea room in Bold Street with another girl. My acquaintance recognised the other girl as the lady's maid to a shipping family. I thought you'd like to know.'

'Do you know how I can contact the lady's maid?' Albert suddenly felt a surge of optimism. He'd been wanting to speak to Clara and now the possibility was opening up in front of him.

Mrs Billinge provided the name of Clara's friend's employer and Albert asked one of the constables to trace a telephone number for them, hoping a call from Scotland Yard wouldn't get the lady's maid into trouble.

An hour later a constable knocked on Albert's door. He'd spoken to the young woman, who'd been fairly easy to find because the family she worked for was prominent in the city. Big noises, was how he put it. Clara, she'd said, had a place of her own now — a rather swish place, the girl had told him with a hint of envy.

Clara wasn't in service any more. And her new

forwarding address was in a very desirable area of Liverpool.

Clara's friend provided them with an address. However, the constable who'd spoken to her had had the distinct impression she was hiding something.

Albert thanked him and said he'd done well. He was always a believer in giving praise where it was due. He sat at his desk, paralysed by indecision and numb from the shock of Mary's death. There was no way he'd be able to spend the night at home. Vera would, no doubt, be keeping vigil over Mary's body and she had made it quite clear he wasn't wanted. It was his own house and, if he'd felt so inclined, he could have made a fuss and insisted on his rights, but that was the last thing he felt like doing. Right now all he wanted was to escape from London and the memories it held. Wenfield held bad memories too, but he had a job to do up there. Only when that job was finished would he be able to make a decision about his future.

As soon as Sam Poltimore returned Albert called him into his office and told him to close the door. Sam looked solemn as Albert broke the news of Mary's death, and disbelieving when he told him about Vera's outburst.

'You can stay with us. It's getting late and the missus won't mind.'

The offer was automatic, made without thinking, and Albert felt his eyes prick with tears.

'That's very kind of you, Sam. It really is. But I couldn't put you to any trouble.'

'It's no trouble. And I reckon after the day

you've had, you'll need the company. The missus wouldn't hear of you being on your own at a time like this. I've got some brown ale in. We can have a drink and a smoke like old times, eh?' He looked at him intently. 'What have you done to your face? Been in a fight?'

'Someone jumped me when I was on my way home. Punched me and made the usual threats. Probably an old customer of ours.'

'Any idea who?'

Albert shook his head. 'Hopefully he'll have got it out of his system and he won't bother you no more,' said Sam firmly. 'Any sign of that MP yet?'

'No, but I think I might have a new lead. Unfortunately, I'm no nearer to discovering the identity of the victim we thought might be him.'

'Is that the one they found in a cave with no clothes on and his face bashed in?'

'That's right. I've got my work cut out up there, Sam.' He wondered whether to mention Mrs Bell's suspicions about her husband's death, but decided against it for the moment. Until Dr Kelly received the results from the lab, all he had were the widow's suspicions.

Sam looked at him, concerned. 'Wenfield. You're all right about staying up there after what happened the last time?'

Albert took a deep breath. 'Flora's gone, Sam. And her father's left the village. I've met the new doctor — nice young chap. Nobody else in Wenfield knew about me and . . . Although I have come across some of the people I met back then, the man Henry Billinge was staying with

246

being one of them.'

'Sir William Cartwright. I've heard he's a bit of a one for the ladies.'

Albert raised his eyebrows. There had been an incident with a maid — one of the murder victims — back in 1919, but he was surprised that news of Sir William's amorous activities had spread to the capital. 'Where on earth did you hear that?'

'My son-in-law's brother works in the House of Commons. He knows all the gossip.'

'Has your son-in-law's brother heard anything about Henry Billinge?'

'Only that he's quite a secretive gent. Keeps himself to himself.'

Albert examined his pocket watch, then gratefully accepted Sam's offer of a bed for the night. He had no desire to travel back to Wenfield through the darkness. And besides, he needed company.

He stayed the night in Sam's spare room. Even though the bed was comfortable he didn't sleep well and the next morning he found himself dozing off on the train back up North, soothed by the rhythm of the wheels on the track. He changed trains at Manchester and arrived in Wenfield at ten thirty. It had begun to rain and as he walked through the streets towards the Black Horse the pavements glistened and people scurried to and fro with umbrellas. They were used to rain up there.

When he reached the Black Horse he hesitated at the door, feeling lost. He'd known for a while that Mary was unlikely to recover — in some ways she'd been dead inside since Frederick went — but as the reality dawned on him he was suddenly engulfed in a pall of heavy sadness.

He made his way to his room, glad that Mrs Jackson hadn't been there to greet him on his arrival. He was in no mood for small talk.

After rinsing his face with water in the basin in the corner of his room, he left the inn. His sense of duty told him that he should look in at the police station to see whether there had been any developments in his absence. The prospect of facing Sergeant Teague at that moment made his spirits sink even lower but it was something that had to be done. After that he would go to Liverpool to find Clara. He had the feeling she was the key to finding Henry Billinge, dead or alive.

When he reached the station he found Teague standing behind the front desk looking pleased with himself. Albert was soon to discover why.

'Morning, sir. Good news. We've charged Rose Pretting with her husband's murder and she's been taken to Manchester to await trial. The stubborn bitch still won't name her fancy man, but we'll get him, don't you worry.'

'You can't possibly think Mrs Pretting knifed her husband in a back alley. The doctor said the attacker was someone a lot taller.'

'That will have been the fancy man. But, mark my words, they planned it together and any decent jury will make sure she hangs with him.'

Albert said nothing but he feared Teague was right. Any jury of men would be bound to convict her. Scarlet women were rarely forgiven.

And yet he wasn't altogether convinced of her guilt.

When he told Teague he was going to Liverpool to follow up a lead in the Henry Billinge case, the sergeant asked if he wanted him to come too. Albert said no. The last thing he wanted was Teague to be with him when he spoke to Clara.

52

It was the middle of the afternoon by the time Albert arrived at Lime Street station. Stepping outside, he was faced with a magnificent, soot-blackened, classical building on the opposite side of the road with pillars that would grace any Greek temple. To his right he could see an array of buildings — galleries and law courts — as fine as any in his native London, reminding him that this was a prosperous city that had made its fortune from the sea. As he left the station he recalled that Henry Billinge served as the Member of Parliament for a nearby constituency, and there was a local connection in another of his cases too: Bert Pretting had lived over the river on the Wirral and it was likely he'd worked in the city. His policeman's instinct made him wonder whether there could be a connection between the two men, one missing and one dead. But Liverpool was a big place.

He took a taxi cab to Clara's address, hoping she'd be at home. After a short journey the cab pulled up outside a grand Georgian terrace near the centre of town. At one time it would have been the residence of a prosperous family but now it was divided into apartments, although, judging by the pristine stucco and the fresh paintwork, these were apartments of the highly respectable kind.

He had been told that Clara lived in flat

number two, so he pressed the doorbell. To his surprise, the young woman who answered the door looked nothing like a maidservant. She was wearing a figure-enhancing black dress and her auburn hair was expensively bobbed. With her cigarette in an ebony holder, she had the look of a film star.

'I'm looking for Clara.'

'You've found her.' There was a hint of insolence in her reply; insolence and boredom.

When Albert introduced himself and explained the reason for his visit, she merely raised her eyebrows and invited him in. He followed her up the graceful staircase to the first floor where the drawing room of her apartment occupied the entire front of the house. A row of tall sash windows overlooked the elegant square below and the furnishings were in the latest modern style, the sort of thing Albert associated with the fashionable London homes of the wealthy.

'I know why you've come,' she said, knocking the ash from her cigarette into an onyx ashtray. 'I knew it would only be a matter of time before you got round to me.' Clara might be dressed like a society girl but the cockney twang in her voice betrayed her roots.

'Really?' Albert was intrigued.

'Who put you on to me?'

'Mrs Billinge. She heard her husband and Sir William Cartwright arguing about you.'

A smile played on her lips. 'Henry's always looked out for me. He's a gent.' She cast an appraising eye over Albert. 'You've been in the wars.'

'Yes,' he said, glancing down at his maimed hand.

'No, I meant all those bruises on your face. Someone resisted arrest, did they?'

Albert had almost forgotten about the attack in London, but Clara's words reminded him of his vulnerability. 'You were telling me about how Mr Billinge looks out for you.'

'He was furious with William when he said he wasn't going to pay for my flat in Manchester no more. I told Henry I could fight my own battles but, like I said, he's a gent. Thought William was doing me wrong.'

Albert took a seat opposite her. 'William? I thought you and Mr Billinge were . . . '

'No. You've got it all wrong. It was me and William . . . '

'You were having an affair with Sir William, not Henry Billinge?'

She giggled. 'I don't think I'm Henry's type — although he is a sweetie and he's been very good to me.' She hesitated. 'Will you promise me that this won't go beyond these four walls? Henry could get into terrible trouble if anyone found out.'

'That depends. If it's anything illegal . . . '

She snorted. 'Why won't you bobbies live and let live?'

'I promise you that if it isn't something that hurts others, like robbery, fraud, assault or murder, I'll say nothing.'

She gave him an uncertain smile. 'Henry might be married but he's not the marrying kind, if you get my meaning. William's son,

Roderick, is of the same persuasion, so he's been . . . sympathetic. Now you see why I asked you to keep it to yourself.'

'You don't need to worry. All I want to know is whether Mr Billinge is safe and well. Tell me about your relationship with Sir William.'

She stubbed out her cigarette angrily and Albert waited. In his experience, people could never resist the urge to fill a silence.

'Me and William met in London when he came to see Henry. I was working for Mrs Billinge back then. Lady's maid. Anyway, William said that if I came up North he'd look after me; promised to set me up in a nice flat in Manchester.' She rolled her eyes. 'I went up there to be near him, hoping for the nice gaff, but he kept making bloody excuses while I was stuck living in a fleapit in some godforsaken suburb. Typical of men. Full of hot air and empty promises.' She lit another cigarette and inhaled deeply.

'Anyway, Henry took pity on me and said I could stay in one of his properties in Liverpool. His constituency's nearby and he owns a few places in town.' She gave a grunt of disgust. 'Haven't seen William since I moved over here.'

'When did you last see Mr Billinge?'

'A couple of weeks ago. He called in to check I was all right before going to stay with William for the weekend. He promised to have words with him — shame him into doing the right thing by me, he said. Told you he was a sweetie,' she added fondly. She suddenly frowned. 'I hope nothing's happened to him.'

'Everyone's worried about him. Including Sir William.' He paused, wondering how much to reveal about the circumstances of Henry Billinge's disappearance. 'It appears that Mr Billinge and Sir William had a disagreement before he left. It was thought it might have been about women's suffrage, but from what you've just told me, they might have been arguing about you.'

She shrugged her shoulders. 'Maybe.'

'You seem to know Mr Billinge well. Where do you think he is?'

She gave the question a few moments' consideration before answering. 'He often talks about how much he loves the Lake District, especially Windermere. He says there's nothing better than walking in the hills and getting lost in nature without anyone knowing where to find you.' She pulled a face. 'Can't see it myself. I prefer the city.'

'Is it possible he's gone there?'

She thought for a moment. 'He told me he's been under a lot of strain recently. A young man he was ... friendly with killed himself about eighteen months ago and Henry hasn't been the same since it happened. It can't be easy for him. Lying to everyone. Parading round with his wife on his arm. Keeping up the act.'

Albert nodded and their eyes met in understanding. As he stood up to leave he noticed a silver-framed photograph of Sir William Cartwright on the marble mantelpiece, suggesting that Clara hadn't altogether given up hope of Sir William resuming their relationship.

He wondered whether Lady Cartwright knew of her existence. Probably not. Lady Cartwright struck him as a woman who preferred to ignore inconvenient truths.

Outside Clara's flat he hailed a passing taxi cab, but instead of telling the driver to take him to Lime Street station, he pulled Gwen Davies's address from his pocket and asked to be taken there. It was an act of impulse, possibly a reaction to the shock of Mary's death; a desire for comfort; for someone who might understand.

Soon the handsome terraces of the town gave way to parkland and leafy outlying suburbs. When they eventually reached Gwen's address the driver stopped and told him the fare.

For a while Albert gazed out of the window at the neat semi-detached red-brick house in the tree-lined road. This was her parents' address and she'd returned there after leaving her post in Mabley Ridge. She was a school teacher, so she could well be home by now, sitting in that house quite unaware that he was so near. His heart began to pound as he realised the idea was foolish. Wrong.

He told the driver to take him to Lime Street where he caught the five-thirty train. First, however, he saw a public telephone box and made a call to the police station in Wenfield, relieved when Constable Smith answered. The young man sounded surprised when Albert asked him to telephone every hotel and guest house in the Windermere area to ask whether they had any guests answering Henry Billinge's description.

And under no circumstances was he to let Sergeant Teague or Constable Wren know what he was doing.

53

Rose

This is a terrible place. It smells of fear and dirty bodies. Worse still, they won't let me have any books. I'm to stand trial, they say. According to them, I'm a murdering whore. An unfaithful wife. A woman of the worst kind imaginable.

They keep on saying I must name my Darling Man. I was tempted to tell them it was Sergeant Teague and see what they made of that. Not that I'd ever have anything to do with that horrible man, but it would have been worth lying to see the looks on their faces.

I kept reminding the sergeant that Bert always had a lot of money but he'd never say where he got it, even though I knew it was far more than his wages. I told him he used to talk about knowing people's secrets, but he'd never tell me what those secrets were because he said I was a blabbermouth and I couldn't be trusted. He was always saying horrible things to me and calling me dreadful names. The sergeant said Bert's money probably wasn't important, but I said he should at least tell the man from Scotland Yard about it. He told me he wouldn't think of bothering him with the ravings of a wicked murderess.

Last night I dreamed I was in the library at Wenfield, surrounded by the characters from my books. I was riding through the countryside on a white horse behind my Darling Man and we were on our way to a ball at a beautiful house — the grand house in *The Duchess's Secret* with a handsome portico and rows of gleaming windows. I was dressed in a fine silk gown and I felt so happy as I clung to him in the sunshine. Then I woke up and I was in my cell lying on a hard mattress with the smell of the toilet in my nostrils.

54

Albert had become sceptical about hunches. He knew they were a popular feature of detective novels but he'd learned from bitter experience that relying on solid police work was safer. Instinct had once let him down badly and, after what happened in Wenfield in 1919, he'd vowed never to trust it again.

His trip to Liverpool to see Clara had temporarily taken his mind off Mary's death but the enforced idleness of the return train journey gave him plenty of opportunity to think. Now the reality had sunk in, Vera's ban on his presence at the funeral felt shocking; as he chugged towards Manchester on the train, gazing out of the window, the thought of ignoring his wife's passing from this world became too much to bear. His eyes swollen with unshed tears, he pulled his handkerchief from his pocket and pretended to blow his nose in the hope that his fellow passengers would assume he was suffering from a cold.

He arrived in Wenfield at seven thirty but, in spite of the late hour, he called in at the police station, hoping Constable Smith would have news for him about the enquiries he'd been making in the Lake District.

Smith had gone off duty, but Albert knew that he shared a small terraced house near the mill with his mother and younger brothers. After he'd called in at the Black Horse for something to eat, he left the inn and walked through the dark cobbled streets.

It had started to drizzle and he could hear his footsteps on the glistening stone pavement — and a slight echo as though there was somebody following behind. But when he turned round there was nobody there. The attack he'd suffered in London had made him jumpy, but he told himself that nothing like that was likely to happen in Wenfield.

It was Smith's mother who opened the door. She was a small, round woman wearing a cross-over apron and a wary expression. 'Not today, thank you,' she said firmly, preparing to close the door in Albert's face.

Albert gave her his most sincere smile even though the effort hurt his bruised face. As soon as he'd introduced himself and reassured her that he wasn't going from door to door selling things she didn't want, he asked to see Daniel. Once his credentials had been established, the woman's manner changed and she invited him in like an honoured guest, apologising that he'd found them unprepared for his visit.

He was shown into the front parlour, the room kept for best, and a few moments later Daniel Smith joined him. The young man looked even younger out of his uniform with his shirt sleeves rolled up.

'Sir, I wasn't expecting . . . Is something the matter?' There was a worried frown on his face as though he feared he'd done something wrong.

Albert was swift to put his mind at rest. 'I was

wondering whether you'd had any luck with that Windermere lead.'

Smith nodded eagerly. 'There was something promising, sir. One of the hotels I telephoned said a gent stayed there last week. He only stopped for a couple of nights and he mentioned he was looking for a property to rent up there. He answered Mr Billinge's description and he was using the name Cartwright.'

Albert raised his eyebrows.

'Thing is, this gentleman arrived in a motor car. Mr Billinge came to Wenfield by train. Didn't have no motor car, according to Sir William.'

Albert paused to mull this over while Smith watched him in silence, awaiting his verdict on this new discovery.

When Albert eventually spoke, his question had nothing to do with the Lake District. 'A couple of days ago I believe someone reported a missing bicycle. Where was that?'

Smith looked surprised. 'It was up at Tarnhey Court. Mrs Banks reported it. One of the lads who comes in to see to the garden asked if he could use it, but when she went to look for it in the stables it had gone. It was only an old bike that used to belong to the chauffeur and she was in two minds whether to report it. She thought it had probably been nicked by a tramp but then she thought of Mr Billinge. If he'd wanted to get somewhere, he might have borrowed it.'

'Why wasn't I told about this right away?'

'Sergeant Teague said not to bother you with it. He said it wasn't important. People pinch bicycles all the time he said.'

'Is there a garage anywhere round here where someone could hire a motor car?'

Smith shook his head. 'Not in Wenfield.' He thought for a moment, brow furrowed. 'But there's one in New Mills that sells new motor cars. They might hire them out and all.'

'Get on to them first thing tomorrow. Ask if Mr Billinge has been a customer of theirs. He might have been using a different name, so give them a full description.'

'Will do, sir.'

'And keep this between ourselves, eh? Sergeant Teague doesn't need to be told unless something comes of it.'

'Right you are, sir.' Smith gave him a conspiratorial grin.

Albert made his way back to the Black Horse through the damp streets, hoping it wouldn't be long before Henry Billinge was found. However, with that case solved, he wondered if his superiors at Scotland Yard would allow him to stay up there to deal with the other cases that he now felt had become his responsibility.

Sergeant Teague seemed convinced that the man at the Devil's Dancers had been a vagrant, fallen foul of one of his fellows who had stolen his clothes and any meagre possessions he might have been carrying. Now that the possibility of the victim being Billinge had been eliminated, the local police were hardly likely to deem this unsolved murder worthy of investigation by Scotland Yard. But, in Albert's opinion, there were features of the case that told another story.

262

And the investigation into Bert Pretting's murder had taken on a new urgency since Rose's arrest. He'd hoped he'd be able to leave the matter to the locals but, now that a young woman was in danger of facing the hangman for a murder she might not have committed, he felt it was up to him to do something about it.

Then there was Mrs Bell's certainty that her husband's death was suspicious. The letter with the enclosed photograph she claimed the reverend received on the day of his death hadn't been found. And the only people who'd had access to his correspondence were Mrs Bell herself and the new vicar, Fellowes. But was Fellowes' secretive behaviour due to his penchant for risqué photographs, or was there a more sinister reason? He had no alibi for the night of Bell's death. And if Bell had decided to nip down the road to have words with his curate, he might not have bothered mentioning it to his wife. Perhaps the letter he'd received that day had contained some disturbing information about Simon Fellowes; something worth killing for.

With all this unfinished business still to deal with, Albert was reluctant to leave Wenfield. Besides, apart from saying his final farewell to Mary at her funeral, he had little to return to London for.

As he neared the Black Horse the rain turned from a light drizzle to a downpour and Albert raised his collar against the cold.

But the sound of the rain dancing on the grey pavements masked the footsteps of the man who'd followed him from Constable Smith's house at a safe distance, keeping to the shadows, determined not to be seen.

55

Constable Smith couldn't conceal his excitement as he went about his work the next morning. He'd been given a special task by an inspector from Scotland Yard and when he'd shared the news with his mother she'd glowed with maternal pride.

As promised, he'd said nothing to Sergeant Teague about the matter and he'd waited until the sergeant was out on patrol before making the telephone call to Riston's Garage in New Mills. He spoke to Mr Riston himself and he almost felt like dancing around the office when he learned that a motor car had been hired out late on the Saturday afternoon Billinge had vanished to a well-spoken gentleman who'd given a London address. The gentleman had matched Mr Billinge's description exactly, although he gave his name as Brown and said he was up North on business. The car was a small Ford, nothing fancy, and he'd told Mr Riston he had some business up in Lancashire and would bring the car back in due course. Mr Brown had arrived on an old bicycle he said he'd borrowed from the bed and breakfast establishment where he was staying just outside New Mills, and he'd paid for the hire of the motorcar in cash without quibbling over the quoted price. The bicycle was still there in the corner of the workshop awaiting his return.

As the disappearance of Henry Billinge had been kept out of the papers, Mr Riston hadn't been aware of it. If he had been, he might have made the connection.

Once Smith had checked the London address 'Mr Brown' had provided and found it to be false, he rushed to Albert's office to tell him the news.

'It's a Ford. Black. And he told me the registration of the vehicle as well.'

'Then you know what to do, Smith. Call the place up in Windermere and ask if the guest's vehicle matched that description.'

Smith blushed. 'I was just about to do that, sir.' He paused. 'If it does, will you have to go up there, sir?'

'I've heard Windermere is lovely in the spring, so maybe I will,' said Albert with a smile, watching the young man's face. It was easy to guess what was on his mind. He fancied a jaunt up to the Lakes as well. 'But it's probably better if I go alone. It's a delicate matter and we don't want to alarm the gentleman, do we.'

The constable's face was a picture of disappointment. 'I'll go and make that telephone call now, sir,' he said. He was about to leave the office when he turned in the doorway as though he'd remembered something.

'My mam was talking to Tess Pollard who helps Miss Hubbard at the library. Tess lives on our street and she went to the grammar school. Always been a bit of a brain box has Tess.'

Albert suspected he hadn't stopped in his tracks merely to share news of Tess Pollard's

266

academic prowess. He waited for the constable to come to the point.

'Tess said she'd seen that Mrs Pretting talking to Edward Price at the library. She said it looked like they were friendly. Very friendly, if you know what I mean.'

Albert straightened his back, giving Smith his full attention. 'Who's Edward Price?'

'He works at the library — part-time. I'll go and make that phone call now, sir.'

56

Smith had been waylaid by Sergeant Teague to carry out some mundane task, so Albert was still waiting for him to telephone the Lake District. Albert knew it would be wise to tread carefully because if the sergeant found out he was commandeering Smith's help to pursue his own lines of investigation, Teague was quite capable of making life uncomfortable for him, even though Albert was superior in rank. As an outsider he was reliant on the men with local knowledge. And there was always the nagging fear at the back of Albert's mind that the sergeant might one day discover the truth about his relationship with Flora Winsmore if he cared to dig into the matter more deeply. And that was something Albert could never allow to happen.

He'd told Smith to say nothing about Edward Price to anyone else for the time being. If Teague got wind of any rumours he would no doubt bring the young man in for questioning and maybe even charge him. Before that happened, Albert wanted to talk to the man himself and hear his side of the story. He was quite confident that he'd know if Price was lying to him.

As he set off to walk to the library, the hills surrounding the village were veiled in low cloud and the only sound he could hear was the distant bleating of sheep in the fields round about. The belching mill chimneys at the far end of the village looked incongruous in the rural scene but he supposed the march of progress couldn't be stopped. Even so, it would be a shame if one day all the green were to vanish beneath factories and houses.

Albert entered the library, aware of the solemn hush. He removed his hat and approached Miss Hubbard, who was stamping books behind the counter.

'Does a man called Edward Price work here?'

'Yes. He's in the stacks if you want to speak to him.'

'In a minute. Tell me about him.'

'He was at Oxford until the war interrupted his studies.' She smiled fondly. 'He's a nice young man. He was badly wounded in the war and he suffers with his nerves, so the quiet of the library suits him.'

'Does he have much to do with Mrs Pretting?'

'I've seen them talking — ' She stopped as though she'd suddenly realised the implications of her statement. 'Not that there was anything improper, of course. Edward's a gentle soul. Hardly the murdering type, if that's what you're thinking.'

'I'm sure you're right.'

'Do you want me to tell him you're here?'

When Albert nodded she vanished through a door behind the counter, returning a couple of minutes later with a young man. His face was badly disfigured, the scarring worse than Albert's own. Before the war he must have been a good-looking lad but now his flesh had burned away and one of his eyes was missing, thick scar tissue grown in its place to cover the empty socket.

'Are you Edward Price?' Albert asked in a whisper.

'That's me.'

'I'd like to speak to you about Rose Pretting.'

For a moment Edward looked flustered. Then, after a brief word with Miss Hubbard, he led Albert to a small, cluttered office off the main library.

'I heard about Rose — Mrs Pretting. I can't believe she'd do anything like that.'

'Has Sergeant Teague spoken to you?'

Edward shook his head stiffly as though the effort hurt him.

'What was your relationship with Rose Pretting?'

'What do you mean?' Albert could hear the alarm in his voice.

'Did you write letters to her?'

Albert saw Edward clench his fists before he turned his head away. 'What good would it have done? Why would a woman like that look at someone like me? Even if I'd wanted to . . . ' His shoulders had started to shake.

'She was seen talking to you.'

'She was kind. Do you think I don't look in the mirror? Do you think I could ever be with a woman like her?'

'Did you want to be with her?'

Edward hesitated before giving a small nod. 'Like I said, she was kind. We talked about books. Beauty and the Beast we would have been if . . . '

270

'You're not a beast, Edward. Never think that.'

'They called us heroes. I wasn't a hero. I was scared out of my wits most of the time. It came as a relief when I was sent back to Blighty.'

'You're not alone there.' Albert would have liked to let Edward talk but time was pressing. 'So you weren't Rose's lover?'

'Fat chance.'

'Any idea who was?'

He slumped down into a nearby chair, shaking his head. 'No. The only person I've seen her talking to was Dr Kelly; deep in conversation, they were. I thought she might have been asking him about some medical problem — trying to get his opinion on the sly without having to pay his fees. On one occasion they seemed to be having words, so maybe he got fed up with it.'

'You've seen them talking more than once?'

Edward shrugged. 'I suppose so. And he often comes into the library just after her, but he never takes any books out. I sometimes wondered if they were hoping to bump into each other but . . .'

Albert thanked him and left. He had a call to make.

He wanted to speak to Kelly. If nothing else, there was always a chance the doctor could give him the results of the tests on the stomach contents of the man in the cave and the Reverend Bell.

271

57

Albert arrived at Kelly's house shortly after morning surgery had finished. He walked up the front path of the handsome stone house where Flora and her father had once lived and rang the bell, suddenly nervous as the memories flooded back — good and bad.

The door was answered by Kelly himself, who greeted Albert like an old friend, which made Albert feel awkward as he followed the doctor into the parlour — a room that had changed a great deal since Dr Winsmore's day. There were two modern sofas and a low coffee table in the latest style and the pictures adorning the wall were no longer the dark Victorian landscapes that once hung there.

One picture in particular caught Albert's attention. At first he thought it was a local scene; an impressionist's view of a stone-built Derbyshire village. But on closer inspection Albert realised that its origins were more exotic.

'It's by Cezanne. Only a print, I'm afraid. I picked it up in Paris.'

'Reminds me of the houses around here.'

Kelly came and stood beside him and both men studied the picture as though they were visitors in an art gallery.

'It's called *La Maison du Pendu*, usually translated as *The House of the Hanged Man*, although it was said to be the home of a Breton called Penn'Du. They got it wrong.'

Albert nodded, his eyes still fixed on the picture.

'That's what I've heard people call this house. *The House of the Hanged Woman*.' He paused. 'I've heard it was you who arrested Flora Winsmore.'

'That's right. Have you had those results back from Liverpool yet?' Albert asked, anxious to change the subject.

'As a matter of fact, I have,' Kelly said, gesturing Albert to take a seat. 'Turns out we were right. Both our friend in the cave and the Reverend Bell were poisoned. A large amount of laudanum was found in the reverend's body — same with our unidentified victim. I suppose suicide's a possibility in the vicar's case.'

'I think that's unlikely.'

'From what I saw of him, I tend to agree. And suicides don't bash their own faces to a pulp, so our man in the cave was definitely murdered. We can only assume that both men were somehow tricked into consuming laudanum.'

Albert took a moment to absorb this new information. Mrs Bell had been right to suspect her husband's death hadn't been natural; he wondered how he was going to break the news to her. And the news that the man in the cave had died in the same way suggested a connection. Although he couldn't imagine what that connection could be.

'The bottle I gave you — the one I found in the stables at Tarnhey Court?'

Kelly sat back in his chair and arched his

273

fingers. 'The bottle contained eye drops. Quite a common remedy. It's a poison and not to be taken by mouth, but it's definitely not an opiate. We can rule it out.'

'Laudanum's easily available.'

'It isn't as easily available as it used to be, but there'll still be a bottle or two in many households. I'm afraid you're looking for the proverbial needle in a haystack.'

Albert watched the doctor's face. It was clear he had no idea of the real reason for his visit and he almost felt guilty. He liked the man.

'There's something else I need to ask you, Doctor. It's a delicate matter.'

Kelly grinned. 'You should have come to my surgery, but I'll make an exception just this once.' He leaned forward. 'What seems to be the trouble?'

The misunderstanding didn't make Albert's task any easier. 'It's not about my health. You were seen talking to Rose Pretting.'

'Oh.' The doctor sat back and arched his fingers again.

'You've been meeting her?'

'I've bumped into her from time to time.' He paused. 'It's an occupational hazard, I'm afraid — patients developing a . . . crush.'

'Letters were found hidden in Rose's house. They're from a man. Did you write them?'

Kelly sighed and shook his head. 'I wouldn't do anything so stupid.'

'But you don't deny she had a crush on you. Did you feel the same?'

Kelly suddenly rose from his seat, a spark of

anger in his eyes. 'I admit she used to contrive meetings, make doe eyes at me, come to my surgery with imagined maladies. She even followed me sometimes when I went out on walks. But I swear I never gave her any encouragement.'

'Was she with you when you discovered the body of the man in the cave?' It was a guess but when Albert saw Kelly's reaction he knew his question had hit home.

The doctor sank back into his chair and took a deep breath. 'I didn't say anything at the time because I was embarrassed. I saw her and I slipped into the cave in the hope of shaking her off.' He shook his head. 'I'm sure she genuinely believed that I was interested in her, but it was all in her imagination. First of all she was married and her husband, in my opinion, was a brute. Secondly there's the fact that she's my patient and I wouldn't risk being struck off the medical register even if I was attracted to her — which I'm not. I felt sorry for her but that's as far as it went. Besides, there's a young lady in Manchester I see from time to time; a sister in the Royal Infirmary there. I wasn't interested in Rose Pretting and I hoped she'd get the message eventually, but in the meantime I did all I could to avoid her.'

'You were seen having words with her.'

The doctor looked exasperated. 'I was trying to explain to her as kindly as I could that there was nothing between us, but she was behaving as though she didn't believe me. In the end I told her to leave me alone and stormed off in

275

frustration. I didn't wish to hurt her feelings, but I couldn't allow her to continue with her delusions, could I?'

Albert watched the man's face and his instincts told him that he was telling the truth. 'Let's return to the day you discovered the body. Did Rose follow you into the cave?'

Kelly's face reddened and he nodded slowly. 'I'd just slipped into the cave when she appeared at the entrance. She came inside and began . . . She was carrying on as though we'd arranged to meet there and before I knew it she was kissing me. I pushed her away. Told her to go home.'

'But she didn't?'

'No. I think she'd have stayed if I hadn't noticed the smell of rotting flesh. There's no smell like it and I knew something was wrong. I took out my lighter and when I flicked it on I saw the body. She saw it and gave a little scream but at least it meant she didn't want to hang around. She ran out of the cave and I assume she went home. Then I informed the police, saying I'd gone there later that day and praying she hadn't said anything. If it had come out that she was there too, people might have got hold of the wrong end of the stick.'

'You know Sergeant Teague is looking for Rose's lover? He's certain the man killed Bert Pretting at Rose's request so they could be together.'

'Unless she was pursuing some other poor chap, I think the lover existed only in her head.' He thought for a moment. 'I don't think her marriage was happy, so it's possible she sought comfort elsewhere — but not with me.'

Kelly looked straight at Albert, anxious to be believed. Everything about his story seemed to fit with the letters from Rose's wardrobe. Albert had encountered many guilty men and women in the course of his police career but he was as sure as he could be that the doctor wasn't one of them.

However he knew it wouldn't be long before Sergeant Teague spoke to Edward Price and made the connection. And he couldn't trust the sergeant not to reach the obvious conclusion.

He left the doctor's surgery, the house that held so many unsettling memories, fearing there might be another arrest. And this one might not be justified.

58

When Albert arrived back at the police station he made for his office and shut the door behind him. As soon as he'd sat down his telephone began to ring. It was Scotland Yard. Sergeant Sam Poltimore.

'Sir, I've found out that your mother-in-law's arranged Mary's funeral for tomorrow. Three o'clock at that so-called church of hers, followed by burial in the municipal cemetery. I called round to offer my condolences and one of her cronies from that church was there. I overheard her discussing the arrangements. Thought you'd like to know.'

'Thanks, Sam. I'll make sure I'm there. Not that I'll be welcome.'

'There's something else you should know. I've been making enquiries into that reverend —Thomas Gillit. My cousin in Kent remembers a Tommy Gillingham who lived in the Rochester area before the war. Used to claim he was some kind of medium and went round big houses getting in touch with dead loved ones. He was quite popular at one time, then there was a bit of a scandal. Some writer exposed him as a fraud and he left the area. Do you think it could be the same chap?'

Albert thought for a while. 'Any way of finding out?'

'I can try,' said Sam cheerfully. Albert knew

that once Sam had the bit between his teeth he wouldn't give up. Since Mary's death, Gillit no longer had the power to affect his life, but it would still be good to be proved right . . . and to save others from Gillit's smooth trickery.

The moment he'd finished the call there was a knock on his door and Constable Smith hurried in. Standing in front of his desk like a schoolboy called to the headmaster's study, he announced, 'You know that Ford motor car hired from New Mills, sir? A constable from Bowness called me on the telephone half an hour ago. It's been spotted.'

'He's sure it was the right car?'

Smith suddenly appeared unsure of himself. 'He didn't get the registration number, but it was a Ford and he hadn't seen it before. It was black.'

'I think they all are,' said Albert quietly, not wishing to dampen the young man's enthusiasm.

'He said the driver fitted Mr Billinge's description. I told him to stop it if he saw it again. Did I do right, sir?'

'You did very well, Smith,' said Albert, favouring the constable with a smile. 'What about the hotel?'

'It sounds like it's our man all right. But he checked out yesterday.'

This wasn't what Albert wanted to hear but he tried to hide his disappointment.

'What if they find him, sir? Will they arrest him or what?'

'What on earth for? I was called up here because it was thought he'd been murdered, but if he's found up there safe and well, the matter will be closed. It's not against the law to go off somewhere on your own to think things over.'

'If it does turn out to be him, will you be going back to London?' Albert saw a forlorn look on Smith's youthful face.

'Not yet.' He paused. 'I've been talking to Dr Kelly and he now has proof that the Reverend Bell was poisoned.'

Smith's mouth fell open. 'Who'd want to poison the old vicar? Everyone liked him,'

'The doctor also says that the unidentified man in the cave was poisoned with the same substance, so there could be a connection. I need to speak to Sergeant Teague — bring him up to date with developments.'

'I'll tell him to come in, shall I, sir?' Smith said before leaving the room to take up his post behind the front desk.

Through the open door of his office Albert saw Sergeant Teague give Smith a curt nod of acknowledgement and, after a moment's hesitation on the threshold, he entered and stood to attention by Albert's desk.

'You wanted to see me, sir?'

Albert told him to sit down and when he repeated what he'd just told Smith he saw a look of disbelief on the sergeant's face.

'The old vicar — murdered? I can't believe that. He was a harmless sort and very popular in the village. Even his sermons weren't too long. He died of natural causes. Everyone knew that. Even the doctor,' Teague said, as though he suspected Albert of lying.

280

'Mrs Bell wrote to me in London to tell me she thought there was something odd about her husband's death, but I decided not to say anything until I had proof. And now I have that proof I want to undertake a full investigation.'

Teague frowned. 'It might have been accidental . . . or he might have taken his own life.'

'I think that's unlikely, don't you? We need to find out who the Reverend Bell visited on the night he died. And that means house-to-house enquiries. Can I leave you to arrange that, Sergeant?' Before the sergeant could answer Albert carried on. 'And if we find out who's responsible for the vicar's death we might be closer to discovering who killed the man in the cave.'

'I don't see how there can be a connection, sir. Unless it's some mad man.' His eyes lit up. 'Or mad woman. That Mrs Pretting was planning to poison her husband. Maybe the reverend found out somehow and she silenced him.'

This scenario hadn't occurred to Albert, but he said nothing as he watched Teague leave his office. Perhaps the man was right about Rose Pretting after all. If Kelly was to be believed, she'd lost touch with reality and lived in a fantasy world. But could Kelly be trusted?

There were times when Albert doubted his own judgement.

59

Rose

I've asked the inspector from Scotland Yard to visit me in this place of smells and wickedness. They've given me a rough dress to wear and taken my clothes and make-up off me. I'm not allowed any comforts, they say. Murderesses don't deserve them.

The wardresses look at me as though I'm an unpleasant insect that's landed in their food. I can feel their disgust and hatred as they bark their orders at me. They tell me I'm to face a trial and they say the jury doesn't like people like me. Women who betray their husbands and then plan to kill them so they can be with some fancy man. They keep telling me I have to name my Darling Man but I won't. Never.

They say I'm going to be hanged. One of the wardresses, the fat nasty one with the eyes like tiny grey buttons, told me how the hangman comes to measure you the night before and how they tie your hands and ankles and shove a hood over your head before it happens. She said it's what murdering whores deserve. But I never murdered anybody. All I did was dream about it.

There is one wardress who's not so bad. She even asked me if I was all right yesterday. I asked her to pass on the message but I don't know if I can trust her, even though she did give me a smile. I told Sergeant Teague about Bert's secret but he took no notice, so I need to see the inspector. I need to make sure he knows all about what Bert was up to. It's my only hope.

60

On Saturday morning Albert asked Mrs Jackson to serve his breakfast early and by seven o'clock he was arranging his knife and fork on his empty plate and taking his final swig of strong tea. He wanted to catch the seven-thirty train to London so he'd have time to call in at Scotland Yard before attending Mary's funeral. He'd telephoned Sam the day before and asked him to contact an expert he'd used in several previous investigations and arrange a meeting. Sam had promised to take care of it.

After speaking to Sam, he'd visited Rose Pretting's home and Dr Kelly's surgery. The doctor had been surprised by his unusual request but Albert had come away from his house with the evidence he hoped would help to clear up the matter of Bert Pretting's death. He hadn't told Sergeant Teague what he'd done, and he wanted the man kept in ignorance until he was certain of his ground.

The uneventful journey to London allowed Albert time to turn the cases over in his mind. He had to acknowledge that he was no nearer to bringing the killer of the man at the Devil's Dancers and the Reverend Horace Bell to justice now than when he'd first arrived in Wenfield. He stared out of the window at the passing landscape with a feeling of helplessness. His only glimmer of light in the darkness was the possibility that Henry Billinge MP might soon be found alive and well in the Lake District.

Once in London he took a taxi to Scotland Yard where Sam was waiting for him with a small elderly woman wrapped in enough furs to face a Moscow winter. Mrs Greenbaum felt the cold, Sam explained.

Albert shook the woman's birdlike hand and she looked up at him through her thick pince-nez and smiled.

'Sergeant Poltimore here says your wife has recently passed away. My condolences.'

Albert thanked her politely, experiencing an unexpected stab of grief at the reminder.

He was relieved when at last he was able to get down to business. He'd used Mrs Greenbaum's expertise with written documents several times before and he trusted her judgement. He took the samples of handwriting obtained from Kelly's surgery and Rose's house from the briefcase he was carrying and told her what he wanted her to do. She promised to let him know the results of her investigations as soon as possible.

When Mrs Greenbaum had gone, Albert headed for his office and Sam followed, picking up a cardboard file on the way which he carried to Albert's office under his arm like an officer's swagger stick.

'Know that cousin I was telling you about? The one in Kent?' Sam said as he sat down and placed the file on the desk in front of him.

'I remember.'

'Well, he suggested I get in touch with the

285

local paper, 'cause there was a bit of a scandal at the time. I telephoned the paper and they sent me some old cuttings from 1912 before the war.'

Sam pushed the file towards Albert, who opened it and scanned the contents with a satisfied smile.

'I'll see you at the funeral,' said Sam.

Albert nodded, grateful that he'd have some support among the members of the League of Departed Spirits.

Once his business at Scotland Yard was over, he took the tram to Bermondsey. The curtains of his house were drawn as was the custom, but the front door was ajar to allow the neighbours to come in and pay their respects.

When he stepped into the house it seemed colder than usual and silent, apart from a low murmur of voices from the parlour. He took a deep breath, summoning his courage before entering the room. He wasn't sure what he'd expected to see but the sight of Mary lying in the centre of the room in an open coffin shook him for a moment. Vera was bent over her daughter's body, gently stroking her hair and muttering what sounded like words of comfort while Thomas Gillit looked on, a benevolent half smile on his face.

There were other people in the room too, mostly women in black gathered near the window like a gaggle of crows. As soon as Albert entered the room all eyes turned on him, some curious, some hostile.

It was Vera who spoke first. 'I told you, you're not welcome here. Get out.'

There was a flurry of anticipation as though the little audience in black were hoping to witness an interesting scene, something they could gossip about for weeks to come. Albert ignored them and stood his ground.

'As Mary's husband I've every right to be here.' He searched for the right words. 'Mary and I went through a lot together. She was my wife.' He glanced at Vera, but she looked away.

Then he turned to face Gillit. 'I'm sure you'll agree that it would be wrong to turn me away, Mr Gillingham. It is Tommy Gillingham, isn't it?' He tried his best to make the question sound innocent.

The man didn't answer and Vera came to his rescue. 'This isn't the time or the place, Albert. I said you're not welcome.'

At that moment the door opened and Sam Poltimore walked in, taking his place at Albert's side. With the arrival of a stranger, Vera's anger subsided into a withering look.

Although Albert was tempted to confront Gillit there and then with the evidence Sam had discovered, he realised that at least he should let Mary be decently buried first. He heard the clip-clop of horse's hooves outside the window, announcing the arrival of the hearse.

In a daze he watched the solemn undertaker place the lid on Mary's coffin and experienced another pang of grief, so strong that it left him shaking. He felt Sam's touch on his arm as, without a word being spoken, everyone left the house and followed the hearse on foot down the street as passers-by bowed their heads and doffed their caps in respect.

Albert walked behind the hearse in a daze with Sam by his side. Before he knew it they'd reached the building that housed the League of Departed Spirits. At one time it had been the large house of a prosperous family and Albert couldn't help wondering how Gillit had raised the necessary funds for its purchase — although he could hazard a guess. The main room with its high ceiling and elaborate cornice was furnished with rows of chairs for the congregation and an impressive table at the front where Gillit presided. Albert sat at the back while Gillit's oily words washed over him. Mary had found happiness and contentment at last, he said. She had been a generous benefactor of the League — a sacrificial giver — and this wouldn't be forgotten now she'd reached the Astral Plain. At the mention of money, he felt Sam nudge his arm.

The strange ceremony involved no prayers or hymns, only a series of testimonials from Mary's departed relatives saying what a good woman she was and how pleased they were to see her on the other side. Albert tried to suppress his anger. Mary deserved more.

The service passed swiftly and soon they were out in the street again making their way to the municipal cemetery, walking in procession behind the hearse. As he watched her coffin being lowered into the grave, he felt strangely detached from what was happening, as though he was watching it in a dream. Perhaps it would take time for the reality to sink in. In the meantime, he was unable to cry, unable to speak. He'd never been so glad to have Sam Poltimore beside him.

When it was finished, he walked away with Sam, not bothering to say his farewells to Vera, who was studiously ignoring him.

'That file — you'll make sure Gillit's dealt with appropriately, won't you?'

'Don't you worry, sir. I can't guarantee you'll get back any of the money your missus spent on him. but I'll see to it he doesn't operate in this manor again. He'll be sent on his way.'

Albert thanked him and, in spite of Sam's insistence that he spend the night at his place, he told him he needed to get back to Wenfield that night. He had unfinished business to deal with.

61

Albert had arrived back in Wenfield late on Saturday night, exhausted and hungry. Mrs Jackson had taken pity on him and heated up a meat pie which he washed down with a pint of ale before retiring to his room.

Sunday was a day of rest when most of Wenfield attended church. Albert, however, still had work to do. As soon as he arrived at the police station, Teague greeted him smugly with the news that Dr Kelly had been arrested the previous day on suspicion of murdering Bert Pretting.

It wasn't just Edward Price who'd seen the doctor and Rose Pretting together. As a result of Teague's investigations in the village several witnesses had come forward to say that Kelly and Rose seemed to be on closer terms than the usual polite distance between doctor and patient. They'd been seen whispering conspiratorially, which suggested to Teague that they hadn't merely been passing the time of day. But the thing that clinched it in the sergeant's opinion was the mention of the ground glass in the letters. Surely only a medical man would possess such knowledge.

Albert's hope that Kelly's name could be kept out of it until he had solid proof had come to nothing. Teague had been happy for Scotland Yard to help out with the Pretting case until

Albert's theories began to contradict his own. From that point on he'd made it plain it was a local matter and he resented some smart alec from London creating complications when he should be looking for the missing Member of Parliament.

Teague also favoured the theory that, if the Reverend Bell had indeed been murdered, then Rose and Kelly had to be suspects. Albert felt control of the case slipping from his grasp. He'd been distracted by Mary's death and funeral, but now it was time to act.

When he asked to speak to Dr Kelly he was told the doctor had already been charged and transported to Manchester. Dr Bone from New Mills was going to take his surgery for the time being. Albert remembered Dr Bone from his last stay in Wenfield. Bone had assaulted Flora while she'd been working as a nurse at Tarnhey Court during the war and left her traumatised. He despised the man.

Albert was furious at this fait accompli and he suspected that Teague had moved swiftly to arrest Kelly while he was away in London in order to spite him. Now all Albert could do was wait for Mrs Greenbaum's verdict and hope her evidence would be enough to save two people from the gallows.

'That Rose Pretting has sent you a message from prison but I'd ignore it if I were you. She's where she belongs and she'll be dangling from the end of a rope before too long.'

To hear the death of a young woman mentioned so lightly and with such relish made

291

him want to punch Teague's grinning face with his good hand. But instead he took a deep, calming breath.

'What did her message say?'

Wren took a piece of paper from beneath the desk; a crumpled scrap that looked as though it had been screwed up in disgust. The man straightened it out before pushing it across the polished counter towards Albert.

Albert picked it up and read.

Dear Inspector Lincoln, it began,
I need to see you urgently. I didn't kill Bert but nobody will believe me. There are things you should know about Bert. He always had a lot of money and I didn't dare ask him where he got it but he told me once that he knew people's secrets and I think one of them must have killed him. I told Sergeant Teague but he wouldn't listen. Please, Mr Lincoln, you've got to help me. I'm frightened they'll hang me when I didn't do nothing.
Yours truly
Rose Pretting (Mrs)

Albert put the note in his pocket, resolving to make the necessary arrangements to see her at the first opportunity and hoping he would hear from Mrs Greenbaum in the next few days. In the meantime he hurried through the streets towards the church. Mrs Bell would be on her way to morning service and he needed to ask her some questions.

As he left the station, struggling to keep his temper under control, he was surprised to see Mrs Bell in the company of Grace, the maid from the vicarage, hurrying towards him, dressed in their Sunday best.

'Good morning, Inspector. Is there any news?' There was a note of anxiety in Mrs Bell's question.

'Not yet, I'm afraid, but I would like to ask you something. Do you keep laudanum at the vicarage?'

'No,' said Mrs Bell. 'Why?'

'The doctor thinks your husband consumed a fatal quantity before he died.'

He'd expected Mrs Bell to be shocked but instead she nodded slowly. 'Then it's as I thought. He was poisoned. But who would do such a thing?'

Grace, in contrast, looked flustered. 'Oh dear, I don't know whether I should . . . It seems like a betrayal . . .'

Albert waited, knowing Grace couldn't be hurried. His patience was rewarded when she continued:

'It's the Reverend Fellowes — I found two bottles of laudanum in his bathroom cabinet. He told me he takes it because he has difficulty sleeping.'

'Lots of people take it,' said Mrs Bell, as though she was trying to make excuses for her late husband's successor. Albert saw Grace give a little shake of her head at her former employer's naivety.

'Thank you for telling me, Grace,' said Albert,

touching his hat. 'And don't worry, he won't hear that I learned about it from you.'

He watched the ladies scurry off towards the church, leaning on each other as if for support. The news had clearly confirmed what Mrs Bell had suspected and, whatever Teague might think, he felt it was up to him to clear the matter up once and for all. He began to walk through the streets without purpose, putting one foot in front of the other until he found himself in Pooley Woods, the scene of so many violent deaths back in 1919. He stood for a while, listening to the breeze rustling the tree branches, now green with new life.

He wasn't sure how long he stayed there but eventually he left the dappled shelter of the woods and returned to the churchyard where he could hear the sound of singing coming from the ancient stone building. As he was walking down the path between the leaning, lichen-covered gravestones the church doors suddenly opened and the congregation began to flood out. Among the first to emerge were the Cartwrights, Sir William arm in arm with his delicate wife, who seemed to be barely aware of her surroundings. They passed Albert without acknowledging him and made straight for the Rolls-Royce parked by the gate that would take them the short distance home. Sir William opened the door for his wife to climb in, the perfect gentleman. But Albert had spoken to Clara, so he knew the truth.

The Reverend Simon Fellowes stood at the church door shaking hands with his departing flock, less relaxed than Horace Bell had looked when he'd performed the same duty.

Albert watched as the people of Wenfield made their way down the path, all on their best Sunday behaviour. The Ogdens were making their way arm in arm to their motor car parked in the lane outside and he saw Mr Jones, the mill manager, deep in conversation with another man, while his wife trailed behind wearing a cloche hat and red bouclé coat that wouldn't have looked out of place in a top London hotel. Some of the clerks from the mill office were trying to avoid their superiors. George Yelland was with his mother, who linked her arm through his protectively. The young man looked shaken and frail and Albert hoped he was having a better time of it at work without Bert Pretting there to bully and mock him.

Once the congregation had dispersed, he saw Simon Fellowes coming towards him, his surplice billowing in the breeze.

'Inspector, may I have a word? There's something I'd like to discuss with you in private.'

'As a matter of fact, I was hoping to speak to you myself.'

Fellowes said nothing as they walked side by side towards the vicarage and it wasn't until they were sitting in the study that the vicar broke his silence.

'Since your visit last week I've been wrestling with my conscience, Inspector.'

'You can rely on my complete discretion,' said Albert quietly, wondering what was coming.

The vicar took a deep, shuddering breath and stared out of the window, avoiding Albert's eyes.

'It might not be important, of course, but as there's been an arrest . . . '

'Are we talking about Bert Pretting?'

Fellowes bowed his head. 'Yes. Pretting. As a man of God I'm supposed to see the best in everybody, but some people are more easy to think well of than others.'

'I've spoken to some of Pretting's workmates. He sounded like a bully.'

'He was. And if his unfortunate wife did away with him, I have some sympathy. Although I shouldn't say that, should I?'

Albert didn't answer the question. 'Did you have any dealings with him?'

'I'm afraid so.' There was a long pause before he spoke again, as though he was gathering his thoughts — or deciding how much to reveal. 'From time to time I meet with a group of like-minded gentlemen in New Mills. We have a mutual interest in photography. The study of the human form.'

'The female human form?'

Fellowes' face turned beetroot red. 'There are certain ladies who are kind enough to pose for us. It's artistic, you understand. Nothing untoward occurs at our meetings and everything is conducted with the height of propriety.'

'I understand,' said Albert, wishing the man would get to the point.

'I'm afraid Bert Pretting found out about our meetings. I've no idea how.'

'And he asked for money?'

'He said that if I didn't pay up everyone in Wenfield would get to know about my

. . . pastime. I've done nothing wrong, but people are so swift to judge, aren't they.'

'Do you know who else was being blackmailed by Pretting?'

'Blackmail?'

'What else would you call it?'

'Pretting called it a contribution. Helping him out because he was a bit short, was how he put it.'

'It was blackmail, Reverend. Do you know anybody else Pretting asked for money in this way?' Albert had a sudden idea. 'The Reverend Bell, for instance?'

The vicar looked affronted. 'Surely not. Although . . . I did wonder about the Cartwrights. I know there are certain family matters they'd prefer didn't come to light. Sir William has a reputation as a ladies' man. There was a young maidservant some time ago; an unfortunate girl who was murdered, I remember. Then there's his son, Roderick . . . '

'I know all about Roderick Cartwright's private life, Reverend. But I agree. Others might not be so . . . slow to judge. Sergeant Teague would probably consider it a matter he couldn't overlook.'

'You're quite right, Inspector. I saw Pretting talking to Sir William once. The gentleman looked quite upset, so I'm sure . . . And if Pretting was so bold as to approach Sir William, who knows what other upright citizens have fallen victim to his . . . requests.'

'Thank you for being so frank with me, Reverend. You've clarified several things in my mind.'

'You won't tell anybody about my . . . ?'

'You can rely on my discretion,' said Albert, registering the relief on Fellowes' face, as though a heavy weight had been lifted. 'Are you in the habit of using laudanum, Mr Fellowes?'

The expression of relief instantly vanished. 'I . . . I do take a dose now and then when I find it difficult to sleep.'

'The Reverend Bell died from an overdose of laudanum. I think somebody gave it to him.'

Fellowes' eyes widened in alarm. 'You surely can't think . . . I assure you that if he did consume any laudanum, it didn't come from me. I admired the reverend greatly. I would never have done him any harm.'

'Even if he found out about your . . . pastime?'

'Even then.'

Albert studied his face for a while, thinking that his look of injured innocence, the look he'd seen so often on the falsely accused, was unlikely to be faked. Then again, he'd been wrong before.

'Just how much did you want to be vicar of Wenfield, Mr Fellowes?'

The man looked hurt. 'Not enough to poison a good man like Horace Bell, I assure you.'

'So he didn't visit you on the night he died?'

'Certainly not.' He hesitated. 'In fact I wasn't even in Wenfield that night. I was at my . . . photography club.'

'Why didn't you say this earlier?'

His face reddened. 'I think you know why, Inspector.'

Albert stood up. 'One last thing before I leave. I asked you about a letter the Reverend Bell received in the late post on the day he died. There was a photograph enclosed in the letter. Do you know anything about it?'

'You asked me that before and I'm afraid the answer's still no.'

'That man who was found in the cave by the Devil's Dancers. Someone went to a lot of trouble to conceal his identity. Did you ever see a stranger who fitted his description around the village? He didn't call at the vicarage asking for help?'

'I would have told you if he had. I never saw him. And in Wenfield a stranger would usually be noticed by someone, don't you think?'

It was a few seconds before Albert summoned the courage to ask the next question. 'When I spoke to you the other day I mentioned the name Charlotte Day. I had the impression it meant something to you.'

Fellowes remained seated, turning a pen over and over in his fingers while he stared at it with fascination. Albert resumed his seat and waited.

'Charlotte is Lady Cartwright's niece and before the war we were ... we had an understanding. But while I was away in France she married somebody else. She had a child, but I heard it died. Influenza.'

The words made Albert's heart lurch as it brought back memories of Frederick. Another child lost to the terrible epidemic. Could it be that the child Charlotte Day lost was his and Flora's — adopted then snatched from her by death? The thought was too painful to bear. Perhaps it was a good thing that he hadn't summoned the courage to seek her out. The quest would have ended in more pain than he felt he could endure at that moment.

'She lives in a village called Mabley Ridge now,' Fellowes continued. 'It's near Wilmslow in Cheshire.'

'I know where it is. I investigated a case there last year.'

'The man she married is a cotton manufacturer. And a war hero.' He looked directly at Albert, who could see the sadness in his eyes. 'What chance did I have? A humble clergyman who hasn't been the same since he witnessed the horror of the trenches. Those horrors are still with me, Inspector. Often I can't sleep without the roar of gunfire and the cries of the wounded ringing in my ears. What did I have to offer Charlotte when she could have a wealthy hero instead?'

The vicar's hands were shaking but Albert couldn't think of any fitting words to say. Nothing that would reassure or comfort. He reached out and touched the man's sleeve. 'There are a lot like us, Simon. It'll get better with time,' he told him, not quite believing his own words.

Albert left the vicarage with a feeling of heavy sadness. It was Sunday so he had the choice of spending the day of rest brooding on recent events or dropping into the police station in the hope that there was some new development.

He chose the latter option.

62

As soon as he arrived at the police station Constable Smith looked up from his paperwork with a conspiratorial smile. As Albert took off his hat, he suspected that the young man was beginning to regard him as his guardian angel in the force. But he'd soon be back in London and Smith would be left to answer to Teague, so he didn't want him to become too reliant on having the man from Scotland Yard to protect him.

'I've heard from the police station in Bowness, sir. A chap answering Mr Billinge's description is renting a cottage near the town. And he's driving a Ford.'

Albert absorbed the news for a moment. 'I don't suppose you can drive, can you, Smith?'

'Oh yes, sir. Before I joined the force I used to do odd jobs up at Tarnhey Court and Mr Pepper, the chauffeur, taught me how to drive. Said if I ever wanted a job at his new garage in Stockport I was to come to him. But I decided on the police instead. Me mam's pleased I stayed in Wenfield.'

'Of course she is,' Albert smiled. 'Is there a police car available?'

'There's one over at New Mills, sir.'

'Ask if we can borrow it. Fancy a trip to the Lakes?'

Smith's eyes lit up with enthusiasm. 'Oh yes, sir.' Then the smile disappeared. 'But what will

Sarge say? I'll have to get his permission.'

'Leave that to me,' said Albert with a confidence he didn't feel. Smith was under Teague's supervision, not his.

He made for Teague's office, resolving to tell, not ask. Teague didn't look pleased, but Albert pressed home the point that his mission was in the national interest and in the end it was agreed that he and Smith would travel up to Bowness in the New Mills police car. Hopefully, they'd return with the missing Member of Parliament.

★ ★ ★

Smith was a good driver. He had learned on the country roads of Derbyshire so the winding lanes of the Lake District held no fear for him.

Albert had never experienced the beauty of that particular part of the world before so he sat in the passenger seat enjoying the passing scenery, awed by its wild magnificence.

They arrived in the small lakeside town of Bowness in the late afternoon. It was a fine spring day and Albert stood by Lake Windermere breathing in the pure air and watching a stately steam yacht chugging across the vast expanse of glistening water. There were other craft too; sailing yachts and rowing boats. Despite all this activity, the scene was peaceful and leisurely as the green mountains beyond the lake reared up to touch the pale blue sky. It was a world away from Bermondsey and Albert's spirits soared. People had written poetry about this place and recorded its loveliness in watercolours and oils. It was a place that could heal the soul and he could have stayed there for ever if he hadn't had a job to do.

Having located the police station, Smith went on ahead and Albert followed. A stiff breeze had begun to blow in from the lake and people were hurrying towards their homes, hotels or guest houses, ready for their evening meals. When they reached the stone-built police station that reminded Albert of Wenfield's own, the sergeant, a large man with a good-humoured smile, invited them behind the front desk and shook Albert's hand heartily. Here the man from Scotland Yard was a welcome guest rather than a usurping nuisance.

'Well, we're honoured. Scotland Yard,' he said, as though he couldn't quite believe it. 'I'll get one of the lads to take you up there, if you want.'

'That won't be necessary, thank you, Sergeant. I'd rather not alarm the gentleman. Discretion's the watchword here.'

The sergeant looked disappointed, as though he'd been anticipating a bit of excitement and his plans had been thwarted. 'I understand, sir. I'll give you the directions.'

He was as good as his word and soon Albert and Smith were driving uphill, making for an isolated stone cottage with a ribbon of smoke rising from the chimney. The small Ford parked near the outhouse bore the correct registration, which told them they'd come to the right place.

'You stay in the car, Smith. It's best if I go in alone.'

As Albert got out of the car Smith wished him

luck, although Albert was sure he wouldn't need it — until he reached the front door and felt a tingle of nerves in his stomach.

He knocked on the door with the knuckles of his right hand, his maimed left hand tucked into the folds of his coat. No matter how many times he told himself that he should be proud of the scars earned in the service of his country, he tended to feel self-conscious when meeting people for the first time, especially individuals of Henry Billinge's social standing.

There was no answer so he knocked again. This time the door opened a few inches, but he couldn't see who was behind it.

'Sorry to bother you. I'm looking for a gentleman called Henry Billinge.'

The door moved as though it was about to be shut in his face. Albert put his hand out to stop it.

'It's nothing to worry about. His family and friends are worried about him and I need to reassure them that he's safe.'

The door opened a little wider. 'Who are you? What's your name?'

Though Albert still couldn't see the man on the other side of the door, he could hear the anxiety in his well-spoken voice.

'My name's Albert Lincoln,' he said. 'Detective Inspector, Scotland Yard. I've spoken to Mr Billinge's wife . . . and Clara.'

Now the door opened fully and Albert recognised the man he'd only seen before in a photograph, proudly posed, every inch the confident MP. The Henry Billinge who stood before him had lost his veneer of pride and prosperity and somehow this made him look more human.

'Mr Billinge? May I come in?'

The man stood aside to allow Albert to enter. As he did so, he removed his hat and found himself in a cosy parlour with a fire glowing in the hearth. The ceiling was low and Albert had to stoop to avoid hitting his head on the oak beams. The diamond-paned windows were too small to let in much light, so it took his eyes a while to adjust to the gloom. It was a few moments before he noticed the other person in the room; a slim, fair-haired man sitting on the edge of a chair beside an old gate-legged table. He was considerably younger than Billinge and dressed casually with his shirt open at the neck. Albert could see uncertainty in his eyes. And something else: fear.

'This is my private secretary, Sydney Wade.' Billinge seemed to be regaining his confidence.

'I expect you needed to get away from London to conduct some parliamentary business that couldn't be done in Sir William's house.' Albert looked Billinge in the eye and gave a discreet nod, as if to let him know that he understood the true situation.

'That's it exactly, Inspector. I'm sorry you've been troubled.' Albert could hear the relief in his voice. And gratitude too.

'You really should have told someone your plans. As I said, people have been worried. They called in Scotland Yard to look for you.'

'I realise that now. I'm sorry. There's no

telephone here, but if you could let people know I'm safe . . . '

'Of course, sir.' Albert caught a meaningful glance between Billinge and Wade.

There was a long silence before Billinge spoke again. 'As you said, I needed to get away. The pressure of . . . You say you've spoken to Clara. How is she?'

'Well, I think.'

'I'm afraid I walked out of Tarnhey Court because I was furious with William for the way he treated her and I couldn't keep up the pretence of civility any longer. I apologise for causing so much trouble. I only intended to be away overnight and return with some excuse about being called away urgently to my constituency, but . . . ' He glanced at Wade. 'When I called Sydney to tell him what I'd done, he offered to come up North to join me. It was then I realised I couldn't keep up the pretence. The life I was living was based on lies — my marriage, my career, everything. I did intend to go back, but in the end I couldn't bear it any longer.'

His eyes widened in panic and Albert could see they were brimming with unshed tears.

'You're a policeman, so I shouldn't be telling you this.'

'I can keep confidences,' said Albert quietly. 'Unless you've committed murder or robbery, whatever you tell me will go no further, I promise.'

It was half a minute before Billinge spoke again. 'I've been making plans,' he said, almost

306

in a whisper. 'Dreaming about disappearing for good — going to the South of France with Sydney. I even thought about leaving my clothes on a beach somewhere to make everyone believe I was dead.'

'What about your wife?'

'My marriage to Anne is one of convenience, Inspector. She has her own private life and neither of us ask too many questions. But I see now that faking my death was a stupid idea. It would have been the coward's way out — and in the war I was never a coward. I realise I'll have to go back and face the music.'

There was a vulnerability about Billinge that made Albert warm to him. 'One of the reasons people were so worried about you is that the body of a man answering your description was found in countryside near Wenfield, not far from Tarnhey Court. The man had been stripped of his clothes and his face battered to a pulp. The post-mortem revealed that he'd been poisoned with laudanum.'

A look of horror passed across Billinge's face. 'And you thought it was me?'

'At first. Until your wife provided us with certain information that confirmed the body wasn't yours.'

'He was like me, you say?'

'The same height and build, although the face . . .'

'Clearly someone didn't want the poor blighter recognised.' He shook his head. 'Which rather suggests he was known in Wenfield, don't you think?'

'Nobody's come forward to identify him or

report him missing.'

The MP frowned, as though he was trying to retrieve some elusive memory.

'I wonder . . . At the dinner at Tarnhey Court on the Saturday night we began discussing the plight of exservicemen; people who'd fought in the war and had come back injured or suffering from shell shock so were unable to resume the lives they'd had in civvy street. Some are homeless, begging in the streets. William and I agreed that something needed to be done. Then one of the ladies said she'd seen a tramp the previous week and she wondered whether he was one of those unfortunate men. One of the men said he'd seen a similar man walking on the road leading to Wenfield. He'd felt sorry for him, so he stopped his motor car to speak to him. Well spoken, he said he was. Possibly a former officer who'd fallen on hard times.'

'Which guest are you talking about?'

'I forget the name. He manages one of the mills in Wenfield. His wife was with him, but she spent much of the evening being lectured by that vicar chap.'

'Mr Jones?'

'That's him. Wife's a lot younger than he is; looked bored stiff.'

'Did he say anything else about the man he spoke to?'

'Afraid not. Soon after that the conversation turned to politics.'

'Surely the problems faced by former soldiers should be the concern of politicians,' Albert said sharply.

'Of course,' Billinge said smoothly. 'That goes without saying.'

Albert wasn't sure whether to believe in his sincerity. His initial humanity had gradually been replaced by the well-practised veneer of the professional politician. He noticed Wade was watching him warily, as though he wasn't quite sure what to do.

'What are your immediate plans, Mr Billinge?'

The politician sighed. 'I'll return to Liverpool tomorrow,' he said with a cold smile. 'If you could let the relevant people know I'm safe and well, I'd be very grateful.'

'I'm sorry to have intruded,' said Albert, reaching for his hat, which he'd placed on a table near the door.

'You were only doing your duty, Inspector.' He hesitated and glanced at Wade. 'And I'm sure I can rely on your discretion.'

'Of course, sir.'

Albert was suddenly anxious to be out of there. He needed to get back to Wenfield as soon as possible. Henry Billinge would have to look after himself.

63

Rose

I cry most of the night and the wardress tells me to shut up. She says if I didn't like it in here I shouldn't have murdered my husband. It's no use telling her I didn't, because she doesn't believe me. Everyone in here swears they're innocent, she says with a nasty smirk on her face.

They still won't let me have any books and I've stopped asking. It was because of a book that I'm in here in the first place. *The Garden of Secrets*. I sometimes wonder what Cecilia Yarmouth is like; whether she actually murdered her husband like in her book. I doubt it. The thought that my dream of being with my Darling Man might one day come true was the only thing that made my horrible existence bearable, but I don't think anyone will believe me. And now Ronald's been arrested, accused of stabbing Bert in an alleyway so he could be with me. I must find a way to convince them that they've got it wrong.

I've asked to see Inspector Lincoln, but they say he won't come. I'm not important enough for a detective from Scotland Yard. I'm just a murdering bitch who did away with her innocent husband.

But there are things I've got to tell him. I need to see him.

64

The return journey to Wenfield seemed to take longer than the drive up to Bowness but Smith assured Albert that it was just his imagination. Albert knew he was right. His impatience to speak to Jones made every minute seem like five.

Smith asked about Billinge, but Albert was discreet. Mr Billinge, he said, had wanted to get away to think over a problem in his political life and make a decision about his future. He'd been so preoccupied that he'd forgotten to inform anybody of his whereabouts. Now that he'd been found safe and well, the matter was closed. It was the truth, so far as it went, and Smith seemed satisfied with the explanation.

When Albert asked Smith to take him straight to Jones's house, the young man looked uncertain. 'Shouldn't you make an appointment, sir? He might not like being disturbed at this time on a Sunday night.'

'I'm investigating a murder, Smith. He might be in charge at the mill, but I need to ask him some questions.'

On the way back from Bowness he'd told Smith about the stranger Jones had encountered a week before the Tarnhey Court dinner. And the constable had put into words what Albert had been thinking. Why hadn't Mr Jones said anything about the incident before?

It was almost eleven by the time they reached

Wenfield and Albert reluctantly agreed with Smith that a late visit to Jones's home might not be welcome. He'd have to curb his impatience and catch the man first thing the next morning.

After a restless night at the Black Horse he rose early but instead of heading for the police station he arrived at Jones's front door at eight thirty precisely. The maid who answered looked flustered by his arrival and told him the master had already gone to the mill. He always liked to make a prompt start. Albert thanked her and set off, arriving ten minutes later at the offices where Bert Pretting's colleagues were working away at their desks. He was surprised when George Yelland rose to his feet and hurried over to him.

'Can I have a word, Inspector?'

'Of course. But it'll have to wait until I've seen Mr Jones. Hopefully I won't be long.'

The young man looked anxious, but then that seemed to be his default expression. Albert gave him a reassuring smile and saw Yelland return to his seat, fidgeting with his shirt cuffs.

He knew Janet Reynolds was at her post from the clatter of her typewriter and when he entered her office she looked up and smiled. 'Morning, Inspector. What can I do for you this time?'

When he told her, she showed no surprise. Instead she made straight for the door which bore the name *A Jones Esq* in gold letters and knocked. When she opened the door, Jones was sitting behind his grand oak desk on a chair that resembled a throne; as he rose to his feet, Albert could tell he was trying to control his irritation.

'I assure you, Inspector, I've already told you

everything I know about Pretting's death and Mr Billinge's disappearance.'

'Mr Billinge has been found. I've spoken to him.'

'I'm pleased to hear it. Now if that's all you've come to tell me, I'm a busy man.'

'Mr Billinge told me you spoke to a man about a week before Sir William's dinner. A tramp — possibly an old soldier, he said. Is that true?'

Jones hesitated, as though he wanted to choose his words carefully. 'I saw the chap by the side of the road and stopped the motor. He was a tramp; shabby clothes, haversack. I asked him if he'd fought in the war and he said he had, so I asked him if he wanted a lift anywhere. I felt sorry for him. Not right for a man to serve his country only to end up like that.'

'Did he tell you anything about himself?'

'I asked him what he did before the war. It was at the back of my mind that I might find some employment for him in the mill, you see. Trouble is, he couldn't remember, poor chap. All he knew was that he'd been injured by a shell blast and he'd lost his memory completely, to the point he couldn't recall anything that might help identify him. Didn't even know where it happened, only that it was somewhere in France. He told me he'd been in a hospital in Buxton for a while, then he'd left once he started to remember bits and pieces about his life before the war.'

'Did he say what he was doing here in Wenfield?'

'Looking for his wife, he said. When he was in

313

hospital he saw her picture in a newspaper. This was a while ago, but he hadn't been well enough to try and find her at the time.'

'Did he say which paper it was?'

'Afraid not.'

'Do you remember anything else he said?'

'He told me that when he left hospital he went to the place where he used to live but he found strangers living there. The lady there had been kind, he said, and she'd told him the last tenant moved out without leaving a forwarding address. But she thought the person had moved to this area. High Peak.'

'Did he say where he used to live?'

'No. It was all rather vague, I'm afraid.'

'Did he tell you his name?'

'The people at the hospital had called him Tommy. He couldn't remember his real name, but he kept saying he was sure he would, given time.'

'What about his wife's name?'

'He called her Flower — said that was his pet name for her. He asked me about the people who lived around here — women who'd be the same age as his wife — and I talked about some of them, more to make conversation than anything. I suggested he try other places around here too — New Mills or Whalley Bridge.'

'Can you describe him?'

The description Jones gave could well have fitted the man at the Devil's Dancers. Only the dead man had been clean-shaven and his hair had been neatly cut, unlike Jones's tramp who'd had a beard and straggly hair. Even so, Albert

314

wondered whether it could be the same man, cleaned up and given a haircut. All he had to do now was to discover whether the man had managed to find his wife during the week between Jones's act of generosity and the discovery of the body at the Devil's Dancers. And whether that reunion had somehow led to his death. On the other hand, the two things might be completely unconnected and the tramp might still be wandering Derbyshire in search of his loved one.

Jones spoke again, interrupting Albert's thoughts. 'I told him the local vicar might be able to help, but he said someone from the hospital had written to all the vicars in the area months ago, enclosing a picture of his wife, and there hadn't been a positive reply.'

This new piece of information caught Albert's attention. Could this be the mystery letter that sent Bell hurrying out on the night he died? It was an intriguing possibility.

'That's all I can tell you, Inspector. Now if you'll excuse me, I'm a busy man. And I'd never seen that man before in my life.'

'Or since?'

Jones lowered his eyes. 'Or since.'

'You gave him a lift in your motor car. Where did you drop him off?'

'In the village.'

'Where?'

'Near Tarnhey Court.'

'Did you see where he went after that?'

'I'm sorry, no.'

'He would have been conspicuous.'

'There are so many vagrants about since the war ended that people have stopped noticing them,' said Jones sadly. 'There is one thing I remember. When I dropped him off, I saw that writer woman who was at Sir William's dinner. She must have seen him. Why don't you ask her whether she spoke to him?'

'I will. Thank you.'

Albert thanked him and walked out through the clerks' room where everyone was bent over their work in a great show of industry. When the door had opened it was clear they'd been expecting Mr Jones to appear; as soon as they saw it was Albert, they relaxed.

George Yelland's desk was nearest the door and as he passed, Yelland cleared his throat.

'Sir, can I have a word? In private?' he said, eyeing the door to Jones's office warily.

Albert left the room and waited outside for Yelland to join him in the corridor. He noticed the young man's hands were shaking again.

'What is it?'

'I was given the job of clearing out Bert Pretting's desk and I found something taped at the back of his bottom drawer. It's a book with names and sums of money. Some of the names are only initials, but there's an address in the back. It's in Liverpool. I told Mr Perkins, the chief clerk, and he said not to bother you with it. He said Bert's missus did him in so it can't be important, but . . . '

He took a small tattered notebook from his pocket and handed it to Albert.

'Thanks, George. You did the right thing.'

'Will Bert's missus hang? And the doctor? Do you think he really was her fancy man?'

Albert didn't answer.

65

George Yelland's question about Rose Pretting's and Ronald Kelly's ultimate fate suddenly made Albert's intention to speak to Rose more urgent.

Her message had been conveyed reluctantly by Constable Wren, who clearly thought the woman had no right to make demands, particularly not to a Scotland Yard inspector. She was being held in Strangeways Prison, Manchester; the place where Flora had met her death. Albert had visited the prison in the course of a previous investigation and the memory of what had happened there made it a place of dread. But if he was going to learn the truth about Bert Pretting's murder he would have to pass through those forbidding gates again.

He hated the sounds and the smells of the prison; the feeling of being trapped. But there was a chance Bert Pretting's widow might have something new to tell him about her husband's death, so he'd be neglecting his duty if he didn't go.

First, however, he asked Smith to call all the hospitals in the Buxton area to ask about the mystery man. One told him they'd had a patient matching his description, but he'd left their care over a month ago. He was a man who had no memory of his former life, although the doctors hoped it would return eventually. Other than that, they could tell him nothing apart from the fact he thought he'd once lived in Liverpool. At the time he left, he told them he was going there to look for his wife.

Albert told Smith he'd done well. But this new information wasn't going to make him change his immediate plans.

Smith still hadn't returned the motor car to New Mills, so Albert suggested he drive them both to Manchester. It would save time waiting for trains and, besides, he'd be glad of the young man's company. Albert suspected that Smith reminded him of himself in his younger days, when he was a youthful uniformed constable just started in the Metropolitan Police. When he was first walking out with Mary.

Smith entered the prison gates at his side but Albert asked him to wait in the governor's outer office while he spoke to Rose. The sight of a uniform might put her on her guard. Besides, it was him she'd asked to see and he wanted her to feel relaxed during their interview.

She was brought to him in the windowless room where lawyers usually saw their clients and a large woman in a warder's uniform insisted on staying with the prisoner, posted at the door and watching with hard, unsympathetic eyes. Albert wished he could tell her to go but he didn't want to make waves.

Rose herself looked gaunt, as though she'd lost weight since he'd last seen her. Her prison uniform hung off her thin shoulders and her face was grey. From the redness around her eyes, Albert could tell she'd been crying.

'You asked to see me,' Albert began gently. He

doubted whether anyone had shown this woman much kindness since her arrest and, in his experience, kindness often worked better than bullying.

'I thought you might understand.'

'Understand what?'

'That I didn't do it. I never killed Bert.'

'Those letters — they described how you were planning to kill your husband. They'll be pretty damning evidence when your case comes to court.'

'But it was all made up. I read this book about a woman killing her evil husband, so I thought if I . . .'

'Who wrote those letters to you, Rose?'

She hung her head as though she was ashamed. 'I wrote them to myself. I disguised my writing so I could pretend they were from . . .'

'Dr Kelly?'

She nodded. 'He didn't write them, honest. He had no idea I was in love with him. I was just a patient to him. I used to say I was ill and go and see him at the surgery and when he was looking down my throat or in my ear, I'd imagine what it would be like if he loved me. He got so close that I could feel the heat from his body and when he listened to my heart he'd say it was beating unusually fast and I wanted to tell him it was beating for him, but I was never brave enough. I wrote the letters and when I read them I'd imagine he'd sent them to me. It was a game of pretend. You have to believe me.'

Albert smiled. 'I've read *The Garden of Secrets*. It's about a woman trapped in a loveless marriage who plots with her doctor lover to kill her husband by putting glass in his food. Did you do that?'

'I tried it once but he found it, so I never did it again. I wanted to know what would happen — whether it would be like in the book. It wasn't.'

'At the end of the book the lovers commit suicide before they can be arrested.'

Rose didn't answer.

'Did you think that was romantic — like Romeo and Juliet?'

She nodded eagerly.

'Only being kept in here and facing a trial isn't very romantic, is it?'

She bowed her head again. 'All the wardresses say they'll hang me. They've told me exactly what's going to happen. How the hangman comes to measure you the night before and — '

'They won't hang you if I've got anything to do with it,' Albert said sharply.

'But what can you do?'

Albert caught the despair in her question. He was still waiting to hear from Mrs Greenbaum, so he couldn't make any promises. 'I'll do my best,' he said. 'It's all any of us can do. You said you had something to tell me.'

She took a deep breath.

'Bert had money. Lots of it. I think that must have something to do with his murder. I told Sergeant Teague but he said it wasn't important.'

'I already know about your husband's blackmailing activities.'

She looked disappointed, as though the last

321

weapon in her armoury had turned out to be useless. 'I never knew what he was up to, I swear. He never told me.'

Albert had been hoping for new information about Pretting, something that would lead to his real killer. But Rose hadn't told him anything he didn't already know.

Then she spoke again. 'A couple of weeks before he died he said he'd found something out and he was due some money. A lot of money, he said. I didn't know whether to believe him 'cause he often said things like that. But this time it was a bit different. He seemed really . . . excited. The more I think about it, the more . . . '

'Can you recall exactly what he said?'

She screwed up her face as though she was making a great effort to remember. 'He came in one evening and said we were going to be in the money. He'd recognised someone from the past.'

'Who?' Albert held his breath.

'Someone at work, he said. Someone who was going to keep us in comfort for the rest of our lives.'

'Did he mean someone from the mill?'

She shook her head. 'I think he said where he *used* to work. I'm sorry, that's all I can remember.'

'You said he lived on the Wirral before the war. Where did he work then?'

'In Liverpool — told me he got the ferry to work every day.'

This caught Albert's attention. The mystery man who'd left the Buxton hospital had mentioned Liverpool and now the name of the city had come up again. 'What did he do?'

'He was a clerk — in insurance. When we were courting he used to tell me how he called at big houses in the nice suburbs. Lovely places, some of them. He said one day we'd have a house like that.' She laughed. 'To think I used to believe him.'

'Do you think the person he recognised was one of his old customers from those days?'

'I don't know. After the war he went to work at a bleach works near Stockport, so it might have been somebody from there.'

Albert looked at her hopeful face and felt a pang of regret. If he couldn't prove her innocence very soon her life would end at the end of the hangman's rope.

But he had the Liverpool address Bert Pretting had written in the back of his secret notebook. All of a sudden those few scribbled words took on a fresh significance. If his instincts were right, they might save the lives of an innocent man and woman.

66

By the time Albert and Smith arrived back in Wenfield it was three o'clock in the afternoon. Seeing Peggy Derwent again was on his list of things to do but when he telephoned her cottage there was no answer, so he made some other calls and the fifth produced the result he wanted. By the time he'd finished it was too late to set off for Liverpool. But Buxton was far nearer.

Smith was happy to drive there and Albert sat in the passenger seat, looking out at the wild, hilly landscape as the young constable steered along the winding pass, avoiding the sheep that wandered into their path.

When they arrived in the town, Albert was surprised by the gracious architecture and the handsome stone-built crescents. He'd been expecting something less grand and more industrial, but Smith reminded him that Buxton was a famous spa town, renowned for its healing waters.

The hospital stood on the edge of town, a classical building with a portico which would grace any stately home. Smith waited in the motor car while Albert went in search of the matron, a tall woman with a straight back and a chiselled face. But her sympathetic manner belied the formidable first impression and she listened with interest to what Albert had to say before summoning a sister who, she explained, had looked after the man in question.

The sister was young and efficient, and matron left her to talk to Albert alone.

'Tommy was better physically, so the doctor said he could leave. He was keen to get out of here because he had some bee in his bonnet about finding his wife in Liverpool. I've been rather worried about him, to tell the truth. Even though his body had recovered from his injuries, he still hadn't fully regained his memory.'

'Tell me what you know about him.'

'He was brought here from a French field hospital in '18 — found wandering in Flanders shortly after the Armistice and shipped back to Blighty. Complete memory loss. Nothing. The doctors said his memory would return eventually but it could take a long time, and he had no ID on him.'

'I understand he was starting to remember things about his past?'

'He remembered he was married. He had a photograph of his wife — his only possession that survived. He didn't even have a uniform — somehow he'd managed to swap it for civvies. Got them from some Frenchman, he said.' She shrugged her narrow shoulders.

'But he was definitely a soldier?'

'He said so, and his wounds seemed to confirm that he'd been in the middle of the fighting. And he certainly spoke like an officer.'

'The picture of his wife, do you have it?'

She shook her head. 'My brother had a photographic shop and he made some copies for him. I had the idea of sending the copies to vicars in the area to see whether any of them recognised her.'

'He might not have come from round here,' Albert said, puzzled.

The sister smiled. 'He said he'd seen his wife's picture in one of the local newspapers, you see. We let our patients read the papers. It gives them an interest.'

'Which one?'

'I don't know, but we don't take any national papers. The news in them is far too disturbing for our patients.'

'When did he see the picture of the woman he thought was his wife?'

'This was a while ago. Must be over six months.'

'Did he show you the picture?'

'He showed me the page, but it wasn't clear which picture he meant. There were a few and I was too busy to take much notice. To be honest, I thought he was probably mistaken, but I thought sending the copies of the wife's picture to some vicars in the area would make him think he was doing something positive. Around that time he'd begun to have longer flashes of memory and I thought . . . Well, it couldn't do any harm, could it? I wrote the covering letters for him.'

'Do you still have a copy of the newspaper photograph?'

'Good Lord, no. Old papers get thrown out. Probably went for chip paper months ago.'

'And the picture of his wife?'

'He kept the original and all the copies were

sent out. I'm sorry. All the vicars replied saying they were sorry but they didn't recognise her. No luck, I'm afraid.'

'All the vicars?'

'There might have been one who didn't, but I'm afraid I don't really remember.'

'Do you know which vicar didn't respond?'

She frowned in concentration, then shook her head. 'I'm sorry. It was so long ago. If someone didn't reply I expect it was because they didn't know anything and they were too busy to write.'

Or perhaps they were dead, Albert thought, although he didn't put this into words. 'Will your brother have a copy of the picture?'

'Sorry. He sold up and moved to London three months back. Says it's better for business down there.'

'What happened when Tommy left your care?'

'As I said, his memory was starting to come back. Just bits and pieces at first. And dreams — nightmares. Then a few weeks ago he told one of the nurses he'd remembered where he used to live in Liverpool and he wanted to go back there to look for his wife. The doctors said he was well enough to leave, but I was worried about him. When he left I told him to write — to keep in touch — but . . . ' She spread out her small hands in a gesture of despair.

'So he went to Liverpool? Did he give you the address?'

'I'm afraid not. He said he remembered the house but not the address, although he seemed quite confident he'd find it. I hope he's all right. I hope he's found his family and he's not living rough somewhere.' Albert heard the anxiety in her voice. She cared.

He didn't tell her about the man at the Devil's Dancers. There was no point burdening the young woman with more tragedy than she'd already had to face.

He took his leave, more convinced than ever that it had been Tommy who'd met his end in that cave. But who would have wanted to kill a soldier robbed of his memory and identity by war?

Unless his killer was afraid that his memory was about to return.

67

That evening Albert found that there were new guests at the Black Horse; a pair of cotton merchants from Bolton visiting one of the mills. They nodded to him at dinner but made no attempt to start a conversation with him; from what he could overhear, their talk rarely strayed from business matters. Albert decided to retire to his room. He'd brought some files back with him and he spent the evening studying them and making notes. The picture was gradually becoming clearer, but he still needed proof.

The following day he walked to the railway station and caught the train to Manchester. From there he caught another train to Liverpool, arriving at Lime Street station in the middle of the morning. He had the address George Yelland had found hidden at the back of Bert Pretting's drawer, but before he went there he decided to visit the Dale Street offices of the insurance company who'd once employed Bert Pretting.

Fortunately their chief clerk had worked there for some years and he remembered Pretting well, although from the guarded way he spoke about him Albert guessed he hadn't liked him very much. The chief clerk was a small, thin man, too old to have served in the war, who wore a stiff collar which looked as though it was biting into his neck. When Albert broke the news of Pretting's murder, the man expressed shock and

329

the customary willingness of the law-abiding citizen to help the police bring his killer to justice. Albert didn't mention the fact that Rose had already been charged. In his opinion this would only prove a distraction.

When he asked for a list of the customers Pretting had dealt with, the chief clerk vanished into a back office and as soon as he'd gone the other clerks looked up from their desks and ledgers and stared like curious cattle. A visit from Scotland Yard was providing some welcome entertainment.

The chief clerk returned with a typewritten list on flimsy paper and presented it to Albert, who thanked him and left, reluctant to study it in front of an audience.

Once he was outside the building he began to read, oblivious to the passing traffic. He was looking for one address in particular, the one he'd found in the back of Bert Pretting's notebook, and when he saw it on the list he experienced a thrill of triumph. In his excitement he was almost run over by a horse-drawn lorry as he crossed the street, but he carried on towards the station where he caught the train to Aigburth. The journey seemed frustratingly slow but Albert fought his impatience, wondering whether his destination — a place called Fulwood Park — was anywhere near Gwen Davies's house.

As it turned out, the address wasn't too far from Gwen's. Only in contrast this house was a large Italianate stucco villa set in its own spacious gardens behind a pair of substantial gateposts. There were steps up to a grand front door with tall bay windows either side overlooking the entrance.

He climbed the flight of stone steps, ignoring the pain in his leg, and rang the doorbell. A maid wearing a starched cap and apron opened the door and gave him a wary look. She was thin and in her fifties, and when Albert introduced himself she looked alarmed and put her hand to her mouth.

'Oh Lord, what's happened? It's not the master, is it?'

Albert interrupted before she could carry on. 'Can you tell me who lives here?'

'Mr and Mrs Bethel. Mr Bethel went to London on business this morning. Has there been an accident? As if losing the boys wasn't bad enough for the poor lady — '

She had obviously jumped to the wrong conclusion and Albert felt obliged to put her out of her misery. 'Mr Bethel's quite safe as far as I'm aware. Can I speak to Mrs Bethel?'

The woman sniffed. 'I'll tell her you're here.'

He waited in the wide hallway with its gracious mahogany staircase, wondering what Mr Bethel did for a living. Trading with the rest of the world had made many in the city wealthy while the not-so-fortunate still lived in poverty, just as they did in his native London.

He didn't have to wait long before the maid returned and showed him into an elegant drawing room where a plump middle-aged woman rose to greet him with a worried frown on her face. She invited him to sit and ordered tea, for which Albert was grateful.

'What can I do for you, Inspector? Mavis says it's not about my husband, so I don't really see . . .'

Mrs Bethel looked the sensible type so Albert decided on complete honesty. He explained about the address at the back of Bert Pretting's notebook and the fact that her address had featured on the list of Pretting's customers at the insurance company. He sat back and awaited her reaction.

Unexpectedly she smiled. 'I'm sorry Inspector, I can't help you. You see my husband and I only moved into this house two years ago. And before you ask, I've never had any dealings with that particular insurance company and I certainly haven't heard of this Bertram Pretting.'

Albert did his best to hide his disappointment. 'Who used to live here?'

'The previous occupant was a widow who'd lost her husband in the war. Terribly sad. I believe her name was Jenkins and her husband was in shipping before he went away to do his bit. Such a tragedy' She looked at Albert's maimed hand, her eyes full of sympathy. 'You were lucky to get through it alive, I see.'

'Yes. I was.'

'Our two sons both died on the Somme,' she said simply, glancing at the pair of silver-framed photographs on the mantelpiece; handsome young men in the prime of life. Beside the pictures were two bronze plaques; people called them 'death pennies', sent to the bereaved by the War Office to acknowledge their relatives' sacrifice. Some people had discarded them in anger. But Mrs Bethel kept hers in pride of place — a permanent memorial to those she'd lost.

'I'm sorry,' said Albert, unable to think of any more suitable words.

She straightened her back and stared ahead. 'You have to carry on, don't you. You can't give up.'

Albert nodded in reply. She was right. Life went on, even though things would never be the same. There was a lengthy pause before he asked his next question: 'Do you know where Mrs Jenkins went?'

'You're the second person to ask that.'

Albert sat forward, suddenly alert. 'Who else has been asking?'

'A man came to the door. Poor chap looked very confused when he saw me, and I assumed he was a tramp. We have them coming to the back door from time to time asking for food and money, but they're not usually bold enough to use the front. He demanded to know what I was doing here and where his wife was, and I had to tell him that I didn't know his wife. Then it dawned on me that he might be looking for the last tenant, Mrs Jenkins, and his eyes lit up as soon as I'd said the name, as though he recognised it. He was fairly polite — unlike some of them. Mavis has had trouble with some who won't take no for an answer.'

'Did he say anything else?'

'He asked where Mrs Jenkins was and I told him she'd moved to Derbyshire. High Peak. A village near New Mills beginning with a W.

333

That's all I remembered. Mavis might have known, but it was her day off.'

'She worked for the Jenkins?'

'That's right. I inherited her, as it were.'

Albert felt a prickle of excitement. 'Would you mind if I spoke to her?'

Mrs Bethel rang the bell at the side of the fireplace.

When Mavis hurried in he asked her to sit down and she glanced at her mistress for permission. Mrs Bethel gave her a gracious nod. 'The inspector wants to ask you about Mrs Jenkins who used to live here,' she explained.

Albert asked his questions and by the time he left the house he thought he had most of the answers he needed. But as Mavis showed him out he had one last question to ask her in private.

'After her husband died, did Mrs Jenkins have a gentleman friend?'

Mavis gave a conspiratorial nod. 'Very soon after she got the telegram this gentleman started to call. She said he was a colleague of Mr Jenkins, but they used to closet themselves away — told me not to disturb them.' She gave him a knowing look. 'Good job Mr Jenkins' old father had passed away a few weeks earlier, so he never knew about his son being killed.' She paused and leaned forward, lowering her voice. 'He never liked the mistress, you know. I overheard a terrific row once — called her a gold-digger, he did.'

'The gentleman who visited Mrs Jenkins after her husband was killed — what was his name?'

'I don't think she ever told me.'

'Can you describe Mrs Jenkins and this gentleman.'

She gave a description that could have fitted a hundred people in early middle age but in spite of this Albert had the feeling that he was on the right track at last.

On the way back to the station he passed the end of Gwen's road. She would be finishing work around now so he lingered, keeping her house in sight. He wanted to speak to her; to tell her about Mary. But she didn't appear so he caught the train back, thinking that it might have been for the best that he hadn't seen her. Besides, he needed to return to Wenfield. And, with any luck, he'd soon be able to make an arrest.

68

When Albert reached the police station, Smith rushed out to greet him before he'd even had a chance to remove his hat.

'I've been looking through the local papers from around six months ago, like you asked, and I found a photograph of Mrs Jones in the *High Peak Clarion*. She was at a dinner in New Mills with her husband. The local Business Circle. Very grand do, by the look of it.'

'Anybody else?'

'Sir William and Lady Cartwright were there too. And Mr and Mrs Ogden. And Mr Perkins, the chief clerk from the mill, with his good lady. Of course it could have been a lady from New Mills — there were a lot of them there. Then there was an article about that writer woman — Miss Derwent. It was about her new book. Big photograph of her, there was.'

Albert raised his eyebrows. 'Any other pictures of ladies from around here in the newspapers from that time — apart from the Business Circle and Miss Derwent, that is?'

'None who'd be the right age, sir. Unless you count a woman who was sent down for pinching from her employer. She got a job as a maid in some big house in Whaley Bridge but her new employer never checked her references so she didn't know she was an old customer of ours. Pinched a load of jewellery she did — and her

336

old man's in Strangeways and all so it runs in the family.'

'Probably not her then.'

'Well, she might have led a double life in the past. Who knows?'

Albert smiled. Smith's suppositions reminded him of Rose Pretting's fantasies. Sometimes, as in Rose's case, an overactive imagination can be a curse rather than a blessing.

'I've got a job for you, Smith. Can you contact all the vicars in the area and ask them if they received a letter from a nurse enclosing a woman's photograph. This would have been about six months ago.'

'All the vicars?'

'All of them in, say, a thirty-mile radius.'

Although Smith nodded, Albert could tell he felt daunted by the task he'd been given. And when Albert said he was going out he saw a look of disappointment pass across the young man's face when he said he wanted to make his next visit alone. Walking to the cottage where he and Flora had once met and made love was bound to bring back memories and he hadn't wanted anyone else to share the journey.

He found Peggy Derwent at home, although he could tell she was irritated at being disturbed.

'I've just got back from London,' she said peevishly as she walked ahead of him into the parlour.

'I'm sorry to disturb you again,' he said as she lit a cigarette and inhaled deeply. She didn't offer him one; clearly she didn't want to encourage him to stay longer than necessary.

'Were you working?'

'I'm always working. That's what writers do. Even when I'm out walking, I'm working. People don't realise that.'

She sat down but Albert remained standing.

'Why don't you sit down. You're making me uneasy, looming over me like that.'

Albert did as he was told. 'About six months ago your picture appeared in a local newspaper.'

'I seem to recall that I gave a talk at a literary society around that time.'

'Somebody saw your picture and recognised you.' He paused. 'Your husband.'

She froze, cigarette in hand, unaware when a worm of ash dropped onto her skirt.

'What do you know about my husband?' she whispered after a long silence.

'That he came here looking for you. That he ended up dead in a cave with his face battered beyond recognition. You were seen with him.'

'Who by?'

'Mr Jones. The manager of Gem Mill.'

There was another long silence before she spoke again. 'Mr Jones can't possibly have seen me with my husband because my husband's dead. All I have left of him is a photograph.'

She rose, walked to the sideboard and opened a drawer. The photograph she took out and handed to Albert was of a man in uniform — only it wasn't the sort of uniform Albert had expected to see. The soldier in the picture was German.

'Now you know why I value my privacy and never talk about my past. I heard that some local

338

women banded together to torment men they considered too cowardly to fight. Can you imagine the reaction if they found out I'd married the enemy?'

'Your husband's dead?'

'Werner was killed at Passchendaele. One of his friends was kind enough to let me know.'

'Mr Jones saw you talking to a tramp about a week before the man was found in the cave by the Devil's Dancers.'

For a moment she looked puzzled. 'Oh, *that* man. He just said good morning. He looked rather confused, then as I walked on a motor car drew up and he spoke to the driver. I saw him get in and I remember hoping he was being taken somewhere . . . safe. I felt sorry for him.'

'Did you recognise the driver who picked him up?'

She lit another cigarette. 'Oh yes.'

★ ★ ★

Albert returned to the station wondering whether there was sufficient evidence to make an arrest. After asking Smith to bring him a cup of tea he closed the office door and sat with the files open in front of him on the desk. After Peggy Derwent's revelation the picture was gradually becoming clearer. But he wanted to keep Peggy's name out of it if possible. If Wenfield found out about her past, life might become uncomfortable for her.

When Smith finally brought in his tea some of it had slopped in the saucer, but Albert said nothing about the constable's domestic failure. Instead he asked him how his enquiries with the clergy of the area were going. Smith said he'd struck lucky with the first vicar he contacted; a vicar whose church was two miles away. He'd kept the letter and the photograph he'd received. Did Albert want him to go and fetch it? The answer was yes. And it would help if he hurried. But before he left he told Smith to ask Teague to join him. He had something to say.

Teague's first reaction was one of disbelief with a hint of defiance. Bert Pretting's killer and his accomplice were already in jail awaiting trial so there was no reason to look elsewhere. As for the man at the Devil's Dancers, he was a vagrant. Probably got into a fight with one of his fellows and the rogue had pinched his clothes. Some people were desperate and the chances of tracking down his killer were slim.

Albert was angered by the man's stubborn disregard for the facts, in his opinion bordering on stupidity. In the end he stood up, no longer able to control his temper.

'I've told you about the latest developments, Teague. It's about time you started to use your brains. I want one of your men to go there with me at midday to bring the suspect in for questioning. Smith will do. He's a bright lad. And nobody's to breathe a word of this before then. That's an order.'

It wasn't often that Albert pulled rank but on this occasion it was necessary. He was almost certain he now knew the killer's identity. All he needed was the photograph. Once he was holding that, he'd have the proof.

'You can't barge in and arrest someone of his standing. It's not right.'

'You were quick enough to arrest Dr Kelly.'

'That's different. We had lots of evidence against him.'

'That evidence is unreliable and I'll prove it. Just do as you're asked, Sergeant.' Albert checked his pocket watch.

Teague struggled to disguise his fury at this challenge to his authority. He was used to the station being his kingdom and Albert was usurping his throne. In the end he couldn't keep his thoughts to himself any longer.

'You're wrong. You were wrong back in 1919 and you're wrong now. If my superiors get to hear you've been bothering people of that sort . . .'

The mention of the events of 1919 made Albert freeze. What if Teague was right? What if he was making a terrible mistake? For a brief moment he began to doubt his own judgement.

'As soon as Smith returns we're going. I don't expect you'll want to come with us.'

'I'd rather slit my own throat,' Teague muttered under his breath, slamming the door as he left the room.

69

Albert approached the front door, suddenly nervous even though he knew Constable Smith was standing behind him. Despite his youth, Smith was a comforting presence.

It was a long time before the door was opened by a tired-looking maid who recognised Albert from his last visit and gave him a wary half smile.

'Sorry, Inspector, they've gone away. Paid the rent that was owing, packed up all their things and moved out. The van came yesterday afternoon. They said an elderly relative of the master's had fallen ill and they wanted to be on hand.'

'You'll be going with them?' Albert asked, looking the girl in the eye.

'I'm just stopping for a couple of days to clean up. Not that there's much to do,' she added with pride as though she didn't want Albert to think she had neglected her duties while she'd been working there.

'Do you have their new address?'

'Sorry, sir, they didn't leave no forwarding address. They said they'd found somewhere temporary to rent but they might not stay there long.'

'Did they say where it was?'

She shook her head. 'I overheard the master talking on the telephone and he mentioned a place. Something Bridge?'

'Whaley Bridge? That's not far away,' Smith piped up. Albert had almost forgotten he was standing behind him. Listening.

'No, it wasn't that. It wasn't a place I knew. I said it was Bridge but it could have been Ridge. The master said it was in Cheshire.'

'Mabley Ridge?' The question was tentative, as though Albert couldn't quite bring himself to say the name.

The maid's eyes lit up in recognition. 'That could be it. Mabley Ridge.'

'Have they left anything here?'

The maid shook her head. 'The place was let furnished so the big stuff's still here. But apart from that they've taken the lot.' She frowned. 'Unusual, that. People normally leave something behind, don't they? Something they've forgotten or they don't want. Anyway, I won't have to worry about other people's mess no more. I've got a job at the mill. Regular hours and better pay. I've had enough of being at people's beck and call.'

'Did you know the last vicar, the Reverend Bell?'

Her expression softened. 'Oh yes. He was such a nice man, the old reverend. So sad about him passing away like that.'

'Do you remember him visiting this house around the time he died?'

She gave the question some thought and when she answered, Albert knew his theory had been proved right.

'Did anyone visit this house about two to three weeks ago. A middle-aged man. A stranger?'

343

She frowned, trying to remember. 'A man did arrive with the master in his motor car, but he wasn't dressed like a gentleman, although he did speak proper. Looked like a tramp, he did.'

'Can you describe him?'

'Not as tall as you. Worn clothes, worn shoes. Straggly grey hair. Beard. Smelled a bit. Like I said, I thought he was a tramp — someone who'd fallen on hard times.'

'What happened?'

'The master took him in the drawing room — which was strange, 'cause usually people like that are given something to eat in the kitchen. I hoped they weren't going to offer him a bed for the night. I mean, I wouldn't have fancied washing them clothes. Anyway, later the master came out and told me he was an old soldier from his regiment and he was going to give him some money and send him on his way.'

'Did he?'

'I suppose so, but I didn't see him go. The mistress said I'd been working hard and why didn't I take the week off to go and see my sister. Said I was to go right away. I wasn't going to argue, was I?'

'Was she usually so thoughtful?'

The maid shrugged. 'Known worse.'

Albert thanked her, raising his hat in salute and wishing her luck before he and Smith returned to the police station in silence, Albert anticipating the smirk on Teague's face when he broke the news that their birds had flown. But he wasn't giving up. There was a constable he remembered at Mabley Ridge police station,

344

Constable Mitchell, a young man who had proved his worth when he'd conducted the investigation there the previous year. Like Smith, he'd been too young to experience the horrors of war and, like Smith, he hadn't acquired the cynicism and arrogance that the likes of Teague sometimes develop as the arbiters of law and order in a small community. As soon as they entered the police station he told Smith he had a telephone call to make.

To his relief, Constable Mitchell was still stationed at Mabley Ridge and the young man seemed delighted to hear Albert's voice. His eagerness when Albert outlined what he wanted him to do reminded Albert of an enthusiastic sheepdog, waiting with pricked ears for his master's next instruction.

When Albert told Mitchell he'd better inform his sergeant, Mitchell replied that he'd received promotion and was now in charge, his pride at the news almost palpable. Albert congratulated him and said the promotion was well deserved. He was pleased for the young man.

Now it was just a matter of waiting for Albert's quarry to be found.

70

Rose

It begins today. When I was growing up my parents used to say that all you can do is tell the truth and you'll be all right, but now I fear that won't be enough. They've made up their minds that I'm guilty. And there's nothing I can do about it.

The wardresses tell me to wash and dress. They've brought me my own clothes — my best blue dress and the hat I bought in a sale in Stockport just after Christmas. That's blue too and Bert told me off for buying it, saying I had too many hats already. Then he hit me across my back so hard I fell over. Bert said it was all my fault. That's what he always said.

My barrister is shabby with a black gown that's faded to dark grey. He barely listens to a word I say and he smells of stale cigars. I can't afford an expensive one from London. The wardresses say that will go against me. They say the prosecution will get a King's Counsel who's very clever and will run rings round my man. They say I'm bound to hang.

It's time to go now. There are steep steps up to the dock and when I stand at the bottom and look up at them I feel dizzy.

I'm scared. I don't want to hang.

71

The next morning Albert was taking off his hat and coat when he was interrupted by Sergeant Teague, who burst in with a grin of triumph on his face, as though he'd been awarded some sort of prize.

'The trial starts today.'

Albert sank into his chair. During the past few days he'd been so busy pursuing his enquiries that the imminent legal process that could well end the lives of Rose Pretting and her alleged lover had been pushed to the back of his mind.

'Don't suppose it'll take long. Open-and-shut case, if you ask me.'

Albert decided not to contradict the man. He was still waiting for Mrs Greenbaum's report from London. Until then he had no solid evidence that Teague was wrong.

The sergeant left him alone with his feeling of helplessness. He was convinced of Rose Pretting's innocence but he knew those letters found in her wardrobe were bound to damn her and Kelly in the eyes of any jury.

He stared at the telephone, wondering whether to call Sam Poltimore to see whether there'd been any word from Mrs Greenbaum, but he knew Sam would let him know if there was any news.

Then there was the other call he was expecting. Sergeant Mitchell had promised to

347

make enquiries, although he knew the maid could have been wrong about Mabley Ridge and Mitchell's efforts might come to nothing.

He was sure Bert Pretting's murder was linked to his blackmailing activities and the fact that he'd kept the secret notebook that appeared to contain details of his victims' payments seemed to be evidence of the connection. There had been no full names; just a single initial beside the sums of money, so the identity of most of Pretting's victims remained a mystery. But Mrs Jenkins was the exception. The fact that her old address in Liverpool was there in full must be significant. And it was up to Albert to discover why.

After losing her husband in the war the woman had moved away from her large and comfortable home in Fulwood Park without leaving a forwarding address — like the people who may or may not have moved to Mabley Ridge. Soon after the telegram had arrived to tell Mrs Jenkins she was a widow, a man had started to visit her; a man the maid, Mavis, thought was a colleague of the late Mr Jenkins, although she'd never been told his name. Albert's instincts, honed by his years at Scotland Yard, told him he was on the right track, especially with Peggy Derwent's statement to back up his suspicions.

He was deep in thought when the telephone on his desk rang. The sudden sound made him jump and he snatched the receiver, his heart pounding.

'Inspector Lincoln speaking.'

It was Sam Poltimore and Albert pressed the receiver closer to his ear, hoping for news.

'Mrs Greenbaum called in first thing. I put her report in the post as soon as she left, so with any luck it should be with you later today.'

Albert sat up straight. 'What does it say? Was I right?'

'You were.'

'I'll wait for it to arrive then. Two people's lives depend on it.'

'And I thought you might be interested to know that Thomas Gillit — alias Tommy Gillingham — has been arrested on a charge of fraud. Found rather a lot of cash in the flat he occupied behind his so-called church. Gifts from well-wishers, he said. When I challenged him about his contact with the 'spirits', he said he was only telling people what they wanted to hear. He was in the business of keeping people happy and they paid for the privilege. I couldn't believe he was so brazen about it. He claims he's done nothing against the law, but I'm sure I can find a few charges that'll stick if I put my mind to it.' There was a long pause before Sam spoke again. 'I called on your mother-in-law to break the good news, but she wasn't in. Do you want to tell her yourself?'

Albert pondered the question. Did he really want to witness Vera's reaction when she discovered she'd been duped? The answer to that question was no. No amount of anger or revenge would bring Mary back — or their little Frederick.

'No, Sam. I think I'll leave it. She's just lost

349

Mary so there's no need to make things worse for her than they already are, eh.'

As soon as Sam rang off another call came through. This time it was from Sergeant Mitchell at Mabley Ridge. And it was good news.

72

Constable Smith's eyes lit up when Albert told him to commandeer the motor car again. The young man had taken to driving, something Albert had never felt inclined to master. For one thing his injured leg would make it difficult. For another, he was uncomfortable with the speed of motor cars, the potential loss of control.

Albert sat back in the passenger seat while Smith crunched the gears, making the engine roar louder as they drove down a series of country lanes until they reached Mabley Ridge, the village that was home to Charlotte Day. Although if — as he suspected from his conversation with Simon Fellowes — the child she'd adopted was dead, then making contact with her would cause both of them immeasurable pain.

Approaching the centre of the village they passed the gate that led to the Ridge itself, an expanse of thick woodland sheltering ancient mine workings and quarries, ending in a dramatic sandstone escarpment; a high place affording a view over Manchester's vast huddle of belching mill chimneys. It was from this place, Oak Tree Edge, that a murderer had fallen to his death all those months before, although his body had never been recovered. It was a brooding, sinister place and Albert had hoped never to set foot there again.

Mabley Ridge itself wasn't a typical Cheshire village. The small terraces clustered behind the shops in the centre mainly housed the staff who worked in the big houses that had become the village's raison d'être. With the coming of the railway, Manchester's wealthy cotton barons had built their grand houses there and when the people in the village centre called them the 'Cottontots', the title had stuck. It was there the previous September that Albert had brought a pair of killers to justice. He'd also managed to rescue a damaged young man and he'd met Gwen Davies, who'd been teaching at the village school. Mabley Ridge was filled with memories. Not all of them good.

Smith parked the motor car outside the police station and when they entered the building Albert was delighted to see Mitchell behind the polished front desk, standing proudly with his sergeant's stripes on his arm.

His open face broke into a smile as soon as he spotted Albert.

'Sir. It's good to see you again,' he said, taking Albert's offered right hand.

'And you, Mitchell. How are things in Mabley Ridge?'

'Quiet since you were here last.'

Albert hesitated. 'I don't suppose you've heard anything about Abraham Stark? Have they found the body?' The question brought back the memory of how Mitchell's predecessor, the man who'd presided over the police station for many years, had been unmasked as a ruthless killer. Together with his female accomplice he'd killed

352

anybody, including innocent children, who'd threatened to uncover their hidden obsession. The very thought of the case still chilled his heart.

'No, he was never found,' said Mitchell. 'Probably crawled off somewhere to die. Bones'll turn up eventually, I dare say.'

'Expect so,' said Albert, before going on to enquire about some of the people he'd encountered in the course of his last investigation, starting with Peter, the boy who lived in the cemetery lodge. Peter had found the body of a woman and later he'd been rescued from certain death at Stark's hands. Albert was pleased to hear that the boy was doing well and that the new schoolteacher, Gwen's replacement, had taken him under her wing.

Once he'd caught up with the news, it was time to come to the reason for his visit.

'You said you'd tracked down my suspect.'

Mitchell nodded. 'A house near the Ridge has been lying empty for a while but it's just been let furnished to new people. A couple answering the description you gave me.' He leaned forward conspiratorially. 'I can give you some men as back-up, if you need any.'

Albert thanked him and said he'd go himself with Smith — although he might need help later if it came to an arrest.

Pleasantries over, Albert told Smith to drive to the address Mitchell had provided and ten minutes later the constable brought the motor car to a halt outside a pretty brick cottage with dusty diamond-paned windows and low gables.

The small cottage garden was overgrown with weeds and the privet hedge needed trimming. Roses grew around the door but the leaves were spotted with black and the blooms dying. A motor car was parked at the side of the house in front of a tumbledown wooden shed. If this was the right place it certainly wasn't as well appointed as the occupants' last accommodation.

'Fallen on hard times?' Smith suggested as they waited at the door.

'Or they wanted to get out of Wenfield fast, which suggests they know we're on to them.'

There was no sign of life in the cottage but as Albert turned to leave a young woman appeared at the gate. She wore a cheap felt hat and a shabby grey coat and she was carrying a wicker basket over her arm. The basket looked full and heavy and when she spotted them she put it down on the ground, her eyes alight with curiosity.

'Can I help you?' she said, eyeing Smith warily. To most people a call from a policeman signified trouble.

'We're looking for the people who've taken this property. I believe they moved in yesterday.' He said the name and the girl shook her head.

'The people who've moved in are called Johnson. Mr and Mrs Johnson from Manchester — renting this place while they look for something bigger, they said.'

'You work for them?'

The girl sniffed. 'I worked for the last people and the new ones asked me to come in to help out,' she said, as though the thought of being in service was beneath her. 'Why?'

'Can you describe them?'

The thorough description she gave hinted at an observant mind. Albert thought she was a loss to the police force.

'Do you know where they are now?'

'When I saw them first thing they said they were going for a walk on the Ridge. People from town seem to like walking there, not that I can understand it — place gives me the creeps. They like the view from Oak Tree Edge, I'm told. I said to be careful,' she added with another sniff.

'What time will they be back?'

'No idea,' she said as though to emphasise that she wasn't their servant.

Albert thanked the young woman and headed back to the road as she disappeared into the house.

'I know the Ridge quite well,' he said to Smith, who was trailing behind him. 'If they've gone to Oak Tree Edge I can find the way.'

'Very well, sir.'

From Smith's tone, Albert suspected that the woman's warnings about the Ridge were making him nervous.

'On second thoughts, maybe we should wait for them here.' Albert had fought bravely in the war and his sudden attack of cowardice took him by surprise. Why should he fear a place so much when he had faced a determined enemy on the battlefield? Ashamed of his own foolishness, he began to make for the road but as soon as he reached the gate he saw two figures in the distance; a man and a woman emerging from the gate on the opposite side of the road; the gate that led to the woodland around the Ridge.

He touched Smith's sleeve and nodded towards the cottage. Concealing themselves behind the hedge would give them the advantage of surprise.

The wait seemed interminable and Albert stood silently, trying to ignore the cramp in his injured leg. He began to flex it to relieve the pain and saw Smith watching him with sympathy in his eyes. Albert stopped moving. He didn't want the young man's pity.

He could hear voices approaching, tense and argumentative. The pair were having a row.

Albert caught the words 'It's your fault' followed by 'They hadn't a clue and now we're stuck in this dump for nothing. We should have stayed put.'

The reply came swiftly and angrily. 'That inspector was sniffing around. We couldn't take the risk.'

He and Smith flattened themselves against the hedge as the gate opened with a loud creak. The couple Albert had once known as Mr and Mrs Ogden were making for the front door, too preoccupied to notice Albert and Smith standing behind them.

'We'd like to ask you a few questions, Mrs Jenkins. It is Mrs Jenkins, isn't it?'

The woman swung round, a look of horror on her face. Albert saw the man take her hand, gripping it tightly.

'I don't know what you're talking about.'

'You used the name Ogden in Wenfield and now you're calling yourselves Mr and Mrs Johnson. Why is that?'

The man who spoke gave Albert the honest smile of a practised liar. 'If you want the truth, we're in debt, old chap. On the run from our creditors. Made some bad investments and the bloody war put paid to my business.' The statement was smooth and confident. If Albert didn't possess the policeman's naturally suspicious mind, he'd probably have believed him.

'We'd better continue this conversation inside,' said Albert.

Reluctantly the couple opened the door and showed the two policemen into a low-ceilinged parlour. The room was shabby and sparsely furnished and Albert noticed several wooden packing cases piled in the corner. The maid hurried in, relieved when Mrs Ogden told her she could take the rest of the day off.

As soon as she'd gone, Albert took a seat on a dining chair and left a long silence before asking his next question. 'Have you ever been to Liverpool?'

'I've visited the city, yes.'

'Are you familiar with Fulwood Park in Aigburth?'

Mrs Ogden's eyes widened in panic. 'I don't think I . . . '

Albert recited the address. 'There's somebody there who remembers you, Mrs Ogden. Mavis still lives there. She will be able to identify you, I'm sure.'

'We don't know Fulwood Park and we

certainly don't know any servant called Mavis. We've told you the truth. We changed our name because of our creditors,' the woman said.

'I never said Mavis was a servant,' said Albert. 'I just assumed . . . '

'According to Mavis, the late Mr Jenkins was heir to quite a fortune. His father had a successful shipping business and he rented a large house for his son, even though he couldn't stand the woman he'd married. Where did the money go?'

It was the man who answered. 'We told you we don't know any Mr Jenkins. And as for where any money went, I'd take a guess at bad investments. The war.'

'Mr Jenkins' life was insured with the Mersey Life Insurance Company.'

'What's that to me?' the woman said.

'A man called Bert Pretting worked for that company. He called at the Jenkins' address; dealt with the couple's insurance matters.'

Mrs Ogden suddenly looked wary. 'What of it?'

'Bert Pretting was also a blackmailer. He was murdered.'

Albert let the words hang in the air as he watched the expressionless faces of the couple in front of him.

'Mavis told me that a gentleman started to visit you, Mrs Jenkins, after your husband was reported missing, believed dead. Was that gentleman you, Mr Ogden? Before you reply, remember that Mavis will be able to identify you.'

358

The man pressed his lips tightly together and said nothing, as though he was trying to think of a way out and failed.

'You were acquainted with the late vicar, the Reverend Bell.'

The woman gave a nervous nod.

'Did he visit you on the evening of his death?'

'Does anybody say he did?' The man's question was sharp.

'Your maid had gone to bed, but the sound of the doorbell woke her up and she came out on the landing to see who was calling. She knew the reverend's voice at once because she'd heard it every Sunday in church.'

'The man was collecting for the church roof or some such,' Mrs Jenkins said quickly. 'We felt obliged to make a contribution.'

'At that time of night? I think he came to see you on a far more delicate matter. Somebody had written to him enclosing a photograph. Now who would that be?'

'I've really no idea.'

Smith cleared his throat, but Albert ignored him.

'Somebody was looking for you, Mrs Ogden. Somebody who'd seen your photograph by chance in a newspaper. Somebody who recognised you from your past life in Liverpool.'

'That's ridiculous.'

'Copies of your wedding photograph were sent to all the clergy in the area, but of course nobody recognised you — apart from the Reverend Bell. I have a copy of that picture. The man it belonged to had lost his memory but he knew it

359

was his wife.' He took the photograph of the woman as a bride that Smith had obtained from the local vicar out of his pocket and handed it to her. 'That is you, isn't it?'

'This man could have found it anywhere. You said he'd lost his memory,' she added with a hint of triumph.

Smith bent towards Albert and whispered in his ear. 'Perhaps we should take them back to Wenfield, sir. Question them properly.'

Albert had spotted a telephone in the hallway and he told Smith to call Sergeant Mitchell and ask for back-up, somebody to help him take the couple in for questioning. When Smith looked at him enquiringly he made the excuse that he wanted to search for evidence in the cottage. He asked Smith to pick him up later.

Once Smith and a young constable from Mabley Ridge station had left with the suspects, Albert made a perfunctory search of the cottage and found a couple of box files containing various documents. He left them in the hall by the telephone, intending to take them back to Wenfield to examine them properly, when one of the boxes fell off the edge of the table, spilling its contents out onto the floor.

He'd begun to replace the papers when he spotted the corner of a photograph peeping out from behind a cardboard file. When he teased it out with his thumb and forefinger he saw that it was the photograph of a man, carefully posed in a photographer's studio. He was sitting on a grand chair against a painted backdrop depicting the library of a stately home, a pile of learned books beside him on a table. His suit looked expensive and he looked every inch the respected pillar of society. Albert turned the photograph over and saw that it had been taken in a studio in Bold Street — the same studio Henry Billinge had used. He studied the man's image again, wondering if this could be the man found naked and mutilated at the Devil's Dancers. He was the right build with similar hair and Albert was as sure as he could be that this was the man who Peggy Derwent had seen being picked up in Alastair Ogden's motor car. But he needed proof — and he'd get it, even if he had to bring Mavis to Wenfield to identify her previous employer, and Alastair Ogden, the man Albert was sure had started visiting Mrs Jenkins after her husband had been reported dead.

He took his watch from his pocket. He had to know for sure whether his son by Flora was alive or dead and he had enough time before Smith's return. He'd committed Charlotte Day's address to memory. It had been too important to forget.

The sun had just emerged from behind the clouds and it was shining down weakly as Albert walked in the direction of the village. His last visit had made him familiar with the various large houses that lined the road to the Ridge, so he knew the whereabouts of Poldean House. It lay down a small cul-de-sac not far from the house where, the previous September, a lady's companion had fallen victim to a terrible murder.

Now as Albert walked down the street it struck him that maybe his lost son had been there when he was last in Mabley Ridge, a hundred yards away from him without him knowing.

He wasn't sure what he was going to do when he got there. Would he knock on the door and ask to see Mrs Day? Would he pretend to be undertaking an enquiry so he could gain access to the house and maybe catch a glimpse of the child who might be his and Flora's son. Or would it be a house in mourning for another child lost to influenza? His thoughts were in turmoil, veering between excitement and dread as he walked up the drive, his shoes crunching on the gravel, announcing his arrival. As soon as he reached the front door, shaking with nerves, his courage failed him and he turned to go. Then suddenly he heard a young child's gurgling laughter. A joyful sound that dispelled all thoughts of death and war.

Albert stationed himself behind a hedge watching as a uniformed nursemaid placed a child in a shiny pram, solid as a motor car, and strapped him in for safety. If there had been any doubt in his mind it vanished now. The resemblance to Frederick was uncanny as the child gazed at his nursemaid with eyes so like Flora's that it made him feel like weeping.

The scene blurred as the tears welled up and he stood there, hidden from sight and unable to move from the spot.

73

Rose

The judge looks at me as though I'm a nasty insect he's discovered in his soup, and the jury, all men dressed in grey and black, glare disapprovingly too. At least I have my darling Ronald beside me in the dock, although he does not look at me. He stands up straight, staring ahead, and from time to time he passes a note to his barrister, who flaps about in front of the jury like an oily crow. My barrister speaks quietly in a high-pitched voice. I don't think the jury will be swayed by him.

The barrister for the Crown also looks like a carrion bird; a fat, malevolent one who feeds on dead lambs in the spring. He calls me terrible names and I can say nothing in my defence. I am supposed to leave that to my shabby man who stays silent most of the time.

This morning a doctor described how Bert died. All the times I'd imagined him dying, I never thought of the reality of what would be done to his body. They say my Ronald did it. They say he has no alibi for the time because his housekeeper had gone to bed and had taken something to help her sleep; something pre-scribed by him they say — which they claim is proof that he wanted her out of the way. They say I couldn't have stabbed Bert because his killer was much taller, so I must have had an accomplice. And they think that accomplice was Ronald.

I'd hoped the inspector from Scotland Yard would be here, but I haven't seen him. Sergeant Teague said he was only in Wenfield to find that missing Member of Parliament and now he's turned up safe and well he'll probably go back to London.

I've asked again for some books to read and they say that once I'm in the condemned cell I can have anything I want.

74

Albert was hardly aware of what he was doing when he followed the nursemaid out of the grounds and watched her turn the pram in the direction of the Ridge.

He kept some distance behind, driven by an urge to be near the child — his and Flora's flesh and blood. At that moment he didn't have any sort of plan — just the need to see his son.

To his surprise, the nursemaid carried on towards the gate that led to the Ridge itself. With his knowledge of what had happened there only months before, he felt it was no place to take an infant. But at least he was there to protect the boy if anything should happen.

He carried on walking, unaware of soft footsteps behind him. The stealthy footsteps of a predator tracking his prey. Suddenly he lost sight of nursemaid and pram. He'd been reluctant to follow too closely so he assumed that she'd slipped out of sight down one of the paths running between the trees towards the other gate that led back to the road and the tea room that was so popular with the visitors from Manchester who came there to walk in the fine weather. Albert had wandered too far into the woodland and he was suddenly alone in the landscape that still featured in his nightmares. His heart pounding, he speeded up, desperate to find them again.

Somehow he took a wrong turning and found

himself at Oak Tree Edge, where he came to a halt, awed by the view; the smoke from Manchester's distant chimneys hanging over the town like a thick mist. There was no sign of nursemaid and baby now. But a figure was emerging from the trees behind him.

It was a big man with a long, straggling beard wearing a tattered army greatcoat. Albert had seen many men like him on the streets of London, begging or selling matches, and he always tried to give them a kind word and some loose change. There but for the grace of God went anyone who'd returned from France with wounds, visible and invisible, and had no family willing or able to care for them.

Albert turned to face the man, assuming he'd come to Mabley Ridge to try his luck at the back doors of the big houses where some cook or housemaid might take pity on him and provide him with food. Likewise, a lot of farms in the area would allow him to sleep warm and safe in a barn in exchange for a day's labour.

'Hello, my friend,' said Albert. He might not be in a position to help the man, but at least he could treat him as he'd wish to be treated himself.

But the man didn't answer. As he walked slowly forward, staring ahead with cold eyes, there was a malevolence about him that sent a thrill of fear through Albert's body. And something else; something familiar. As the man came closer, Albert suddenly realised he'd seen him in that very place the previous September.

'I never thought you'd be stupid enough to

come back to Mabley Ridge.' Albert was trying his best to keep his voice calm and even. 'Aren't you afraid you'll be recognised?'

'Did you recognise me?' the man asked with a smirk. 'Thought not. I'm a new man now. Changed my name to Aloysius Spring. But I haven't forgotten the man responsible for my Ethel's death. Hanging's not a pretty way to go.'

The vicious hatred in the man's eyes made Albert shrink back as though he'd been struck. He was between the murderer he'd once known as Abraham Stark and the long drop to the rocks below. He moved slowly away from the edge. He needed to keep the man talking.

'Lots of people will remember you around here. You were a prominent man in Mabley Ridge. Everyone knew you. The station sergeant everyone trusted.'

'Memories fade. And admit it, even you didn't know me when I gave you a good hiding in London.'

'That was you?'

The man smiled but didn't answer.

'What do you want?'

Stark ignored the question. 'Once I've dealt with my unfinished business I'm going back to London. Or Manchester. Anywhere big and anonymous. Maybe I'll make something of myself. I put all that on hold in the hope that one day I'd be able to avenge Ethel. I would have finished the job in London if we hadn't been so rudely interrupted, but you won't get away so easily this time. And once I've dealt with you, I'll be a free man.'

'How did you escape? I saw you fall,' Albert asked, playing for time.

'Some might say I had the luck of the devil. I was winded but I'd landed on a ledge, so I escaped with little more than a twisted ankle. Hid up in Farmer Brace's barn until the fuss died down, then I caught the train to London.' His lips formed an unpleasant sneer. 'Not much of a detective, are you, Lincoln? I've been keeping an eye on you down there and you never even realised. Tracked you up to Derbyshire as well. With that limp of yours, you're an easy man to follow.'

Albert was aware of his adversary edging closer. In spite of living rough for so long, he still looked powerful.

'Ethel deserved all she got. She was a killer.'

'She disposed of inconvenient people. People who didn't matter.'

'She killed an innocent child.'

Albert could see the fury burning in Stark's eyes. Albert had been the one who'd brought his lover to justice so, in his mind, he was the guilty one. No argument could prevail against that kind of twisted obsession. He needed to get away from there. Fast.

Stark was coming for him now, his greatcoat flapping out like the wings of a bird of prey. Closer and closer, determined to knock Albert over the edge into oblivion. Nobody knew he was there, and he suddenly felt alone and more vulnerable than he'd ever felt before. Even in the trenches at least he'd had his comrades.

With a primal roar, Stark descended on him,

arms outstretched, hands like grasping claws. Albert braced himself for the impact and when it came he felt himself being thrust backwards towards the long drop to the rocks below. He doubted whether he'd have Stark's luck and land on a ledge halfway down. He'd die, probably slowly, of his injuries.

The wounds sustained in battle had weakened his body. As a younger man, he would have wrestled his adversary with an even chance of coming off best. But now his hand throbbed and his leg felt useless as Stark tightened his grip on his right arm, steering him towards certain death. Albert shut his eyes and let his body go limp, preparing for the inevitable while praying for a miracle as he had so often on the battlefield. Then suddenly he felt the man release his hold as he stumbled and uttered an oath. Albert seized his chance and threw his weight to one side. He opened his eyes to see that the momentum had made his adversary topple forward and vanish from sight. Gone.

Albert crawled to the edge, hardly aware of the vast vista of green Cheshire fields with the smoking chimneys of Manchester in the distance. He lay on his stomach to look down into the abyss. This time Stark's devil's luck had abandoned him. His body was lying spread-eagled a hundred feet below. Perfectly still with a slick of fresh blood spreading around his head like the halo of a wicked saint.

75

Albert limped back to the road then down the hill into the village, ending up at the police station where he'd arranged to wait for Smith to arrive with the motor car to take him back to Wenfield. A constable he didn't recognise was stationed behind the front desk and he wondered whether to report what had happened; to tell him that the body of the sergeant who'd once presided over that very station — the man who'd been presumed dead ever since he'd been unmasked as a murderer — was lying at the foot of Oak Tree Edge.

He knew where his duty should lie. On the other hand, as far as the police were concerned, Stark had died the previous September. Besides, he really couldn't face reliving his ordeal, so when the constable asked him what he'd been doing to get himself into such a state he lied and said he'd fallen. All he wanted was to get back to Wenfield to question his suspects and he also needed to clear the names of an innocent man and woman before the judge placed the black cap on his head and pronounced the sentence of death.

He was relieved when Smith and Mitchell returned, having deposited the Ogdens in the cells at Wenfield police station. The two young police officers seemed to have established a friendship and they shook hands heartily before parting. Albert watched them, glad that they'd both been too young to experience the horrors of war; confident that nothing like that would ever blight young lives again.

On the drive back he found himself thinking of his son, seeing the boy's face each time he closed his eyes. He managed to field Smith's enquiries about the state of his clothes, telling the same lie as he'd told the constable at Mabley Ridge. The body of Abraham Stark would be found soon enough, he supposed, and his death would, no doubt, be treated as a mystery — although it was one puzzle Albert had no desire to help them solve.

As soon as they reached Wenfield, Albert asked Sergeant Teague whether there were any letters for him. The sergeant produced a large envelope bearing a London postmark.

Albert took it into his office and tore it open, impatiently scanning the contents. To his relief, the evidence was there: the handwriting on the letters found in the bottom of Rose Pretting's wardrobe did not match that of Dr Ronald Kelly. In Mrs Greenbaum's expert opinion, the letters had been written by Rose herself, slightly disguising her writing. Albert couldn't help smiling as he returned the report to its envelope. Now all he had to do was make sure the jury believed in Mrs Greenbaum's expertise.

He checked his watch. It was too late to put the information before the court that day, so it would have to wait until tomorrow. But there was something else he could check in the meantime. He went to his office door and called to Teague to find him a magnifying glass. The sergeant looked puzzled but obliged without question. Once he'd gone, Albert made a detailed examination of the photograph he'd found at the Mabley Ridge cottage — the man who'd posed in the same Bold Street studio as Henry Billinge. And when he'd finished, he sat back in his seat, confident he now had the proof he needed.

The couple he knew as the Ogdens were waiting in the cells and Albert saw no reason to delay the interview any longer. Half an hour later he was sitting opposite the woman in the claustrophobic room used to interview suspects. He'd been in that room before; he'd even faced the woman he'd loved across the same table when she'd been unmasked as a killer. The small windowless chamber held a lot of bitter memories, but at that moment he tried to forget them.

He had the photograph from the Mabley Ridge cottage in his pocket and he placed it on the table in front of the woman. 'Who is this?'

'I don't know.'

'It was found among your papers.'

She gave a shrug.

'This photograph was taken at a studio in Bold Street in Liverpool. That's where you used to live.'

She shook her head vigorously. 'My husband's visited Liverpool on business, but I don't know the city at all.'

'And yet this photograph of a man was taken there and it was in your possession.' He paused.

'I've had a chance to study it in detail. The subject has a blemish on his right hand. Some sort of birthmark. It's quite clear. The right hand of the dead man found naked and mutilated at the Devil's Dancers bore an identical mark. The photograph is of that man. What's his name?'

'I don't know.'

'The maid, Mavis, told me about the birthmark Mr Jenkins had on his hand. Do I have to get her over here to identify the photograph — and identify you as the man's wife and her previous employer?'

Albert could tell the woman was searching frantically for a plausible answer. He folded his arms and leaned back, apparently relaxed. Eventually she spoke, the words flooding out.

'How was I to know my husband had survived? I'd had a telegram from the War Office, telling me he was dead. I moved on with my life and married Alastair.' She blushed. 'Alastair and I had been . . . friends for a while when I received the news of Geoffrey's death. We thought it would cause a scandal in Liverpool if I was seen to re-marry with such haste, so we came to Derbyshire where nobody knew us. Alastair had often visited the area as a child and said it was a lovely part of the world. Then a few weeks ago Geoffrey turned up out of the blue saying he'd survived but he'd lost his memory. I panicked. I'd claimed the insurance money and inherited all the money his father left him, and now I learned that I'd committed bigamy when I married Alastair. But honestly, Inspector, I had no idea he was still alive when we married. I swear I didn't know until he turned up that evening. You have to believe me.'

Albert looked her in the eye. 'When Geoffrey was in hospital in Buxton he saw your photograph in a newspaper, along with Mr Ogden, who was a former employee at his father's shipping company. Unlike your husband, Alastair Ogden hadn't gone to war because of a health problem.' He paused. 'You were having an affair with him while your husband was away at the front. In my opinion, that's pretty despicable behaviour.'

'I was lonely.'

'So were a lot of other women.' Albert usually tried not to judge people but on this occasion he couldn't help himself.

'Geoffrey had lost his memory but gradually he started to remember certain things about his former life — his house in Fulwood Park, for instance. He left hospital and set out to find you, and when he called at his old home the present tenant told him you'd moved to this area. Eventually he came to Wenfield where he was spotted by Alastair Ogden, who picked him up in his motor car. Ogden brought him home and the two of you decided to dispose of him.'

Margaret Ogden didn't bother with a denial. Instead she sat in silence with her head bowed.

'It wasn't the first time you'd killed to keep your secret, was it? Six months earlier you poisoned the Reverend Bell.'

Her eyes widened. 'That was Alastair. He panicked when the vicar came round saying he'd had a letter from my husband. I didn't know

374

how Geoffrey found out I was in the area, but he'd written to the vicar asking if I was living in his parish and enclosed a photograph of me on our wedding day; one that Geoffrey must have kept with him when he went to France. Mr Bell recognised it at once and came to see us. He said he hadn't told anyone yet because it was his duty to respect confidences. But he told Alastair that unless we came clean he'd be obliged to inform the authorities.'

'Why kill him?'

'Alastair said we had no choice — the reverend was an honest man, we'd never be able to bribe him to keep quiet. And once he went to the authorities, not only would we have to give back the insurance money and the money I'd inherited that should have been Geoffrey's, we would have been sent to prison for bigamy. If the truth came out, it would have ruined us.'

'So you poisoned the vicar?'

'No. I mean, Alastair did. I honestly didn't know he'd done it. He didn't tell me until afterwards, and I was horrified. You have to believe me.'

'The vicar was given laudanum.'

'I take it to help me sleep. Alastair told me he'd put some in the reverend's whisky. When he left, it was beginning to affect him, but I tried to put it out of my mind. Alastair made sure he kept the letter and the photograph so there was no proof, and we hoped that was the end of the matter.'

'Until your first husband turned up in Wenfield six months later. Did he recognise

Alastair when he picked him up?'

'He said he was sure he recognised him from somewhere and asked if he knew where I was, because he was looking for me. Alastair brought him home.'

'And Geoffrey didn't realise he was walking into a trap?'

She bowed her head and Albert saw tears trickling down her cheeks.

'It's been a strain . . . living with what we've done.'

'When Alastair brought him home, you told the maid to take time off to visit her sister. You didn't want any witnesses to what you were about to do. What happened when you met Geoffrey?'

'He just stood there as though he didn't know what to say, but I could tell he'd recognised me. As the evening went on I realised how much he'd changed, not only in appearance but his whole manner. He was brusque, bad-tempered. Unpredictable. One moment he was trying to take my hand, the next holding his head and sobbing. I was afraid of what would happen if he found out Alastair and I were . . . '

'War changes people. What did you do?'

'We told Geoffrey he could stay while we worked out what to do. As far as Geoffrey was concerned, I was his wife and he expected me to look after him. He had a bath then he asked me to cut his hair. He said he'd been living rough for a few weeks while he was searching for me and he was tired of looking like a tramp. Then I gave him some of Alastair's old clothes and once he was dressed he said he felt much better.'

376

'You poisoned him.'

'He stayed with us about a week, but we realised we needed to deal with the situation. Geoffrey kept asking Alastair what he was doing there. I think he was starting to remember who he was. Alastair had worked at Geoffrey's father's firm, you see. That's how we met. We both knew that if Geoffrey left the house he'd give the game away and ruin everything.' Her eyes started to fill with tears of self-pity. 'Alastair kept telling me that people go to prison for bigamy, but if Geoffrey was out of the way permanently then nobody need ever know and we'd be safe for ever. As far as the authorities were aware, Geoffrey was dead anyway. Alastair said that if I left them alone together he'd deal with the problem.'

'So that's what you did.'

'I went up to bed and I thought they were having a drink together. I thought Alastair intended to buy him off.'

'With money that was rightfully his?'

She ignored the question. 'I came downstairs just as they were both leaving the house. Alastair said Geoffrey wasn't feeling well so he was taking him to see Dr Kelly. Only he told me later that he'd given him a large dose of laudanum and led him to the Devil's Dancers. He waited until he was dead then he made sure nobody could identify him.' She put her head in her hands. 'It's not my fault. It was all his idea.'

'What about Bert Pretting?'

She looked up, her expression suddenly dark. 'He was a horrible man. He called at the house

377

one day saying he recognised me from Liverpool. When he'd worked in insurance he'd called at our house in Fulwood Park to see Geoffrey on business. I remembered that I hadn't liked him then. He was cocky, full of himself. He had no respect.'

'So you killed him too.'

'He started demanding money to keep silent. He said he'd seen Geoffrey getting into Alastair's motor car and he'd recognised him as my husband. Said that if Geoffrey was still alive then Alastair and I must be living in sin — or worse, committing bigamy. We paid him. What else could we do?'

'The trouble with blackmailers is that they keep coming back for more. You had to put a stop to it.'

She shook her head. 'Can you really imagine me stabbing someone in an alleyway?'

'I expect you got Alastair to do it. He seems to have done all your dirty work, Mrs Jenkins.'

'Alastair was with me all that night.'

'Can you prove it?'

'You'll have to take my word for it.'

Albert leapt to his feet, sending his chair skidding backwards with a loud scraping sound on the linoleum floor.

'I wouldn't take your word for anything.'

He strode out of the room, no longer able to face the woman who'd been complicit in the murder of her innocent husband and the gentle Reverend Bell. He knew he was going to have to break the news to Mrs Bell and it was something he was dreading.

He told Smith to return the woman to the cells. His next task would be to interview Alastair Ogden, but before he faced him he needed a break. He returned to the Black Horse where Mrs Jackson looked surprised when he asked for a brandy.

'We're not serving yet, Inspector. You should know that.'

'I won't tell anyone if you don't.'

Mrs Jackson gave him a conspiratorial smile and went behind the bar to pour the drink.

'On the house, sir,' she said as Albert delved into his pocket. 'You look as though you need it.'

76

Rose

My barrister came to tell me he had good news. He had a telephone call from Inspector Lincoln to say that there's new evidence. Something to do with a handwriting expert from London. He didn't give me any details but he said the inspector would bring the evidence to him in time for the trial tomorrow. Tonight I'm going to say my prayers like I used to when I was younger — before I met Bert who told me that sort of thing was rubbish and I was stupid for doing it.

How I wish I could speak to my darling Ronald, but when he stands beside me in the dock he won't look at me.

Soon, though, we'll be free to live and love as we choose.

77

Margaret Ogden blamed Alastair Ogden, and Alastair Ogden blamed Margaret Ogden. According to him, she was a woman who could poison without conscience. He claimed he'd tried to stop her but she'd been determined. Poison was a woman's weapon, wasn't it? That proved he was telling the truth. She should be the one who was due for an appointment with the hangman, not him.

With each blaming the other, Albert had no choice but to charge them both and leave it to the court to decide who was lying. Yet, to his surprise, although Ogden admitted that Pretting had been demanding money in return for his silence — bleeding them white was how he put it — they both denied his murder. Albert was tempted to add Pretting's murder to the charge sheet, but something stopped him. He would hold that one in reserve.

As for the case against Rose Pretting and Ronald Kelly, Mrs Greenbaum's evidence appeared to prove that Rose was a fantasist, a woman whose miserable marriage had caused her to take refuge in stories of romance. The letters had been written by Rose herself, disguising her handwriting slightly so she could make believe they were written by a lover. It looked as though Dr Kelly was guilty of little more than the crime of being handsome, single and sympathetic. Rose had projected her dreams onto him and he probably hadn't even been aware of it.

He hoped Mrs Greenbaum's expert evidence, together with the likelihood that the Ogdens had disposed of Bert Pretting because of his blackmail attempt, would be enough to see Rose and Kelly acquitted and released from custody the next day. However, it would depend on the judge and jury. In Albert's experience, the justice system moved at the pace of a snail and could be unpredictable.

He left the station without telling Teague where he was going and made his way back to the Black Horse. His fight with Stark on Oak Tree Edge had drained him of energy and he was desperate to return to his room and sleep, preferably after taking a bath to soothe his aching limbs.

The green-tiled bathroom at the end of the upstairs corridor was shared with other guests, but there was nobody about so he ran the bath and relaxed in the warm water, eyes closed, thinking of the case. He hadn't yet broken the news of the Ogdens' arrest to Mrs Bell. She'd known her husband's killers as a highly respectable couple; a pair she'd dined with at Tarnhey Court, which was bound to make the news even more shocking.

But Mrs Bell would have to wait because first he had to attend court in Manchester to ensure Mrs Greenbaum's evidence was heard. At least having so many things to occupy his mind stopped him brooding about the child he'd seen in Mabley Ridge — the boy with Flora's eyes. He'd found his son at last and yet he had no idea what to do about the discovery.

The water was growing cold, so he hauled himself out of the bathtub and reached for the towel, looking down at his scarred body and glad that the Jacksons hadn't thought to provide a full-length mirror. His mangled leg ached as he dried himself and put on his clothes. The hot water had aggravated the sensitive flesh which stood out shiny and red. As he stared down at his injuries he felt a stab of despair. He'd almost been within touching distance of his lost son, the thing he'd dreamed about ever since he'd found out about the boy's existence. It had seemed then that he had been given a chance, however small, of replacing his lost Frederick. But things were never that simple.

He was unsure how Charlotte would react; she was the child's mother now. Then there was Charlotte's war hero husband. What would he think of a man who turned up out of the blue wanting a role in the boy's life — carrying a reminder of the child's unfortunate origins?

He slept fitfully that night, Mrs Jackson's sausage and mash, excellent though it was, lying heavy on his stomach. He had a nightmare about fighting Abraham Stark on Oak Tree Edge — a nightmare that ended in Albert plummeting to his death rather than the killer. He awoke suddenly with a looming sense of fear, as though he was in the presence of some creeping unseen threat.

When the morning came he dragged himself out of his twisted sheets, evidence of a restless night. He arrived downstairs to find that there was a new guest already tucking into his bacon and eggs. He didn't look like the usual sort who visited the mills on business, and when Albert nodded to him the man stood up and walked across to his table.

'You're the Scotland Yard man, aren't you? I understand you found Henry Billinge in a nice little love nest. Am I right?'

'Who told you that?'

The man, young and florid in a checked suit, tapped the side of his nose. 'I never reveal my sources. Am I right? I'd like to talk to the lady in question — hear her side of the story. In the interests of the public, of course. We need to know whether our politicians can be trusted, don't we?' He held out his hand. 'Jerry Buckle, by the way. *Manchester Clarion*. Weren't you the detective who arrested that Flora Winsmore back in 1919? I'm sure my readers would like the inside story of that particular case. Can we arrange an interview?'

Albert ignored the question, but the man carried on.

'And I hear you've charged someone with the murder of that tramp they found in the cave. Are you going to tell me who it is?'

'The press'll be informed in due course.'

Albert stood up just as Mrs Jackson bustled in with his breakfast. 'Sorry, Mrs Jackson. I've got to go.'

He saw the look of disappointment on the

reporter's face but going hungry was preferable to enduring one minute more in his company. He made straight for the station where he rushed into his office and slumped in his seat, surprised that the encounter with the reporter had disturbed him so much. He was used to hard-faced journalists at Scotland Yard — Fleet Street was full of them. But something Buckle said had got to him. Perhaps it was the mention of Flora, a subject still as raw as the flesh on his injured leg.

He tried to forget the incident. He was going to court in Manchester that morning, sure that the evidence he'd provided would alter the course of the trial. When he asked Smith to drive him, Teague didn't look too happy about his constable taking orders from the man he considered to be an outsider. But Albert had more important things to worry about than the sergeant's sensibilities.

By the time he made it to the court, the trial was about to resume. He had Mrs Greenbaum's report with him and when he asked to see Rose Pretting's defence counsel, the man pored over the file with a widening smile on his face.

'This is pretty conclusive. The woman's been living in a fantasy world. Too much reading, if you ask me. She keeps going on about wanting her books. Doesn't seem to realise the gravity of her situation.'

The man shook Albert's hand and said he'd see that the new evidence was presented to the court. He seemed confident, but Albert wondered if he always acted that way; keeping up the appearance of optimism even in the most hopeless cases.

Albert was tempted to stay for a while and watch the trial from the public gallery, but he had things to do back in Wenfield. He'd just have to trust Rose's barrister to present the evidence properly. He'd done his bit and now things were out of his control.

78

Rose

It seems like a miracle. My barrister read out the report, strutting proudly in front of the jury who, I must say, looked convinced. But my barrister says you can never tell for sure until the verdict comes back. Sometimes juries surprise you, he said.

A lady from London, a Mrs Greenbaum who's a handwriting expert often consulted by Scotland Yard, examined the letters from my wardrobe. When she compared them with samples of my own writing and Ronald's, she said it was obvious I'd written them myself. My barrister said this was evidence that I'd been playing out a romantic fantasy, fuelled by my love of novels. He even called Miss Hubbard from the library to say what sort of books I liked to read and how often I went there. He made me sound quite mad. But escaping from reality is never mad when reality is so terrible. Even being in prison is better than putting up with Bert. A lot of people would call that a wicked thing to think, and say that he was my husband till death did us part. But his death came as such a relief. I've been told to act like a grieving widow in front of the jury and I keep dabbing my eyes with my handkerchief. I hope it does the trick. Sometimes I catch Ronald glancing at me. His glance is cold, as though he hates me for all the trouble I've caused him. But I know that's a pretence as well.

My barrister tells me the police have arrested someone for the murder of that man we found in the cave. He says they killed the old vicar too, which came as a shock. He says Bert was a blackmailer and that's why they killed him, and he says their arrest, coupled with the handwriting evidence, is good for me. The more doubt we can put in the minds of the jury, the better.

When the judge says it's time for lunch and I'm taken down to the cells again, I notice the manner of one of the wardresses has softened. She even gives me a smile before leaving me alone and locking the door. It's as though she knows I'm innocent and I'll soon be a free woman.

79

Albert hadn't heard from Henry Billinge MP since their meeting in the Lake District and he'd had little time to wonder when the man would return to public life. However, when he arrived at the Black Horse that evening and picked up the newspaper lying on the sideboard in Mrs Jackson's saloon bar, a headline caught his eye. Billinge had resigned from his seat for personal reasons. There was to be a by-election in Liverpool East.

Albert smiled to himself, thinking of Anne Billinge. He'd liked the woman and he knew she'd ensure the situation was treated with discretion to avoid a public scandal. He wondered whether Sir William Cartwright would do his bit to support his erstwhile friend, or whether Sir William's shabby treatment of Clara would continue to come between them. Whatever the case, it was none of Albert's business. He'd established Billinge was alive and well, so he'd done his duty as far as Scotland Yard was concerned. What the various parties decided to do in the future was up to them, although it did worry him that, should the truth emerge about the nature of his relationship with his private secretary, Henry Billinge might face imprisonment for a crime that Albert didn't think warranted the name.

Before leaving Wenfield police station that

evening he'd received a telephone call to say that the jury in Rose's and Kelly's trial had retired to consider their verdict. He felt unusually nervous about it, even though he was convinced of their innocence. In his opinion, Alastair Ogden had disposed of Bert Pretting because he was the victim of blackmail. Pretting hadn't realised he was dealing with people who'd killed before. That had been his grave mistake.

He was about to make for his room when, to his horror, Jerry Buckle walked through the hotel entrance, his small eyes lighting up as soon as he saw his prey.

'I saw you at the trial this morning.'

'I didn't see you,' said Albert, as he put the newspaper back where he'd found it.

'Jury's out.'

'So I've heard.'

'I understand you arrested the little tart and her fancy man, is that true? The village doctor! Who'd have thought it? And that doctor's daughter lived in the same house back in 1919. Wonder if that house is cursed. The House of the Hanged Woman, eh? Just like she wrote in those letters that were read out in court. Like the painting — *The House of the Hanged Man* — the letter said. Who'd have thought Mrs Pretting would know about something like that — in French and all. Mind you, she did spend a lot of time in that library — when she wasn't up to other things.' The reporter's eyes were glowing with what looked like lust, no doubt picturing Rose Pretting's alleged sins and the headlines he'd be able to write about them if the jury's verdict went against her.

Albert felt his heart rate quicken. 'Until the trial's over I can't discuss it. You'll have to attend court like everyone else.'

'But then I'd have exactly the same story as my rivals. I'm looking for background; the story behind the story.' He paused. 'If you don't say anything, I'll make it up.'

'You do that.'

He climbed the stairs to his room. Since his arrival in Wenfield the Black Horse had seemed like a haven. But Buckle's appearance on the scene had changed that. He kicked off his shoes and lay on his bed, wondering how he could avoid the man at dinner.

Exhausted, he closed his eyes and a phrase began to echo through his head. Jerry Buckle's words had triggered a faint memory; something about the letters Rose Pretting had written to herself. But the more he tried to remember what it was the more it eluded him. In the end, hunger got the better of him. Despite the risk of running into the reporter, he decided to go downstairs for dinner and then retire for an early night.

Luckily there was no sign of Buckle in the dining room. When Mrs Jackson put his plate in front of him, he asked where his fellow guest was. He'd eaten early, she said. Then he'd gone to the Cartwright Arms to look for someone who knew Bert Pretting, eager to get a new angle for his story. It was clear from her face she shared Albert's distaste for the man, but he said nothing.

He didn't sleep well that night. His work in

Wenfield was almost done and yet he felt uneasy. Perhaps it was the thought that he'd soon have to return to London to get on with his life. A life without Mary, living alone in the house they'd once shared. At least he'd set eyes on his son at last; he had to find some consolation in that.

The following morning he arrived at the station, having avoided Buckle at breakfast. When he asked for another word with the Ogdens, Sergeant Teague didn't look pleased but he raised no objection.

'Jury'll be back in the Pretting case soon,' he said to Albert's disappearing back. 'The bitch'll hang. No doubt about it.'

Albert didn't reply. He waited in the interview room for the Ogdens to be brought to him. He would speak to them together; easier to see how they reacted to the other's words.

'Bert Pretting,' he began as soon as they were seated in front of him. 'Who made the decision to kill him?'

'Neither of us,' Alastair Ogden replied swiftly. 'We've already told you. We didn't do it.'

'You killed the Reverend Bell and Geoffrey Jenkins.'

'We panicked.' Margaret Jenkins bowed her head. 'We could see no other way. The vicar was an honest man. He'd never have kept silent.'

'What about your husband, Geoffrey? Was that a spur of the moment thing too?'

'He could have ruined us,' said Alastair.

'So could Bert Pretting.'

'Pretting was greedy. Money would have dealt with him.'

Albert sat back in his seat, his eyes fixed on Ogden's face. 'I don't think you want to admit to such a sordid murder, do you, Mr Ogden? A knife in an alley. Hardly the sort of crime a person of your class commits, am I right?'

'Quite right,' the woman said quickly.

Albert resisted the urge to smile at the discovery that there was snobbery even in murder.

There was a knock and Smith poked his head round the door. Albert told the constable who'd been standing in the interview room to return the prisoners to their cells, and hurried out to hear what Smith had to say.

'The jury, sir. They haven't come back yet.'

Albert thought for a moment. 'Can you drive me to the court? Best you don't let Sergeant Teague know where you're going.'

Smith nodded eagerly and Albert wondered whether he was eager to get away from Teague. He'd felt an atmosphere between the two men, but he'd put it down to Teague's resentment towards the up-and-coming youngster.

It took them an hour to get to court and take their places in the public gallery. Jerry Buckle was in the front row, leaning over to get the best view, his pencil poised over his notebook. Albert suspected the reporter was longing for a guilty verdict because it would make a better story. He knew from experience how much the public relished the hanging of an attractive young woman.

It wasn't long before the jury filed in, their faces serious, and Albert began to wonder whether the male jury's disapproval of an unfaithful wife would trump Mrs Greenbaum's evidence.

He saw Rose Pretting and Ronald Kelly being brought up from the cells and watched them standing in the dock, both looking ahead as though they were pretending the other wasn't there. Kelly's expression was blank and devoid of emotion. Rose, in contrast, looked terrified.

The courtroom was filled with hushed expectation as the jury took their seats, leaving only their foreman standing.

'Have you reached a verdict upon which you are all agreed?' The question was asked in sepulchral tones.

The foreman of the jury replied in a reedy voice that belied his stern appearance. 'We have.'

'Do you find the defendant Rose Pretting guilty or not guilty?'

The answer caused a gasp from the public gallery.

'Do you find the defendant Ronald Kelly guilty or not guilty?'

When the words 'not guilty' were pronounced again there was another gasp which sounded like relief. The pair, the judge said, were free to go. Albert wondered if he was fingering the unseen black cap with disappointment.

Kelly and Rose stood as still as the waxworks of murderers Albert had seen in the Chamber of Horrors at Madame Tussauds. After a few seconds the verdict sank in and Rose slumped onto the chair that had been placed behind her, apparently in a faint. Kelly immediately came to her aid, his hand on her wrist to feel her pulse. The gesture was tender, even loving, and Albert watched with fascination until Smith nudged his arm.

'Better be off, sir. Beat the rush.'

Albert nodded and followed the young man out, deep in thought.

They drove back to Wenfield in silence until they reached the outskirts of the village.

'Think the jury got it right, sir?' Smith said.

'The handwriting evidence seemed conclusive. Mrs Greenbaum's an acknowledged expert. Scotland Yard's consulted her many times.'

'Doctors' handwriting's always unreadable anyway. They're known for it, aren't they?'

Albert didn't reply.

80

Rose

It is over. And we are victorious.

When the foreman of the jury was standing there looking so solemn I thought it had all gone wrong. I didn't dare to look at my darling Ronald in case I betrayed the truth. Only after the verdict did I succumb to my emotions and it was so wonderful to feel his touch once more, knowing we were safe at last.

I'm so glad my darling insisted that I copy out his letters and destroy the originals. He knew everyone would recognise his terrible doctor's writing if they were ever found. But I didn't mind; his spidery scrawl was so hard to make out that copying them made it easy for me to read them over and over again.

I have the inspector from Scotland Yard to thank for our freedom. If he hadn't decided to send the letters to that lady expert in London, we might have been done for.

Now that I'm safe I can be like the heroines in my books, living happily ever after with the man I love; the man who had killed for me as a knight would slay a dragon for his lady. He waited for Bert and thrust a kitchen knife between his ribs when Bert went down an alley to relieve himself after a night drinking at the Carty Arms. He knew the best way to make sure the knife hit its mark. He is a doctor, after all.

We will both leave Wenfield after a suitable interval, of course. Ronald — I must get used to calling him that — says it would be foolish to parade our love in front of the village gossips even though the law cannot touch us now. He told me that once you have been acquitted of a crime you cannot be tried for it again, so we are perfectly safe — provided we commit no other murders and I don't think that is at all likely.

He says I must play the devoted widow for a while and he is certain the Ogdens, who have so shocked the village with their wickedness, will get the blame for Bert's death.

I will go to the library now and take out more books to read. My books will have to suffice until Ronald and I can be together. The library is my castle of stories. Where else would I have found the perfect answer to all my problems?

81

Albert stood in front of the doctor's house, staring at the front door. He knew he should have guessed the truth a long time ago, as soon as he'd read those words in the letter Rose Pretting had, allegedly, written to herself — certainly when Buckle mentioned it. Would Rose have known about Cezanne's painting and its title if Kelly hadn't told her? She might have done, of course, being a regular at the library, but he thought it unlikely.

The print hung in Ronald Kelly's drawing room, a room Rose would never have entered as a patient. It was a favourite image of his, so he'd shared it with the woman who'd become his lover, telling her the variation of the title that he'd given to his own house. The House of the Hanged Woman. The house of Flora Winsmore.

For the second time in his life Albert had failed and both failures had taken place in that very village. Perhaps it would be best if he returned to London as soon as possible. According to the legal principle of Double Jeopardy, Kelly and Rose could never be brought to justice now they'd been acquitted of the crime of murder. And Margaret Jenkins and Alastair Ogden had been taken to Manchester to face trial for the two murders they'd committed — although there hadn't been enough evidence to add Bert Pretting's murder to the charges.

But he still had unfinished business in Wenfield. He hadn't spoken to Mrs Bell since the arrest of her husband's killers and he owed the lady a visit.

He walked slowly to the cottage, glancing back once at the doctor's house, committing it to memory before moving on. When he knocked on Mrs Bell's front door it was answered almost immediately by Grace, who gave him a reproachful look.

'Better late than never,' she said with a sniff. 'We were wondering when you'd get around to paying us a visit.'

'I'm sorry. I've been busy,' he said meekly.

'You'd best come in. I'll put the kettle on.'

The maid opened the drawing-room door and ushered him in before disappearing into the back of the cottage. When Albert stepped into the room he saw Mrs Bell sitting on a faded chintz armchair by the unlit fire. She greeted him with a smile before inviting him to sit in the armchair opposite hers. It was a worn chair and Albert recognised it as the one her husband used to sit in when he was alive.

'I heard about the Ogdens,' she said. 'They seemed such a nice couple. Respectable.'

'Appearances can often be deceptive, Mrs Bell. You find that out in my job.'

'I can't believe anybody could do anything so wicked. My dear, gentle Horace never harmed a soul.'

'Because of his honest nature they couldn't trust him to keep their secret. Their deception meant they could have gone to prison, so they knew Horace was a danger to them. That's why he died. You're right, it was a particularly wicked thing to do. But they'll face the full force of the law, don't worry about that.'

'That letter Horace received — it was from the real husband?'

'It was from a nurse at the hospital where he was being treated. It said one of her patients had lost his memory and he was trying to find his wife. A copy of a photograph of the woman you knew as Mrs Ogden was enclosed and your husband recognised her at once. He called on the couple the same evening to ask them what was going on.'

'If only he'd confided in me.'

'The Ogdens knew your husband's reputation for discretion. But once he knew they'd broken the law they assumed he'd feel obliged to inform the authorities.'

'Horace was used to keeping people's secrets but in this case he'd have felt obliged to do the correct thing otherwise the worry would have gnawed away at him.'

'You're right. Leaving him alive was a risk they couldn't take.'

'And they murdered that poor husband of hers too. Blighted by the war and then killed by his own wife and her lover.' She gave a heavy sigh, just as Grace entered with a tray of tea and scones. Albert had smelled the scent of fresh baking when he'd entered the house and now he realised he was hungry. Grace poured the tea and offered a buttered scone on a dainty plate. Once Albert had taken one, Grace left them alone.

'I heard that Dr Kelly and Mrs Pretting were acquitted.'

For a split second Albert was tempted to confide in this woman who reminded him in many ways of his own late mother. Then the moment of temptation passed. He'd share his mistakes with nobody, not even with Sam Poltimore when he got back to Scotland Yard.

'The Ogdens killed Mrs Pretting's husband too of course. It's obvious.' She took a sip of tea and replaced her cup in its saucer. 'You don't look happy, Inspector. I would have thought you'd be pleased to have brought the matter to a satisfactory conclusion. And Mr Billinge has turned up safe and well too. You've done well, Inspector. Do help yourself to another scone.'

Albert gave her a grateful smile and did as he was told. After a while she spoke again.

'I called on Lady Cartwright yesterday. She mentioned her niece, Charlotte. She had an understanding with Simon Fellowes before the war, you know. Then she met her husband and . . . She's a lovely woman, according to Lady Cartwright. And a good mother. She lost her own child to influenza, you know, and then she adopted a little boy. Horace arranged it all. The child's very fortunate to have such a loving mother.'

The words left Albert stunned and when he looked into Mrs Bell's eyes he realised she knew the truth, which was something he hadn't expected. The Reverend Bell's famed discretion apparently hadn't extended to all matters. It was

401

possible he'd sought his wife's advice as to how best to deal with a delicate situation. Or perhaps, being an intelligent and observant woman, she'd guessed about his relationship with Flora.

'You can rest assured that young Johnnie has the best of everything,' she said quietly. 'And most important of all he is loved.'

'She called him Johnnie?'

'At the real mother's special request. John was the name of her brother who was killed in the war.'

This confirmed that Mrs Bell knew everything. Flora had been close to her brother, John, who had wanted to become a doctor like his father. John had died because the women of the Society for the Abolition of Cowardice had pressured him to return to the front. Because the wounds he'd received in war weren't the visible kind, they'd accused him of being a coward. Flora had blamed them for his death and taken her revenge.

'You know he's Flora Winsmore's child?'

'I know a lot of things, Inspector. I guessed at the time that you were the father of Flora's child.' She smiled. 'But I can keep secrets. I've had a lot of practice.'

'If Johnnie's my son, what should I do?'

'As I said, Charlotte's a loving mother to him and he wants for nothing. But you must do what you think best. The only thing I would ask is that you consider the matter carefully.'

Albert drained his teacup and stood up. On impulse he bent to kiss Mrs Bell's cheek and she took his maimed hand gently.

'God bless you,' she said. 'I know you'll do what is best.'

Albert left the house, more perplexed than ever.

★ ★ ★

Albert's mother had always told him that if you slept on a dilemma, things would seem clearer in the morning. But on this occasion her advice didn't work. When he left the Black Horse that Saturday morning he felt more confused than ever.

Instead of reporting to the police station he took the train out of Wenfield on impulse, making the change in Manchester that would take him to Mabley Ridge.

When he reached the village he walked from the station to Charlotte's house. He thought of her as Charlotte. Even though he'd never met her, the fact that she was caring for his son, his own flesh and blood, seemed to create a sort of intimacy between them. On arriving at the front door he raised his hand to knock. But at the last moment his courage failed him and he stood there, head bowed, Mrs Bell's words echoing in his head.

He heard voices coming from the garden at the side of the house and without thinking he began to walk towards the sound. Then he saw her, Charlotte sitting on a wicker garden chair, dressed in a low-waisted white dress, smiling at the child playing with his coloured bricks on a tartan rug, chattering away to him. He watched

403

the child toddle over to the woman and hand her a couple of bricks, which she took from him gently with a kiss and a show of thanks.

She looked up for a second and when she spotted Albert the smile vanished, to be replaced by a wary frown. 'Can I help you?'

Albert thought quickly. 'I'm sorry to bother you, madam. Inspector Lincoln. I'm a detective. Scotland Yard,' he said, fumbling for the warrant card in the inside pocket of his jacket. 'There's been a report of a suspicious man in the area. Somebody said he was seen coming this way. I'm just checking that you're safe.'

The smile reappeared. 'I haven't seen anybody, Inspector. If I do, I'll be sure to let you know. It's good to know that the boys in blue are taking such good care of us.'

'It's what we're here for, madam.' He paused, unable to take his eyes off his son.

'Lovely little chap. What's his name?'

'Johnnie.' She picked up the child and as she kissed his cheek he grabbed hold of her hair with his chubby fist. She untangled it with great gentleness and bestowed another kiss. 'He's a great blessing. I lost a child and the doctors told me I could never have another. Then Johnnie came along.'

'He seems very happy.'

'We both are.'

The child turned and gazed at him with Flora's eyes. Albert hesitated. It was now or never.

'I'm afraid I wasn't telling the whole truth, Mrs Day.'

He saw curiosity in her eyes — and a hint of fear.

'I knew the late Reverend Bell and his wife. And . . . and I was a friend of Johnnie's mother.'

'I see.' Her expression was hard to read. She drew Johnnie towards her and held him protectively, as though she feared that Albert might have come to take him away from her.

'I don't know how much you know about . . . '

'The reverend told me he'd been born out of wedlock to an unfortunate girl who died. I thought it best not to ask too many questions. As far as we're concerned, Johnnie is our son.'

'Of course,' said Albert quickly, his eyes fixed on Johnnie, who favoured him with a smile that melted his heart. 'Actually I happen to be a relative of the father. He wasn't in a position to do the right thing and marry the mother but . . . he still takes an interest in his son's welfare.'

He saw Charlotte back away with alarm, her grip tightening on the child.

Albert raised his hands, a gesture of appeasement, of reassurance. 'I promise you that he has no wish to interfere in Johnnie's upbringing. As you say, Johnnie is your son now and obviously happy, so that is the last thing he would want. But if you were to allow me to visit from time to time — with your husband's permission, naturally . . . ' He searched for the right words. 'A boy can't have too many uncles to take an interest and provide gifts on special occasions, can he?'

Charlotte looked at him suspiciously. 'You say you're a Scotland Yard detective?'

405

'I am.' He blurted out that he'd just lost his wife and how he was up there investigating a case. He told her he'd made an arrest in Mabley Ridge — and that he'd been the detective who'd solved the murders there the previous year.

She listened with interest and he waited for her answer, his heart beating fast.

'I think you're right,' she said at last, her lips forming a smile that lit up her face. 'A child needs exciting uncles.'

Johnnie toddled over to him and placed a brick in his hand and he felt his eyes prick with tears.

'I'd better be off then,' he said, wanting to be out of there before he gave himself away.

'Thank you, Inspector,' Charlotte said as the child returned to her arms. 'For everything.'

Albert turned and walked away.

82

When Albert reached Manchester, still in a daze, he saw the Liverpool train standing on the platform, belching smoke and steam like a captive dragon.

He bought a ticket and rushed to catch it, wrenching open the door of a second-class carriage with his good hand as the wheels were preparing to move, narrowly beating the guard's flag. Once in Liverpool he caught another train out to Aigburth, determined that this time his courage wouldn't fail him.

He walked to Gwen Davies's road as quickly as he could manage, ignoring the pain in his leg. Eventually he found himself standing opposite a red-brick semi-detached house with a small, neat front garden and a bottle green front door. It was an unremarkable house like so many others but the sight of it set Albert's heart racing. Last time he'd seen Gwen they'd been in Mabley Ridge. She'd endured pain of her own in the past and they'd become close. Because of Mary they'd agreed that nothing could come of their embryonic relationship and she'd returned to her family in Liverpool. But now the world had changed.

He knew that lurking in the street staring at the house might arouse the suspicion of the neighbours. He had already seen a lace curtain twitch next door, so he straightened his back and walked to the front door. It was a Saturday, not a working day, so there was a chance she'd be at home.

He removed his hat before ringing the doorbell and waited, more nervous than he'd felt in a long while. After what seemed like an age the door opened.

Gwen Davies was standing there in a well-worn dress and long cardigan. She stared at him in disbelief for a moment, then her lips turned upwards in a smile.

'I'm sorry to call on you unannounced.'

She took a step forward. 'Don't be sorry.' There was a long pause, as though she was trying to find the right words. 'Actually, I hoped you'd turn up one day.'

'Did you? Did you really?'

Albert saw a blush appear on her freckled cheeks. 'Why do you think I gave you my address last time we met in Mabley Ridge? Give me a moment,' she said quickly, glancing behind her.

She disappeared into the depths of the hallway and returned a few seconds later wearing her hat and coat. 'Let's go for a walk,' she said.

Albert nodded, relieved that he hadn't been forced to give awkward explanations to her family. Gwen shut the front door behind her and linked her arm through his. He walked in silence, unable to find the words to express how he felt about seeing her again. Elated. Hopeful. Nervous. He'd experienced the depths of despair but now he was filled with optimism for the future; a happiness he thought he'd never know again.

'How have you been since Mabley Ridge?' she asked once they'd reached the bottom of the road, turning to look him in the eye.

He told her. Everything. About Johnnie. About Mary's death. About the Reverend Bell and Abraham Stark. And she listened, saying nothing until he'd finished.

'Will you be going back to London soon?'

With those few tentative words everything became clear. 'Not necessarily,' he said softly. 'There's not much to go back for. And I dare say Scotland Yard can manage without me.'

She nodded, unsmiling, and he watched her face, fearing that he'd been too honest; said too much too soon. Then she touched his hand.

'Let's walk in the park. You can see the river from there. My dad says it's wider than the Thames.'

She turned to face him. Then she stood on tiptoe and they kissed, gently at first then with more passion. They walked towards the park arm in arm and, as he felt the warmth of her body next to his, London and his old life seemed very far away.

Other titles published by Ulverscroft:

THE BOY WHO LIVED WITH THE DEAD

Kate Ellis

It is 1920 and DI Albert Lincoln is still reeling from the disturbing events of the previous year. Before the War, he'd investigated the murder of a child in a Cheshire village, and now a woman has been murdered there and another child is missing. With the help of the village schoolmistress, Albert closes in on the original pre-war killer. He soon realises the only witness is in grave danger, possibly from somebody he calls 'the Shadow Man'. And as he discovers more about the victims he finds information that might bring him a step closer to solving a mystery of his own — the whereabouts of his son.

THE BURIAL CIRCLE

Kate Ellis

On a stormy night in December, a tree is blown down on an isolated Devon farm. A rucksack is found caught amongst the roots — and next to it is a human skeleton. The discoveries revive memories for DI Wesley Peterson: a young hitchhiker who went missing twelve years ago was last seen carrying a similar backpack. Suddenly a half-forgotten cold case has turned into a murder investigation. Meanwhile, in the nearby village of Petherham, a famous TV psychic is found dead in suspicious circumstances whilst staying at a local guesthouse. Could a string of mysterious deaths in Petherham over a hundred years ago be connected to the recent killings? As Wesley digs deeper, it seems the dark whisperings of a Burial Circle in the village might not be merely legend after all . . .